Little Bits of Sky

S. E. Durrant

Holiday House New York

Text copyright © 2016 by S. E. Durrant
Inside illustrations © 2016 by Katie Harnett
First published in the UK in 2016 by Nosy Crow Ltd, London
First published in the USA in 2017 by Holiday House, New York
All Rights Reserved
HOLIDAY HOUSE is registered in the U.S. Patent and
Trademark Office.
Printed and Bound in July 2017 at Maple Press, York, PA, USA.
www.holidayhouse.com
First American Edition
1 3 5 7 9 10 8 6 4 2

Library of Congress Cataloging-in-Publication Data

Names: Durrant, S. E., author.
Title: Little bits of sky / S.E. Durrant.
Description: First American edition. | New York : Holiday House, 2017. |
"First published in the UK in 2016 by Nosy Crow Ltd, London." | Summary:
"Siblings Ira and Zac know the foster system inside and out, but it's only
when they are sent to Skilly House, a children's care home in London, that
their lives truly start to change"— Provided by publisher. | Summary: Ira
and her little brother, Zac, know the foster system well but their lives
start to change for the better when, in 1987, they go to Skilly House to live.
Identifiers: LCCN 2016056932 | ISBN 9780823438396 (hardcover)
Subjects: | CYAC: Orphanages—Fiction. | Orphans—Fiction. | Brothers
and sisters—Fiction. | Foster home care—Fiction. | Civil
disobedience—Fiction. | London (England)—History—20th century—Fiction.
| Great Britain—History—Elizabeth II, 1952—Fiction.
Classification: LCC PZ7.1.D875 Lit 2017 | DDC [Fic]—dc23 LC record
available at https://lccn.loc.gov/2016056932

For Duncan, Rosie, and Oliver

Today

This is the story of a time when my life turned upside down. Not that it was the right way up before, but for a while it felt like that moment when a clown juggles plates and they're all up in the air, and the only thing you can do is hold your breath and hope they don't come crashing to the ground.

I've put this story together from the diaries I kept when Zac and I were children. I wrote them because I felt we were almost invisible and I wanted to make sure our story was told, and also in the hope that life would get better for the small unloved girl that was me, and my even smaller unloved brother. And if life didn't get better or at least more interesting, I was going to make it up—to put in witches and castles and rides in fast cars. But I didn't need to. Life got exciting all by itself.

My story starts at Skilly House. The garden there was the wildest place I had ever seen. There was a patch of grass big enough to run around in, and on all sides a tangle of scratchy bushes and shrubs, trailing ivy and a convolvulus that climbed the walls in summer, dotting the garden with flowers. There was a small overgrown pond covered with chicken wire, and there was the fallen tree.

I never felt entirely comfortable in Skilly House itself—it was too full of ghosts—but the garden was special. It was the first place I ever felt truly happy. I think Zac felt the same. Not that we wanted to go there, of course.

Skilly House
October 1987

My name's Miracle, but I don't tell anyone. It's embarrassing, especially for a care kid. Maybe my mum thought life would be wonderful and perfect when I was born, but it wasn't and it never has been. That's why everyone calls me Ira. My brother's called Zackery or Zac. Both names are okay, but Zac suits him better because he's always running. If you call him Zackery, he's gone before you get to the end of his name.

We didn't want to come to Skilly. We'd never been in a children's home, and anyway it wasn't fair we had to

3

move so suddenly. One minute we were eating dinner with Brenda and Alf, seeing how much ketchup we could balance on a chip, the next Anita was chasing us up to our room to pack our bags. I banged my suitcase all the way down the stairs, which is unusual for me. I normally keep my feelings to myself, being the oldest. Zac stood in the hall with that awful sad face he has when misery's wrapped itself around him so tight he looks like he's choking, and I know it will take ages to dig him out.

"Make sure you come and see us, won't you?" Brenda said as she hugged us good-bye.

And that made me feel really sad because I was nine years old and Zac was seven, and we already knew we'd never see them again. And she was the grown-up and she didn't know.

After that Zac made his mouth into a thin, flat line and that was that. There was no point trying to talk to him. We sat in Anita's car and watched the world go by. Our bit of the world, that is: South London.

At first Anita tried to chat. She told us about a James Bond film she saw. She said the actor was really handsome. She probably has his poster on her wall. But we didn't answer, so she gave up trying. I couldn't even think about James Bond. All I could think was, the car windows needed cleaning.

4

Anita's our social worker. She dyes her hair to match her lipstick. It's usually red, but we never know what kind of red it's going to be. Sometimes it's pink or orange. It takes our mind off things. Maybe that's why she does it. That day it was red like cherries. She looked like a film star stuck in the wrong film with two miserable kids in the back of her car, when really she should have been sky-diving or kissing a double agent.

It took us ages to get to Skilly. The traffic was all jammed up, and I thought the cars must look like ants from the sky. And I know ants are meant to know exactly what they're doing, but it made me wonder if they felt like we did inside. Lost.

When we finally stopped, we were on a street just like the one we came from. Nothing was any different. There were no fields or mountains or waterfalls or chimpanzees or kangaroos. There wasn't even a park. It was just a normal London street with all the houses and flats squeezed in together like rotten teeth. If we hadn't been in the car for an hour, we'd have thought we just went around the corner.

As Anita parked the car, my heart started jumping around. It always does that just when I wish it would stay still, like if I want people to think I don't care what happens when really I do. It's hard to look like you don't care what happens when your heart's doing somersaults.

Anita got out our suitcases and opened the gate to a crumbling old house. I had to pull Zac to make him come. He didn't want to move. He just wanted everything to stop there and then, like if the world could stop that would be good. When I pulled him he banged his head on the window. He didn't say anything, but I knew he hated me.

The house was tall and scruffy with white paint peeling off, like it had been painted a hundred years ago and nobody had bothered to tidy it up ever since. A man was tying a rosebush to the wall. He was trying to stop the roses trailing on the ground. They were small and red and their petals were falling off, but he still wanted to tie them up. I expect they looked nice in summer.

Anita said, "Hello," and the man turned around.

He was wearing an old leather jacket and his hair was full of ringlets, not shiny like a princess but all tangled and sticking out. He smiled when he saw us, and his face filled with creases. I didn't want to like him, but I couldn't help it.

"I think the wind's going to blow up a bit," he said.

He waved a bit of string.

He shook Anita's hand, and then he shook ours. I acted like I always shake hands, but really it was the first time it ever happened. Zac's hand went all floppy like when he pretends he's ill. People don't normally shake hands with care kids. Sometimes they don't even look at us.

"I'm Silas," the man said. "Welcome to Skilly."

He's the only Silas I've ever met. He's probably the only one in London. People don't call their kids Silas anymore. It's an olden-days name.

We walked to the front door, and he rang the bell. There was a sign on the wall that said SKILLY HOUSE 1887, which means it was built a hundred years ago, which is a century. I thought of all the kids who must have stood on the doorstep before us, wondering what would happen next. Maybe their mum had been run over by a horse and carriage or their dad had gotten stuck up a chimney, or maybe they just ran out of luck. I turned my face to stone so whoever opened the door wouldn't see how I felt inside. Zac was taking lots of breaths like he was tired out. Only he wasn't tired out. He was scared.

But the woman who opened the door wasn't scary at all. She was beautiful. She was smiling and smiling, like she'd been looking forward to seeing us all day, and finally we'd come.

"Children!" she said. "Come in, come in. We've been waiting for you."

She put out her arms and wrapped them around us. It felt so nice. She had yellow beads on the ends of her dreadlocks, and they bounced like bees. I wanted to hold one, but I didn't. I just touched one really gently so she wouldn't notice. It felt lucky.

Silas said, "This is Hortense. She'll settle you in."

Then he went back to his rosebush.

We went inside with Hortense and stood in the hall. It was dark and the stairs went up and up, and I tried to imagine them going all the way up to the sky and at the top there'd be a big burst of light. Then I had a feeling someone was watching us, and when I turned around I saw a woman standing in a doorway. I thought she was a ghost at first. A shiver went right down my spine. She was very thin and she was standing as still as a skeleton and she was staring at me and Zac like she wished we'd never arrived. Like if she could wind back time, she'd make us walk right back out of the door and lock it behind us.

Hortense said, "Meet Mrs. Clanks, manager of Skilly," and the woman came over.

She walked really straight like a soldier and her shoes went *tap-tap* on the floor, so I knew she was real. Ghosts don't make noises. It takes all their effort just to be here at all. That's why you don't see them much.

She was old and her hair was tied back, and she had a frown between her eyes that looked like it had been there forever. Like she might have been the first baby ever to be born with a frown. She was wearing boring grown-up clothes, except for one thing: she had a pink shiny ribbon in her hair. I wondered if someone had put it there and she didn't know yet. But it didn't make me want to laugh. It made me embarrassed.

She shook Anita's hand and said, "Good afternoon."

Then she smiled at me and Zac. Only it wasn't the kind of smile that makes you glad to be there. It was the kind of smile you give someone when you wish they lived hundreds of miles away, like in Australia.

"Hortense will show you your room," she said.

She said it just like that. Not "Hello" or "How was your journey?" She said it like a plumber had come to fix a leak, and she had to tell them where the pipes were. And they better get on with it before everything flooded. Not like some kids had come to their new home where they might have to stay forever.

I wanted to shout that we weren't staying. I had to grit my teeth to stop it coming out. I wanted to shout that we hated it here already, and we were going back to Brenda and Alf. But I couldn't. Zac would be upset, and anyway it never works. Even if the cutest little kid makes a fuss, nothing changes. Not if they're a care kid.

Anita usually smiles when she leaves us because smiles spread. If one person smiles, that makes the next person smile and it goes on and on. You can cheer up a whole crowd of people that way. It's like magic. But that day she couldn't smile. Her face just wouldn't make the right shape. She knelt down in front of me and Zac and gave us a kiss.

"Off you go," she said. "I'll see you soon."

She still looked like a film star, only now she was in a war film watching her children be evacuated to the country, and she was being brave. She left cherry lipstick on Zac's cheek, then she wiped it away.

We followed Hortense up the stairs. I pretended she was an angel taking us to heaven, but I couldn't do it for long. Kids were peering at us through the banisters and sticking out their tongues. A tall boy threw a ball of paper at my shoulder. I pretended I hadn't noticed, but I could hear him sniggering.

The stair carpet was so old you could see threads where the soft bits had worn away. It might have been nice once because it still had flower patterns, but now they were muddy like at the bottom of a pond. Every step creaked, and the creaks were all in different places. Some were in the middle of the step and some were on the edges and some steps seemed fine, but when you took your foot off they gave a little squeak. You could never go up or down those steps quietly; you'd have to learn where the creaks were.

There were drawings on the walls and writing that had

been smudged out, maybe because it said someone loved someone else and they changed their mind, or maybe because it said something horrible.

And there was dust on every step. I had to try really hard not to think about it because dust comes from dead skin, so it must have come from the children who walked up the stairs before us. Maybe even from children who are dead. I just concentrated on counting the steps. I always do that in new places. I always count the steps going up so I know how many I have to go down. It's one of my habits. From the hall up to our room is forty-seven steps.

Our bedroom is right at the top of the house. You can't go any farther. It's nice like that. No one walks past. When we got there Hortense said, "Best room in the house," and opened the door like we'd just arrived on holiday or something, not in a children's home.

But actually it's okay. It's got a sloping roof on one side and a window on the other, and from the window you can see the garden. There were two beds with duvets and bobbly blankets, and there was a sink with yellow stains going from the taps to the plughole. There was a wardrobe and some drawers and a table, and there was tape stuck to the walls where kids had taken off their posters. There was a rug on the floor that was so old the color had faded away, and under the rug were floorboards.

11

Hortense put her head to one side and looked at us like a heron searching for fish in a pond.

"It'll feel very different when you've settled in," she said.

Then she opened the window and a breeze came into the room, and it felt lovely. I looked out and saw a bird fly into a tree.

"Now," Hortense said, "come and see the garden."

The garden at Skilly is amazing. It's huge and raggedy and full of hiding places, and even though there are buildings all around, it feels like it's on its own. There was a shed and a pond with chicken wire over the top, and there was a huge tree in the middle. When the sun came through the leaves, it made patches of light on the grass.

We had the garden all to ourselves that afternoon. We didn't know then, but that's what they do with new kids. They let them play in the garden on their own. At first Zac wouldn't let go of my hand, but then he found a stick and started hitting the tree. Bits of bark were flying off. I didn't say anything. I just walked away. Then I spun around and around until I was so dizzy I had to lie down, and as I lay there I let my head fill up with the blue sky, and then I didn't want to shout anymore. That's the thing about the sky. No matter how bad things are, you can always look up at the sky, and then you feel better.

Afterward we had tea in the kitchen with the other kids. They hardly even looked at us. I pretended not to look at them either, but really I kept taking glances. They all did different things with their food. It showed their personalities. Some ate really quickly and wanted more, some only ate the best bits; some just pushed their food around their plate and didn't eat at all. Some kids made a mess, and some were really tidy and put their knives and forks together when they finished like they were in a restaurant and the waiter would come and take their plates. The boy who threw the paper at me didn't even chew. He gulped his food down like it was melted ice cream even though it was shepherd's pie. When Hortense wasn't looking, he put some mashed potato on his fork and flicked it at me. It landed in the middle of my plate. I didn't eat after that. It put me off.

As soon as we could get away, we ran up to our room and looked out at the garden. It was nice to be so high up. It's like being invisible. It was dark and windy outside, and the tree was shaking. Two pigeons were sitting in the branches, but they didn't mind. They just rocked from side to side. They were used to it. Silas was carrying some tools into the shed, and his hair was blowing in his eyes.

Then we got into our beds and just sat there for ages. I didn't read or draw or anything. I wanted to be paying attention for when Zac spoke.

13

At last he said, "Why are the walls so high?"

It was the first thing he said since we left Brenda and Alf's.

"It's an old house," I said. "That's how they made them."

"Were people taller then?" he said.

"No," I said. "I think they were smaller."

He looked annoyed.

"Why then?" he said.

"I don't know."

"Can I get in with you?" he said.

I nodded.

He ran to my bed and curled up beside me. People like Zac because when he's not sad or angry, he's funny. He makes up games and he can run really fast, and he likes to chase people or be chased and to run down the street ringing doorbells. And kids like that even if grown-ups don't. Especially old ladies don't.

But Zac doesn't like other people. Not really. He doesn't trust them. The only person he trusts is me, so I can never let him down. He's my responsibility.

"What will it be like here?" he said.

"It'll be okay."

We could hear people talking downstairs.

"Do you think there are ghosts?"

I shook my head, but really I was wondering too. I

wasn't worried about the kind you can see through, or the kind that look like sheets. I was worried about all the children who lived in Skilly before us and all the clues they left behind, like the scribbles on the walls, and all the sad eyes that must have looked out of the windows and wished they were somewhere else.

"No," I said. "There's no such thing as ghosts."

Zac's mouth was wobbling.

"Shall I tell you a story?" I said.

"The special one?"

"If you want."

He nodded.

I always make up stories for Zac. Usually he kills a monster and rescues the villagers or the schoolchildren or the sailors who are drowning because a sea monster sank their boat. But the special story is different because I don't know if I made it up or not.

Zac always says things like, "What was Mum like? Did she cuddle me?" And he doesn't want me to say I don't know, so I have to give him an answer. And that's how we got our story.

"Mum was holding you," I said. "You were really tiny and you were holding her finger like you'd never let go, and she was kissing you and her hair was curly like ours, and she thought we'd be happy forever."

I stroked his hair and his eyes flopped shut and then he was asleep. That's what he's like. All he has to do is close his eyes.

I couldn't get to sleep. I kept thinking about all the people we'd lived with before we came to Skilly. I always knew we wouldn't stay with Brenda and Alf for long. They were old, and Alf kept losing things. He needed Brenda to look after him, not us. Before them there was Petra, who got a job working night shifts so she couldn't look after us anymore, and there was Alara, who kept telling us we wouldn't be there for Christmas (and we weren't). There were the Grimbles, who said they'd keep us forever, but then their new baby arrived. And there was Adam, who didn't have enough chairs for everyone to sit down at the same time. And then there were all the short stays with people we called Nan or Auntie but who weren't relatives at all, and the woman who was mean to us so Anita had to take us away.

I used to tell Zac we were like gypsies—always traveling to exciting places—but I stopped saying it because it didn't make moving exciting. It made it worse. But that night I pretended there was a horse sleeping outside and an old-fashioned caravan with flowers painted on it, and in the morning we'd go on an adventure. We'd go down a long road with grass on both sides and trees blowing in the wind, and there'd be hills in the distance, and me and

 16

Zac would be holding the reins and singing. And then I realized I didn't know if horses sleep standing up or lying down and I was trying to work it out, and I think that's when I fell asleep.

The Storm

At first I thought I was having a nightmare. I was bumping all the way down the stairs. The banging was really loud, and I was trying to count the steps and thinking it's going to really hurt when I got to the bottom. But when I woke up, I could still hear banging. Zac was holding on to me really tight and digging his fingers into my arm. His eyes were squeezed shut.

"Ghosts!" he whispered.

But I knew it wasn't ghosts. I could hear the wind howling outside. I jumped out of bed and ran to the window. It was the middle of the night, and a storm was crashing through the garden. It was pulling up bushes and ripping pieces of wood off the shed and throwing them into the air. The tree was rocking from side to side, and all the time the wind was wailing. It was like when a kid has the worst tantrum ever, and you know you won't be able to calm them down. You just have to wait for it to be over and hope they don't break too much.

"Zac!" I called. "Look!"

Zac got to the window just as the tree blew over. It was amazing! The wind was pushing it so hard, it went diagonal, and then suddenly it couldn't get up again and crashed to the ground. As it fell it howled like it was a dying animal, and its roots came up and they were being blown by the wind, so it looked like the tree was still alive. Like an antelope being eaten by lions. Only it wasn't alive. It was dead.

At first me and Zac could hardly breathe. Then we started laughing like we were on a ride at the fair. We felt sick, but it was brilliant. We could hear people running around downstairs, but we didn't go down. We just sat on my bed and listened to the storm, and I crossed my fingers and hoped the house wouldn't blow over.

Seeing the tree blow down was one of the best things I ever saw. I know it shouldn't be, but it was.

The storm was gone by the next morning. I don't know if it went somewhere else, but it wasn't in London. We couldn't wait to see what had happened. All the Skilly kids ran out into the street. We didn't even have breakfast. Another tree had blown down right across the road and landed on a car. There was a dent in the roof, and the windscreen was smashed into tiny pieces. I don't think you could ever fix it.

Bins were blown over too, and rubbish had gone everywhere. There was a banana skin stuck in the branches of the tree and some plastic bottles and lots of wrappers. An old man wearing a bathrobe was sweeping glass off his path, and two women were trying to get a bike off some railings. It was twisted on so it looked like a cartoon, and there was a crisp packet stuck in the wheel. The women were half laughing and half annoyed. Because even though the storm was amazing, the bike was ruined.

Silas's rosebush had completely disappeared. Even the string was gone. It probably went miles. It might even have landed in someone else's garden, and in summer people would wonder where the red roses came from, because maybe they only planted white. Silas wasn't annoyed, though. He was laughing.

"I didn't think it was going to be *this* windy," he said. "Go down in history, it will."

And it really will, because it was the biggest storm for three hundred years. That means even before Skilly was built and when women wore long dresses and couldn't vote or go to school. And there were no cars or TV and there was no electricity, and people played the piano in the dark and the whole family would sing along. Me and Zac might be in history books too, because we saw what happened.

19

On the news it showed what else the storm had done. There was a house with its roof blown right off. You could see into the bedroom. You could even see what kind of wallpaper the people had and what books they were reading.

The wind blew lorries over too. It just picked them up and threw them on to their sides, and they were lying across the motorway like elephants that poachers had killed to take the tusks. And the wind threw trailers into the sea so all the pots and pans were floating around.

We Skilly kids were really excited. We already knew everything could be turned upside down at any moment, and now everyone else could see it too. We ran into the back garden and climbed onto the tree and just kept staring at it because we couldn't believe it was lying on the ground when it used to be up in the sky. We kept running along the trunk and jumping off the roots, and we did it over and over, and every time felt just as amazing as the first time.

Silas cut the branches off the tree, and we gathered them up and put them in a pile with the wood from the shed. And as the leaves and twigs crunched under my feet, I had to stop and take a deep breath because I realized I was happy and I was so surprised.

"We'll have a great fire with this lot," Silas said.

And we did. On Bonfire Night we stood in the garden and ate hot potatoes and watched the flames flickering in the big hole where the tree used to be.

The tree's been lying in the garden ever since. Silas cut steps into it so the little kids can get onto the top. The bark's crumbling and covered in moss and kids have written their names on it. I scratched *Ira and Zac were here 10/16/87* into one of the steps, because we saw the tree fall and that makes us part of its history, and also because it was our first whole day at Skilly. The kids here call the tree the ship or the raft, and we run along the top of it or hide behind it and ambush each other. And when the garden's quiet I lean against it and draw, or just shut my eyes and listen, because when no one's outside the garden sort of hums.

Photo of a Dog
March 1989

It's been nearly a year and a half since me and Zac came to Skilly. All the kids who were here when we first came have gone, apart from the boy who flicked mashed potatoes at me. The others have been fostered or adopted or gone home and new kids have come instead, but Jimmy's still here. He goes away, then he comes back, then he goes away again. Nothing works out for him. Maybe it's because he's so tall. Maybe it's even worse than having curly hair like me and Zac. But I don't think so. I think it's because he's angry. Even when he's happy, he's angry. Even when he's laughing and telling jokes, you can tell he's a little bit angry underneath.

I never know what he's going to do next and he makes me nervous, but he's still one of my favorites because he's full of life. He doesn't like life very much, but it bursts out of him anyway. He can't help it. It's like he's got bouncy shoes.

He does little skips and jumps when he walks, and if his favorite song comes on the radio, he dances. He knows all the words and moves. He looks like a pop star. Sometimes Hortense joins in too. She can't help it either, and then they're both dancing and laughing. That's the thing about Jimmy. Even though he's angry he makes people happy.

But apart from Jimmy, me and Zac have been here longest. Hortense says that means we're old hands. We're supposed to show new kids what to do, but usually they don't want anything to do with us. Being old hands isn't something to be proud of. It's something to be ashamed of.

When new kids come to Skilly, they're either loud and angry or secretive and quiet. The angry kids tell everyone about their lives, what their families are like and where they've come from. They say they're not staying, and they try to fight other kids because they don't want to fit in. They tell lies too. One kid said his mum was a millionaire, and another said her dad was a TV chef. But I'm sure they were lying, because rich kids like that don't go into care. Someone always wants them.

The quiet kids are the opposite. They don't say anything. They keep their secrets to themselves so no one can take them away. Really, they want to be invisible. Usually the angry kids have to fight each other because the quiet kids don't want to.

People probably think me and Zac are the secretive kind, but we're not really. It's just that we don't have anything to tell. We don't have parents, and there's nothing to show we ever did have parents. We've got a Memory Book full of photos and birthday cards, but everything in the book comes from being in care.

Except one photo.

There's one photo of us that was taken somewhere else. If you look at it quickly it looks like a photo of a dog—a big black hairy dog jumping towards the camera, his tongue poking over his lips. The dog takes up nearly all the picture, and when people see it for the first time they say, "Oh look, a photo of a dog."

But if you look closely, you can see the dog's jumping out of an armchair and me and Zac are sitting on each side. We're almost squashed out of the picture, but not quite. Zac's a baby and he's propped up with a cushion and he looks surprised, and I'm on the other side, a bit blurred, as if I jumped when the dog jumped. I'm nearly two years old. We know it's us because the photo has *Miracle and Zackery, July 1980* written on the back in someone's writing. I don't know whose, and I don't know where the chair was, and I don't know who the dog was. And that's it. It's hard to get any information from a picture like that. I sometimes wonder what happened to the dog, but I expect it's dead by now.

And apart from that photo, there's nothing to show we ever had a family. Except we look the same—two curly-haired kids. Same but different.

Anita says we had a mum once, but she couldn't look after us any more. It's what people say to care kids. It doesn't really mean anything. It's like saying it's cold outside when really it could be stormy or wet or snowy or icy and you haven't got a window so you can't check. All you know is you'd better put your coat on.

I said, "Can't she come to visit?" but Anita said, "We don't know where she is."

Then she looked so sad, I wished I hadn't asked. She looked like she'd come for a party and arrived on the wrong day.

I don't think me and Zac will ever get a family. This is why, in no particular order:

We're not little anymore.

Every time someone doesn't want us, it shows a little bit.

We want to stay together.

Anita keeps trying to find us a family. She doesn't give up. When we came to Skilly, she advertised us in the paper next to the holiday cottages so people would see us if they were looking for somewhere nice to stay. They might even think of us if there was a spare room, so as not to waste it. A photographer hung a sheet in the hall and Hortense threw a ball in the air, and me and Zac sat in front of the sheet and looked at the ball and smiled. We've got the photo in our Memory Book and we saw the advert in the paper. It said:

Sister and brother, aged nine and seven, need a family. Ira loves reading and drawing; Zac loves being outdoors and takes a while to settle.

But the trouble with photos is people can see what you look like. There's nothing you can do about it. I think people would like us better if they got to know us first instead of looking at a photo. We tried to look sweet, but nobody came. I curled my fingers into my palm to hide my chewed nails, but nobody came.

 26

And now I'm ten and a half and Zac's nine, and Anita said as we get older it'll be harder to find us a family. I said, "Well, no one wanted us anyway." She said maybe the right people don't know about us yet. But I think there are too many people for the right ones to find us. There are millions of people just in London, so the chances of finding the right two must be really tiny. By the time they find us we will be grown up, and it'll be too late. And that would be even worse than not finding us at all.

I try not to think about my dream home too much because it makes me sad, but I'm going to write it down just this one time. Because writing things down makes them real, and things don't happen if they're not real. You have to tell someone, even if it's just a diary.

My dream home will have a front door just for me and Zac and our mum and dad, and a key we hang in the hall. There'll be wallpaper and flowers and not too many rooms. There'll be stairs that don't creak, and I'll have my own bedroom with a desk and drawers for my art materials. There'll be a goal in the garden for Zac, and at the end of the road there'll be a sweetshop with old-fashioned jars and flying saucers and sherbet lemons.

I haven't imagined my mum and dad, but if they're not beautiful or handsome or clever or rich it won't matter as long as they're nice.

Skilly's nothing like my dream home, but it's okay. Even

though me and Zac share a room, it's okay. Zac put up his Arsenal poster because that's his favorite team. He knows the names of all the players. I put up my *Matilda* poster because *Matilda*'s my favorite book. It's about a girl who's got horrible parents, but it doesn't matter because she can make things happen just by thinking. I've tried to do that myself, thinking really hard, but it doesn't work. It feels like it should, but it doesn't. My poster's a drawing of Matilda thinking really hard, but you can't tell what she's thinking and you can't see what she's changing. Sometimes I imagine she's thinking about me and Zac and she's going to make our life much, much better.

But the problem with the posters is that Zac's Arsenal poster is above his bed so I have to look at it, and my *Matilda* poster's above my bed so Zac has to look at it. We tried it the other way around but it didn't feel right— it's one of those problems people don't realize if they don't share a room.

The very best thing about our room is the only thing above it is the sky. When I wake up in the morning, I think about the birds flying over me, and when Zac can't sleep I tell him there's an owl sitting on the roof and the owl knows all the secrets of the world. And that makes him feel safe.

My favorite hobby is drawing. I draw flowers and

nature and people, and sometimes I do sketches called caricatures. I started doing caricatures when I was trying to draw Zac; I couldn't get him right, so I gave him a long nose and he looked really funny. I like drawing people this way—the way I see them instead of the way they actually are.

I've done lots of pictures of Skilly kids. I've drawn the boy with the knobbly knees who stayed for a week, and the kid who gelled his hair into a spike, and the girl with rings in her nose. I've drawn the short kids, the fat kids, the tall ones and the thin ones. Sometimes I put them in a line with the really tall ones next to the really small ones, and sometimes I make up kids who've never been here.

I've also drawn Silas with his hair tangled like a lion and Hortense with wings because she's like an angel, and Mrs. Clanks as a skeleton. I've drawn Zac riding a dinosaur and as a pirate and as a strongman at the circus. I've even drawn him as a bouncy ball, because that's what he's like. He always bounces back.

The only people I don't draw are the children who lived here before us. I try not to think about them because they must be old now or dead. If I see reminders like scribbles on the wall, I think about something else.

But there's one girl I can't help thinking about. She

scratched her name into our windowsill, so every time I look at the garden I think of her. It says *Glenda Hyacinth, 1947*, which is forty-two years ago. She must have stood at the window too, and that means she lived in our room and she's probably dead now and that makes her a ghost. And then I remember that I scratched me and Zac into the fallen tree, and we'll be ghosts one day too. And that makes me feel horrible.

But mostly Skilly's okay. And when I feel sorry for myself, I talk to Silas. He tells me one day things will be different.

Silas

Silas is the best person ever. He's not like a grown-up. He doesn't mind mess, he doesn't get angry and he can fix things. He always smells of fresh air. It's like he's got the outdoors wrapped round him. If someone made that smell into perfume, they'd be rich. It could go in a little green bottle with a daisy lid. Everyone would want to buy some.

Silas is full of life like Jimmy, but he doesn't have bouncy shoes. Life comes out of him in a different way, like leaves in a breeze. He's never still for one minute. He can't help it. Sometimes he has tea with us in the kitchen, and even though he's sitting at the table, he's rocking and his fingers are moving and his face is smiling and laughing and frowning all at the same time. It's because his head's full of memories.

He's been all over the world and done loads of things. We get him to tell us his stories over and over again. Sometimes he says, "Haven't I told you that already?" but we always say no, because Skilly kids want to know his stories by heart so we can pretend we were there ourselves.

When he was younger he lived in Australia. He rode horses and looked after cattle. It's called being a rancher. If you could dig a hole right down through the pavement and keep digging, you'd end up in his ranch. Only there's fire in the middle of the world, so you can't go through. You have to go around. When it's daytime in Australia it's night here, so when everyone in London was sleeping Silas was riding his horse, and when everyone in London was having breakfast he was looking at the stars. It sounds confusing, but it isn't, because the sun tells you when it's time to get up or go to bed.

He's been in the rain forest too. He says if you stand really still and listen, you can hear insects running over the leaves and little drops of water falling. He's also been to India and he's seen cows sit in the middle of the road and not move, even though cars are hooting at them and there's a traffic jam. The cows even go to sleep there. They don't mind. And he's seen spices so bright they made his eyes hurt.

One time he was camping in a forest, and when he woke up there was a python in his sleeping bag. Pythons can swallow a crocodile whole, so it could easily have eaten Silas. He had to lie really still until the snake woke up and slithered out. He lay there all day, just keeping calm and hoping the python wasn't hungry. You have to be very brave not to move if a python's in your bed. Me and Zac tried pretending, and we couldn't do it. And that's without a real python. If we had been there, we'd have been eaten.

"I dreamed of that snake," Silas said. "I dreamed it was there and I knew not to stretch out my legs, and that dream saved my life. Sixth sense, I call it."

We don't learn about sixth sense at school. We just learn the five main ones: hearing, smell, sight, touch and taste. My teacher said to imagine using them when someone's cooking dinner, but it's more fun to imagine them when someone's burning dinner. You hear hissing, you smell burning, you see the burned pan, you touch the hot handle and you taste the burned food. Then you spit it out.

But sixth sense is different. It's sort of invisible. I think it's like knowing someone's burned the dinner even though you're not back from school yet. Silas says we'll recognize it when we need it. He says if you trust it, it can get you out of trouble.

But the best thing about Silas is he's a care kid like us, so he understands how we feel. All he knows about his family is his dad was named Bernard and his mum was named Hilda. He doesn't even know why they named him Silas. He was born in London in the war, and when he was a baby a bomb landed on his house and killed his mum and dad. They just couldn't get out quick enough. Hilda was probably trying to get him into his little jumper and Bernard was probably getting him some milk.

"I was pulled out of the rubble," he said, "and passed from one pair of hands to the next. Just like you lot."

He went to live on a farm away from the bombs, and when the war finished he didn't have anywhere to go, so he stayed in the countryside and got moved from one place to the next.

"I used to think I could be picked up and carried any-where," he said, "but I learned something you lot should understand. They can take you anywhere they like, but they can't choose where this goes."

And he banged his hand on his chest where his heart

must be. I know what he meant. If you don't have a family, you have to hold on extra tight to what's inside. I hold on to my heart really tight. Zac holds his even tighter.

Skilly Kids

Apart from me, Zac, and Jimmy, there's six other kids at Skilly. This is them—not in any special order, just how they come into my head.

Sophia's the oldest. She's fourteen. She's kind and quiet and doesn't say anything about herself. She's like me and Zac in that way. She writes poems on a little typewriter, and sometimes you can hear her typing in her room. But then she hides her poems so you can never read them. She braids her hair and wears bright shirts, which is funny because she doesn't really like to be noticed, and if you wear bright shirts people notice you. She looks like a pop star, but I've never heard her sing.

Ashani's the youngest. She's eight. She wishes she was a boy because she wants to be a footballer when she grows up and she wants to play at Wembley. She supports Crystal Palace, and when she talks about football she says things like, "We only lost because the ref was rubbish and our striker was injured." She makes it sound like Crystal Palace played best even if they didn't win.

She's got a Crystal Palace shirt, but it's too big for her. It's probably big enough for Jimmy. Hortense sewed it up, but the shoulders still come to her elbows.

Ashani's everyone's favorite. She makes funny faces and she laughs a lot and she's easy to make happy. If I was going to adopt someone, I'd adopt Ashani. Then I'd buy her a Crystal Palace shirt that fits and take her to a real live football match so she didn't have to watch it on TV. And I'd buy her chips afterward, and Coke.

Esther's nine. She loves yellow. She doesn't feel like herself if she's not wearing it. She feels like someone she doesn't like. She gets upset if her clothes get messy, and when she came to Skilly she was angry because she wants to live somewhere pretty. She's the same age as Zac, but he doesn't like her. Sometimes she plays dressing up and wants him to be her husband. But Zac doesn't want to play families. He wants to play knights and soldiers. And he doesn't want to rescue a princess either.

Miles is thirteen like Jimmy, but he's small so you can't tell. When he first came, Jimmy wanted to fight Miles but Miles just walked away. He's got tiny hands, and he spends ages in his room making things with sticks or taking things apart and putting them back together. Hortense gives him matches when she's used them, so they can't catch fire, and he makes stick men or houses out of them. One time Silas made holes in chestnuts, and Miles put matches through the holes so they were like wheels on little cars, and we had races with them. They didn't last long, though. They kept breaking.

Milap and Harit are ten and nine, and they're brothers. Milap is really good at magic. He can make little red balls disappear and then appear somewhere else. He can do card tricks too, and he knows what your card is even though he can't see it. Harit likes animals, especially extinct ones. He's like Zac because he knows all the names of dinosaurs. His favorite is *Triceratops*, which is the one with three horns. Zac likes *Tyrannosaurus rex* best.

But Milap and Harit are always waiting to leave Skilly. You can feel it. Even if you're talking to them, it's like a bit of them isn't listening properly in case the doorbell rings and it's their mum come to get them. Their mum's in the hospital because she got worried and her brain needs a rest, and their dad couldn't look after them because he got sad thinking about their mum. It's called mental illness. You can't see it like a broken leg, but it's just as bad. Maybe worse. When their mum gets better they're all going to get back together again, because then their dad will be happier too. Then they can go home.

Easter

We all got Easter eggs today with our names written on them in squiggly chocolate writing. Ashani said she saw Mrs. Clanks taking them out of a bag and putting them on the kitchen table, but I don't think so. I think Mrs. Clanks was taking them off the kitchen table and putting them in a bag. That's what she's like. She doesn't want us to have fun. It was lucky Ashani walked in.

After breakfast Silas hid the eggs in the garden, and we had an egg hunt. Jimmy found his first. I found Milap's, Milap found Esther's, Esther found Sophia's and Sophia found mine, so we all swapped. It's the first time I ever saw "Ira" written in chocolate. It looked so nice. If it was always written in chocolate, I'd like it much better.

We all found our eggs really quickly, apart from Zac. Jimmy had nearly eaten his and Ashani kept getting us to hide hers again, but Zac hadn't even found his for the first time yet. He was beginning to get upset. Silas looked worried because he hid eight eggs and he couldn't remember where they all were.

Esther said, "You can have mine if you like," but Zac said, "No thanks, it's got *Esther* on it!"

I was thinking how quickly things get spoiled when

Harit said, "Look!" and there was Zac's egg hidden behind the ivy, high up on the wall. Silas was surprised because he'd hidden them all low down, so I think Jimmy moved it. Anyway it was all okay.

Eating an egg with your name on it is one of the nicest things in the world. But it does have to be your own name.

My Perfect Day
April 1989

There's daffodils and daisies in the garden now. It shows summer's coming. I tried to draw them today, but I couldn't even make them look like flowers, so I put little legs on them and made them into insects. They looked funny crawling across the page.

Zac and Harit were chasing each other with bows and arrows but I didn't mind as long as they kept away from me. I was sitting in a patch of sun, and it was really warm on my back. Silas was in his garden next door.

Silas lives in the bungalow next to Skilly. We're not allowed in his garden, but if we see him we talk to him over the fence. Unless Mrs. Clanks sees us, because then she comes out and tells us off. She says things like, "Isn't Silas allowed some time to himself?" And all the time she's flapping her hands to keep insects away. She doesn't like nature. She's an indoors sort of person. Zac says he's going to put a spider down her back one day, but I know he won't. She's too scary. It's just one of his dreams, like fighting dinosaurs. I don't think even Jimmy would do it.

But Silas likes talking to us. He says things like, "How's it going?" or "What you up to?" One time he showed us a beetle. It had a green and blue shield on its back that looked like a shell. It's called a shield bug. The shield's meant to protect it, but it hadn't worked because the beetle was dead when Silas found it. Now Zac's got it. He put it on our windowsill, next to Glenda Hyacinth's name. I moved it along in case she didn't like insects, but she might not mind. It's quite pretty.

Silas is always finding things. That's why his garden's full of junk. He says it'll come in handy one day, but I don't know how. He's got an old table and piles of wood and pots of paint and a broken chair and a cage with a wheel but no hamster in it. Usually he's got a pint mug of tea, which is a whole teapot full.

One time at school everyone had to say what their perfect day would be and I couldn't even imagine because I've never done anything perfect. My heart was beating so loud, I thought the whole class would hear. Other kids were saying things like going to Disneyland or camping next to a stream, but when my turn came I had to say I didn't know. It was embarrassing. But actually, I think my perfect day is drawing in the garden with the sun shining and Zac playing and Silas in his garden too. So I think today was my perfect day.

When I finished drawing I went to talk to Silas over the fence. He was hammering a nail into some wood.

"What are you making?" I said.

"I'll show you."

He lifted up a stick with a bit of board nailed to it. It looked like a giant lollipop.

"Is it a placard?" I said.

He nodded.

"It's just to tell people what I think."

Me and Zac see placards every day on the way to school. People stand outside the library with them, even if it's pouring with rain. I think they must take sandwiches, because they're still there when we're walking home. They've usually got No Poll Tax or Can't Pay, Won't Pay written on their placards, but they don't look too fed up.

41

"Are you going to stand outside the library?" I said.

"No," Silas said. "I'm going on a march."

"About the poll tax?"

He nodded.

"With other people?"

He laughed. "I hope so."

Hortense says the poll tax isn't for kids to worry about. It's a grown-up thing. She says it's money grown-ups have to pay, but lots of people are worried because it costs too much. That's why they have placards. So they can tell everyone it's a bad idea. She says history's full of people holding placards.

I've seen lots of placards. Sometimes they say ONLY GOD CAN SAVE YOU, and sometimes they say CHARLIE'S JERK CHICKEN 99P. It all depends.

But I think life would be more straightforward if everyone had a placard, because then you don't have to say what you think out loud so you don't have to be rude. It's like shouting without making a noise. You could maybe even stop a war that way.

"I wish I had a placard," I said.

Silas said, "What would you write on it?"

"I'd write 'Leave Me Alone' for when kids keep pestering me."

He laughed. "Mine would say 'Any Chance of a Cup of Tea?'"

After that I kept thinking of different things to write.

Zac's placard would say ARE YOU MY MUM? Because every time he sees a woman who looks like us, he thinks she's our mum. If he had a placard, he could stand in the street and people could come up and say yes or no, or they could just walk past but at least he wouldn't have to keep asking me. I expect most would walk past. Maybe all.

Esther's would say HAVE YOU GOT THAT IN YELLOW? Milap and Harit's would say WAS THAT THE DOORBELL? Ashani's would say CRYSTAL PALACE FOREVER or THAT WAS A FOUL or THE BOYS WERE UNLUCKY.

I'd have different placards for different occasions. I'd have the one saying LEAVE ME ALONE for if I was reading or drawing. I'd lean it against my chair so I could hold on to my book. And I'd have one for when people are being horrible or telling me off. I'd hold it up in front of Mrs. Clanks or my teacher or Skilly kids when they're making me feel bad. It would say STOP NOW! And I'd have another one for when Zac's embarrassing me, like when he rings people's doorbells and runs away. It would say THAT BOY IS NOT MY BROTHER.

My Favorite People

These are my favorite people. There aren't many. If I die and there's a funeral, not many people will come because I don't know many people. If I had a family, I'd have cousins and aunts and grandparents, but I've only got Zac. I've written a list just in case. Zac's at the top, even though he's annoying sometimes.

Silas and Hortense are next. Silas because he's the best person in the world, and Hortense because sometimes she puts her arm around me and gives me a kiss and I don't even know why, and apart from Anita she's the only person who's kissed me for years and years. Also, she goes to church to say prayers and sing hymns, which makes her really good. I hope she says prayers for me and Zac because if I was God, Hortense is exactly the sort of person I'd listen to because she's like an angel.

Anita's on the list as well; she's always looking out for us, and even though she must be fed up of looking out for two kids nobody wants, she doesn't show it. She just keeps on trying to cheer us up and surprising us with her hair.

The Skilly kids are on my list too. I put Jimmy and Ashani at the top because they're my favorites. All the others are on the same line because I can't choose between them. I like them all the same.

I also put Amanda and Kaleigh from my class on the list, but I put them at the bottom. Because I don't always know if they're going to be nice, and I'm not even sure if I like them. I put them at the bottom so I can tear them off or fold the paper over if I change my mind.

Mrs. Clanks isn't on my list because she makes me feel bad. At first I thought she was a ghost, but now I know she's just a horrible living person. I hope she never becomes a ghost because if she does, Skilly will be haunted forever, and nobody will want to come in because all the kids would die of fright. Even as a living person, she spoils things. She's always trying to catch kids doing something wrong, and she's always thinking things and you can't tell what they are, except they're not very nice.

Jimmy said she locked a boy in a cupboard once and left him there, and he died. He told Zac, and Zac told me. Zac's eyes were really wide like he was scared and excited. Like when the tree blew down.

He said, "And when the boy died he became a skeleton, and someone opened the cupboard and the skeleton fell out, and no one knew who he was or even if it was a boy or a girl because you can't tell with skeletons."

I said, "Don't be stupid, Zac; she couldn't do that. Someone would find out."

But Zac said, "It's true. Jimmy says so, and he's been here the longest."

I said to Hortense, "Did any kid just disappear in Skilly and never be found for years?"

She said, "No, what a strange thing to say. Kids leave to go somewhere else, but they don't just disappear into thin air."

I said, "I think the kid was found in the end, but by then he was a skeleton."

Hortense laughed. She said, "Who's been telling you stories?"

I said, "No one."

Then she looked up at the sky in case God was watching. It's what she does when she's thinking how stupid the world is. And then she hugged me so I think it's okay. Hortense has been here even longer than Jimmy, so she knows.

But even if Mrs. Clanks didn't lock someone in a cupboard, I don't want her on my list, and I don't want her to come to my funeral because she's not very nice. She hates being here, and she hates us being here too.

One time her husband came to get her after work. He waited outside in his car. I didn't even know she had a husband, but Hortense said that's who he was. When she got in the car she gave him a proper smile, not like the ones she gives us. She was just so glad to get away from Skilly.

I think Mrs. Clanks probably wanted to be a flight attendant or a trapeze artist when she was a child, and she's disappointed she ended up here. That's why she makes so many rules. She wants everyone else to be unhappy too.

Some Skilly rules:

Don't drop your bags and coats on the floor.

Don't bother adults if they're busy.

Don't fight with sticks.

Don't bother Silas if he's in his garden.

If the toilet paper roll runs out, tell Hortense.

Don't put toilet paper roll down the sink.

Don't run in the house unless something bad happens, like a fire—and if there is a fire, don't run, because you have to walk out of the house in an orderly fashion.

Don't put anything in front of the fire exits, because then you can't get out.

Don't take food up to your bedroom.

Glenda Hyacinth
May 1989

Something amazing happened today! I'm not going to tell anyone, because it's my secret. I'm so happy, I have to stop myself dancing around, because when Zac saw me he said, "What's up with you?" and I'm not telling anyone what's up.

This is what happened.

I dropped a pencil down the side of my bed, and when I crawled under to get it, a bit of floorboard moved. And under it was a letter! I've been sleeping above a letter since

I was nine, and I didn't even know! All I was thinking about was the birds on the roof. It was in an envelope with stars drawn on it and writing that said *To Whom It May Concern*, which means the person who wrote it didn't know the name of the person it was for.

When I found it I could hardly breathe. I didn't know what to do. I sat on the floor and just stared and stared at it. And then I thought, If it's not for someone special, it could be for me, so I opened it. And inside was a letter from Glenda Hyacinth!

It says *1947* on it so it's really old, but the paper isn't yellow or falling apart. It looks like she wrote it yesterday. I don't think anyone ever touched it apart from Glenda and now me. The writing's old-fashioned and neat; all the letters are the same size, and they all lean in the same direction. This is what it says.

24th September 1947

To Whom It May Concern,

I hope whoever finds this letter is a girl. There are too many boys here already. If you are a boy, please put this letter back.

My name is Glenda Hyacinth, and I am eleven years old. I live in Skilly House, which is an orphanage. I don't remember my family, but I miss them terribly. I especially miss my mother. I hope whoever is reading this has a family and there are no orphanages anymore and everyone has somewhere nice to live.

I got the cane at school today because I didn't know my times tables. I was supposed to recite them all the way to twelve, but I couldn't even remember them up to eight. I had to stand in the corner and practice over and over and I missed my break, and I had to hold my breath so I didn't cry.

The thing I'm best at is handwriting. Even my teacher says so. I hope you think so too. I always make sure the letters touch the lines.

What I like doing best is playing in the bomb site across the road. There used to be a big house there, but now there's only rubble because the Germans bombed it. I pretend the house is still there and I live there and I'm helping my mother cook dinner and lay the table. Once I found a red ribbon and I washed it and kept it and now I wear it, and once I found a photograph of a family, but I didn't keep that. I dug a hole and buried it in the ground.

I also like climbing the tree in the garden. If I could fly, I would climb to the top of the tree and fly away and never come back.

With love from
Glenda

I was so amazed, I read it over and over just to make sure it was real. And all the time I was reading, I kept checking the door in case Zac came in because I don't

50

want him to laugh or tell everyone. And now I know the letter by heart. I've always thought about Glenda, and now I feel like I've met her. Then I wrote a letter back.

14th May 1989

Dear Glenda,

I hope you don't mind me writing, but I found your letter under the floorboard. I am a girl, though I share the room with my brother, Zac. I hope that's OK. He always wants to share, but I don't really mind. I think I'd be lonely on my own. I hope you weren't too lonely here. I'm ten and three quarters. Zac's nine.

My real name's Miracle, but everyone calls me Ira. Zac's real name is Zackery.

It's really nice to read your letter. I know your name because it's on the windowsill. You must have pressed really hard, because it's gone in really deep. I think it will be there forever.

I'm sorry you got the cane for not knowing your times tables. If I was hit for getting my times tables wrong I'd be black and blue, but my teacher doesn't hit me for not knowing. She just rolls her eyes.

There isn't a bomb site across the road anymore. There's a block of flats, and lots of people live there. I don't think they know ghosts are watching them when they're making cups of tea or eating breakfast. There isn't a tree in the garden at Skilly now either. A storm blew it over. Me and Zac saw it. It was amazing.

Skilly House is still an orphanage, but people call it a children's home now. Me and Zac don't have parents either, and I miss them too. Missing them is like a hole in my heart.

I'm going to put your letter back under the floor and I'm going to put this letter there too, and in the future maybe another girl will find them. Maybe by then people will think care kids are special and treat them even better than other kids, and Skilly will be like a palace and everyone will want to go there. Can you imagine it?

I know you must be really old now or even dead, but I'm going to think of you as my friend. You can think of me as a friend too if you like, even if you are a ghost. And if you want to watch me and Zac some-times, that's OK.

Love from Ira

PS Your writing is much better than mine. I can't make all my letters touch the lines. I can't stop them going in all different directions.

Then I got an envelope that was left over from a birthday card, and I put my letter in it and wrote *Sorry about the envelope* on the back because it was pink. Then I wrote *To Glenda* on the front and put it under the floorboard with Glenda's letter.

And now I feel like I've got a new friend, even though she's a friend from the past. Even though she's probably dead. I've always wanted a special friend, and now I've got one.

City Kids, Country Kids
June 1989

Me and Zac are going on holiday! It's our first ever! All the Skilly kids have been on holiday except us. I don't know if it's because there's two of us and we want to stay together, but we've never been. We've been on outings, just not holidays. Anita took us to the National Gallery in Trafalgar Square to look at the old paintings. I really liked them, but Zac got bored and set off an alarm by going over the rope that stops people from touching them. Afterward we had a picnic in Trafalgar Square and climbed on the

 54

lion statues and fed the pigeons. The pigeons went crazy. All you could see was their fluttering wings and nodding heads.

I've been on a boat on the Thames with my class too. We went under the bridges, and a man told us the history of London and pointed out special buildings. We couldn't see him. His voice was coming out of the ceiling, but I think he was standing on the top. I didn't enjoy it though. I felt so sick, I couldn't look up.

But me and Zac have never been away for a week, or even for a night, and come back. If we ever go away for a night, we don't come back. Ever.

The holiday's organized by City Kids, Country Kids. It's a charity where people who live in the country let city kids stay with them. It's like when country people had evacuees like Silas—only now they don't have to keep them for years; they can keep them for a week and send them back. It's better that way in case they don't like them.

Mrs. Clanks called us into her office. We were worried because kids usually go in there to be given bad news or told off. I've been in twice before today. Once was because I lied to cover up for Zac when he took a packet of cookies from Hortense's tin that was hidden behind the rice in the pantry. Now the tin's behind the cereals on the fridge and he can't reach it, even standing on a chair. I got into as much trouble for lying as Zac did for stealing the cookies. Mrs. Clanks said if we did that sort of thing we'd ruin our lives. She didn't shout. She just stared at us like she could see how awful we were inside. She made me feel cold.

The other time was when my school report said I was looking out of the window in lessons. Mrs. Clanks tapped her finger on her desk and said, "If you're not careful, you'll come to nothing," which means my life will be wasted. But I think my life's wasted anyway. What sort of life is a care kid's except a waste?

But this time when we went in, she was sort of smiling. It made my heart jump (not in a good way), because I wondered if she was going to send us away and that's why she was happy. She had a yellow ribbon in her hair.

Wearing a ribbon is Mrs. Clanks's distinguishing feature, which means it's the thing that makes her different. If someone didn't know what she looked like, you'd say the woman with the ribbon. It's like burglars wear striped sweaters and Frenchmen have curly mustaches. I don't like it though. It just looks weird. Maybe she wants to look young, but it doesn't work. It makes her look even older.

When we sat down she said, "I have good news. I've found someone to take you for a holiday."

Then she waited for us to say something. But we didn't speak. We were too shocked.

"It wasn't easy to place you together," she said, "but a lady called Miss Freeman will take you. This is a big opportunity. You are going in the summer. I will take you on the train, you will stay for a week, and I will pick you up and bring you back to Skilly."

I felt faint after that. I couldn't work out if I was happy or worried, and I felt dizzy with it. Because going on a train with Mrs. Clanks is the worst way to start a holiday. But then she's going to leave us there, so that's okay.

"You must be polite at all times," Mrs. Clanks said, "and do any jobs required of you, and afterward Miss Freeman will tell me how you've behaved. What do you think?"

I wasn't sure what I was thinking, so I nodded and said, "Thank you."

Zac screwed his eyes tight shut and just sat there. It's what he does when he wants to hide. It's like when little kids put their hands over their eyes and they think you can't see them. Except Zac's nine years old. I'm hoping he'll grow out of it soon.

Mrs. Clanks looked at Zac for a few moments.

Then she said, "Well, off you go then."

I pulled Zac's arm and he followed me out. He didn't

even open his eyes. He was tripping over me. When we got in the hall, he leaned against the wall because he felt wobbly.

He thinks Mrs. Clanks is going to leave us in the forest like Hansel and Gretel and let the animals eat us. I'm worried too. Not about being left in a forest but in case we don't come back.

I told Hortense and she said, "Ira, don't you worry, you'll have a wonderful time. You won't want to come back, but when you do we'll be here."

Silas said, "You'll never forget it, Ira. Take it with both hands."

When he said that, it made me think of Christmas dinner because I always take that with both hands. It's my favorite meal apart from the stuffing. My other favorites are sausages and mash when Hortense cooks it, and fish and chips eaten on a beach when you have to chase the seagulls away. I haven't had fish and chips on a beach yet. It's a favorite for the future.

After I talked to Silas and Hortense, I didn't feel so worried. Then I told everyone else. Esther got a bit huffy, even though she's had two holidays and we've had none. I expect she wants another one. Jimmy's annoyed too. He said, "How long for?" and I said, "A week," and he said, "Oh yeah . . . ," like "yeah" had lots of dots after it, like we weren't really coming back. And now he's ignoring me. Sophia and Miles wish they were going and Milap said, "That's nice," and Harit said, "I'm going to get you for that!" and chased Zac around the garden.

Ashani's really excited. She said, "You've got to start packing NOW," even though we're not going for weeks, and then she wrote me a list. It said:

What to take on holiday
faverit toy
faverit outfit
faverit thing to do

All the *favorites* were spelled wrong. I didn't say anything. I just gave her a hug and said, "This is for my faverit girl."

I've told Glenda about the holiday too. I told her in my head. I wonder if she ever had a holiday. I hope she's pleased because she can have our room to herself for a week.

Ashani
July 1989

Ashani went to see her new family yesterday. It's the third time she's been. They might adopt her. They've got a garden, and if she goes to live there they'll buy a goal so she can play football. They've got a grown-up daughter who's at university. Ashani met her and said she's nice and wears glasses and green nail varnish, and she smokes so her breath smells funny. Ashani said she likes the family, but last night she came into our room in her bunny pajamas and she was crying. She didn't know why. She just felt all mixed up inside.

I let her sleep in my bed. Zac didn't mind. He doesn't come in my bed now, and anyway Ashani's his favorite. This morning she was back to normal. She did bunny jumps all the way down the stairs while Zac was a fox chasing her.

I hope Ashani's family don't just want to foster her so she has to move again.

Milap and Harit

Milap and Harit went to see their mum and dad today. They were so happy. They couldn't stop talking about it. They went on a rowing boat in the park, and then they went to a café. Milap had egg and chips and Harit had egg, beans and chips, and their dad had egg, beans, chips and tomato and their mum wasn't hungry so she just had a cup of tea. It sounded lovely.

But when we were having tea, Milap wouldn't eat anything.

Hortense said, "Go on, have a little bit; you'll be hungry later."

She said it nicely but Milap suddenly jumped up and threw his plate on the floor. The plate smashed and the food went everywhere and it was spaghetti Bolognese, so it made a big mess. Bits of spaghetti were stuck to the cupboards. They looked like worms.

Then Milap shouted, "I hate it here!" and after that he couldn't stop shouting it, like it was the only thing in his head. He shouted, "I hate it here! I hate it!" over and over and then he ran up to his room, and even though he slammed his door we could still hear him shouting.

Harit didn't say anything. He put his hands over his ears and opened his mouth like he was screaming but no sound came out. Not even a whisper. It made me feel awful because I couldn't tell how bad it was, but I knew it must be very bad. It was even worse than Milap shouting out loud.

Hortense took Harit away and Silas sat with us while we finished our tea, except no one did finish it because we'd all lost our appetites. Because if Milap can shout like that and throw his plate and he's really gentle and sweet, it made us think what the rest of us could do. Because we aren't like other people. Other people have all their emotions spread out like all different shades of color, like if you go from red through purple until you end up with blue. But we have our emotions right next to each other so one moment we're happy and then suddenly we're angry and sometimes we don't feel anything at all. It's scary being like that.

Packing
August 1989

Me and Zac go on holiday tomorrow. While we were packing Ashani came in with her Crystal Palace shirt.

She said, "Do you want to take this with you? You can if you like."

She meant me because Zac supports Arsenal.

I said, "No thanks, Ashani. It's too precious."

She looked glad.

Then I said, "I wish I could take you instead," and I tickled her and she laughed and said, "Me too."

Going on Holiday

Zac felt sick this morning. He said he was too ill to go on holiday.

I said, "You have to go. It's a big opportunity."

He said, "We won't come back, will we?"

I said, "Of course we will. We're only going for a week."

He didn't believe me.

Then I said, "Well, I'm going anyway, even if you don't come," which wasn't true. I'd never go away without him. I didn't think he'd believe me but he did. He stuck out his bottom lip and didn't say another word.

Mrs. Clanks told us to put on our best clothes, the ones we don't normally wear because they're so uncomfortable. Zac wore his white shirt with the collar that digs into his neck and his shorts with the itchy waistband. I wore the green dress I've had since I was nine. It was too big when I got it, and now it's too small. We looked like cartoons with wobbly faces drawn on. Only we didn't look funny.

Hortense gave us sandwiches for the train. Her eyes were shiny, and when I said "Bye," she hugged me really tight. I wanted to stay like that forever. Zac stood completely still when she hugged him, but I knew he didn't want to move either. He wanted to stop time. I wish Hortense could adopt us. I wish she was our mum.

Then I said, "See you," to Jimmy, but he looked away.

We got in the back of Silas's old car that he always has to empty before we get in because he's always picking up junk. Then Mrs. Clanks got in the front. She had a polka dot ribbon in her hair. She didn't say, "Good morning." She just said, "Seat belts on?" After that no one talked. It reminded me of when we came to Skilly.

Silas waited with us at the station. When the train came Mrs. Clanks said, "Coach C, this way," and ran down the platform. I thought her ribbon would fall out. I imagined it lying in the dust, but it stayed in.

As we got on the train Silas said, "Now, don't you forget why you're going—to have some fun."

I had a lump in my throat and it was hurting. Zac pressed his face into Silas's jacket.

"And you, little one," Silas said. "Run and run and use up that energy, eh?"

We got a table on the train. Me and Zac sat one side and Mrs. Clanks sat on the other. Silas put our bags on the rack and said, "I'll see you next week. I'll be waiting for you."

He waved us good-bye from the platform, and we watched him get smaller and smaller until the train turned a corner and he was gone. Zac was nearly crying.

 65

Mrs. Clanks got some papers out of her bag.

"Do you mind if I work?" she said.

We shook our heads because we didn't mind. We were glad. We didn't want to talk to Mrs. Clanks. We never talk to her, except when she tells us what to do, and then we don't talk anyway. She does.

Sometimes we imagine she's a robot and we pretend to be her. We wind her up and do her stony face and make her move faster and faster and crash into things. Zac's really good at it. Even when he falls on the floor, his face stays completely blank. He's really funny.

But I think it's best to be like a robot if you do Mrs. Clanks's job, because whatever happens she always looks the same. You need to be like that when you look after care kids. She doesn't shout and she doesn't cry even when kids are really upset, and her smile's the same whether she's saying "Hello" or "Watch out!" It's the kind of smile you need if you don't know if the news you're giving is good or bad.

As soon as we couldn't see Silas anymore, Zac started wriggling. I got out my sketchbook.

"Do a picture of Mrs. Clanks," he whispered.

I drew her with a tiny head and tiny hands reading a gigantic bit of paper. Zac tried to draw a mustache on her, but I wouldn't let him. He made such a fuss, I shut the book.

66

"Let's count animals," I said.

London was flying past. It felt like it would go on forever. There were streets and shops and flats and houses and parks, and all of them had people in them. We must have gone past millions and millions of people, but the only animal we saw was an angry dog chewing a bit of wood.

"Boring," said Zac, and he pressed his tongue against the window and began to lick down the glass.

"Zac, don't do that," Mrs. Clanks said.

He didn't hear her at first. He just kept licking. Then he realized she was watching and he put his tongue in. He looked annoyed.

"Please don't do that sort of thing while you're away," Mrs. Clanks said. "I'm sure Miss Freeman won't appreciate it."

There was a smear down the glass like a giant snail trail. Mrs. Clanks gave Zac a tissue, but it wouldn't wipe away. I think you'd need soap to get it off.

I tried to change the subject so we could all stop thinking about it.

"What's Miss Freeman like?" I said.

"I haven't met her yet myself," Mrs. Clanks said, "but I understand she's very nice. She used to be a headmistress, so she's had plenty of practice looking after children. She'll be old-school, so she won't put up with any nonsense. You will have to behave yourselves."

Then she looked at Zac.

"Zac?" she said.

She put a question mark after his name. She meant "You will behave yourself, won't you, Zac?"

Zac didn't answer. He just sighed. He didn't even try to keep it inside. He went "Hhhhhhhh" for a really long time. He didn't care what she thought.

I tried to smile because I didn't want Mrs. Clanks to think other kids might be more grateful and then take us back to London. But old-school made me think of Glenda getting the cane for not knowing her times tables. It didn't sound fun at all.

Suddenly, Zac shouted, "Cows!" There was a field of cows, not just one like at the city farm, but lots of them chewing and flicking their tails.

"And sheep," he said, because then there was a field of sheep all walking in a long line like they were queuing up for the best bit of grass.

After that we looked out the window for the rest of the journey. It was so nice. We just ignored the smear on the window. There were farms and fields and rivers and woods and people fishing and walking their dogs and little towns and villages. We saw a big bird fly through the sky, and we argued about whether it was a crow or an eagle. Zac thought it was an eagle. Then it rained and the raindrops came sideways across the window so they looked like tadpoles racing each other. And when we ate our sandwiches, the sun came out, and there was a rainbow.

By the time we got off the train, I felt all scrunched up, like I'd been stuck in a little box. Zac felt the same. As we stood on the platform he swung his arms around like a windmill. Then he tried to do a cartwheel.

"Please, Zac," Mrs. Clanks said. "Do you want to come back to London with me?"

When everyone had gone, the only person left on the platform was a funny-looking woman with her head pushed forward like a chicken, nodding and bobbing. When she saw us she hurried over. Her hand was stretched out.

"Mrs. Clanks?" she said.

She smiled and looked serious all at the same time, and her voice was soft and high like a child's, even though she was quite old. Mrs. Clanks shook her hand.

"Miss Freeman, pleased to meet you," she said.

"Do call me Martha," said the woman.

She had glasses with silver rims and a chain that went down from her glasses and all the way around her neck in case they fell off. Her hair was brown and speckly gray and it was tied up, but bits were dropping out. She was wearing a yellow dress with no sleeves like a little girl's, and she was very tall and had paint on her dress and big feet like a man's, and she was wearing red sandals. Zac nudged me. I knew he was smirking, but I wouldn't catch his eye.

The woman bent down to look at us. She was a mixture of old and young. She was wrinkly but she had bright shiny eyes like Ashani's. Then I noticed something I've never seen in a grown-up before—she was shy! I've never met a grown-up who's shy. I didn't think grown-ups could be shy because they have to do so many grown-up things. But that's how she looked—shy.

"You must be Miracle," she said.

I nodded. Even though I hate that name, I didn't want to be rude.

"Pleased to meet you," I said, and I gave a little curtsy, like I was meeting the queen. I felt stupid. I knew Zac would think I was an idiot. Martha bowed back.

"And Zackery, lovely to meet you."

Zac scowled.

"Come on then," the woman said. "It's a bit of a drive, but it won't take long. Let me take your cases."

She hurried off, pulling my case and pushing Zac's.

Mrs. Clanks followed her. Then she turned back to us and mouthed, "Come on!" Zac scuffed his feet. He was disappointed already.

"She's just like a teacher," he said.

Appleton House

Martha's town is called Wellsbury. It's not like London at all. The streets have trees on both sides and I only saw one NO POLL TAX sign and no people with placards. There are no sirens either, and no traffic jams.

Martha's house is at the end of a cul-de-sac, which is a street that stops so you can't go any farther. Her house blocks the road so if you kept on driving you'd crash right into it, and it's got sky around it instead of being squeezed into a gap like Skilly.

There's a window above her door and it says APPLETON HOUSE in gold writing. I thought only children's homes and prisons had names. It's nice for a normal person's house to have a name too. It gives it personality. Martha said it's called Appleton House because there used to be apple trees there.

At first I thought loads of people must live there because the coat rack's covered in coats and hats and old-fashioned umbrellas that don't fold up. But it's only

Martha. All the things are hers. There's an old mirror in the hall, with silver coming off so it's like looking into a frozen pond. And there's a black-and-white photo of a man with a beard dressed like a vicar, and wherever you stand it looks as though he's staring right at you. It's like he's reminding you God's always watching. You can't get away from him.

Martha's sitting room is the nicest room in the world. There's a rocking chair with a torn cushion, a lumpy yellow sofa, a footstool covered in roses that have nearly faded away and a table with books and magazines on top. There's a fireplace with dusty bits of coal in it, and there are bookshelves all the way from the floor to the ceiling, and everywhere that's not covered in books is covered in plants and paintings. I was trying to work out why it looks nicer than Skilly even though everything's scruffy, and I think it's because Martha loves it. Skilly looks like nobody ever loved it at all.

But Zac didn't look at the room. He went straight to the window and stared at the garden. It's got a lawn like a bowling green that no kids ever play on, and there are no tall buildings all around. And there are flowers all down the sides of the grass, and at the bottom there's a tree with leaves that go all the way to the ground.

Martha said to Zac, "Do you like it?"

Zac shrugged, which gave the wrong impression. It was because he liked it too much.

"That tree," Martha said, "is called a weeping willow because it looks like it's weeping."

And it did. Its leaves looked like they were tears falling to the ground.

"Why don't you have a look," Martha said.

She opened the windows and they weren't windows at all. They were doors, and you can walk right through them.

"Off you go," she said.

Zac didn't move. He was frozen.

"Can I go too?" I said.

"Of course," said Martha.

I took Zac's hand and pulled him, and suddenly we were running on the grass under the big, blue, perfect sky.

"There's a stream at the bottom of the garden—take your shoes off," Martha said.

But we weren't paying attention. Zac was doing somer-saults and I was spinning around and around because my dress was too tight to do anything else in. When we got to the weeping willow, we stood underneath it and looked up. Light was streaming through the leaves. It was like being in a church.

Behind the tree there's a stream that goes under the fence at the bottom of the garden and out into some woods. Zac crouched on some stones across the stream and pulled a handful of mud out of the water. Then he rubbed it all over his face.

"Zac! You idiot!" I said.

He stuck out his tongue. "What do I look like?"

"Stig of the Dump."

He grinned. It's his favorite book.

"You do it," he said. "Go on."

I shook my head. "I'll watch."

"Okay," said Zac. "I'll catch a fish and you can have it."

He leaned out to where the water was deeper, and then he began to wobble. I knew he'd fall in. That's what he's like. If he wants to do something he will, even if it means trouble later. He had a big smile on his face because he knew he was about to get wet and no one could stop him.

When he fell it was like slow motion. Even the splashes looked like they came up slowly. Then he got on his hands and knees and began to bark like a dog, and then he dipped his head in the water and shook it. He's good at being a dog. He's always wanted one, and he's always pretending to be one. He's had lots of practice.

But even though I was laughing on the outside, a bit of me was thinking, what if Mrs. Clanks and Martha come? Because Zac didn't look like the boy who got off the train. He looked like a different boy. He was covered in mud, his curls were stuck to his head and his shirt wasn't white anymore. Martha might be shocked to see him.

"Zac, get out," I said.

He shook his head. "Nah-nah-na-na-nah."

But then his face went tight and he wasn't looking at me anymore. He was looking behind me, and when I turned around I saw Mrs. Clanks and Martha coming through the willow. The lines between Mrs. Clanks's eyes were really deep. She was shaking her head, and her spotty ribbon was bobbing from side to side.

"Get out, Zac," she said.

Her voice was extra calm. She must have been really angry.

Zac tried to get out but he kept slipping. In the end I had to pull him. Then he just stood very still and squeezed his eyes shut. Water was dribbling out of his shoes. Martha was staring at him through her silver glasses. She was probably wondering what happened to the nice boy in the white shirt. I crossed my fingers and wished she wouldn't send us home.

"I'm terribly sorry," Mrs. Clanks said. "He's full of beans."

Martha made a little "um" noise.

Then she said, "Why don't you take off your shoes and socks, Zackery, and your nice shirt, and have a play."

Zac didn't even open his eyes to take off his socks and shoes. He did it with his eyes shut. It took ages. It was embarrassing. I picked three bits of grass and braided them together so I wouldn't have to watch.

When they walked back to the house, Martha was holding Zac's shoes by the laces and her hand was stretched out like when she met us at the station, only this time it was because she didn't want to get mud on her clothes. Mrs. Clanks was carrying Zac's shirt and her hand was stretched out too, and her other hand was flapping at flies.

Tea with Martha

Me and Zac stayed by the stream for ages, but it was no fun. I kept thinking Mrs. Clanks would take us back to Skilly. I was trying to imagine what expression I could have on my face when we got there to make it less awful. I decided to look like I was pleased to be back and a bit annoyed about the whole experience.

But then Mrs. Clanks came to tell us she was getting a taxi back to the station. She gave us a look and said, "Behave yourselves," and then she went. I took such a deep breath, I felt dizzy.

After that Martha came to get us for tea. She made us wash our hands under a tap in the garden. The water was so cold I thought my fingers would drop off. It probably turns to ice in the winter. Then she took us up to our room. It was only fourteen steps.

"I'm told you like to share," she said, "but there's a room each if you'd like."

Zac shook his head.

"We'll share," I said.

"Very well," said Martha. "Then this is your room. I hope you like it. Come down to the dining room when you've cleaned up."

Our bedroom looks like it hasn't changed for fifty years, or maybe a hundred. It's got two beds with metal frames and a dressing table with drawers and a mirror shaped like a heart. There's a sink with HOT and COLD written on the taps, and a wooden desk with a lid that lifts up and an inkwell where people used to put ink when they used pens made of feathers. There's faded wallpaper with leaves on it and they're all lined up, and there's a wardrobe that's got the same wallpaper inside, only it isn't faded. I'm going to keep the wardrobe open the whole time we're there so it matches the walls.

Zac put on his shorts and Arsenal shirt, and I put on my jeans and T-shirt. I'm not going to wear the dress again. Not if I can help it. I'm going to leave it here and pretend I forgot it. Before we went downstairs I tried to wash Zac's face and his hair, because it still had loads of mud in it. The mud got stuck to the sink, though at least he looked better.

You can tell which is the dining room because there's a table and chairs in the middle. There are books and boxes and plants all over the floor, but if you saw the table on its own you'd think you were in a restaurant. There was a tablecloth and there was a teapot covered in purple flowers and matching cups and saucers. The teapot was chipped, so I think the tea set was really old, but Martha loved it too much to get rid of it. There were even little glass pots with silver lids with salt and pepper in them, like you get in cafés. There were napkins too, and sandwiches and sausage rolls and crisps and small tomatoes and chocolate biscuits. It was like a birthday party where there were hardly any guests and someone had forgotten the cake.

Martha was sitting at the table when we went in. She hadn't eaten anything. She was just waiting for us. She was very polite. She said, "Please tuck in." She looked a bit worried, as if the tea wasn't good enough for us. Or maybe it was too good, or maybe she was worried that we'd left mud in the sink.

Zac ate a sandwich so fast it made his eyes water. He just stuffed it in. Then he took another.

78

"Miracle, help yourself," Martha said. "And drink your tea. It's not too hot."

I didn't want to say we don't drink tea and we've never drunk out of a cup and saucer either, so I put my finger through the handle and lifted the cup really carefully. I pretended I was in an old film and the waitress was waiting to see if I liked it. If I did she would top up my cup with some more. But the tea tasted like warm water. Maybe it's better with sugar like Silas has it. I told the imaginary waitress not to worry. When I put the cup back in the saucer it made a little clink.

After that we didn't talk. We just ate. Zac made a mess like he always does. Hortense says she needs a dog to eat the food he drops on the floor. Crumbs kept falling out of his mouth on to the tablecloth. I had to be extra tidy to make up for him, so Martha might think the mess came from two kids. Martha looked very serious. She was cutting bits off her sausage roll and putting them in her mouth with all different expressions on her face, like she didn't know what to think.

"I do hope you'll be happy here," she said at last.

"It's a lovely garden," I said.

"It's so big," said Zac.

"We have a garden at Skilly," I said, "but we have to share it with lots of other kids."

Then Zac said, "How long have you lived here?"

Martha made a little cough and said, "All my life."

Zac's mouth fell open. It was embarrassing. It was full of food and he didn't shut it. He just kept staring at her. I tried not to stare, but I was shocked too.

"I was born in this house," Martha said. "I lived here with my parents and brother. My father was a vicar. My parents are dead now, and my brother lives in Australia. This has always been my home."

It was hard to understand what she meant. I didn't know someone could live in the same place all their life, right from being a baby to an old person. I'd never even thought of it.

Martha's cheeks went red and then the red went all the way down her neck.

"Please don't worry," she said. "There may be old things here, but there's nothing valuable."

After that everything felt funny in a bad way. I don't even know why. I just felt really bad. Like we'd come to a different planet that we didn't even know existed.

Martha pushed Zac's cup of tea toward him.

"Have a little drink, Zackery," she said.

He shrugged, then he picked up the saucer with both hands, balancing the cup on top. It was fine at first, but when he tried to drink, the cup slid off the saucer and fell down his front. Tea poured down his Arsenal shirt and onto the floor.

Martha jumped up.

"Oh dear me. Are you burned?"

Zac shook his head. He was looking at his shirt. It was stuck to his chest.

"We don't normally drink out of this sort of cup," I said.

"Of course not," Martha said. "Silly me."

She ran out and came back with some towels.

"There you go, Zackery. Dry yourself down."

Zac looked so sad. He loves his shirt so much he even sleeps in it. Martha began to mop the floor.

"Can I help?" I said.

"No, no, no, Miracle," she said. "Please don't worry."

She was kneeling under the table.

Zac was nearly crying.

"I think we'll go upstairs now," I said.

"Are you sure you've had enough to eat?" she said.

"Yes, thank you. We're full, aren't we, Zac?"

Zac nodded.

"Very well," she said. "Good night."

As we were going upstairs I had a thought, so I ran back.

"Martha?" I said.

She looked up.

"Yes, Miracle?"

"Could you call me Ira instead of Miracle?"

She nodded.

"And Zackery, Zac?"

"Yes," she said. "Of course."

Her face was very hot and her glasses were falling off her nose. It was lucky she had the chain.

When we got upstairs Zac kicked the wall so hard, he made a dent in the wallpaper.

"Zac, be careful," I said. "She'll send us away."

"I don't care. It's too fancy here. I hate it."

He sat on the bed, and I put my arm around his shoulder.

"Will my shirt be okay?" he said.

"Yes," I said. "We'll soak it in the sink."

We sat there for a while just thinking, and then he said, "I don't really hate it here."

"I know," I said. "It's just different. I think it'll be okay if we try to be good."

And now he's asleep and he looks like an angel, and I wish Martha could see him, because then she'd understand that he's all different things all at the same time. He's clumsy and he always finds trouble and he pretends he doesn't care, but he's also very sweet.

 82

Chickens

I couldn't sleep last night. I was worried we'd upset Martha, and anyway it's too quiet here. There's hardly any noise except for animal sounds, and I don't know what animals they are. Birds, maybe, and foxes. They squeak and yelp and all around them is silence. I tried to picture them in my head, but I couldn't. I just lay there wishing I could hear a siren or traffic or people shouting in the street. Just so I'd know we weren't on our own.

When it was morning I was worried in case Martha wanted to send us back to Skilly. But she said, "Morning, children!" in a singsong voice and didn't seem cross at all. At breakfast there was no tablecloth, and we had mugs and plates that didn't match. I expect she thought it wouldn't matter if we broke one. Me and Zac didn't drink tea either. We had juice.

After breakfast Martha said, "We're going to get eggs for lunch." We climbed over the fence at the bottom of the garden and into the woods and walked along a path. There were so many trees that when I looked up I could only see little bits of sky. Apart from that, it was all green leaves. Zac was chasing squirrels, but they were too quick for him. He couldn't even touch their tails. It's the nicest walk in the world. It was two miles there and two miles back. I don't know if I've walked that far before, but I could have walked forever.

We got to a farm with a field full of chickens. There was a table next to the gate and a saucer with money in it and some empty egg boxes.

"There's no eggs left," I said.

Martha smiled.

"We collect our own."

"What do you mean?" said Zac.

"We collect them from the chickens."

She gave us a box each, and we went into the field. The chickens started squawking when they saw us and ran around making bubbling noises and shaking their feathers. Me and Zac were frightened. Zac kept screaming and jumping around. His eyes were nearly popping out of his head. Martha said the chickens wouldn't hurt us. They were only excited because they thought we were going to feed them. But we kept running away. We couldn't help it.

After a while Martha said, "If you don't calm down, I'll get the eggs myself."

So we calmed down and the chickens calmed down too, and then they were just clucking.

We found eggs hidden under straw in the field and also

 84

in the chicken coop, which is where they sleep. Some had feathers stuck on and bits of mud, and most were white, and some were speckled and one was brown. When we filled our egg boxes we had six each, which makes a dozen. Martha put some money in the saucer. She said the farmer would get it later.

I said, "What if someone takes it?"

She said, "Who's going to take it?"

I looked around. There was no one there except us.

"No one," I said.

As we walked back Martha said, "I hear even people in London keep chickens."

"That's the sort of thing Silas would do," I said.

"Who's Silas?" Martha said.

"He looks after Skilly," I said. "He's the caretaker."

Then I said, "He was an evacuee," and Zac said, "He's traveled the world."

We wanted Martha to know how interesting he is.

Later we had eggs with toast fingers. Martha called them *soldiers*. I think it's because she lived in the war. The eggs were really nice. I'd never had an egg that was just laid. Then we played in the garden and Zac fell in the stream again, but he didn't get into trouble so I jumped in too.

But after that things went wrong. Zac climbed the

willow and broke a branch off, and it fell down with all its leaves just lying there.

Martha said, "Do you have to climb everything?" She said it quietly, but that made it worse.

Zac shrugged, which looked not very nice.

Then we fell on some flowers and they broke. Martha took them inside and put them in a jug, but they looked better in the garden, and now they'll die soon.

Later on Zac broke the rocking chair. Rocking chairs are for old people, not kids, so he should never have sat on it. He was rocking really hard. He looked like he was about to take off and then he flew right over the back and one of the rockers snapped. I expect the chair belonged to Martha's parents or grandparents even, and that means it's *priceless*, which means you could never have enough money to pay for it because it's worth more than money. Martha probably sat on it when she was a little girl, so it's full of her dreams.

I was so upset, I had to stop myself from crying. Zac said to keep it a secret but I told Martha because she'd find out anyway, and if we didn't tell her she wouldn't trust us. When she saw it her face went red. Then she put it in the corner and said not to touch it.

When she'd gone Zac called me a snitch.

"I'm not a snitch," I said.

86

"Yes, you are," he said. "I hate you."

And we had a fight and a cushion got torn and this time I didn't tell Martha. I just turned the cushion over so she wouldn't see it yet, because I thought if she saw one more thing go wrong today she might send us home. If it was on TV people would laugh, but in real life it wasn't funny at all.

At teatime Zac ate really quickly and I kept saying please and thank you and didn't eat much, and Martha hardly ate anything at all. She just looked sad. She was probably thinking if we stay for a week she'll have nothing left that isn't broken. She must be disappointed, especially as she's old-school.

And now Zac's asleep and I don't even want to cry anymore.

I think me and Zac are in the wrong place. It's like if you play a football match on an ice rink, and the players keep falling over. Or if you put a teacher in the jungle, and there's nowhere for the desks and chairs. We're always in the wrong place. Me and Zac don't belong in a normal house—we belong in a *children's home*.

Zac wants to go back to Skilly, but I want to stay here. I'm crossing my fingers and saying prayers in my head in case God's listening, even though I'm not sure if I believe in him.

Reasons to stay:
I want to collect more eggs.
I like the garden.
The house is full of interesting things.
I want to get used to the quiet at night.
We can see stars.
I like Martha.
Martha might like us if she knew us better.
If we go back to Skilly, the others will laugh at us and Hortense and Silas will be disappointed, and Mrs. Clanks will be angry and like us even less.
If we can't be happy here for one week, people will think we can never be happy and no one will want us for good.
I want to do some drawing in the garden.

Reasons to go back early:
None.

Bats

Me and Zac didn't break anything today. We were extra careful. We didn't touch anything unless we had to, like if we had to pick up a cup to have a drink. Martha was quiet. I kept thinking she wished she'd never invited us to stay, but she was too polite to say.

She told us to make ourselves at home, but we didn't feel comfortable in the house so we stayed in the garden. When we came in she kept clearing up after us. She put our shoes into pairs when we left them in the hall, and she picked up our cups as soon as we'd finished with them. You'd think in such a messy house it wouldn't matter where things are but they must be in a special order, even though other people can't tell.

For dinner we had shepherd's pie. It wasn't as nice as when Hortense makes it. Martha isn't the best cook. It's probably not worth cooking for just one person, so she doesn't get much practice. She probably mostly eats sand-wiches. Then we went back in the garden.

We had ham sandwiches for tea and little pink cakes called fondant fancies, but I lost my appetite and couldn't eat any. I was waiting for Martha to tell us we were going back to London early. I didn't want to be swallowing when she told us. I kept my fingers crossed under the table. She looked funny—not funny ha-ha, but funny like she was thinking something she wasn't saying. When she finished drinking her tea she put the cup in the saucer and made a little cough.

"Ira and Zac," she said. "I do hope you'll be patient with me."

Her head was bobbing.

"I haven't had children of my own," she said. "I've

rather missed out, I think. So I tend to be set in my ways. You two will be an education to me."

I wasn't sure what she meant but I thought she wasn't sending us back to Skilly, so I uncrossed my fingers. Zac took one of the pink cakes, bit off the top and licked out the cream.

"The funny thing is," Martha said, "when I was a headmistress I would speak to hundreds of children at a time, but I don't think I have ever sat down to tea with just two."

She smiled.

"Can you understand that, Zac?" she said.

Zac looked surprised, like if a teacher asked him a question and he hadn't been paying attention. He pushed the whole cake into his mouth so he wouldn't have to answer. Then he started coughing.

Martha's face went all out of shape.

"Spit it out, Zac," she said.

Her voice was wobbly.

Zac spat the cake into his hand. It was all soggy and pink and crumbly. He looked at it for a moment and then he shrugged and put it back on the plate with all the other cakes no one had touched. I felt so ashamed.

At first I thought Martha was crying. Her eyes were wet and her face was all screwed up. But then I saw she wasn't crying at all; she was laughing. She laughed quietly at first, but then she was laughing really loudly and she was rocking from side to side, and her glasses went lopsided. Zac was laughing too and making faces like he thought he was the funniest kid in the world, and I just thought how stupid everything was and I started laughing as well. And then we were all laughing and looking at the pink blob on the plate.

We laughed for ages. Just when we all stopped, someone started again.

Then Martha said, "Fill up your plates; take what you like. Bring a drink too and follow me."

And we carried our plates down to the stream.

"Now," Martha said, "whatever we spill, the birds will eat."

We stayed out by the stream until it was nearly dark. Me and Zac tried to build a dam, but the water still got through. We told Martha about Skilly and Silas and Hortense and the tree blowing down. She told us about her life with her big brother Douglas and her dad the vicar and her mum who used to make tea for the congregation, who are the people who go to church. It's her dad in the picture in the hall. He's the one who's always watching.

And she told us her full name is Martha Bonita

Freeman. Bonita's a Spanish name. It sounds quite funny next to Martha. It was her gran's name, but her gran never went to Spain. She didn't even like going on holiday. It's a mystery why she was called Bonita. Martha said all families have mysteries.

And she told us one time Douglas found a baby hedgehog, and they fed it bread and milk until it got bigger and then they set it free. It crawled into the grass by the stream, and now she thinks its great-great-great-great-grandchildren might live in the garden.

And she also said she always wanted to prove she was as clever as Douglas because in those days people thought boys were cleverer than girls. That's why she became a teacher and a headmistress. But her real dream was to be an artist, and now she's stopped being a headmistress, and she's got a studio at the top of the house. She said she'll let us see it tomorrow! And then I remembered seeing the paint on her dress when she met us at the station and it didn't seem funny at all anymore; it seemed wonderful.

We all stayed outside really late. When it got dark bats came out and swooped around us, and we sat by the stream and watched and didn't talk at all and everything was perfect.

Martha's Studio

Martha's studio is in the attic. It's sixteen steps up from our bedroom and thirty steps from the hall. But apart from being in the attic, it's nothing like our bedroom at Skilly. For one thing, there's no bed or wardrobe because it's not for sleeping or getting dressed in. It's just for painting. A whole room just for painting!

When we went in the smell of paint made me feel dizzy. But when I saw the paintings, I forgot the smell, and all I could think was how amazing the colors were. There are loads of paintings just leaning against the walls. Some are small, but some are even taller than Martha. They're not paintings of things, they're just colors and shapes. One's a red square with yellow and green lines on it, and the lines look like they're moving. I couldn't stop looking at it.

"Did you do these?" I said to Martha.

She nodded. It's amazing to think all those colors are in her head.

"What are they?" Zac said.

"You just have to look," I whispered.

"Look at what?" he said. "What are they?"

"I don't know what they are, Zac," Martha said. "They're feelings, I suppose. You know when you run around and that shows how you're feeling inside—well, these paintings show how I feel inside."

"Can't you paint properly?" Zac said. "Dogs and people and houses and things."

Martha smiled. She didn't seem annoyed.

"Well, yes, I can paint things and I did for a long time," she said. "But now I paint feelings."

"Why?"

"I don't know," Martha said.

She picked up a bit of paper.

"You know, Zac, the older I get the less I ask why. Does that make sense to you?"

Zac shook his head. "No."

"Would you like to paint something?" she said.

Zac shrugged. "Okay."

Martha squeezed three colors onto a bit of plastic she called a palette. It's what artists put their paint on. The colors were red, yellow and blue, and they looked like shiny slugs. Then she gave Zac three brushes.

"Use a different brush for each color," she said. "Paint what you like."

Zac took a brush and stuck it in all the paints and swirled them together until most of the color went brown. Then he painted a big swirly circle on the paper and put some yellow on top and then red and then blue, and he kept making really big lines. He did it fast like he knew exactly what he was doing, and then he stopped. He looked pleased. So did Martha.

"That looks like a painting about feelings," she said.

"No," Zac said. "It's a velociraptor fighting a triceratops."

When it was my turn, I tried to be really careful so the colors wouldn't mix together. It was meant to be a garden, but it wasn't very good. Zac's painting was better. But I was so happy I didn't care.

"If you like," said Martha, "I can set you up in the garden to do some painting."

So that's what we're doing tomorrow!

Painting

There were two easels in the garden this morning with canvases on them, just like artists use. And there was a table with paints and brushes, and they were for me and Zac! I could hardly eat my breakfast. I just wanted to get started.

Zac didn't want to paint, so Martha came in the garden with me and explained everything. She said the paint was acrylic, which means it dries quicker than the oil paint she uses in her studio, so I can take my painting back to Skilly if I like it. It's not as smelly either. Oil paint is what van Gogh used. Van Gogh was the one who painted sun-flowers and cut his ear off. Acrylic's more modern.

Just as Martha was showing me how to squeeze the paint from the bottom of the tube, Zac shouted from the house. We ran in. He was standing in the kitchen with sugar around his mouth and down his front and all over the floor. The sugar bowl was broken into pieces.

"Zac!" I shouted.

I couldn't help myself. He didn't say anything.

"Go and get cleaned up, Zac," Martha said, and he ran up the stairs.

Martha picked up the broken bowl and swept up the sugar. I tried to help but I kept getting in the way.

"Don't worry, Ira," she said. "I'll sort it out. Go and do your painting."

But I couldn't go. I just couldn't.

I kept saying, "I'm really sorry. He didn't mean any harm."

"I know, Ira," Martha said. "I know."

When I said, "Maybe I should see if Zac's all right," she got annoyed.

"Ira," she said, "you worry too much about Zac. Maybe you should worry about yourself sometimes."

"What do you mean?" I said. My voice sounded really small.

"Maybe worrying about Zac is easier than worrying about yourself," Martha said. "You're always thinking about what Zac wants. What I wonder is, what does Ira want? Do you know?"

I couldn't look at her. I had to look out of the window. Silas asks me that sort of thing but no one else does, and with Silas there's never time to talk properly. Someone always interrupts. Martha looked like she was waiting for an answer, like she had all day, but if I told her the truth I would die of shame. Anyway, what I want wouldn't be what I want if I have to ask for it. What I want is for someone to want me and Zac.

I shrugged.

"I don't know what I want," I said.

"Well," she said, "how about that painting you were going to do?"

I felt really bad after that, but when I started painting I forgot. I was just thinking about the colors. I used two different greens and made another green by mixing blue and yellow together. I painted the willow and the lawn and the flowers down the sides, and a little bit of the blue stream poking through the leaves.

And then I saw Glenda under the willow. It really was her. It's the first time I've seen her. She was jumping up and touching the leaves. She looked so happy. She kept disappearing and then coming back again. I waved to her but she didn't wave back. I didn't mind. I'm just pleased she didn't stay on her own at Skilly. I put her in my painting, very faint so if you didn't know she was there you wouldn't see her. Or you might think she was a dove.

Martha said my painting is impressive, which means not bad for a beginner. I'm going to take it back to Skilly so I can remember this holiday forever.

Paint Colors

Artists' paints have really complicated names. They're not just green and blue and red and yellow. They're all the colors in between. Some of them are colors I never even knew existed. The names are really hard to remember, so Martha said I should make up my own. These are my names next to the proper artists' names.

Cerulean blue	Summer sky
Ultramarine	Stormy sky
Prussian blue	School uniform
Chromium green	Grass stains
Sap green	Martha's lawn
Cadmium yellow	Sherbet lemons
Burnt sienna	Spaghetti Bolognese
Cadmium red	Anita's lipstick

Raw umber   Skilly stairs

Magenta   Pomegranate seeds

Afterward Martha stuck my names onto the tubes of paint. It means Zac can use them too if he wants. Martha doesn't need to.

My Favorite Things

We're going back to Skilly tomorrow. I want to see everyone but I don't want to leave, because then Martha and Appleton House will be a memory. And memories mean things are *gone*. I don't want here to be gone.

I haven't even written in my diary properly, so these are some of my favorite things so I'll never forget them:

Zac found a frog the size of his fingernail and put it in the stream.

We walked to the farm four times. Two times we went just for fun, not even to buy eggs. We're going again tomorrow to get eggs for Skilly. That means we will have walked twenty miles altogether, because we'll have been five times and every time is four miles.

We had tea in the garden four times, even one time when it was raining.

One evening we counted eight bats in one go.

Martha showed us photos of when she was a
child playing under the willow, and the tree
was much smaller. Now that she's grown up
she looks like her mother, the vicar's wife.

We drew pictures on blank cards and sent them
to Skilly.

I saw Glenda dancing under the tree, and one
time she was splashing in the stream.

Zac climbed to the top of the willow when
Martha wasn't looking, and he didn't break
any branches. He said he felt like a bird.

Doves sit at the top of the willow and they make
cooing noises, but when Zac climbed up they
flew away.

I like it being quiet at night now. It's like being
wrapped in a big, soft blanket.

Martha doesn't go to church, even though her dad was
a vicar. She says God is in the garden.

Back to Skilly

This morning we collected twelve eggs in one long box
to take back to Skilly. Me and Zac aren't frightened of the

chickens anymore so it was easy. We didn't take the plain eggs. We just took the speckled ones because they're the prettiest. Then we said good-bye to the chickens because we won't see them again. As we walked back we didn't talk at all. Zac just chased the squirrels. I was too sad to talk.

When Mrs. Clanks came to get us, she gave Martha a form with CITY KIDS, COUNTRY KIDS at the top. I wonder if Martha will ever take care kids again.

I didn't want to bring my dress back to Skilly, so I left it in the wardrobe and shut the door. It's the first time the door's been shut all week.

Martha drove us to the station, but she didn't wait with us. I think she wanted to get back to Appleton House so she could have it all to herself. Maybe she wanted to fix the rocking chair and see what else was broken. She said good-bye on the steps. First she shook hands with Mrs. Clanks, and then she leaned down and kissed my cheek. I could see myself in her glasses.

"What do you say, Ira?" Mrs. Clanks said, which was annoying because I was going to say thank you and her saying that made it seem like I'd forgotten.

"Thank you for having us," I said, and then I did a stupid curtsy. I couldn't help it. I don't think Zac saw. He was looking at his shoes. Martha had polished them and the sun was bouncing off them.

"Thank you," said Martha. "It's been a pleasure."

Then she kissed Zac's hair. She knew he'd jump if she touched his face. He stood really still but didn't move away, so it was okay.

"Zac?" said Mrs Clanks.

"Thank you," said Zac.

Martha had wrapped my painting in newspaper. When she gave it to me she said, "Look after it; it's a beauty."

Then she gave Zac the box of eggs. He wrapped his hands around it like it was a new baby and he couldn't drop it. Probably it was even more fragile than a new baby, like lots of new babies.

I looked back at Martha as we went into the station. She should have looked funny with her big feet and her bobbing head, but she didn't. She looked nice and a bit worried, like she thought Zac might drop the eggs.

All the way back to London, I felt like I'd left a bit of myself at Martha's house. Like part of me will always be a little ghost painting in her garden. Zac held on to the box of eggs the whole way back. He didn't even wriggle.

Mrs. Clanks got out her papers again so we didn't have to talk to her. The only thing she said was, "I think you made a very good impression. Well done."

I felt bad when she said that, even though I think she

102

was trying to be nice. I expect she's pleased because Martha might let other kids go there.

Silas was waiting at the station like he said he would. It was like he'd been standing there the whole week. He had a big smile on his face. I ran along the platform and gave him a hug. Zac did a funny sort of skip because he didn't want to drop the eggs.

"You look different," Silas said.

"What do you mean?"

"More grown up, I suppose. Like you've seen something of the world, and it's changed you."

I said, "Is that okay?"

And he said, "Oh yeah."

It's strange being back at Skilly. Everything seems so noisy and busy. Someone's hung a sheet on the flats across the road with STOP THE POLL TAX in big black drippy letters. When the wind blows it flaps against the wall. Skilly looks the same though. It looks like we never even left.

Zac gave Hortense the box of eggs. She opened it carefully in case they were broken, but all twelve eggs were perfect.

"Did you carry them the whole way?" she said.

Zac nodded.

"It's a small miracle," she said.

Because miracles can be big or small. Miracle isn't just a name for a kid somebody doesn't know if they want or not. Miracles can be big, like someone walking on water, and small, like eggs not getting broken.

Me and Zac told everyone about our holiday over and over. Sometimes I told a story one way and then Zac told the same story in a different way, but nobody minded. They couldn't believe Martha lived in the same house all of her life. Everyone's mouth fell open. Even Hortense was surprised. We sat at the kitchen table, and everyone listened and looked at the speckled eggs. Ashani sat on my lap and put her head on my shoulder. She seemed a bit sad. She liked the eggs with the feathers on top, so I gave her a feather to cheer her up—a really soft white one. I expect she wishes she'd come.

Everyone liked the cards we sent, and my painting. I didn't tell them Glenda was in it. They all thought the little Glenda shape was a rabbit.

Hortense said, "It's beautiful, Ira. Can we hang it in the hall?"

But I don't want it in the hall. Someone might kick a ball at it or scribble on it. I want it in my room so I can remember the holiday forever.

Hortense said, "Well, I'll just have to come up and look at it sometimes, to get a taste of the country."

We had the eggs with toast, and we told everyone about Martha's toast soldiers. It was nice sitting at the table together, but the more we told our stories the more it felt like they happened a long time ago. Silas must feel like that. He must feel like his stories happened a hundred years ago. Or in another lifetime.

When I saw Jimmy he said, "So you came back then?" and I said, "Yeah. . . ." And this time I put lots of dots at the end of it.

I hope I never forget what Martha looked like or how lovely her garden was or what it felt like to stand under the willow or walk two miles to get eggs or go to sleep when all you can hear is animals in the woods.

The trouble with holidays is they make ordinary life feel even more ordinary.

Ashani's Gone

Ashani left today. She went to live with her new family. It was all arranged while we were on holiday. I think that's why she was sad when we came back. Probably she was happy-sad.

When she said good-bye, she made funny faces and she kept tickling everyone and laughing. I picked her up and held her tight and she wrapped her legs around me

like a monkey. I wished and wished I didn't have to let her
go. When she got in the car, she was smiling and waving
and sticking her tongue out of the window. But as the car
drove away I couldn't tell if she was smiling anymore, but
I thought maybe she wasn't and I felt awful.

Zac was annoying all day and I hated him, but then I
saw his eyes were red and I thought maybe he was upset
because he liked Ashani too. Now everything feels like
the sun's gone in and it's going to be cloudy forever.

I told Glenda about Ashani and how bad I feel now
that she's gone. I haven't seen her since we got back, but
I told her in my head. I keep looking out of the window
in case she's in the garden, but she's not there. Maybe she
stayed at Martha's.

Silas Is in the Paper
September 1989

Silas has his picture in the paper. He's standing with some other people, and they're holding placards with STOP THE POLL TAX written on them. Some people are holding a sheet with CAN'T PAY, WON'T PAY, and the sheet's drooping onto heads of the people in the middle, but they don't seem to mind. Everyone's smiling like they're having a nice day out. It's not a very good picture of Silas though.

"You look like you're wearing a wig," Hortense said.

And he does. He looks like he's in disguise, like he's a spy or something.

Hortense stuck the picture on the kitchen board and somebody wrote *Who is this man?* next to it.

Back to School

We went back to school today. It's my last year before I go to secondary school. Some of the new little kids were crying because they wanted to go home, and others were running around thinking they were really grown up, when they looked really small and sweet in their tiny uniforms.

I told Amanda and Kaleigh about my holiday. I usually tell them I don't like holidays, but this time I told them about Martha and the chickens and the garden. They laughed when I told them about Zac pretending to be a dog in the stream, and for a moment I felt like a proper friend. I didn't tell them about City Kids, Country Kids. I said Martha was our aunt! Now I'll never be able to invite them to Skilly in case they find out.

We got a new teacher called Miss MacDonald. She's Scottish and she's young and she's got a really nice accent. I really like her already. She's going to teach us French in case we marry someone French or just want to go there on holiday. And we're going to do science and write lots of stories. It's cheered me up having Miss MacDonald as my teacher.

Postcard from Martha

We've got a postcard from Martha! It's a picture of a chicken. She didn't write much because there wasn't much space, but me and Zac know it by heart. She said the house was quiet without us, and it wasn't as much fun collecting eggs on her own, and she hoped we didn't have to work too hard at school. At the end she put *Martha* and a squiggle that might have been a kiss but might just have been a funny loop she does on the end of her name.

"Do you think we'll go back?" Zac said.

I shook my head. "I expect she'll take different children if she does it again."

He looked sad, so I said, "Maybe if we wait a couple of years, we'll get another turn."

And he shouted, "A couple of years?!!"

After that he was really upset. Every time he saw me he said, "I hate you!" and "You're rubbish!" and pushed past me. He was like that all day until he went to bed, and then he said "sorry" really quietly so I could only just hear. I'm going to stick the postcard on the wall next to his bed so he'll see the chicken when he wakes up.

Pip

A new girl came to Skilly today. She's called Pip. She's ten, but she looks eight. She's moved into Ashani's room, but she's completely different from Ashani. She's small and thin and wears a purple jumper that's too big for her, and her sleeves are all soggy and the wool's come undone because she's always chewing them.

She didn't say anything at tea, and she didn't look at anyone. I tried to catch her eye, but it was like she had a wall in front of her face. She looked sad sitting there looking at her wall. She didn't eat. She just chewed her jumper.

Hortense took some food up to her room later. It's against the rules to take food upstairs, but if I was in charge I'd say the rules don't matter because if Pip doesn't eat she'll starve to death. I'm going to try to make friends with her.

The Mouse

We got a computer at school. Miss Campbell showed us. She said one day everyone will have one. It's a big gray box with lots of wires, and the screen lights up and all

110

the letters are on a special board. When she was plugging it in she said, "Now, where's the mouse?" and everyone looked at the floor in case a mouse ran up their legs. But she wasn't looking for a real, squeaky mouse. She was looking for a thing with buttons on it.

It's quite good because it's got games, but the best thing is it's quieter than a typewriter. When you tap the letters they don't make such a noise.

Glenda

Glenda's back. I'm sure she is. I keep seeing her out of the corner of my eye. I'm sure it's her. I can feel her in our bedroom too. I just know she's there. I showed her the chicken postcard, but I didn't tell her about Martha's because she knows what that was like because she was there too. I'm so glad she's come back.

Steps

These are the steps of all the places I've been since I could count. I always count the steps, because then I know that whatever happens, I only have to go that many steps down to get to the ground. And then I'll be outside and I can look at the sky. It makes me feel better.

Our bedroom at Skilly	47 steps
Mrs. Clanks's office	2 steps
Martha's studio	30 steps
Our room at Martha's	14 steps
Brenda and Alf's flat	32 steps
Petra's flat	1 step
Our room at Alara's	13 steps
Adam's flat	28 steps
Our bedroom at the Grimbles'	10 steps
Woman who was mean to us	17 steps
Nan in Greenwich	55 steps
Nan next to the garages	3 steps
Auntie with dyed blonde hair	18 steps
Auntie in Brixton	22 steps
The National Gallery	22 steps
Upstairs on London bus	8 steps
Boat on the Thames	12 steps
Dentist	4 steps

Pip's in My Class

Pip's in my class. She walks to school with me and Zac. Well, she doesn't exactly walk with us, she walks behind. It's a bit embarrassing in case anyone finds out she lives with us, because I don't tell people I'm a care kid if I can help it. But I don't think I need to worry because Pip doesn't speak to anyone. She just sits at the front of the class and looks down, and at break she stands on her own on the playground and won't play.

Amanda and Kaleigh tried to be friendly with her, but she didn't even look at them. She just chewed her sleeve. She wears her old jumper everywhere, even to school. She won't take it off. She won't even let Hortense wash it. Some people might think she's spoiled, but I think she's sad.

Dogs

Zac got a book from the library called *Dog Facts for Dog Lovers*. I don't think I'm a dog lover because I wouldn't have chosen that book, but Zac is because he talks about dogs all the time and wishes he had one, and sometimes he strokes the pictures.

He said, "Do you think our dog's still alive?"

He meant the one in the photo.

I said, "I doubt it."

He got annoyed and wanted to check, so Hortense got out our Memory Book and we opened it to the photo and tried to work out what type our dog was, because the book said how long dogs live depends on what kind they are.

This is some examples of how long some dogs live. How long they live is called their lifespan.

Beagles	12 to 14 years
Boxers	11 to 14 years
Bulldogs	8 to 10 years
Chihuahuas	15 years or more
Dachshunds	12 to 14 years
German shepherds	10 to 12 years
Golden retrievers	10 to 12 years
Great Danes	6 to 8 years
Labradors	12 to 14 years
Poodles	12 to 14 years
Pugs	12 to 14 years
Rottweilers	8 to 10 years
Yorkshire terriers	12 to 15 years

If our dog was a Labrador, it could live for fourteen years or maybe even longer if it's well looked after.

But our dog doesn't look like any of the dogs in the book. It's got big ears and a long nose and little eyes, and it's hairy. It's hard to tell, but it might have thin legs. Hortense said she thought it was a mongrel, which is two sorts of dogs mixed together, and Zac said that was okay because the book says *Mongrels make wonderful companions and are just as lovable as pedigree dogs.*

Then he said, "That's a puppy; in the photo. It's a puppy."

I said, "It's not a puppy; it's grown up. Mum wouldn't get a puppy after we were born. You don't get a dog when you've got babies. It's too much work."

"She would," Zac said. "To help look after us."

"You don't get a dog to look after children," I said.

"You can," said Zac, "if you can't look after them yourself."

Then he went quiet and his face was like a sand castle, all sliding out of place, and I couldn't tell if he was crying because my eyes went all blurry and my face was like a sand castle too. I had to take a deep breath and wait for the moment to end, and in that moment I thought maybe our mum kept the dog but got rid of us.

Then Zac said, "That's why I like dogs. Because a dog looked after us."

He said it like suddenly everything made sense, but he didn't look like everything made sense. He looked like nothing made sense and he hated everything.

I wish wish wish wish we knew why our mum left us and who she was and where she is. Because not knowing anything means anything could have happened and whatever me and Zac imagine might be true.

Sometimes I think the dog ran onto the road and Mum ran too and they both got run over, or maybe she married someone who liked dogs but not children. Zac thinks she was a spy and the dog had a microphone hidden under its ear, and then she had to go back to her own country and really we're foreign. When he was little he thought she was a prisoner and he would rescue her, but then he had nightmares, so I told him she definitely wasn't a prisoner. He made me cross my heart and hope to die, so I hope I wasn't wrong.

What I really think is that she's probably ordinary like us and has bobbly old cushions on her chairs and dust in her hall like most people do. And then I feel angry with her for being mysterious, when probably she's no different from anyone else. Except most people don't leave their children. So that makes her different, I suppose.

Anyway, we couldn't decide what the dog was, and Hortense said we should think of it as an average dog with an average lifespan, and that's about ten years. So if it was a puppy in the photo, it might still be alive, and if it was an old dog, it probably died of old age. That is if it didn't get run over.

Alice

October 1989

Pip spoke to me today. It's the first time ever. She was leaning against the tree talking to herself, and I thought she might be talking to a ghost, so I went and sat beside her. I was going to tell her about Glenda.

At first I didn't say anything, and then I said, "Who were you talking to?"

And she said—really quietly in a tiny little voice so I almost couldn't hear—"My sister."

I said, "Is she staying somewhere else?"

And she shook her head and said, "No. She's dead,"

and her face was really flat like it was all so horrible inside her head she had to switch everything off, and then I understood why she has a wall in front of her face.

I wanted to cry but I didn't, because it's her that should be crying, not me, so I took a deep breath like I was about to have an injection. My throat hurt because there was such a big lump in it.

"What's her name?" I said.

She said, "Alice. She's twelve."

After that all the words went out of my head, so I just sat there. I don't think Pip minded. We sat like that for ages and didn't say anything, and Pip chewed her sleeve.

Then I said, "Is that her jumper?"

And she nodded and got up and walked away.

Pip's sister dying is the saddest thing in the world. If Zac died, I'd die too. My heart would stop beating, and I wouldn't live a moment longer. I wouldn't even know how to breathe. It makes me afraid to think about it in case it happens. I know it won't make a difference, but I feel like it might. It's called being superstitious.

Usually Zac is superstitious, not me. If I tell him about Pip's sister he'll think I'm going to die, so I won't tell him. He already thinks something bad will happen if some-one puts up an umbrella in the house or walks under a ladder, and if he's worried about something at school he tries not to stand on cracks. We can be walking along as if everything's normal, and suddenly he shouts, "Don't stand on the crack," and I have to jump to make sure I miss it. Or if I did stand on it, I have to go back and walk along that bit of pavement again, but this time not stand on it.

I tried to explain that superstitions are made up by people and they're not real, but he said even if people made them up they're still real.

I said, "Yes, but they're not magic; they won't come true."

He said, "How do you know?"

And when someone says, "How do you know?" and you can't prove it, you can't really say anything.

Me and Zac made up our own superstitions. These are some of them:

Changing how you part your hair.

Eating green and red food on the same plate (e.g., lettuce and tomatoes). This means we can't eat salad.

A hedgehog getting run over (that was Zac's idea, but I don't think it's a superstition—I think it's just bad luck for the hedgehog).

Wearing socks that don't match.

Falling out of bed.

Looking at your reflection in a window.

Putting your pants on back to front.

The Wall
November 1989

Miss MacDonald told us about a city called Berlin that's got a wall going right through the middle so people can't go from one side to the other. It's called the Berlin Wall. It's been there for nearly thirty years, which is almost forever. Some people have been stuck on the wrong side their whole lives. If they were out shopping when the wall was built they'd be stuck without their families forever. They can't even climb over because soldiers would shoot them.

I think it's like being a care kid. There's a great big

wall and your family's behind it, but you can never climb over. The only thing you can do is not look at the wall too much, because if you do, you can't think about anything else. Like Pip. You just have to pretend it's not there and get on with everything else.

But Miss MacDonald told us now people are breaking the wall down. It's amazing. She showed us some film. She said it's a historic moment, like when the tree blew down. People were smashing the wall with hammers and putting bits in their pockets and climbing onto it and waving from the top and jumping over to the other side. They were crying and smiling and laughing all at the same time and looking for the people they'd lost, and some people recognized them even though they're really old now.

And the soldiers weren't even shooting because there were too many people to shoot, and they probably wanted to go over the wall too. They probably have aunties or grandmas on the other side.

It was so amazing!

Photo of Glenda

I've seen a photo of Glenda! Hortense found a box of photos of Skilly kids and tipped them out onto the kitchen table. It was like looking at hundreds of ghosts. We knew they were Skilly kids because they're sitting in front of Skilly House or under the tree before it was blown down. One picture is so old it's brown and white, and the girls are wearing long dresses and they all look miserable, but Hortense said in the olden days people had to sit really still for a long time when they had a photo taken, and it's hard to smile for a long time, so they might not be sad at all. They might just look that way because of all the waiting. Me and Zac tried smiling for a long time and after a while it didn't look like a smile at all. It looked like a scream.

The photo with Glenda isn't as old as the brown and white one, but it's in black and white because they still didn't use colors then. There are seven children in the photo, standing in a row. All the girls are wearing skirts and all the boys are wearing shorts, and all the kids have their socks falling down. On the back of the photo it says *1948*, which is the year after she wrote her letter. The names of the children are written in order, and the last person in the row is Glenda Hyacinth! She's standing next to a boy called Bill Glover. I couldn't believe my eyes. I stared and stared at her.

She doesn't look exactly how I thought she would. She's got long hair and bangs, and she has a ribbon in her hair. I expect it's the ribbon she found on the bomb site. The ribbon's slipped a bit, and it looks like it's going to fall off at any moment. She's not smiling, though she could have done because it was 1948 and cameras were better then, but she's looking at the camera and her face is all flat. She's probably fed up waiting for Bill to stop talking or for everyone to get in a line, or maybe she's fed up of waiting for life to get better. Or maybe she doesn't want to move in case the ribbon falls off.

Mrs. Clanks stood behind me when I was looking at the photo. I felt a bit awkward, so I said, "What happened to them?"

She didn't say anything for a moment. She just looked at the picture.

Then she said, "They grew up," and she walked away.

She made me feel stupid. Hortense patted my arm.

"It's lovely you're interested, Ira," she said. "These children were here before you. It's lovely you can see their photos."

Now I can imagine Glenda properly. I've seen her running through Skilly and I saw her in the garden at Martha's house, but I never got a good look at her. Now I can really imagine her. I wanted to put a ribbon in my hair too, because we're friends, and friends do that sort of thing. But I haven't got a ribbon, so I put a hairband on instead.

Zac said, "What you wearing that for?"

But I didn't tell him. I just shrugged.

My Story

At school today Miss MacDonald told us about Scotland. She said there's lots of countryside and mountains and lots of rain, so things grow really fast, like enormous carrots, and there's lots of potatoes called tatties.

She showed us tartans, which people make kilts out of. Each family has its own tartan, so people know if they are a Campbell or a MacDonald just by looking at their clothes. It made me wonder if anyone in our family is Scottish and if so what their tartan is. Maybe they're Campbells. If they're Scottish, I hope their tartan's got lots of green in it. Green's my favorite colour.

While Miss MacDonald was talking, some people climbed up the lampposts outside the school and hung a sheet between them with No Poll Tax written on it. It was amazing how they did it so quickly. They just slid right up the poles and down again, and Miss MacDonald didn't even notice. I expect they've done it lots of times before.

Afterward Miss MacDonald got us to write stories. She said to use our imagination and write about something from the past. She says a good imagination can make something ordinary extraordinary.

I wrote about a ghost called Glenda who never grows up but is always dreaming about what she might become. It's based on my Glenda, but it's not really her. Miss Mac-Donald liked it so much she wrote on the bottom of my page *Ira has been working hard and has written a beautiful story. She has a wonderful imagination.*

At the end of school when everyone had gone, she said, "You've quite a talent, Ira," and she told me to show it to Mrs. Clanks. I didn't want to, but because I nodded I had to, so when I got back to Skilly I went to see Mrs. Clanks.

After she read Miss MacDonald's note, she said, "Well done, Ira. Shall I read your story?"

I wanted to say no because she's not the sort of person who believes in ghosts, but she wasn't asking me as a question. Her face went funny when she was reading it. She didn't like it at all, even though it's not very long. When she finished she put it on her desk.

"Who is Glenda?" she said.

"She's a girl in the Skilly photo that's got nineteen forty-eight on the back," I said. "She used to live here."

Mrs. Clanks said, "I see."

Then she said, "Perhaps you should write about people you know—real people, not imaginary ones."

"She is real," I said.

"What I mean, Ira, is it would be better if you lived

125

in the real world. Keep your feet on the ground. Don't dream your life away."

I felt horrible when she said that.

"The real world's no fun," I said.

"You had fun with Martha, didn't you?"

I said, "Yes, but I'm at Skilly now, and it's no fun here at all."

Then I picked up my story and walked out. Just like that. It wasn't even true what I said, but I wanted to hurt her feelings like she hurt mine. When I came upstairs I tore my story into lots of pieces and threw them in the bin. They looked like confetti that you throw at a wedding, only instead of happy confetti, they were sad confetti, like you might throw at a funeral.

I hate writing, I hate drawing, I hate everything. I don't ever want to grow up and be like Mrs. Clanks, but I don't want to be a child either.

Ghosts

I couldn't sleep last night. I was too upset about my story. Even imagining an owl on the roof didn't make me feel better. I got out of bed and looked out the window. There was a big moon in the sky, and I was just thinking how lovely it was when I saw Glenda. She was running through the garden and she looked really happy and free, and I wished I could be outside with her.

And then I thought, Why can't I? I can if I want to.

So I decided to go out too.

Zac was asleep. His foot was sticking out from the blanket and it kept twitching. He was probably dreaming about playing football. I opened the door really quietly and crept down the stairs. I didn't make a single sound because me and Zac have learned where the creaks are. We did it by pretending we'd get blown up if we stood on a creak. You learn really quickly if you think you might be blown up.

When I got downstairs I unlocked the back door and crept outside. It was quite light because of the moon, but it felt really scary. The grass was cold and wet on my feet.

Then I saw the bushes move so I whispered, "Glenda! Glenda!" but she didn't come out. I was just thinking I'd go back in, but then I saw her running through the garden. She looked like a little wisp of smoke.

And then I noticed lots of leaves were shaking as if children were running their fingers over them, and I realized the garden was full of ghosts, all running around and touching the leaves. So I began to run too. I ran along the trunk and jumped off the end, and then I ran around the pond and peered into the water and saw the reflection of the moon and insects jumping across the top. And all the time I was running, my fingers were touching the bushes. It was so nice.

But then suddenly the garden felt scary again, so I ran back inside and locked the door, and even though I was scared, I raced all the way up the stairs without making a single creak.

I felt better after that, because now I know that, while we're asleep, Glenda's playing in the garden with the other kids who used to live here. And that makes me feel less lonely.

Zac hadn't moved when I got back to our room. Even his foot was still twitching. He looked so warm, I climbed into bed with him, and when he felt my cold feet he curled up and rolled over.

Mrs. Clanks

I had to go to Mrs. Clanks's office again today. I didn't look at her when I went in, and I wasn't going to listen either. I just hoped she hadn't seen me in the garden.

She told me to sit down, and then she said, "It was very rude of you to walk out when we were talking."

I said, "I'm sorry," even though I didn't mean it.

"Actually," she said, "I wanted to apologize to you. I'm sorry if you thought I didn't like your story. I liked it very much."

She looked strange. Her face didn't look stony anymore. It looked like it was bubbling out of shape.

"What I was trying to say was," she said, "what I've learned in life is that the only way to make things happen is to live in the real world, to make the best of it. Do you know what I mean?"

"To grow up?" I said.

"Yes. That's one way of putting it. Not to live in a dream. If you live too much in your dreams, you will always be disappointed."

I shrugged.

"But I was very impressed with your story, Ira. You must show Silas. You know how he loves a good story."

"I tore it up," I said. "I tore it into a hundred pieces and threw it away."

Mrs. Clanks looked away. It was like she'd cry if she spoke. She made her face even harder than usual and kept swallowing, like she was trying to stop the tears coming.

She said, "I'm sorry if I made you destroy your story. I'm sorry if I was too harsh. Will you write another?"

I was going to say, "No, I won't, never again," but then she said, "One thing you'll learn as you get older is adults are often wrong—maybe you will be one of those people who is able to live in their dreams."

I felt like crying too, but I wasn't sure why.

I just said, "Okay," and she said, "Very well."

Then she said, "You have a talent. It's quite special. Not everyone is so lucky."

I nodded.

Everything feels funny now. Like it's upside down. I like it better the right way up. Then I know what's happening.

I wonder if Mrs. Clanks did bring the Easter eggs.

Invitation from Martha!
December 1989

Martha's invited us to stay for New Year's! She didn't even arrange it through Country Kids, City Kids. She just did it because she felt like it, and that means she wants us to come. Even though we made lots of messes, she wants to see us again. Me and Zac can't stop smiling, and Zac's jumping all over the place. He'd better calm down before we get there.

When I told Silas he said, "Seize your moment, Ira, seize your moment."

Everyone's happy for us this time, even Jimmy. I expect because he knows we'll come back. The only person who didn't seem happy or sad or anything at all was Pip. She just stared at her wall.

Christmas Tree

We put up the Christmas tree today. Silas got the biggest one he could find. I thought he'd have to cut the top off to make it fit under the ceiling, but it was okay. Jimmy helped him carry it in. They put it in a bucket of water, even though it's already dead. Water keeps it looking alive longer. It makes it think it's still alive.

Hortense got out the decorations, and we hung them on the tree. Pip was really happy. She couldn't help it, even though she doesn't want to be happy ever again. She kept touching all the shiny things.

Sophia decorated the top of the tree because she's the tallest apart from Jimmy, and he didn't want to help. He only wanted to carry it in. Her bit looked best because she didn't put too many baubles on it. Hortense said she's more sophisticated. That means she knows when to stop. Esther got one of her dolls, and Hortense wrapped it in tinfoil and Sophia put it on the top like a fairy. There were so many baubles on the bottom, you could hardly see the branches, but when Hortense put the fairy lights on it all looked lovely. We stood in the dark and stared at it for ages. It felt like magic.

Jimmy

Jimmy keeps disappearing. He's too big to lock in a cupboard, so I think he just goes out. He doesn't want to be at Skilly anymore. He wants to be grown-up. He's so tall, his ankles always stick out of his trousers, and he's got pimples, so I think he feels bad on the outside now as well as on the inside. He might be trying to find his family, or he might just want to get away from us.

Christmas makes care kids feel bad because it reminds us we haven't got a family and other kids have. All the ads have perfect families laughing and pulling Christmas crackers and eating toffees their granddads gave them. Hortense says they're not real families at all, they're just actors, but they still look happier than care kids. I don't feel sad at Christmas though, because all my Christmases have been in care, so I don't know any different. At least the ones I remember. But Jimmy feels sad. Jimmy doesn't like Christmas at all.

I asked if he'd play with us today, but he shook his head and didn't even look at me. Then he went out. He didn't come back until we were going to bed. Mrs. Clanks told him off and Silas said, "Come on, lad," and Hortense gave him a hug and made him some supper because he hadn't eaten anything.

Hortense says teenagers need family more than anyone else, which is a shame because teenagers are the least lovely sort of kid.

Christmas Day

Today I got colored pencils, a sketchbook, felt-tip pens and a slap bracelet, which is what everyone has at school. We all got slap bracelets. Mine's green, Zac's is red, Esther's is yellow. They look like rulers, but when you slap them on your wrist, they turn into bracelets. I also got marbles and a little teapot that opens up into a house. There's a bedroom inside with two tiny beds, and a kitchen with a cooker and a sink and a table and a toilet, and there are three little badgers—mum, dad and baby. Mum badger's wearing an apron and Dad badger's wearing jeans. The baby's wearing a T-shirt and shorts. I wanted to make the dad wear the apron and the mum wear the jeans, but the clothes are stuck on. It doesn't matter though. I still love it.

Zac got the same as me, but instead of the sketchbook

and the teapot, he got a bow and arrow and a Batman model. He's really happy. He's wanted a Batman for ages. Esther got yellow plastic shoes and a bag, and Miles got a Game Boy and some tools, and Jimmy got a portable CD player. It's got plugs he puts in his ears so he can walk around and listen to his music without us hearing or him hearing us. It's good because he doesn't like dance music anymore. He likes bands that scream because that's how he feels inside. Sophia got a CD player too, and Milap got a magic kit and Harit got a Batman like Zac. Pip got a new jumper, but I don't think she'll wear it. I think she'll just keep wearing her old one. She also got a craft kit and lots of sequins and tinsel because Hortense saw how much she loved the shiny things when we did the tree.

At dinner we had red napkins and pulled gold Christmas crackers. The little prizes kept falling on the floor. We had to get under the table to look for them. It was very funny. Zac got a plastic ring he didn't want, and I got a key ring. He wanted to swap, but I wouldn't. I'm going to keep the key ring for when I've got my own door key, even if I have to wait until I'm grown up. Hortense got a fluffy hair clip she put in her hair, and Silas was wearing a paper hat that kept slipping over his eyes. Mrs. Clanks came too. She was wearing a ribbon that looked like holly with two red berries.

I always think Christmas dinner is the best one I ever had, and this year's was the same. I gave my stuffing to Silas because he loves it and I hate it, but I had seconds of everything else. Milap and Harit were the only ones who didn't eat. They just pushed their food around their plates because they wished they were with their mum and dad, and that made them lose their appetites. We read jokes from the crackers to cheer them up, but most weren't very funny. The best ones were:

Why did the raisin go out with a strawberry?
Because it couldn't find a date.

What do you get if you sit under a cow?
A pat on the head.

Glenda came to Christmas dinner too, but no one knew except me. They couldn't see her. She didn't sit at the table because she couldn't eat anything, but she kept popping up all over the place.

After dinner I gave Hortense and Silas some drawings I did in the garden. I gave Mrs. Clanks a drawing too, because since she said sorry for telling me off about my story I've thought of her a bit differently. And when I gave it to her, she gave me a kiss. Zac had a big smirk on his face.

I gave Zac a box to keep dead insects and stuff in. I made it out of a box I covered and painted a hen on. The hen looks like a dog, but he likes it. He loves dogs anyway. He gave me peppermint creams he made with icing sugar and green coloring and mint flavor. The first one was nice, but the second one tasted like toothpaste.

Back to Martha's

We've come back to Martha's! We came on the train with Mrs. Clanks, and we weren't even nervous. We just felt happy. Martha was waiting on the platform. She was wearing a fluffy green coat and orange earmuffs and big boots. I had to stop myself running to her in case I looked too keen and embarrassed myself. When she came up to us she gave a little bow.

"Ira, Zac," she said.

She was smiling.

Mrs. Clanks didn't come to the house this time. She chatted to Martha and then she waited for the next train back to London. When we went she said, "Have fun."

On the way to the house, Martha said, "I was going to get a Christmas tree this year, but I wasn't able to, so I do apologize. You'll see why when we get there."

I tried to think why she couldn't get a tree. I wondered

if she'd lost her decorations. I even thought maybe her roof had fallen in because the house must be very old, but when we arrived the roof looked fine.

But when we got out of the car I heard barking and when Martha opened the door, a puppy jumped out. Me and Zac screamed when we saw her, and she jumped all over us and licked our faces. She's brown and white with floppy ears and big black eyes like marbles, and she's a spaniel and she's four months old and she's Martha's. And she's the most beautiful puppy I've ever seen.

When Zac saw her he was like a puppy too, jumping up and down and rolling on the floor. I felt all soft inside. I kept saying, "Oooh."

"She's called Dash," Martha said.

"Because she dashes?" I said.

Martha nodded. "She doesn't stop. She's wearing me out. I'm glad you two are here."

Me and Zac played in the garden with Dash all afternoon. It was really cold, and she was wearing a little tartan coat that buttoned up under her tummy. Martha said it's just for this winter, as she's a puppy. I don't know if she's Scottish, but it suited her anyway. She's so funny. There's an icicle hanging off the tap in the garden where the water drips. She kept licking it and yelping. She wouldn't stop. She couldn't work out why the water was hard.

Martha gave me and Zac some earmuffs like hers.

 138

Mine are purple and Zac's are blue. Zac didn't want to put his on because they're very big and fluffy, but then his ears got cold so he had to. I tried not to laugh.

Dash makes even more mess than we did when we first came to Martha's. She digs up the plants and breaks things, and she peed on the kitchen floor. Martha keeps mopping up after her.

I think about her all the time. She reminds me of the dog in our photo because even though she's completely different, she's still a dog.

Our black dog compared to Dash:

Our dog
Big
Black
Probably not a puppy
Thin legs
Wet nose
Jumping
Good with children (because you wouldn't put a big
    black dog on a chair with two small children if he
    wasn't)

Dash
Small
Brown and white

Puppy
Short legs
Wet nose
Jumping
Good with children

Martha took some photos of us playing with Dash. She's going to send them off to be developed tomorrow. They should come back soon, and then she'll send us the best ones. I can't wait to see them. I hope Zac wasn't moving.

Later when I opened the wardrobe in our room, my green dress was still hanging next to the leaf wallpaper. I took it downstairs when Martha wasn't looking and put it in Dash's basket under her blanket. Now it's extra comfy.

New Year's Eve

It's New Year's Eve already! The whole week's nearly gone.

Martha said, "Time's gone in a flash," and it feels like that. Like it was a firework, lovely for a moment and then gone. It's New Year's Day tomorrow, and after that we have to go back to Skilly.

We've taught Dash loads of tricks. If we throw a stick

and shout "Fetch!" she'll bring it back, and when we say "Sit," she sits up and holds her paws out. Zac taught her how to run along next to his ankles. When he slows down she slows down, and when he goes fast she goes fast too.

She falls asleep on my lap sometimes, and I have to sit very still because I don't want to disturb her. It's like when Silas had the snake in his sleeping bag, except it feels really, really nice. She's not allowed upstairs, but in the morning she barks until we come down. She's always awake before us. It's like she waits for us all night.

I've done an abstract painting, which is a painting about feelings. Martha left all my paint names stuck on the tubes, so it's easy to remember which color is which. My painting's got lots of greens and blues in it. I did it when I was happy, so it's about being happy. Martha kept looking at it, and then she cleared a space for it on the mantelpiece to keep it safe. She said she'd wrap it up really well so I can take it back to Skilly, but I said it was my Christmas present for her.

When I said that her mouth went funny and she fiddled with her glasses as if they were about to fall off, even though she had her chain. Then she said, "Well, in that case you'll have to come back and do another one."

So we're coming back at Easter!!!

New Year

January 1990

Today's the first day of the first month of the first year of the 1990s! It's a whole new decade. I was awake when the New Year happened. Nothing really changes that you can see, but it felt different.

Martha said if we were still awake at midnight, we could go downstairs. Zac's eyes just flopped shut as soon as he got into bed. He couldn't stop them. I kept myself awake by thinking about my impossible dreams.

One of my impossible dreams is to be an astronaut so

I can look at the world from a long way away, like from the moon. The world must look beautiful from far away, where you can't see all the things that go wrong. You can just see the blue sea and the mountains and the trees and the grass. Another impossible dream is to fly to the top of the willow and sit with the doves. Another is to go back to when Glenda was a little girl and play on the bomb site with her. Another is to make things happen by thinking about them like Matilda does. I've got loads of other impossible dreams, but those are my favorites. I've got ordinary dreams too, like going in a black cab or eating fish and chips on a beach.

When it was very late, Martha put her head around the door.

"Still awake?" she whispered.

She let me borrow her soft, fluffy, yellow dressing gown. Esther would love it. Then she made some hot chocolate and we sat on the sofa and drank it and watched TV. The program showed what was happening in different places in the world. There was a big party at the Berlin Wall. Thousands of people were there, sitting on the wall and waving flags, and there were fireworks, and other people were still pulling the wall apart and smashing it because it goes on for miles. Some people were crying and some were dancing and some were looking for their relatives,

143

but there were too many people so I don't think they could have found them. Everyone looked like they were in a dream. Like a day had come they never imagined.

Martha said, "This is one New Year's they'll never forget."

I thought, This is one I'll never forget too.

After that the program showed a big crowd of people in Trafalgar Square in London. They were singing and sitting on the lions and splashing in the fountains even though it was really cold. I couldn't see any pigeons, but I think they'd gone up into the tall buildings to keep away from the noise. They were probably looking down in case anyone dropped some food. Then it showed a party in Scotland with people in kilts singing and playing bagpipes. Miss MacDonald might have been there, but I couldn't see her. Scottish people love New Year's. They organize the parties.

When it was ten seconds until midnight, there was a countdown. It was like when a rocket goes to the moon. Everyone counted ten, nine, eight, seven, six, five, four—right down to zero. Me and Martha joined in for three, two, one, and when it reached zero they all cheered and kissed each other, and Martha gave me a hug.

"Happy New Year, Ira," she said.

It's the best New Year's I've ever had. I'm going to

remember it for all the New Years in the future when I'm on my own or just with Zac and for all the other decades when I'm old and it's even the next century. At the Scottish party everyone sang a song called "Auld Lang Syne," which is about old friends, and I thought about everyone at Skilly and Zac sleeping upstairs and I felt really happy.

When I came back to bed, I looked out the window and saw Glenda skipping around the willow under the stars.

I hope the 1990s will be better for me and Zac. I hope it'll be like when the Berlin Wall came down and we'll get to see our mum and everyone will be happy.

And when we get to the end of this decade, I'll be twenty-one. And even if we don't meet our mum, it won't matter so much because we won't be care kids any more. We'll be grown-ups. And there'll be robots to do all the jobs, and I might be able to fly or go to the moon, and my dreams might not be impossible.

New Year's Resolutions

Martha's New Year's resolution is to worry less. She says she spends too much time worrying, and it doesn't help. I feel like that about crying. That's why I don't do it anymore.

I've made three resolutions. I could have made ten, but I wouldn't be able to remember them all. My first resolution is the same as Martha's. Second, I'm also going to do more drawing so I get really good, and third, I'm going to concentrate more at school so Mrs. Clanks doesn't tell me off.

Zac said his resolution was to eat more sweets.

I said, "That's not what New Year's resolutions mean— they're supposed to be about being a better person."

So then he said, "Okay, my resolution is to keep my feet off the chairs."

I said, "I bet you can't do it even for one day."

Then he said, "I have a real New Year's resolution, but I'm not telling you what it is."

Then he was all smug like he had a secret. It was quite annoying. But I didn't ask him again, even though I knew he wanted me to.

Jimmy's Disappeared

We've haven't even been back at Skilly for one week, but everything's horrible already. Jimmy's disappeared. No one knows where he is. He went out yesterday, but he didn't go to school and he didn't tell anyone where he was going and he hasn't come back. He was out all night. Silas went looking for him, and every time the phone rings, Hortense grabs it and then she looks upset because it's not Jimmy.

Silas and Hortense really like Jimmy. They probably even love him. He helps Silas in the garden and they chat when they're working, and Hortense has known him since he was a little boy. Jimmy really is the old hand at Skilly. Even Mrs. Clanks looks worried. I hope they find him soon. Tea tasted horrible today, like all Hortense's worry had got into it.

Zac said, "Where would he go at night?" but I don't know the answer. It makes me afraid to think of Jimmy out all night. I wonder if he slept on the pavement or if he just walked around. I hope he's got some money so he can phone Silas if he needs help.

Zac thinks he's been kidnapped, but I don't think so— he hasn't got anyone to pay money to get him back, so he's not worth kidnapping. People only kidnap rich kids. Otherwise it's not worth it.

Jimmy's Back!

Jimmy's back, but he isn't happy to be here. He's angry. He's got dark lines under his eyes, so I don't think he's had any sleep. Silas brought him back when we were having breakfast. Hortense said not to ask Jimmy anything so when he came in everyone just said "hi" like he hadn't been away at all. Except for Hortense. She put her arm around him. Usually Jimmy loves food, but he didn't eat anything. He didn't even pick up his knife and fork. He's got a wall up in front of him now, like Pip.

I don't think he'll stay for long. I think he's just pretending to be here. I think he's gone already.

Back to School

We went back to school today. It felt funny writing *1990* in my book. Miss Campbell got us to think about new things that might be invented in the 1990s.

One girl said everyone will be able to talk to each other through computers. Her dad told her about it. She said people won't have to work in offices anymore. They can just stay at home and work. They could even stay in their pajamas and no one would know. They'd still have to get dressed to go shopping though.

One boy said there'll be backpacks with engines, and if you pull a string, you'll be able to fly. Kaleigh said maybe everyone would be able to change the way they look just by eating a pill. I said I think we might live on the moon because it's getting too crowded down here.

Pip doesn't normally say anything, but she said maybe there'd be special helmets and if we put them on and shut our eyes we could go anywhere we imagined, even back to the past. It was the best idea of all.

More Photos of a Dog

Martha sent us some photos. They came today! There's one of me in the garden with Dash, one of Zac throwing a stick to Dash and one of us all on the sofa on New Year's Day. Me and Zac are sitting on each side and Dash is in the middle. Martha's not in it because she took the photo.

Hortense said why don't we put the one with all of us in our Memory Book, so we did. We glued it in really carefully, and I wrote *Dash, New Year 1990*. I tried to write neatly like Glenda, but I couldn't. All the letters went in different directions.

Then Zac said, "Can I look at the other photo of the dog?" So we looked at the photo from when we were babies. Then we looked at the other pages, and the memories seemed such a long time ago and so far away. I felt quite sad.

Hortense said, "That was then and this is now, and now's okay isn't it?" And she smiled, and me and Zac nodded. Because it is.

Snow

It snowed all night, and now it feels like the world's stopped turning, like nothing's moving anymore. Everything's white and soft and the garden looks beautiful, and all the cars are stuck so if you want to go anywhere you have to walk.

Hortense and Silas took us sledding in the park. Everyone went except Mrs. Clanks. Even Jimmy. Esther wanted to wear her yellow shoes, but she put on wellie boots because she wasn't allowed to come if she didn't. There's a cupboard full of wellies, and someone would have to have really enormous feet like Silas's or tiny feet like a baby's for there not to be some that fit. There weren't any yellow ones though. She had to wear green.

Pip came too. She didn't mind what she wore as long as she had her jumper. She wore her Christmas jumper underneath, and Zac gave her his earmuffs, and Hortense put a coat on top and wrapped her in a scarf and put a hat on her head. You could hardly tell who she was. She looked like a bundle of clothes. When we were walking to the park I put my arm through hers, and she didn't mind. It was really cold, and our breath was like smoke, and it felt so nice.

We went to the park early because people go crazy on sleds there. You could get killed even, because they go so fast. People make sleds out of anything. They use bits of metal and big wooden doors and canoes. Last year a girl went down on an office chair with wheels on. She was spinning around and screaming, but she didn't fall off until she got to the bottom. Then she climbed back up the hill but left the chair, and people did all sorts of things with it, and when the snow melted it was still there for weeks afterward. But I don't think you could use it as an office chair anymore. It was falling apart.

Because we went early there was only a man with a little girl on a sled and some people on trays and some teenagers on skateboards and us.

We only had four sleds, so we had to take turns. I went down with Pip. I sat behind her, and she leaned back and looked at the sky and she had a big smile on her face. And for that minute I don't think she was even thinking about her sister. I think the sky was just filling her head. I held her hand when we walked back up. I had to pull her, but I didn't mind. Every time I looked at her, she was smiling.

Sophia and Miles went down together. Sophia was steering, and they went really fast and screamed all the way down.

151

When Esther went down with Hortense, I thought Esther would be thrown into the air because they were almost flying, but Hortense held her all the way down. Then they lost the string and were about to hit the tree, so Hortense pulled her off the sled and they rolled through the snow. There was so much snow stuck to their coats, you couldn't even see Esther's was yellow.

When Milap and Harit went down, Milap kept his heels on the ground the whole way so they couldn't go too fast. He didn't want to risk losing his brother because he's already lost his mum and dad. It didn't look any fun.

Then Harit went down with Zac, and neither of them put their feet down. They just went as fast as they could, and everyone had to jump out of the way. When they stopped they were laughing so much they couldn't stand up.

Jimmy found a tray someone left behind. He didn't want to share. First he went down facing forward, then he went down backward so he couldn't see what was happening. Then he went down standing up. Everyone had to watch out in case he hit them because he didn't care. He was smiling a great big smile, but he didn't look exactly happy. He looked a bit mad.

Then Esther got cold and wanted to go back, and Zac said he couldn't feel his fingers so he wanted to go too.

152

Harit just kept going up and down and up and down with anyone who wanted a go, but he never makes a fuss so he just came.

Jimmy had one last go standing up, but this time he crashed into the man with the little girl. They weren't hurt, but the little girl got frightened and started to cry. Jimmy swore at the man even though it wasn't the man's fault, it was Jimmy's. Silas had to run down and check they were okay and apologize, and Hortense said we had to go NOW.

On the way back Pip's boot came off and her sock got wet, so Silas put her on his shoulders so she was up in the sky. As we walked the snow crunched under our feet, and Silas kept pretending to slip and Esther was dancing around and Pip was laughing. It was so lovely.

When we got back to Skilly, I saw Glenda playing in the garden. She was picking up handfuls of snow and throwing them into the air. When she saw me she waved.

Dressing Up

Pip's social worker came today. She's called Sharon. She ties her hair up with a scarf, and she always wears a woolly jacket and brown shoes or wellies. When she was waiting for Pip, she was standing really still with a smile on her face, like she was on top of a hill looking at a beautiful view.

She took Pip to meet a family, and when they came back Pip was all muddled up. She was sort of smiling, sort of sad. She didn't say anything about the family, but she told me about the games she used to play with Alice when she was younger. They especially liked dressing up, and I said, "Do you want to dress up now?" and she said, "Yes." So we got all the funny clothes we could find and some things from Hortense, like tinfoil and sticks and swords, and we dressed up as soldiers and had a big fight. We raced around screaming and shouting.

Everyone joined in except for Jimmy—even Sophia and Miles, and they're teenagers. Esther put on a fairy dress and pretended she was a princess. In the end I had to rescue her because Zac wouldn't. But it was still really fun.

The Worst Month Ever
February 1990

February is the worst month of all. Christmas feels like ages ago, and Easter's so far away I can't believe it will ever come. Jimmy's angry all the time, and Hortense has a cold, and Zac got into a fight at school, and now he can't go out to recess for two weeks. He has to stay in his classroom.

Me and Zac are going to Martha's for Easter. Martha sent a letter to Mrs. Clanks, so now it's official. We're going for the whole holiday. I've drawn a calendar with the dates on, and every day we tick off another one.

155

Zac's got a little notebook, and he's making up tricks for Dash. He's going to make her an obstacle course in the garden and teach her to go over jumps and through tunnels. I'm going to do a painting of her when she's sleeping as long as she's not on my lap.

Jimmy's Not Coming Back

Jimmy's not coming back. He's been missing for four days, and now he's not coming back to Skilly at all. Silas has been looking for him every day. Then the police came last night, and this morning Mrs. Clanks said, "Jimmy's not coming back."

Zac said, "Is he dead?" and Mrs. Clanks said, "No. I can't say any more except that he will be moving to a new home." She didn't make it sound good. I don't think someone nice wants to adopt him. I think he's in trouble.

I asked Silas what happened, but all he said was Jimmy's okay. But he couldn't smile, so Jimmy's not very okay.

Hortense and Silas had to take the stuff out of Jimmy's room and put it in boxes. Usually they laugh when they do things together, but they weren't laughing at all. At tea Hortense looked like she was crying. She said she'd been peeling onions, but we didn't have onions for tea. We had baked potatoes and beans.

Everyone's sad because everyone knows Jimmy's not okay, but nobody's saying it out loud. We know because if he was okay, he wouldn't have run away. He would say at least good-bye.

If I had a placard now, it would say WHAT HAPPENED TO JIMMY? and JIMMY, COME BACK. It would have one message on one side and one on the other, and I would walk around the streets with it, and maybe someone would help or maybe Jimmy would even see it.

But I can't do that because I'm just a kid. I can't do anything. I'm so sad because Jimmy's one of my favorite people and he was the old hand, and now he's gone me and Zac have to be the old hands.

I think Zac was right. Jimmy was kidnapped, only he was kidnapped by aliens who made him into someone different. Zac says he doesn't want to be a teenager because it's even worse than being a child. I hadn't thought of it before, but now I wonder what happens if we grow up and we still haven't got a family. What happens then?

The Poll Tax March
March 1990

Silas is going on a big poll tax march in London. He's taking his placard. He says there'll be thousands of people there. He might even be on TV.

Me and Zac will be at Martha's, but we're going to look on the news in case we see him, because then we can show Martha. I think she'd like him.

Zac's going to teach Dash to count. He's drawn a chart. First he'll show her two sticks and teach her to bark two times, and then he'll go up to ten. He's going to teach her to count to one hundred if he can find enough sticks.

Pip's Gone

Pip's gone! Sharon took her away this afternoon. Sharon was smiling like they were going on a lovely picnic on a beautiful hill, but Pip wasn't smiling. She looked like I felt when my class went on a boat on the Thames, and even though the boat was slow, I felt really sick and dizzy and kept putting my head down. My teacher said it was because of the different movements. And that's how Pip looked. She looked as though she were seasick and she couldn't keep her head up and she just wished everything would stop still.

When I said good-bye I hugged her really tight so the hug would last forever. Everyone hugged her or waved, but we didn't say things like "See you soon" or "See you at Christmas" because probably we'll never see her again, and if we do it'll be because things have gone wrong and she has to come back. We just waved. As she walked to the car, she curled her fingers up, and I knew she was holding Alice's hand because she wouldn't leave without her.

I hope Pip's okay. She was trying not to cry because she doesn't know what's going to happen next, but she managed because she's spent a lot of time trying not to cry. I was trying not to cry too.

When I went to my room, there was a bit of paper pushed under the door. It said:

Dear Ira

Thank you for being my friend. When we went sledding it was really good, wasn't it? And the dressing up too.

Pip x

My favorite kids are all leaving Skilly—Ashani, then Jimmy and now Pip. I haven't even seen Glenda since the snow. Everything's horrible.

Mum

Something happened today. I can't stop thinking about it. It's stuck in my head and it just keeps going around and around.

Zac was watching *Newsround* and I was drawing, and then Zac shouted, "Look, Ira, look! She looks just like you!"

He was pointing at a woman on TV who was holding a No Poll Tax placard. She was standing with other protesters, and she did look just like me and Zac. Her eyes and nose were the same shape as mine and she was angry, and her face was exactly like Zac's when he's angry. She was saying things like "It's not fair," and the protestors were nodding. Then she ran her fingers through her hair, and a curl flopped right in front of her face.

"That's our mum," said Zac.

I shook my head. "She's too young."

The woman said, "We hope as many people as possible will join us at Trafalgar Square for the march. We need to make our voices heard."

Then the reporter said, "This is Bill Jenkins with the poll tax protestors," and the camera moved back, and as it did I saw a dog at the woman's feet. A black dog!

Zac shouted. "Ira, Ira, did you see the dog?"

"Yes."

"That was Mum."

"No, it wasn't."

"It was!"

He pestered me so much I had to walk away, but he grabbed me in the hall.

"That was Mum. That was the dog from the photo."

"No, it wasn't. That dog's dead."

"It isn't! How do you know?"

"I don't know," I said. "But the woman's too young."

"How old do you think she is? How old?"

"I don't know."

"Go on," he said. "Tell me! How old?"

"Twenty-six?"

"Well, you're eleven so that makes her fifteen when she had you. Lots of people have babies when they're fifteen."

I know it's true. Some kids at Skilly, their mums were fifteen when they had them, even fourteen sometimes. And the woman had a black dog. I didn't know what to say, so I shouted, "Don't be an idiot!"

Zac's face went really angry. And now he keeps going on about it. And I can't stop thinking about it too. The woman looked like us and she seemed so nice. She's got a black dog. It might not be the same dog, but she likes black dogs. She wants everyone to go to Trafalgar Square on Saturday, but we'll be at Martha's. Zac says we can't go to Martha's; we have to go and find Mum. He'd even rather do that than see Dash because he says we can see Dash another time.

Zac asked Silas if he could go to the poll tax march and Silas didn't even think about it. He just said, "Nope."

Zac's really upset. He says it might be our only chance to find our mum. I don't know what to think. I wish he hadn't watched the program.

Before I went to bed tonight, I kept looking in the

garden for Glenda. I stood at the window for ages, but she wasn't there. I was just about to give up when I saw her running along the top of the tree. She had her arms stretched out like she was on a tightrope. I hoped she'd look up and see me, but she didn't.

Back to Martha's

Zac was trying not to cry on the train to Martha's today. I was too, because the train was taking us miles away from where our mum might be, but it was also taking me to the place I wanted to be most. I didn't know how to think about the two things at the same time. It made me feel sick. Mrs. Clanks asked us what was wrong but we didn't say anything. She'd think we were stupid.

Martha and Dash were waiting for us at the station. Dash isn't tiny anymore. She's bigger and stronger. She jumped up and kept licking us and barking, and then she tripped Zac over, even though Martha had her on a leash. Zac couldn't be sad after that. He just lay there and let Dash climb all over him. He couldn't help smiling.

"I think she remembers you," Martha said.

And now we're back at Appleton House, and I feel really happy again. Martha's got the photo of me and Zac and Dash on her mantelpiece. She's got my painting on the wall too, and it looks just right with all the other paintings. It reminds me of when we came at New Year's. The garden isn't wintry anymore, and Dash doesn't need a coat. Crocuses are poking through the grass. I'm going to paint them.

Before we went to sleep I said to Zac, "It's okay here, isn't it?" and he said, "Mmm," and his eyes were watery. He's still a bit sad.

The Worst Day of My Life

Today was the worst day of my life. It's the last day of March 1990. I'll never forget that date, because it was even worse than when Mum couldn't look after us anymore, because I was too little to remember that.

After breakfast we walked to the market in Wellsbury. It was sunny, and we were all smiling. Dash was running along beside Zac's ankles, looking up at him all the time like a pony in a circus. When we got to the market, we looked at a stall with shapes dogs can chew. There were mice and balls and little rabbits, but in the end we got Dash a rubber bone. I thought she might be disappointed to have a rubber bone instead of a real one with meat on it, but she liked it. She kept chewing it and dropping it on the ground and then chewing it again. It was covered in spit.

Then we went to the cattle market. A little black calf was poking his nose through his pen. He kept sucking our fingers. He didn't want to let go. Our fingers got really wet and slimy. He was happy too. He didn't know he was going to be sold and eaten. Dash started yapping and Martha had to take her away, so it was just me and Zac and the calf.

I said to Zac, "If I had loads of money, I'd buy him and put him in a field and let him live forever."

And Zac said, "Is he going to die?"

I wished I hadn't said anything.

After that we went to the market square. Three coach buses were parked next to the square, and people were waiting to get on them. They were holding NO POLL TAX placards like Silas's, and they were happy and smiling too.

"Where are they going?" I said.

"London," said Martha. "There's a march on."

Zac stared at the coaches.

"Can we go?" he said.

Martha laughed.

"No, Zac. When you're older you can do that sort of thing, but I can't take you. Anyway, you don't have to pay the poll tax. Come on."

She hardly even looked at the coaches. She just walked

over to a fruit stall. Zac's face looked like it was melting. I couldn't even look at him.

The stall was covered with grapes. There were green grapes on one side and black grapes on the other. The woman serving said, "Very tasty, best this year," and she let us try them.

Zac said, "They're all horrible," and spat his on the ground.

Martha didn't say anything, but I could tell she was annoyed. She smiled at the woman and rolled her eyes like Hortense does. She didn't know Zac was feeling so bad. Then she bought one bag of green grapes and one bag of black.

After that we walked around. I kept thinking we'd lost Zac and Dash, but then we heard Dash bark, and when I crouched down I could see Zac looking for her slobbery bone.

Then Martha stopped at a stall selling brushes and paints and chalks. Martha picked up a paintbrush that had all the ends splayed out like a fan, instead of making a point like most do.

"This would be good for you, Ira," she said. "Give you more freedom."

What she meant was I wouldn't be able to do little details with it; I'd have to stop being so careful. She says sometimes things look nice by "happy accident," which means you do something by mistake and it works.

She bought the brush and held it out to me like it was a present. It wasn't even my birthday. I was so happy.

After that we lost Zac and Dash, and when I bent down and looked between everyone's feet, I still couldn't see them. We called them but Dash didn't bark, so I knew she couldn't hear us.

Then I saw two of the coaches had gone and I had an awful feeling. I was thinking, He wouldn't be such an idiot, he wouldn't be such an idiot, but another voice in my head was saying, Yes, he would.

I left Martha and ran to the last coach. An old man was waiting to get on. He was wearing a straw hat with No Poll Tax written on it, and he was carrying a bag of apples. He smiled at me.

"I'm afraid your brother got on the other coach," he said.

I must have looked surprised because then he said, "The little boy who looks just like you. Wasn't that your brother?"

My heart was flapping like it was a bird trapped in a cage. It was banging its wings on the bars, and it was really hurting.

"Did he have a dog?" I said.

 167

"Oh yes."

The man was happy.

"A little dog called Dash. Is that the one? He got on with his grandma," he said. "I'm terribly sorry you've missed him."

I tried to smile. I didn't want to spoil his day. Then I ran back to Martha.

The only way I could talk without crying or losing my voice was to pretend I was a social worker. Social workers are good at giving bad news. They do it all the time.

I made my face like a mask and I said, "Zac got on one of the coaches that's gone. He's on his way to London."

All the blood ran out of Martha's face. Even her cheeks went white, and they're usually pink. She took a deep breath like she was counting to ten.

Then she said, "What do you mean?"

Her heart was pounding too.

"We saw a woman on the news," I said. "She was going on the march in Trafalgar Square. Zac thinks she's our mum. I think he's gone to find her."

Martha shook her head like she had a fly whizzing round her ear. But there was no fly.

Then she said, "Surely he wouldn't do that?"

I nodded. "The man over there saw him get on."

"And taken Dash?"

I nodded again.

Martha counted to ten again.

Then she said, "Let's not panic."

Her voice was trembling like she had a bird inside too, but hers was stuck in her throat.

"I should call the police," she said.

When she said that, I wasn't a social worker any more. I was a care kid, and I was crying.

"Please don't! We'll be in so much trouble. Mrs. Clanks will never let us come again. Can't we just go and get him?"

Martha looked shocked. Then she touched my cheek really softly.

"Okay," she said. "We'll assume the best. If we can get on that coach, we'll go ourselves. He's probably not far ahead."

There were lots of seats on the coach. Most people had gone on the first two. The old man with the apples was sitting at the back with some other old people. He waved at me and I waved back. I wondered if he thought Martha was our other grandma, and I wondered who the first grandma was, though I expect she was just some old lady. People always try to make sense of things the easy way so they don't have to worry about what's going on.

I sat next to the window, and Martha sat next to me. I

was still holding the paintbrush, but I was embarrassed because we weren't happy anymore and Martha wouldn't have given me a present if she'd known what was going to happen. I pushed it up my sleeve so I wouldn't have to look at it. Then I leaned on Martha's shoulder. She smiled, but she looked worried.

I suddenly felt really old, like my life would never be simple and I was tired of it already. I didn't even know what to wish for. Part of me was wishing we'd find Zac quickly before something terrible happened, and part of me was thinking that we mustn't stop him before he finds our mum. And then I wasn't even sure if I wanted him to find our mum because she hadn't come to find us, so maybe she didn't want to be found.

I wanted to tell Glenda what was happening but I couldn't, because I had to keep Zac in my head in case I lost him, and there wasn't room for two people who weren't really there.

The journey took hours. We ate all the grapes except the squashed ones at the bottom of the bags. They made my teeth feel furry. The coach couldn't go all the way into London because there was so much traffic, so the driver stopped early.

"Where are the other coaches?" Martha said as we got off.

"Not sure, honey," said the driver. "Pandemonium today."

Pandemonium means "chaos." *Honey* means "sweetheart" or "darling." If Zac had been there, he'd have smirked at the driver calling Martha honey, but Zac wasn't there. He was the little space beside me all the time. Missing.

We had to get two trains and one bus to get near Trafalgar Square, and then we had to walk. There was a big crowd of people going to Trafalgar Square, and they were singing and chatting like they were at a carnival or going to a picnic. Some had placards like Silas's, and some had banners with different people holding each end. There was even a baby in a buggy with No Poll Tax written on the back.

At first it was quite nice, but then it got scary because there were so many people. Martha held my hand, and I was glad because everyone was taller than me. You could drown in a crowd like that. You could run out of air and fall down dead and no one would notice. Or you could trip and be trampled to death, and the pigeons would find you when everyone had gone and peck through your pockets for food. I hope somebody took the baby out of the buggy and cuddled it.

There were so many people at Trafalgar Square, I didn't recognize anything. It was like if you spill juice in the summer and wasps crawl over everything until you can't see the juice anymore. I couldn't even see the lions.

Martha put her mouth next to my ear and shouted, "We won't find them here! We need help."

The bird in my chest was fluttering so hard it was hurting. I didn't say a word, but I kept calling in my head.

Zac, where are you? Zac, where are you? Zac! Zac!

And then I heard his voice in my head. He was calling my name over and over.

Ira! Ira! Ira!

I looked up and saw the top of the National Gallery where Anita took us to see the paintings and Zac set off the alarm, and suddenly I just knew where to go.

I pulled Martha's hand and shouted, "That way!" and we pushed through the crowd. I didn't even say sorry or excuse me. I just kept pushing. And all the time Zac was calling my name.

I kept pulling Martha until we came to a lane behind the National Gallery where there weren't so many people. Two women were sitting on the pavement eating sandwiches. When they saw us they smiled, and one said, "We've walked miles." Martha smiled back but I didn't. I just let go of her hand and ran down the lane. I didn't even check she was behind me. I just kept running, and all the time I could hear Zac in my head.

And then I saw him. He was sitting on a step with Dash on his lap.

I shouted, "Zac!"

He looked like a rag doll.

"Zac!"

I ran to his side and knelt beside him, and he lifted his head and looked at me for a moment. Then he looked away. His eyes were all glassy, as though his tears had made a new skin across them. Dash didn't move. Not even a twitch. Blood was coming out of her ears.

Martha came up behind me and crouched down too. She was panting. She touched Zac's cheek like she touched mine at the market.

"It's all right now," she said.

Zac didn't look up.

Then she ran her hand over Dash's face.

"Is Dash okay?" I whispered.

She shook her head. She was gritting her teeth, and the bird in her throat was making her shiver. It took all my strength not to cry. I had to push my feelings right back inside. I kept telling myself, At least Zac's okay, at least Zac's okay.

Martha wrapped her jacket around Dash and picked her up.

Then she said, "Take Zac's hand, Ira, and stay close."

She carried Dash like she was a baby, even though it was too late to help her now. Even though she was dead. Me and Zac followed her back down the lane, all our happiness gone forever.

When we got to the end of the lane, everything had changed. It was like someone had thrown a bomb into the crowd. Only the crowd was the bomb, and it was exploding everywhere. People were running and shouting and grabbing their children, and police in yellow jackets were charging into the crowd on their horses and waving sticks, and everyone was angry and upset.

The women who were eating sandwiches had gone. They probably dropped their sandwiches and ran. I expect the pigeons will find them tomorrow. Some people were throwing bottles and bits of wood, and if those didn't get you, the policemen might hit you with a stick. A woman was sitting on the curb with blood running down her face. She was so surprised, she couldn't even cry. She couldn't work out if she was in a dream or real life. I couldn't work it out either.

An old man was telling everyone to calm down, but he was like a leaf blown about in a storm. Nobody was paying any attention. A little girl who was being carried by her mum tried to reach her hair clasp, which had fallen to the ground. It had a ladybird on it with glittery red wings.

I picked it up and gave it to her, and she snatched it and turned away. I didn't mind. I knew she was scared.

But Zac and Martha and I just kept on walking. I wasn't scared at all, because the worst thing that could possibly happen had already happened. Zac had killed Dash. I kept looking at Zac's eyes and wondering if they would be glassy like that for the rest of his life.

It took a long time to get away from Trafalgar Square, but at last we came to a bridge. People were leaning over looking into the Thames or sitting on the pavement staring at the curb. They looked confused, like they'd gone on a long journey and arrived at the wrong place. We could still hear shouting, but it was far away. I looked into the water, all shiny and smooth, and wished we could disappear into it forever.

After we had been walking for ages, Martha stopped a black cab and it took us back to Skilly. Even though one of my dreams was to ride in a black cab, it was the saddest journey of my life. Martha put Dash on her lap and covered her with her jacket but her paw poked out the whole way.

Back to Skilly

It was horrible at Skilly. Silas was already upset about the march, and when we arrived everyone felt even sadder.

It was like we were all sitting in a great big cloud. Zac ran straight up to our room and got under his duvet. He wouldn't come out. He wouldn't eat or speak. He wouldn't even put his pajamas on. Silas took Dash away, I don't know where. I'm trying not to think about it. Hortense made a bed for Martha in Pip's old room. Afterward me and Martha ate in the kitchen with Hortense and Silas.

"It wasn't meant to happen like that," Silas said. "It wasn't meant to happen like that."

He had been right in the middle of the fighting. He was lucky he didn't get hit. He said he was one of the first ones to get to Trafalgar Square, and everyone was singing. And then suddenly, it wasn't all right. He said it was like a storm coming.

"If only I'd known Zac was there, young Ira," he said.

When I went up to bed, Martha gave me a hug. She started to say something but then changed her mind; there's nothing to say. We couldn't even really say good-night because it could never be a good night.

I'd hoped Zac would be asleep when I came upstairs, but he wasn't. When I pulled back the duvet, he looked like a different boy. His face was all screwed up like he'd been beaten up from the inside.

"I just wanted to find Mum," he said. "That was my New Year's resolution. I just wanted to see her for one minute because I can't remember her. I'm sorry."

I wanted to tell him it's all right and it doesn't matter and everything's fine, but I couldn't because it's not true. Nothing will ever be fine again. I wanted to be like Matilda and make Dash jump out of wherever Silas put her and come running up the stairs, but I couldn't. I couldn't do anything.

When I took off my jumper, the paintbrush fell out of my sleeve. The bristles aren't shaped like a fan anymore; they're bent.

I wonder if the little calf's dead yet.

The Day After the Worst Day of My Life
April 1990

Martha's gone. She didn't even say good-bye. Silas drove her and Dash back to Wellsbury this morning when we were asleep. We'll never see them again.

Zac's eyes are still wet and he's got that horrible choking look, only this time I don't think he'll ever get out of it. He'll be stuck there the rest of his life. It's April Fool's Day, but nobody's playing tricks.

Hortense gave us pancakes and honey for breakfast, but they tasted horrible. Honey only tastes nice if you're happy. Otherwise it tastes all wrong.

 178

The other kids were nice, but they didn't really say anything. I think Hortense had told them not to ask questions, like when Jimmy came back that time he went missing. Esther sat next to me at breakfast and snuggled up really close. She knew we were sad.

After breakfast Hortense went to church. She said the world is so ungodly, she needs to say a prayer. I hope she says a prayer for all the people at the march and for Martha and Dash and the kids at Skilly and for Silas. When she left I waved to her from the door and she gave me a little wink. She looked lovely.

Later Mrs. Clanks called me and Zac into her office. I thought this time she'd shout, but I think she was too disappointed to be angry.

"Martha was sorry to hurry away," she said, "but Silas wanted to miss the traffic."

"Can we ring her to say good-bye?" I said. "And say sorry?"

"She's going to ring you later," Mrs. Clanks said. "You can make your apologies then."

Then she said, "What you did yesterday was very wrong and very dangerous. You won't find your mother by searching the streets. Seven million people live in London."

Her face was hard when she said that.

"You will have to wait until you are grown up."

179

And she smiled her smile that isn't a smile at all. And that's why she has that smile. So she can say terrible things.

When Silas got back he said Martha told him about me finding Zac.

"How did you know where to find him?" he said.

I tried to explain it was like there was an invisible string leading me to him, and I knew that I had to follow it.

"That's your sixth sense," he said. "I told you it'd come in useful."

Normally I would smile, but I couldn't because I was sad all the way through, like a stick of rock nobody put any sugar in.

Then Silas said, "Don't worry, Ira. Give things time."

That's like saying "Time heals." It's what grown-ups say because the one thing they can be sure of is time, because they've had so much of it. It means after time passes you forget things, and then they don't hurt so much. But I don't want to forget. There are too many nice things to remember, and there might not be any more.

I asked Silas why people were fighting at the march.

He said, "Feelings. Too many different feelings all felt too strong. It's always feelings that get things out of control. If you took the feelings away there wouldn't be any fighting, or anything else good neither."

I don't want to feel anything ever again.

I felt sick waiting for Martha to phone. I didn't know what to do. I tried to write in my diary, but that made me feel even worse. Then I sat in the kitchen with Hortense and just stared and stared at the phone in the hall and waited for it to ring. I wanted to tell Martha how sorry I am and how I wish and wish everything wasn't spoiled.

But when she rang I couldn't say anything. Zac wouldn't come to the phone, so it was just me. My mouth was full and empty all at the same time. A scream was trying to get out but I wouldn't let it, because if it did it might not stop.

At last I said, really quietly so the scream wouldn't escape, "I'm sorry, Martha."

And she said, "I know. Me too."

Then a funny sound came out of me and I was nearly crying, but I stopped myself by pretending to be a receptionist, because receptionists don't cry on the phone. You could never be a receptionist if you cry on the phone.

"Where's Dash?" I said.

"Silas helped me bury her under the willow," Martha said. "When you come back you can take her some flowers."

 181

"Will we come back?" I said.

In my head I was sort of screaming, but on the outside my voice was really small and trembling.

"Yes," Martha said.

"Zac too?"

"Of course."

And now I feel like jumping. Not jumping like every-thing's fine again, but jumping because I'm alive and I want to be alive tomorrow too.

That's what Silas meant by "Give things time."

What Happened to Zac

Zac told me what happened. He said he's never going to talk about it again, so I'd better listen.

When me and Martha were looking at the brushes, he said he and Dash went to look at the coaches. He didn't exactly think he'd get on one; he just wanted to get closer. The first coach set off when Dash dropped her chewy bone, and he was looking for it but then he got in the queue for the second coach, just to see what it felt like to be queuing to go to the march. He stood next to an old woman, and she was stroking Dash and making a fuss of her, so when she got on the coach, Zac got on too and sat next to her. Nobody asked for money or anything.

 182

The woman said, "Don't you want to sit with your mum?" And Zac said, "No, she's got the baby and the baby frightens Dash."

The words just popped out, like someone else had said them.

Then the woman said, "Well, all the better for me then," and she got out a paper bag and said, "Here, have a mint." Dash put her nose in the bag and the woman said, "Bit of an outing for him too," and Zac said, "She's a girl."

The woman talked the whole journey and shared her chicken sandwiches. Zac had the bread and Dash had the chicken. She said, "You're a very little boy to be going to London," and Zac said, "I've been there before."

When they got to London, Zac said, "Thank you very much for the sandwiches," and the woman said, "Lovely to meet you," and Zac and Dash jumped off the coach and ran into the crowd.

Everyone was going to Trafalgar Square, so he just followed them and looked all around for Mum, but he couldn't see her anywhere. The women were all too old or too young or their hair wasn't curly or their faces were wrong.

At Trafalgar Square the crowd was really big and noisy, and people were pushing, and Dash got frightened and was barking. Zac tried to tell her it was okay, but then the crowd moved like a big wave and Zac nearly fell over, and then Dash wasn't barking anymore. She was lying on the ground and people were standing on her. They didn't even know she was there. He shouted but no one heard.

Then he picked Dash up and carried her away from Trafalgar Square. She was really floppy and blood was coming out of her ears but he kept walking and telling her it was all going to be okay. When he got to a doorway, he sat down and put her on his lap, but she wasn't moving. He kept wishing I would come but he didn't call my name. He didn't make a single sound. And when he realized Dash was dead, he wished he was dead too, and he still does.

Silas

Silas might have to go to prison because he won't pay the poll tax. He didn't even wait for the poll tax people to ask for the money. He just wrote and said he wasn't paying because he thinks it costs too much and it isn't fair. Me and Zac were in the kitchen when he told Hortense.

I said, "Will they send you to jail?"

"It's not likely they'll put me in jail," he said. "There

are a lot of people not paying. The jails aren't big enough for all of them."

Hortense was sitting at the table with her hands around a mug of tea. When Silas went out into the garden, she said, "Bloody man." I was so surprised. I never heard her swear before.

"He just has to go that much further than anyone else, doesn't he?" she said.

"That's because he likes traveling," said Zac.

It was the first time since the march that Hortense smiled. Zac didn't smile though.

Back to Martha's

We came back to Martha's today. At first Zac refused to get off the train. He screwed his eyes shut and wouldn't move. It was like he was stuck to his seat. Mrs. Clanks put her face close to his and said, "I'm not putting up with any nonsense from you, Zac, so get up."

Martha was waiting on the platform. When she saw us she ran toward us with her arms stretched out. She was wearing a blue dress and her head was bobbing, and she was sort of smiling like she didn't know whether to be happy or not, but she thought she should try to be. She looked like a puppet with strings attached to bobbing clouds.

She didn't tell us off. She gave us a hug, and after she said good-bye to Mrs. Clanks, she said, "Come along."

Zac didn't speak all the way from London to Appleton House. He hates himself.

Saying Good-bye to Dash

The house is horrible without Dash. All her doggy things are here. Her basket's next to the kitchen door. It looks like she just got out. The blanket's all crumpled, and you can see a bit of my green dress.

She's buried under a little heap of soil under the willow. Me and Zac picked some daisies and put them in a jar next to the soil, but it's so beautiful when you look up into the tree, she probably doesn't need them. Martha said we were saying good-bye.

Afterward she put her hand on Zac's shoulder.

"You had better forgive yourself," she said, "or I will never forgive myself for not taking better care of you. A lot of things went wrong that day. You weren't to know. No one was to know."

Zac's face was all twisted. He looked like he was drowning. Martha knelt down in front of him like she was saying a prayer.

"Do you understand me, Zac?" she said. "This is

where we let it rest. Sometimes things happen that no one could predict, and sometimes someone gets hurt. You did everything you could to look after Dash, and when she needed you most, you didn't leave her. I trusted you with Dash because you loved her. And I was right to trust you. I would again. It was the world I couldn't trust."

Then Zac began to cry. It was like the water over his eyes was holding back a flood and it burst. Tears poured down his cheeks and dripped onto his shirt. They just kept on coming. He cried all afternoon. He couldn't stop. Then when he had no tears left, he curled up on the sofa and went to sleep.

Now he's sitting by the stream.

The Promise

Martha was nervous at tea today. I thought she was going to tell us this was our last visit. She drank her tea, filled it up again and then drank the next cup all in one go.

Then she said, "I wonder if I could make you two a promise, but I will need a promise in return."

"What sort of promise?" I said.

She took a deep breath.

"My promise is that my home will be your home for as

long as I am here," she said, "which I hope will be a very long time indeed. If you would like that, of course."

"In the holidays?" I said.

"Not just the holidays—always."

"Forever?"

"Yes."

"Here?"

"Yes."

"To live here in this house?"

"Yes. You will have to argue over bedrooms."

I could hardly breathe. My head was so full of thoughts, it was hard to remember to breathe too. I was thinking it doesn't matter which room I have, Zac can choose; it doesn't matter if I sleep on the floor or in the garden, even.

"Zac can choose," I said.

"Well, they both overlook the garden," she said.

"To have our own wardrobe?" Zac said.

"One each," said Martha.

"With a sink in the bedroom?" I said.

"Yes."

Martha was smiling now.

"And go to school here?"

"Yes."

"And come home for tea?"

188

"I think that would be a good idea, don't you? You'll be hungry."

Me and Zac were nodding.

"But I need a promise from you if we're to do this," she said. "I need you to promise that if you come, you'll stay."

Of course we'll stay, I thought. Of course we will.

"Not go running off back to London, chasing dreams," Martha went on. "At least not until you're grown up. I'm too old to run around after you."

"Will we see Silas?" I said.

"Of course," said Martha. "I'm not going to let you lose him. He'll visit or we will."

"And Hortense?"

"And Hortense," she said.

I looked at Zac. He was staring at Martha. His mouth was wobbling.

"Can you promise, Zac?" Martha said. "This is a serious promise."

He didn't move. I crossed all my fingers and wished and wished he would promise. For a moment I thought he wouldn't, that maybe he liked Skilly too much, but then he nodded.

"Yes," he said.

He walked round the table to Martha and put his head on her shoulder. She smiled.

"Ira?" she said.

"Me too," I gulped. "We both promise."

"Right," Martha said. "That's settled then."

It's the most impossible of all my dreams. I can't believe I'm writing about it as if it's real. But it is real! I have to keep telling myself me and Zac have a family! Martha will be our family. We won't be Skilly kids anymore. We'll live in a proper home. Me and Zac can't stop smiling and Martha too.

Zac's asleep now, and I've been looking out of our bedroom window at the stars and the garden and the willow. I keep thinking of that day at Trafalgar Square, and I wonder how the two moments could even happen in the same world. I don't think I'll ever understand.

Things I won't miss about Skilly:
Rules
Scribbles
New kids
Bobbly blankets

Things I will miss about Skilly:
Silas
Hortense

Skilly kids
The tree
The kitchen table
Glenda
Even Mrs. Clanks

In my head I told Glenda what's happened. I didn't tell her about Dash, because I don't want to think about it anymore. I expect she knows anyway. I wonder if she'll come to Appleton House with us. Maybe she won't want to leave Skilly.

Last Week at Skilly
June 1990

We have one week left at Skilly, and then we go to Martha's. It feels so strange. We've got to pack and take down our posters and sort things out at school and say good-bye. Hortense keeps giving me extra hugs. She knows there's not long left, so she has to give me as many as she can.

Silas said, "Just make sure you're happy, Ira."

The other kids look fed up. It's because when me and Zac go there's only going to be Sophia and Miles and Milap and Harit and Esther at Skilly, and that means lots

192

of new kids will come. And nobody likes it when new kids come. I feel all mixed up happy-sad.

I haven't seen Glenda since we came back from Martha's. I hope she's not annoyed with me for going. I'm worried she might think I don't want to be her friend anymore, but I don't even know if she's here. I haven't seen her anywhere.

Mrs. Clanks

This morning we had to see Mrs. Clanks in her office. I wasn't nervous because she can't tell us off much longer. But anyway she was nice. She had a silver ribbon in her hair as though it was a special occasion. When we went in she smiled, and it looked almost like the smile was real.

"We will be very sorry to see you go," she said, "but it is a wonderful opportunity for you. We will keep in touch, and if ever you want to come back you will always be welcome. If you're not happy, I mean."

Zac shook his head. He knows he'll be happy.

"I expect you won't want to come back," Mrs. Clanks said, "but you are always welcome to visit. We'd like to know how you get on, and of course Silas and Hortense would love to hear from you."

Our Memory Book was on her desk.

"We mustn't forget this," she said. "No doubt you'll have lots of new things to put in it soon."

She put it in a big brown envelope, then she signed her name on a letter.

"Just a few details for Martha," she said.

I was watching her sign the letter and thinking how neat and slanted her writing was when I saw she'd written "Glenda Clanks"! My chest went funny and tight like I couldn't breathe properly. I thought of the girl in the photo with the ribbon sliding down her hair, and I looked at Mrs. Clanks's ribbon, and I had a thought that seemed impossible.

"There," she said. "All done."

I didn't hear anything she said after that. I was just waiting to get out of her office. I didn't even say thank you when she finished. I just ran out. Zac did too. He wanted to play with Harit.

I ran straight up to our room and pulled the letters out from under the floorboard and opened the one from Glenda. Then I just stared at it. The writing was really neat and it sloped up, just like Mrs. Clanks's writing, only hers was more grown-up.

I kept walking from one side of the room to the other holding the letters, like a detective trying to work out who did the crime, because I was trying to work out something too. I was trying to work out if Glenda became Mrs. Clanks. But even though I walked across the room a hundred times, I couldn't make sense of it.

I thought of putting the letters back and not saying anything, but then I thought of Silas saying "Seize the moment," so I took the letters and ran downstairs. As I was running, Glenda was suddenly running beside me. It was like she was keeping me going in case I changed my mind. When I got to Mrs. Clanks's door, she sort of pushed me in. I didn't even knock. I just fell into the room.

I think Mrs. Clanks would have told me off if I wasn't leaving.

Instead she said, "Ira, come in."

I was shaking. "I just wondered . . ."

"Yes?"

". . . if you lived at Skilly when you were a child."

Mrs. Clanks nodded. "I did."

I took a deep breath.

"Were you Glenda Hyacinth?" I said.

She nodded again.

I looked at her for ages. I couldn't work it out. She's so different from how I think of Glenda.

"Sit down, Ira," she said.

But I didn't want to sit down. I just stood there holding the letters, trying to understand it all.

"You wrote your name on the windowsill in my bedroom," I said at last.

"That was my bedroom."

"But you're so scary," I said, "and Glenda isn't scary at all. She's my friend."

Mrs. Clanks said, "Am I scary? I don't mean to be."

I nodded.

"You know, Ira," she said, "it's too hard to love all the children who come to Skilly, all the children who come and go. It was too hard when I was a child, and it's too hard now. I'm sure you know that. My job is to try to make things the best I can for you and if possible find a way for you to leave here and go somewhere happier."

"Did you ever get a family?" I said.

"Yes, in the end. I spent eight years here and then I met Mrs. Clanks—my husband's mother. I worked in her shop. She took me in, and then I got to know Albert. He was a boy then, and well, I've been lucky."

And then she smiled, and she didn't look hard at all. She looked strong.

"Have you got any children?" I said.

"No, I decided I wanted to look after children who don't have families."

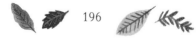

196

"Like us?"

She nodded.

Then I said, "I found your letter," and she just stared at me. She was so surprised.

"I'd forgotten," she said.

"I wrote a letter back," I said. "You can have both. I don't want to take them away. Will you keep them at Skilly?"

She nodded.

I gave her the letters and she put them on her desk. I was a bit embarrassed. My pink envelope looked horrible, but she didn't seem to notice. She walked around to me and put her hands on my shoulders and kissed the top of my head. She smelled of ink and paper.

"Now things will get better for you," she said.

As I was leaving the office, I turned around and looked back at her.

"Why do you still wear a ribbon in your hair?" I said.

She thought for a moment.

"Maybe it's the girl in me," she said.

Then she smiled.

When I got out Glenda wasn't in the hall anymore. I thought she'd be waiting for me, but she'd gone. I looked all around but she wasn't there. I wanted to tell her what happened. She's the only one who'd understand. If she'd waited I could have told her about her future. But she's gone, and I've lost her forever. Because now she's become Mrs. Clanks, and Mrs. Clanks has become Glenda, and I don't think of either of them the same way anymore.

I remember Mrs. Clanks was rude to me when I showed her the photo of Glenda and when she read my story, but now I understand. Because maybe thinking about Glenda makes her sad. Zac's always rude when he's sad.

Leaving Skilly

Today we left Skilly. Anita came to get us. Her hair was the color of cotton candy, and she was wearing pink lipstick and a flowery dress. She might have made the dress out of curtains like in *The Sound of Music* because the flowers were really big. She looked like she should be singing and running over a mountain because she was so happy. Because today was a good day and she didn't have to pretend.

When everyone stood outside Skilly and waved us good-bye, I had to look away. I couldn't watch. They were turning to ghosts right in front of my eyes. I felt a huge sob coming up inside of me. It made my chest hurt. Zac looked away too. His face was moving all over the place like jelly wobbling on a plate. He can't make his mouth flat anymore. He can't hide his emotions at all. One moment he's sad, then he's worried, then he's happy, then he's sad again.

Mrs. Clanks gave us the envelope with our Memory Book, and Zac held it on his lap for the whole journey. Anita said he could put it down if he wanted, but he wouldn't let go. He just held on to it really tight all the way to Martha's.

Today

Zac and I spent the rest of our childhood at Appleton House, and twenty-five years on we still think of it as home. It was as though there were two child-shaped holes waiting to be filled, and we fitted them perfectly. Martha got another dog, a black-and-white spaniel this time, and we called her Zip. She was just as lively as Dash and soon she was running along beside Zac's ankles, looking at him adoringly. We also discovered that dogs can count, though possibly not to one hundred.

Silas didn't go to jail, and not long after the march the

poll tax was abolished and the posters and sheets came down. We still have our Memory Book and the photo of the dog, but neither Zac nor I have looked for our mother since that afternoon in Trafalgar Square. Perhaps one day we will, but for now we have all the family we need.

Martha has been my inspiration. I have moved back to London and work as an illustrator, but there is nowhere I would rather be than with Martha in her studio. She still paints, and though her hands are less steady, her colors are just as vibrant.

Zac became a teacher and is married with a daughter, Bonita. He has promised to take her to Spain one day. He is the sweetest dad you could imagine, and the kind of teacher who spots the sad, sullen kid at the back of the class and tries to help.

Skilly House has been sold by the council and is due to be demolished so flats can be built. Last week we gathered for a final good-bye. Silas and Hortense were there, as warm and energetic as ever, packing and organizing and piling the table with food. The only difference is, a few years ago they married. Zac and I were so surprised. We had been so wrapped up in our own lives, it never occurred to us that adults had feelings too.

Mrs. Clanks was also there with her husband, Albert. She is much older now, but her back is still straight and she still wears a ribbon in her hair. At a quiet moment she took me aside and pulled two envelopes out of her bag.

"I thought you might like these," she said.

And there were the letters we had written so many years ago, the pink and the white envelopes as fresh as if they had been written yesterday. I didn't need to read them—I know them by heart—but I carried them with me all afternoon.

There were many past Skilly kids at the gathering, some I knew and most I didn't, but we were all there for the same reason—because Skilly was part of our lives. Amazingly, Jimmy was there, tall and thin and urgent with life. He told me the night he left Skilly, he'd slept under Waterloo Bridge. He'd felt too old to live in a children's home, but he'd had nowhere else to go. On the second night he stole a blanket and got into a fight; on his third night he was moved to a hostel. His life has been tumultuous, but throughout it all he has stayed close to Silas and Hortense. He now works with young people, and he finally feels he is keeping his head above water.

Wonderfully, Pip was there too. I have often worried about the small, sad girl stuck behind her wall, but there she was, smiling and happy with two small daughters of her own and no possibility of a wall because her girls are completely enchanting. If ever there was a small miracle, it was for me the sight of Bonita playing with the two little girls while Zac stood proudly by.

The garden at Skilly was overgrown and bursting with flowers, and clematis and ivy almost covered the walls. The tree had been sliced into pieces and piled high, the names we carved into the bark buried in the heap.

Later Silas lit a fire and we gathered around, a circle of ghosts watching the flickering flames, and I thought of all the lost children who had gazed out on that garden and wondered what the future would bring, or even if there would be a future.

I walked over to Mrs. Clanks and held out the letters. She nodded. There was no need to speak. We took a letter each, crumpled them into balls and tossed them into the flames. They twisted and tumbled a little, and then they caught light, scattering their embers into the fire.

Acknowledgments

I would like to thank my agent, Gillie Russell, for her support and encouragement and for making so much possible. Many thanks also to the wonderful team at Nosy Crow for believing in this book from the start and picking it up and running with it with such enthusiasm. I could not have asked for more. Huge thanks also to Katie Harnett for her beautiful illustrations.

I would also like to thank my friends and family for their support, in particular Paul, Hilary and Kate for their patient encouragement, Phoebe for her excellent advice and Tess for being a breath of fresh air.

Finally, thank you to Rosie and Oliver for being a constant source of inspiration—and distraction—and for putting up with my moods (sorry about the spinach incident). Many thanks also to Duncan for believing in me and my stories, even when things showed no sign of working out.

The Instant Handbook of

Boat Handling,
Navigation,
and Seamanship

The Instant Handbook of
Boat Handling, Navigation, and Seamanship

A Quick Reference for Sail and Power

Nigel Calder

Richard Clinchy

Bill Gladstone

Peter Nielsen

John Rousmaniere

Bob Sweet

Charlie Wing

International Marine / McGraw-Hill

Camden, Maine • New York • Chicago • San Francisco • Lisbon • London • Madrid • Mexico City • Milan • New Delhi • San Juan • Seoul • Singapore • Sydney • Toronto

*The **McGraw·Hill** Companies*

1 2 3 4 5 6 7 8 9 RRD SHEN 0 9 8

© 2008 by International Marine
All rights reserved. The publisher takes no responsibility for the use of any of the materials or methods described in this book, nor for the products thereof. The name "International Marine" and the International Marine logo are trademarks of The McGraw-Hill Companies. Printed in China.

Library of Congress Control Number: 2007928466

ISBN 978-0-07-149910-1
MHID 0-07-149910-5

Questions regarding the content of this book should be addressed to
International Marine
P.O. Box 220
Camden, ME 04843
www.internationalmarine.com

Questions regarding the ordering of this book should be addressed to
The McGraw-Hill Companies
Customer Service Department
P.O. Box 547
Blacklick, OH 43004
Retail customers: 1-800-262-4729
Bookstores: 1-800-722-4726

All art courtesy the authors unless otherwise noted:
Rick Barrentine/Corbis: 17; Ed Bohon/Corbis: 143; Dana Bowden: 18; FEMA: 228 (second from top); Christian Février, Bluegreen Pictures: 159; Pip Hurn: 133–38, 140–41 (illustrations only); www.mirtoart.com: 162 (bottom), 167 (bottom), 168 (bottom), 171 (top), 192–96, 197 (top and middle), 198–99, 203, 204 (top), 205 (top); Maptech: 44 (top); Nick Noyes: 161 (bottom); Ritchie Navigation: 60 (bottom), 62; Hal Roth: 162 (top), 171 (bottom), 172; Fritz Seegers: 180 (top), 181 (bottom), 221; David Shuler: 1, 191, 197 (bottom); Tom Upham: 224 (top); USCG: 204 (bottom two); Volvo: 175; West Marine: 63, 95, 111, 207; Yanmar: 176.

CONTENTS

On the water, when questions arise, there is often no time to spend searching through an exhaustive manual. *The Instant Handbook of Boat Handling, Navigation, and Seamanship* provides all the answers you need—fast.

Each of these chapters has been written by a leading expert (see pages 223–24 for a list of the contributors), and every page is designed to impart vital information with maximum ease and efficiency. We feel confident in saying that there has never been another seamanship book as authoritative and at the same time accessible as this one.

With the sole exception of Chapter 3, each of these chapters is also available as a stand-alone Quick Guide—a foldout, accordion-style, heavily laminated resource that is waterproof and virtually indestructible. We present the full product lineup below. With a folded size of just 4 inches by 9 inches, the Quick Guides are perfect for onboard use. They are available as Captain's Quick Guides from marine stores, from online book and marine retailers, from the U.S. Power Squadrons, and from www.internationalmarine.com. They are also available as West Marine Quick Guides from West Marine's stores, catalog, and website.

We hope *The Instant Handbook of Boat Handling, Navigation, and Seamanship* makes your time on the water more enjoyable, more rewarding, and safer.

—the editors of International Marine

CHAPTER 1

Boat Handling Under Power

Bob Sweet

Know Your Boat

Every boat under power moves in reaction to the thrust of water discharged from its propeller. When the discharge stream is directed astern, the boat moves ahead, and vice versa.

turn left turn right

thrust trim in

trim out

① The operator of an outboard, sterndrive (inboard/outboard or I/O), or jet-drive boat steers by directing the discharge stream from side to side—and that makes these boats highly maneuverable as long as the engine is engaged.

② In boats powered by a conventional inboard gas or diesel engine, the propeller is mounted on a fixed shaft, so the boat must be steered solely by means of a rudder. Add a second engine, however, and the engines and steering working in concert make the boat highly maneuverable, as we'll see.

The following table is for comparative purposes. Any production boat will handle sufficiently well provided you adapt your handling techniques to your boat's tendencies rather than trying to fight them.

Type of Propulsion	Outboard or Sterndrive (I/O)	Jet Drive	Single-Engine Inboard	Twin-Engine Inboard	Sailboat Auxiliary
Directional Control	Directed thrust propeller(s)	Directed thrust nozzle(s)	Rudder	Rudders + Engines	Large rudder
Low-Speed Handling					
Forward	[1]				
Reverse					
Maneuvers					
Turn in place					
Propeller Side thrust	Moderate	None	Significant	None[2]	Significant
Docking					
Forward					
Backing in					
Cruise-Speed Handling					
Turns					
Trim Front-to-back	Drive trim, Trim tabs	Trim tabs	Trim tabs	Trim tabs	☐
Side-to-side	Trim tabs	Trim tabs	Trim tabs	Trim tabs	☐

Legend: ▪ Excellent ▪ Very good ▪ Good ▪ Fair ▪ Poor ☐ None

1. with engine in gear—does not respond to helm when engine is in neutral

2. with both engines engaged ahead or astern

Slow-Speed Maneuvering

A powerboat turns on a center of rotation that is typically about one-third of the way from the bow to the stern ⒜.

Forward | Reverse | Sailboat

In effect, your boat's propulsion system pushes the stern *away* from the turn so the bow will rotate *into* it, and the stern swing is wider than the bow swing. Also, due to its momentum, your boat *slides* into a turn rather than carving it like a car on a curve ②.

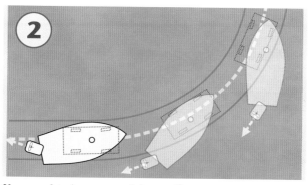

You need to be aware of these effects or you are likely to strike with your stern the very boat or dock you turned your bow away from ③. In time you will learn what clearances your boat requires for turns at various speeds and in various conditions of wind and current.

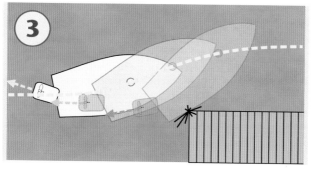

In reverse, a powerboat's pivot point typically moves to about two-thirds of the way from the bow to the stern, so the bow now swings more widely ⒝.

The pivot point on a sailboat is more nearly amidships ⒞.

Single-Engine Inboard

A single-engine (single-screw) inboard powerboat depends on its rudder for steering. When the engine is in forward gear, the rudder turns the boat by deflecting the prop discharge (often called "wash") as well as the current created by the boat's motion. At slow speeds the boat depends heavily on prop wash for steering control; the smaller the rudder, the more true this is.

Forward—prop wash makes rudder more effective.

Reverse—no prop wash.

The propeller also produces a small side thrust that pushes the stern to port or starboard. Most boats use a "right-handed" prop, which turns clockwise in forward gear when viewed from astern, pushing the stern to starboard. Take your cue from the direction the blades are moving at the top of the swing; that's the direction of this so-called prop walk. Prop walk will give your boat a tighter turn to port than to starboard in forward gear.

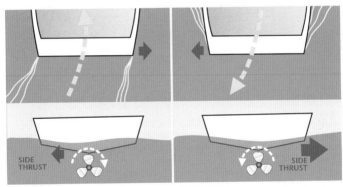

Side thrust in forward pushes stern to starboard.

Side thrust in reverse pushes stern to port.

When you put the single engine in reverse, however, the direction of side thrust also reverses, and the impact is greater in reverse than in forward since the propeller is not as efficient in reverse. To compound the problem with a single-screw inboard, in reverse there is no prop wash on the rudder to help with steering. To counter the stern moving to port, briefly shift the engine from reverse to forward and apply a brief burst of power while you steer hard to port. Then shift back to reverse. You won't make any forward headway, but the stern will kick over to starboard.

You can use prop walk to help you make a slow close-quarters turn to starboard. First turn the wheel hard to starboard and apply a brief burst of power ①. This should turn the boat 20 degrees or more. When you start to make forward progress, apply a brief burst of reverse power ②. The resultant side thrust "walks" the stern to port, continuing the turn while slowing your forward motion. Repeat the process ③ until your turn is completed. With practice, you'll be able to turn a clockwise circle within the boat's length.

Turning counterclockwise is more difficult because prop walk—while it aids the turn in forward—opposes it in reverse.

Twin-Engine Inboard

Twin inboard engines with a rudder behind each prop make a highly maneuverable boat. Usually the starboard propeller will be right-handed and the port prop will be left-handed , so that their side thrusts cancel when both engines are in forward ① or reverse ②. A twin-engine boat will therefore back straight when you center the rudders (absent wind or current) and is steerable at low backing speeds.

When one engine is in forward while the other is reversed ③, the side thrusts combine to make a turn even tighter. When rudder action is added, the boat can even spin within its own length.

You can often maneuver with engines alone. E.g., backing with more throttle on the port engine turns the stern to starboard ④.

On some boats, you can even slide the boat sideways. Try putting the starboard engine in reverse and the port engine ahead with left rudder.

Outboard and Sterndrive (I/O)

Single-engine outboards and sterndrives steer by turning the propeller so as to direct its discharge current. These boats permit easier steering in reverse and tighter turns than you can possibly get from a single-engine inboard.

Without a rudder, however, there is little steerage with an outboard or I/O if the propeller is not engaged. This means it's more difficult to approach a dock with the engine in neutral. Also, most outboard- and sterndrive-powered hulls are designed for planing, not slow speeds. But you soon learn how to use throttle and helm to handle the boat.

Twin outboards or sterndrives offer some of the same handling benefits as twin inboard engines, but not to the same degree, since the propellers tend to be much closer together and farther aft from the boat's center of rotation than inboard props.

Planing hulls are designed to go fast, and track better going forward than in reverse.

Jet Drives

A jet drive has no external propeller. Instead an internal impeller mounted in a tube sucks water in through a grate in the hull bottom and forces it out toward the rear to produce thrust much like a jet aircraft. Steerage is accomplished by turning a nozzle to direct the discharge. When it's time to back up, a deflector shield swings down over the nozzle outlet, directing the discharge thrust forward. This produces a small and relatively ineffective reverse that can be steered for directional control.

Jet drives operate like outboards or sterndrives with nearly instantaneous response. However, the jet drive has no steerage without power applied.

Auxiliary Sailboats

A sailboat's larger rudder makes it slightly more steerable in reverse when the boat is moving than a single-engine inboard powerboat. The sailboat's keel or centerboard will help it track through turns and provides a pivot point fixed nearer amidships. That means the stern kicks out less in a turn ahead, and the bow kicks out less in a turn astern.

However, a typical lack of horsepower imposes restraints. Prop walk is likely to be significant, especially in reverse. Adapting the approaches for single-engine inboards as a starting point, experiment in open water to see how your boat turns and backs. Do not expect great maneuverability under power from a boat designed primarily for sailing. Maneuver upwind or upcurrent when possible and avoid situations that might demand more precise handling than your boat can deliver.

Docking

Docking techniques depend on current and wind. Current affects all boats equally, but wind has a greater influence on a light boat with high topsides and cabin structures and a shallow underbody that offers little resistance to leeway, which describes a typical planing cruiser.

Before you dock, look at flags or ripples on the water to determine wind strength and direction. Note which way moored boats are pointing in response to current and wind—especially boats similar to yours. Or simply stop your boat at a convenient location, observe which way it drifts, and plan your docking maneuvers accordingly.

Deploy lines and fenders in advance, briefing the crew on your intentions and their roles. Leave yourself an escape route in case other boats invade your path or your approach goes awry.

The angle of your approach will depend upon the direction of the wind. For a wind blowing off the dock, you will need to increase the angle.

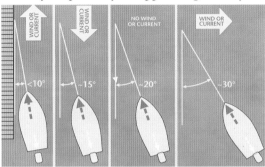

Single-Engine Inboard Powerboat or Auxiliary Sailboat

A port-side-to landing is most convenient, especially if you have a right-handed prop. If wind and current are negligible, approach at roughly 20 degrees, slow to bare steerageway, and just before touching turn parallel with the dock and apply a touch of reverse power. The resultant prop walk will nudge your port quarter into the dock. Have your crew step onto the dock with docklines (inboard ends cleated in advance).

When there is a significant wind or current parallel to the dock, approach into the wind (or current) if you can ①. Pass a bow line or forward spring line to a dockside helper, who will tie off the line forward of the boat ②. (If a crewmember takes the line ashore, he or she should step—not leap—onto the dock.) As the boat is pushed back by the wind or current, the line will come taut and the stern will settle in toward the dock ③.

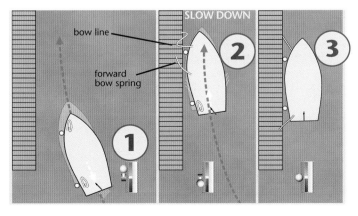

If the wind is blowing toward the dock, turn parallel when farther out than usual and let the breeze nudge you in.

If there is a strong wind blowing off the dock, or if the available dock space is not much longer than your boat, approach at a steeper-than-normal angle and have an after spring line ready—i.e., free to run, with one end cleated at or slightly forward of amidships ①. As your bow quarter approaches the dock, have the spring line led back to a dock cleat or bollard near the "aft" end of the available space and attached there without slack ②. Now when you turn your helm away from the dock and apply gentle forward power, the resultant forces against the spring line will "warp" the boat into the dock ③.

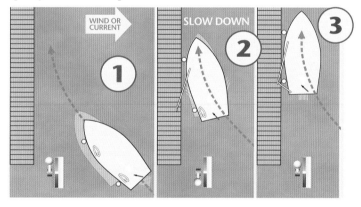

If forced to dock with wind or current behind you, approach at a shallow angle ① and get your stern line or after spring line fast to the dock quickly ②. Gentle forward power with starboard helm (assuming a port-side landing) will hold the stern against the dock while you get the other lines ashore ③.

Outboard and Sterndrive (I/O) Boats

Generally you can use the single-engine inboard docking techniques just described. There is an additional technique with the wind off the dock or when fitting your boat into a short space. As your bow approaches the dock ①, apply a little reverse power while turning the wheel toward the dock to stop your forward motion ②. Now lead a bow line fast to the dock. Backing against the bow line with the wheel to port will move the stern in ③.

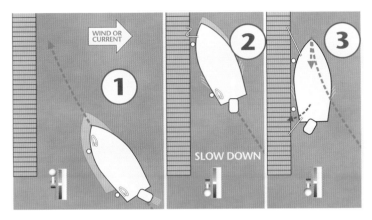

When docking with wind or current from behind ①, hold the boat in a fixed position by applying just the right power in reverse ②. The bow will simply point downwind or downcurrent, and steering gently toward the dock moves the boat sideways to its destination ③.

Twin-Engine Inboard

Adapt the twin-engine techniques described earlier to the docking techniques for a single-engine inboard. A twin-engine boat is more maneuverable and thus easier to dock, and the absence of propeller side thrust means you can land on your port or starboard side with equal ease. You can dock using engines alone to maneuver your boat, but rudders may help.

Boat Handling Under Power

Departing the Dock—All Boats

In the absence of wind or current and with plenty of room ahead, simply ease forward and away from the dock, turning gently so as not to clip it with your stern quarter.

If the wind or current is ahead of you or off the dock, untie the bow and let it swing clear. Then apply forward power, steering to keep your stern quarter clear.

When the wind or current is directly on the dock, pinning you to it, cast off all docklines except your after-bow spring line ①. Make sure you have fenders in place. Turn your helm toward the dock and apply gentle forward power against the spring line, and your stern should swing away from the dock ②. Now release the spring and you should be able to back clear ③. This method also works when the wind or current is pushing you from behind.

(Hint: If you double the spring line around a dock cleat or bollard, with both ends aboard the boat, you can recover it from the boat simply by releasing one end and pulling in the other.)

To clear a tight berth going ahead rather than astern, back down on a forward quarter spring line with your helm centered ①. The forces working against the restraining line will swing your bow out ②. Then apply forward power, recover your spring line, and proceed ③.

Docking in a Slip

When entering a slip bow first, aim toward the inner corner with slow steerageway, fenders deployed, until your bow quarter almost kisses the dock ①. Then apply light reverse power to halt your forward progress and get a bow line around a cleat or post at the inner end of the slip ②. Another burst of reverse power with helm toward the dock will pull the stern in ③, either from the directed thrust of an outboard or sterndrive or the prop walk of an inboard. With a twin-engine boat, use the engine away from the dock.

Backing in is more challenging, especially in a single-engine inboard boat or auxiliary sailboat. Get properly aligned in front of the slip. Punctuate your backing with brief bursts of power ahead under port or starboard helm to get back on course without halting sternway. If necessary, pull out and realign your boat for another attempt. Have docklines ready, and don't hesitate to use them to warp yourself in.

Backing into a slip can be challenging. As soon as you touch, have a crewmember or dockhand tie a stern line, and then use gentle forward power to pull you to the dock.

Boat Handling Under Power

Handling at Cruising Speeds

Most boats handle best when running more or less "on their lines"—i.e., parallel with their at-rest waterline. A slight bow-up trim will increase the efficiency of a planing hull, but excessive bow-up trim increases slamming in a chop and impedes visibility ahead. A little bow-down trim can give a more comfortable ride and better steering at slow speeds or in a chop but may also increase spray and might cause "bow steering" or even bury the bow at cruising speeds in following seas.

Neutral trim

Trimming Your Drives

Outboards and sterndrives typically provide a powered adjustment for the trim angle of the drive unit. When the drive is trimmed "out"—i.e., away from the transom—the bow will rise. When the drive is trimmed "in," the bow falls.

drive trimmed out

BOW UP

stern down

Bow up, drive trimmed out.

drive trimmed in

BOW DOWN

stern up

Bow down, drive trimmed in.

Generally you will trim the drive in for steering, visibility, and wave-handling at slower speeds unless you need some "bow-up" trim to counterbalance weight in the bow. Drive-in trim will also help you accelerate to a plane by lifting the stern. Once on plane you will probably want to trim the drive out, but if you go too far, the bow may begin to porpoise up and down. Trim in until the porpoising stops.

Using Trim Tabs

A trim tab is a hinged plate mounted at each side of the transom's bottom edge. When a tab (or "flap") is in the raised position—flush with the bottom—it has little effect. When it is lowered, it lifts its side of the stern and depresses the opposite bow. The angle of the flap is controlled

Rocker switches at the helm adjust each trim tab up or down.

hydraulically from a pair of rocker switches at the helm. Since each trim tab can be controlled separately, you can adjust side-to-side as well as fore-and-aft trim.

When both tabs are trimmed down, the stern will rise and the bow will drop. This can be essential for getting an inboard boat to plane and can also augment a trimmed-in outboard or sterndrive. Once on plane, adjust the tabs to suit. Raise them to decrease drag, keep the bow up in a following sea, or fall off plane again; or lower them slightly to maintain planing at a lower speed or to reduce slamming in a chop.

With both trim tabs down, the stern of the boat is lifted, which helps get it on plane. This is particularly helpful with inboard engines. Used in concert with the drive trim on an outboard or I/O, it gives you added flexibility.

If your boat is unevenly loaded, you can level it side-to-side using one trim tab. Similarly, if you're heeling into a crosswind, lower the tab on the side of the boat you want to raise. Do it incrementally. Gauge the effect of the trim before you lower the tab farther.

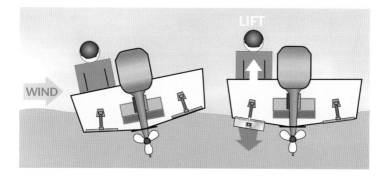

When the Seas Build

To reduce pounding in a seaway, lower the bow to slice through the waves. Trim tabs will accomplish this while slowing the boat, possibly without falling off plane. Trimming in an outboard or sterndrive will accomplish the same thing without slowing the boat. Be careful not to trim the bow down so far that it buries itself into the back of a following sea or digs into an oncoming one.

Boat Handling Under Power

Negotiating Rough Seas and Running Inlets

When the seas surpass what you can handle with trim adjustments alone ①, it's time to slow down and focus on steering and throttle. Treat the waves much like hills that you would rather ski around than over.

Handling Oncoming Waves

Taking the waves at an angle will increase the effective distance between crests and lessen their slopes ②. Too great an angle, however, might allow your bow to be forced downsea, leaving you broadside to the waves and vulnerable to a capsize ③. The better your boat tracks, the greater the angle you can risk.

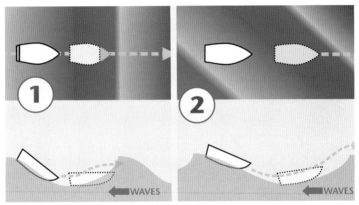

When waves get too steep (left), take them at angle (right).

① Head on—waves too steep. ② Ideal angle. ③ Angle too great—possible risk of capsize.

Pick your path through the waves, altering course and speed to avoid steep and breaking seas. A quick burst of throttle will lift the bow to meet a wave; throttle back when you reach the crest to lower the bow and avoid slamming into the next trough.

Boat Handling Under Power

Running with the Waves

When running downsea, you could be in danger of digging the bow into the back of the wave ahead ①, which would halt your progress and allow the next following wave to lift your stern or break aboard. In extreme circumstances you might broach (turn broadside to the seas) or even pitchpole (somersault the stern over the bow). For a smoother, safer ride, try to position yourself about a third of the way down the backside of a wave and use your throttle to stay in that position ②.

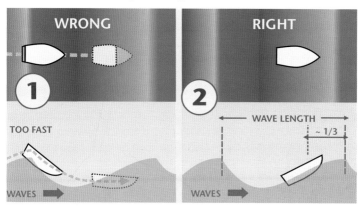

Running Inlets

Inlets can be treacherous. When an outgoing tide meets an incoming wind, the waves become higher, steeper, and more closely spaced. In a narrow, shallow inlet under the influence of swift tides and a strong onshore wind, the resultant seas can be spectacular.

When possible, wait for slack or flood tide or use a deeper, wider inlet. If you must proceed, make sure everyone is wearing life jackets and use the same techniques as when running with following seas. Using your throttle, stay on the backside of the most benign wave you can find. DO NOT ride over the crest, since that might cause you to broach or swamp, and would certainly leave you no room to maneuver.

To exit an inlet under these conditions, take the waves nearly head on, staying midchannel where the water is deeper, and use your throttle to raise and lower the bow over the waves. This is tense, tricky work. Do not allow your bow to be turned by the oncoming waves, as this will limit your ability to maneuver or even swamp you.

CHAPTER 2

Bill Gladstone

Sail Trim and Rig Tuning

About Sails

Sails are marvelous things, deceptively simple in appearance but in practice more complex and variable than an airplane wing ①.

The wind on your sails is the *apparent wind*—the sum of the true wind and your boat's forward motion—and this is the wind you must trim to ②.

This wind bends as it approaches your sails, putting the jib in a relative lift and the main in a relative header ③. Thus the jib is trimmed more outboard than the main.

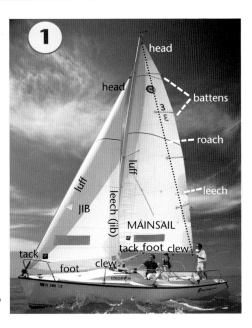

As the apparent wind flows around a sail, for reasons that remain difficult to summarize, the flow over the leeward, convex surface travels faster than the flow over the windward, concave surface. This faster flow exerts less pressure on the leeward (outside) surface than the slower air on the windward (inside) surface. The result is *lift*, which is everywhere perpendicular to the sail surface. Much of this lift is useless, serving only to heel the boat; only a small component drives the boat forward. One goal of your trimming and sail shaping—and of sail design itself—is to improve the ratio of useful (forward) to useless (heeling) forces, often by shifting the maximum

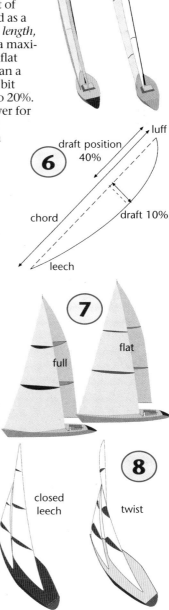

acceleration differences and resultant lift toward the front half of the sail, where the forward component is greater ④.

Even so, the side force of the sails would leave us unable to sail to windward were it not for the keel (or centerboard), which generates an offsetting hydrodynamic lift.

A Sail Has Three Sources of Power

Proper trim achieves the optimum mix of all three:

1. Angle of Attack. This is the angle at which the wind hits the sail. At an angle of zero the sails are luffing. As we trim in sails, move the main traveler to windward, pull the jib lead inboard, or bear away, the angle of attack and the power both increase ⑤.

2. Shape. *Depth* is the amount of curve, or camber, in a sail, measured as a proportion of the distance, or *chord length*, from luff to leech. A mainsail with a maximum depth, or draft, of 10% ⑥ is a flat sail, while a draft of 15% would mean a deep or full main. Headsails carry a bit more draft than mains—say, 12% to 20%.

A deep sail provides more power for punching through waves. A flatter sail creates less drag and is faster in smooth water, and also creates a wider angle of attack for closer pointing. A flatter shape is better when a boat is overpowered in heavy air ⑦.

In addition to controlling the *amount* of depth in the sail we can also control its *position*. The usual goal is to put the deepest draft about 40–45% of the way aft from luff to leech in a mainsail, and 30–40% of the way aft in a jib. Moving the draft forward makes for less drag and more forgiving steering in waves, while moving the draft aft enables higher pointing.

3. Twist. A sail with lots of twist is open at the upper leech, spilling power aloft. A sail with little twist—i.e., a closed upper leech that is nearly parallel to the lower leech—is more powerful. Some twist is usually necessary because the wind is stronger aloft, which makes the apparent wind angle more open near the top of the sail than down low ⑧.

A sail can be depowered either by easing the sheet to increase twist or by flattening. The former is preferred in a chop, while the latter is better in smooth water.

Mainsail Upwind

Your boat will have some or all of these mainsail controls to work with ①:

Mainsheet. Trimming to close-hauled increases the angle of attack. As the boom nears the centerline, further trim pulls the boom down more than in, reducing the sail's twist and tensioning the leech.

Telltales stream back from the leech when the air flow is smooth ②. When the flow around the outside surface separates, the sail is *stalled,* and the telltales disappear behind the leech ③. For good all-around upwind performance, you want the upper batten parallel with the boom and the leech telltales flowing with just an occasional stall. From there, try further adjustments for specific conditions as on pages 23–25.

Traveler. Except when overpowered, adjust the traveler to windward to keep the boom nearly over the centerline, maximizing angle of attack. In overpowering conditions, ease the traveler to leeward to reduce power and relieve weather helm ④. Racers sometimes play the traveler to dump power in puffs.

Boom Vang. This is primarily an offwind control. Upwind, remove the slack to help control twist. In light air, leave the vang eased to avoid a closed leech or stalled flow.

Mast Bend. After the mainsheet, this is the second most powerful controller of mainsail

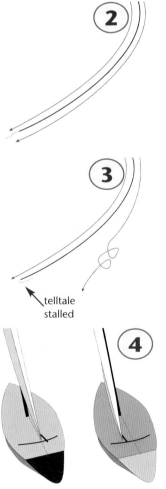

telltale stalled

shape. Increasing mast bend flattens the mainsail and reduces its power. The biggest impact is in the middle and upper portions of the sail. Mast bend also adds twist aloft ⑤.

When the boat is fully powered (and only then), adding mast bend can increase speed by reducing heel and weather helm and the drag associated with them.

Outhaul. Pull the outhaul tighter as the wind builds to reduce depth in the lower portion of the mainsail, and ease it gently for extra power in light air or chop.

Halyard and Cunningham. To hold the draft in its designed position just forward of the middle of the sail, use these controls to tighten the luff as the wind builds. Use the halyard first, and when at full hoist, use the cunningham. When you bend the mast the draft will move aft, so add luff tension as you add mast bend.

leech　　head　　luff

⑤

Mainsheet tight for little twist and extra power and pointing.

Mainsheet eased to add twist and spill power.

Mast straight leaves the sail deep and powerful.

Mast bend makes the sail flat and depowered.

Traveler up for higher angle of attack and more power.

Traveler down reduces angle of attack and power.

Little luff tension allows the draft to move aft.

Luff tension added with halyard or cunningham pulls the draft foward.

Headsail Upwind

If you have a choice, select a headsail that matches the wind conditions. Then try any or all of the following sail controls:

Halyard. In light air, an overly tight halyard hurts performance. As the wind builds, increase halyard tension to keep the luff firm and the draft in the desired position.

Sheet. Trimming to close-hauled adds power by increasing the sail's angle of attack. As the sail nears full trim, the sheet pulls the clew down more than in, which reduces twist and adds further power. For close-hauled trim, the middle leech of the jib should be parallel to the centerline of the boat. The foot of the jib should be a little rounder than the foot of the main, and its overall shape should match the shape of the main ①.

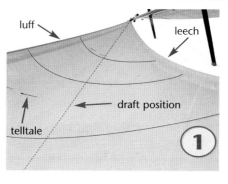
luff　　leech　　draft position　　telltale　　①

As you trim, pointing will improve, with some loss of speed. When further trim fails to improve pointing, the sheet is overtrimmed. Ease slightly—just a few inches—to optimize trim.

Headstay Sag. This can be controlled with an adjustable backstay. A tight headstay flattens the sail, while extra sag adds power. Let the headstay sag in light air, and add tension as the wind builds ②.

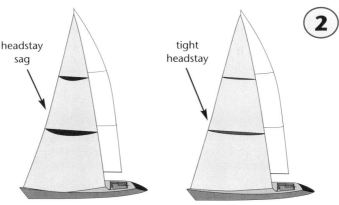

headstay sag

tight headstay

2

Genoa Leads. These change the fore-and-aft sheet position along the genoa tracks. Start by adjusting the lead so the sail luffs along its entire height as you pinch up above close-hauled. From this initial setting, moving the leads forward makes the sail fuller with less twist. Moving them aft makes the sail flatter with more twist ③. See pages 23–25.

3

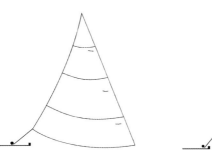

Initial lead position: Genoa shape matches mainsail. Upper telltales break just before lower ones.

Lead foward: Deeper shape, closed leech.

Lead aft: Flatter shape, open leech.

Leech Cord. This merely prevents leech flutter, which can quickly stretch the leech of a jib. Tension it just enough to stop flutter, and no more.

Upwind Sailing

With the jib close-hauled, steer so the lower jib telltales are streaming aft. Head up just short of the point where the inside, or windward, telltales break. The sector you can steer through with the telltales flowing—a range of a few degrees—is the steering groove ①. If you head up too high the inside telltales will break, and soon thereafter the sail will start to luff. But even before that point you will feel the boat starting to lose power and speed. Aim to steer as high as you can in the groove while maintaining full power ②.

If you fall off too far the outside telltales will stall, and you will lose power and speed, not to mention pointing.

Moderate-Air Trim

In moderate winds of 8 to 17 knots (the upper limit will be less for some boats), trim for full power and maximum pointing ability. Start as follows:

- Main boom on or near centerline.
- Mainsail twist adjusted with sheet so that telltale at top batten is flowing most of the time but stalling occasionally.
- Mainsail depth adjusted to achieve slight weather helm and a comfortable heel angle.
- Jib trimmed to close-hauled, just shy of a spreader tip or to the point of occasional mainsail backwinding (then steer as described above).
- Jib leads set so that the curve of the leech matches the mainsail shape, and the telltales break evenly from top to bottom. (As you pinch up above closed-hauled, the upper inside telltales should luff *just before* the lower ones.) ③
- Headstay tightened just enough to flatten the jib and improve pointing while still maintaining enough draft and power for a slight weather helm and a comfortable heel angle.

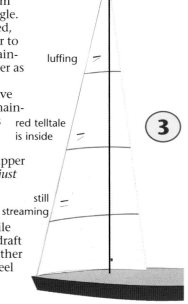

In Smooth Water. Try flatter, more closely trimmed sails with less twist for higher pointing. Trim the mainsail until the telltales stall more than half the time. Use more mast bend and a tighter headstay, move the jib leads aft to flatten the jib, and then trim the jibsheet harder to take out the extra twist.

In Choppy Water. Straighten the mast, sag the headstay, and move the jib leads forward to add depth and power to punch through the waves. Then ease the jib-sheet a few inches to restore the twist that moving the leads forward removed. You want the twist to prevent stalling and give your pitching boat a wider steering groove. Finally, bear off a couple of degrees to increase the angle of attack ④.

smooth water   choppy water

Light-Air Trim

Speed comes first in light air. Bear off a few degrees from the moderate-air baseline.

You want deep sails, so ease the backstay to straighten the mast and put sag in the headstay. Move the jib leads forward and ease the main outhaul. Make sure your halyards are loose—leave a few wrinkles along the luff of each sail.

Leave enough twist to encourage easy flow. You may have to ease the sheets a foot or more from their moderate-air positions to keep the telltales flowing. Easing the sheets reduces power, but you won't get any power without flow, and overtrimming will stall the sails. Another reason for twist is that in light air the wind at the masthead will be stronger than the wind at the deck, resulting in a wider apparent wind angle aloft.

As your speed builds, head up while trimming to reduce twist and maintain angle of attack ⑤.

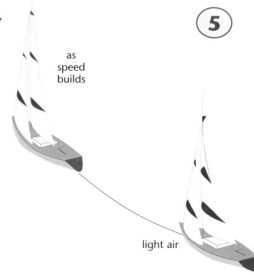

as speed builds

light air

Heavy-Air Trim

Once a boat is fully powered, performance improvements hinge on the ability to reduce drag. Deep, luffing, or overtrimmed sails are sources of drag in heavy air. Excessive weather helm creates enormous underwater drag, and excessive heel also causes drag. So in a strong wind we need to depower in this sequence:

Reduce Sail Power
- Reduce power by flattening sails:
    Bend the mast
    Tighten the mainsail outhaul
    Reduce headstay sag
    Move the jib leads aft
- Reduce power by reducing the angle of attack:
    Feather the boat up (head up slightly)
    Lower the traveler
- Reduce power by adding twist:
    Ease sheets a few inches

Reduce Sail Area
- Roller-furl the jib a few turns or change down to a smaller jib
- Reef the main
- Stow the jib and motorsail

In flat seas, flat sails or reduced sail area work well. In wavy conditions, the challenge is to keep enough power to punch through the waves without being overpowered.

Try to achieve proper power without compromising angle of attack. Focus on flat sails and additional twist before dumping the traveler (or moving the headsail leads outboard). An aft sheet lead position flattens the foot of the jib by pulling out on the clew. Think of it like the outhaul on the main. Moving the lead aft also increases twist, spilling power from the upper part of the sail. More twist widens the sailing groove and prevents being overpowered. In heavy air we want the top of the sail to luff before the lower section.

Steer to maintain a consistent heel angle. Head up slightly to feather through the puffs, and foot off a few degrees to maintain power in the lulls. This is much more critical than telltale activity. The jib telltales may stand up or even flutter on the inside.

A big backwind bubble in the main is preferable to the excessive heeling that further trimming would generate. When you must choose between a flogging main or excess heel and helm, it's time for less sail area. Try lots of twist, and perhaps an outboard jib lead, until you have a chance to change down your headsail or reef.

It is best to reduce headsail area before reefing the main. A small jib/big main setup gives quicker control over power, as we can dump the mainsail traveler in gusts. Further, a small jib is easier to handle, and a big jib/small main configuration creates pointing problems.

The one advantage of reefing is that it is often easier to accomplish than changing to a smaller headsail.

Sail Trim and Rig Tuning

Symptoms/Solutions

The boat is slow.

Try deeper sails for more power. In light air or sloppy seas, add twist for easier flow and bear off a couple of degrees. In a moderate breeze over smooth water, try trimming the deep sails hard (to the point of nearly stalling the main).

In heavy air, reduce sail depth and power to reduce heel and restore helm balance.

Poor pointing.

You may have too much twist. Trim the main to the verge of stalling the top leech telltale, and trim the jib until you get a hint of backwinding in the main.

When overpowered, it is common to lower the main traveler or ease the sheet, but it is better to keep the main trimmed and the main leech firm while feathering the boat or depowering the jib.

The boat is slow and low.

Usually this is a sign of being overtrimmed or undercanvased. Ease the sheets to build speed. Add power all around. Change to a bigger genoa. Work on speed first, then pointing.

In a fresh breeze you may have too much sail shape and the jib leads may be too far forward, creating too much drag.

Too much weather helm.

Reduce heel. Try flatter sails with more twist, and feather up in the puffs to reduce the angle of attack. If that doesn't work, try adding power to the jib and easing the main. Failing in that, shorten sail.

Too little weather helm.

Add power—traveler up; backstay, outhaul, and halyards eased; jib leads forward. Bear off a couple of degrees. Move weight to leeward to increase heel.

In light air, you might be overtrimmed. Ease the main and jib sheets and bear off to add power and speed.

Hypernarrow steering groove.

Tighten halyards to pull the draft forward and round the entry. Perhaps more effective, ease the genoa sheet a couple of inches. Sagging the headstay can also help.

Overpowered one moment, upright and luffing the next.

The entire sail plan is filling and dumping at once. Adding twist will give a more gradual onset and release of power. Move the jib leads aft and ease the mainsheet while pulling the traveler to windward. This will also help an overworked autopilot.

Excessive pitching.

You are sailing too high or your sails are too flat. Foot off for speed, add depth for power, and add twist to widen the sailing groove and control heel. Get weight out of the ends of your boat.

Pounding in waves.

You need more power. Fall off slightly and add twist to keep from being overpowered.

Sail Trim
off the Wind

Close Reaching. As you bear away from close-hauled, ease the jib. Move the lead outboard and forward, chasing the clew of the sail. Otherwise the top of the sail will twist open, spilling power, and the bottom of the sail will hook in toward the boat, creating drag. In a fresh breeze, keep the halyard firm to hold the draft forward.

With the jib trimmed outboard and the vang tight, ease the mainsheet or lower the traveler. As the main goes out, the vang will prevent the boom from rising and the leech of the main from spilling. When overpowered on a reach, easing the vang will spill power, reduce heel, and balance the helm.

Trim to keep the leech telltales flowing. Ease the outhaul and backstay slightly to add power to the main.

Beam to Broad Reaching. As you bear off further, the boat stands upright. Ease sails. The top of the jib will spill open. Trim to keep the middle of the sail working.

The main should go way out—even against the rig if it doesn't luff first. Keep the vang firm enough to hold the top batten of the main parallel to the boom. If the jib jibes itself unexpectedly on a very broad reach, beware an uncontrolled jibe of the main. Turn immediately to windward, and straighten out once the jib returns to its normal position.

Running. Running dead before the wind under jib and main requires careful steering to avoid an accidental jibe. In light air, it often pays to reach up and sail with the jib in normal position, as the extra speed will make up for the extra distance.

When running wing and wing, especially in big following seas, a poled-out jib allows sailing above dead downwind, providing a wider steering lane and reducing the chances of an accidental jibe. Rig a whisker pole with topping lift, afterguy, and foreguy; trim it to position; then trim the genoa sheet through the end of the pole. Rig a preventer from the end of the mainboom to a block well forward on the rail, then back to the cockpit where it can be cast off easily. Anytime you ease the mainsheet, tighten the preventer just enough to prevent the boom from jumping around.

topping
lift

foreguy

afterguy

sheets

Rig Tuning

An improperly tuned rig makes optimal trim and performance unattainable. Fortunately, rig tuning is straightforward. The goals are to:

- Eliminate mast side bend and lean.
- Set mast rake for proper helm balance.
- Tune pre-bend to match the mainsail design.
- Control mast bend and headstay sag.

Masthead Rigs

Side Bend and Lean

1. Check that the mast step is centered and the mast butt is secured to it.

2. Center and block the mast at the partners. (Before stepping the mast, run a line from stem to midstern to check that the partners are centered in the deck.)

3. Tighten the upper shrouds evenly, counting turns and keeping the mast centered. Measure to chainplates and other points of symmetry with main halyard and shock cord to make sure the mast is centered. Do not overtighten. Back off if the mast goes out of column. Be careful not to strip the turnbuckle threads.

4. Proceed to the intermediates and lowers, tightening the shrouds evenly on each side and keeping the mast straight. This is the initial setting, with mast centered, straight side to side, and all shrouds firm.

5. Go sailing in a moderate breeze. Sail a series of tacks, counting turns to maintain symmetry as you tighten the leeward shrouds. Start with the uppers to eliminate lean; then tension the lowers to eliminate side bend.

6. Sight up the mast to check for side bend. If the middle bends to leeward, tighten the lowers. If the top appears to fall off to leeward, it may be the middle popping to windward. Either loosen the lowers or tighten the uppers. Overly tight lowers or loose uppers allow tip falloff and a narrow angle of intersection between the uppers and the mast. This can overload the shroud fittings and cause rig failure.

7. Proper tension will leave the leeward upper shrouds taut at 15 degrees of heel with a full crew on the rail. The uppers should be tighter than the lowers to allow for greater stretch over a longer distance.

8. Check the rig periodically, particularly after sailing in heavy air. Stretched uppers or overtensioned lowers can overload the upper spreaders.

9. From this base setting you may find it pays to fine-tune your rig to sailing conditions. Generally this would mean adding tension to the uppers in heavy air, and backing off a couple of turns in light air. Sometimes fine-tuning is best done with headstay adjustment.

Rake

Rake is the fore-and-aft lean of the mast. Raking the mast aft creates weather helm. Changing the rake may simply require easing the forestay and tightening the backstay, or it may require moving the mast step.

You want a setting that provides some weather helm upwind in light air without becoming unbearable in a blow. Most boats are designed for some rake, but the amount depends on sail design, predominant conditions, and even crew size. Experiment with several settings in a variety of conditions. You want 3–4 degrees of weather-helm rudder angle in moderate conditions. You may find it pays to change rake to match conditions, adding headstay tension on heavy-air days.

Pre-Bend

Pre-bend is tuned into your rig by a combination of compression (rig tension) and mast blocks at the deck partners. Your mast will need some pre-bend—from an inch to a few inches—depending on the luff curve of your main. If your main tends to be too deep, add more pre-bend. If you cannot get enough power from your main, straighten the mast by putting blocks in front of the mast at the partners. As your main ages you may find you need more pre-bend to remove depth from the stretched sail, but this will exacerbate the other problem of age—the draft creeping aft. Stiff, tapered, full-length battens can alleviate that problem.

Mast Bend and Headstay Sag

Working with the backstay and a combination of running backstay, baby stay, and/or vang, it is

running
backstay

possible to control mast bend and headstay sag separately.

Backstay tension will bend the mast through compression as well as tighten the headstay. The mix depends on running backstay tension. If the runners are tight, they restrict mast bend, and the backstay impacts headstay sag. Looser runners allow more mast bend.

With a stiff mast, backstay tension translates primarily into headstay tension, controlling sag. A baby stay is then used to add bend. The backstay contributes to bend as well, particularly once bend has been initiated by the baby stay.

Fractional Rigs

The varied configurations of fractional rigs (swept spreaders versus straight with runners, B&R rigs, etc.) make it difficult to generalize. The procedure described here is for swept spreaders. The straight-spreader procedure is a hybrid of this and the masthead procedure described above.

With swept-back spreaders, adjusting the shrouds affects lean, side bend, rake, sag, and mast bend.

1. Spreader sweep should be fixed. Use pins and/or epoxy to secure swinging spreaders.

2. Center mast at step and partners.

3. With lowers loose, pull the backstay to max. Tighten the upper shrouds, keeping the rig centered and the mast straight side to side. If the mast tends to bend sideways, you may have to ease backstay slightly.

4. Release the backstay. The mast will still have bend. Tighten the lowers to remove bend as necessary to fit the main.

5. The rig is now tuned for headstay tension. Adding backstay tension will bend the mast and add more headstay tension.

6. To get bend more easily, ease the lowers. To translate backstay to headstay tension, tighten the lowers. There is a limit to the headstay tension you can achieve without running backstays. If your mast bends too much, try less spreader sweep. To encourage bend, add more sweep and ease the lowers.

7. Upwind in a breeze, the top of the mast will fall off to leeward and the middle will bow out to weather. This side bend depowers the rig to a greater degree than fore-and-aft bend. Easing the lowers may reduce side bend but will allow more headstay sag and fore-and-aft mast bend. The other solution is longer spreaders, which will push in harder on the middle of the mast. This can reduce but will not eliminate side bend, and may interfere with genoa trim.

8. Changing rake requires a complete retuning of the shrouds. Rake should be set for a balanced helm.

9. Shrouds may be adjusted to achieve proper mast bend and headstay sag for varied conditions. Upper and lower shrouds should be eased in light air for less bend and less headstay tension, and tightened a couple of turns for best performance in a big breeze. Keep track of base, light-air, and heavy-air settings.

10. Running backstays are required if sag is to be properly and independently controlled with a fractional rig.

Small changes in rig tune can have a surprising impact on your boat's performance. Carefully mark and note your current settings. That way, you can revert if you are unhappy with the changes you make.

CHAPTER 3

Bob Sweet

While GPS (Chapter 4) represents a quantum leap in navigation, it alone cannot provide safe navigation. Formal or informal, electronic or traditional, piloting always starts with a nautical chart. We offer this primer on chart reading and navigation for those who are new to the topic or seeking a refresher.

Nautical Charts

Unlike highway maps—on which roads are already plotted— nautical charts require you to plot your own routes, or courses. Chart information typically comes from hydrographic organizations within each country of jurisdiction. In the United States, the National Oceanographic and Atmospheric Administration (NOAA) is the source. (Actually, charts are prepared by the National Ocean Service [NOS], which is part of NOAA.) In Canada, the Canadian Hydrographic Service provides charting information. In the United Kingdom, it's the British Admiralty. International standards are developed by the International Hydrographic Organization. Usually, commercial chart publishers will scan or copy charting information from these sources and perhaps annotate additional information to them. Updating charts is a constant task. Storms change features both above and below the water. Navigation aids are moved or replaced, depths change, and so on. The process of updating charts is expensive, so the responsible organizations only do it periodically. It's not uncommon to come across a chart that has not been updated for some time.

The title block provides important information like the vertical and horizontal datums used to make the chart. If your GPS is not set to the same datum, you will not be able to plot your position accurately.

GPS makes very accurate positional information available, and today it's common that your GPS is more accurate than the chart you are using. This poses a dilemma—which to believe? Prudent navigators treat charts as essential but not absolute. You must use your eyes and observations to refine what they tell you. Nonetheless, they are your primary source of information.

Over the centuries, cartographers have developed several ways of portraying a nearly spherical Earth on a flat chart. For the most part, nautical charts are prepared using one of two projections—*Mercator* and *polyconic*. Mercator projections maintain directional relationships better over long distances, making them the projection of choice for coastal and offshore navigation. Polyconic projections maintain proportions better and tend to be used for inland waterway and lake charts.

Virtually all coastal and offshore navigation charts are Mercator projections. Imagine a sheet of paper wrapped around a globe to make a cylinder that is in direct contact with the globe only at its equator. Now imagine that globe being lit from within so that its landmasses and other features are projected upon the paper cylinder. The result would be a Mercator chart of the world. In a Mercator projection, all parallels of latitude are horizontal and straight, and all meridians of longitude are vertical and straight. The parallels intersect the meridians at right angles. The result—and this is the great advantage of a Mercator projection—is that the navigator can measure and plot directions and distances directly on the chart and use them for navigation.

In the real world, of course, meridians aren't parallel. Thus, Mercator projections distort the shapes and relative sizes of landmasses and ocean basins. This distortion becomes exaggerated near the poles. Remember how huge Greenland and northern Canada looked in the Mercator maps in your school textbooks? However, this distortion is so small it's unnoticeable in Mercator charts covering local regions in low and middle latitudes.

The accompaning figure shows how a Mercator chart is made by projecting the surface of a globe onto a cylinder. Near the equator, the globe and the chart match closely, but the chart stretches as you approach the poles, and landmasses appear larger than they actually are.

The polyconic projection is used for charts of the Great Lakes and some major rivers. An example of this projection can be seen in the paper masters that are wrapped and glued on a sphere to form a globe. When flattened, the result is complex. Using a polyconic chart to travel over great distances would be

Coastal and offshore charts use a Mercator projection. Imagine a light at the center of the Earth projecting the Earth's surface features onto a cylinder that wraps around the equator. The resultant flat projection provides straight and perpendicular grid lines, making plotting easy. Feature shapes and relative positions are accurate, but there is an artificial enlargement of features toward the poles as compared with regions closer to the equator.

A map shows land features but tells little about the water other than the shorelines.

When underwater features such as depth contours are added, the map becomes a chart.

Maps of highways define paths and any marked features along the way. But there are no such features on the water. Therefore, a chart needs to provide a frame of reference. This is indicated by the grid. The grid comprises latitude and longitude lines, and a pair of latitude and longitude coordinates provide your location in numerical form.

Depths

Nobody wants to run aground. Fortunately, nautical charts plot depth measurements, known as *soundings*, that help you avoid this unpleasant experience. The illustration shows how soundings appear on a chart. This might be the single most useful category of information a nautical chart offers.

No nautical chart is complete without soundings. These specific measurements of depth are plotted on the chart to reflect the average least depth at each location. Today, most charts reference these soundings to a tidal datum called *mean lower low water.*

Because water levels fluctuate, particularly in tidal regions, soundings must be referenced to a vertical *datum*, or standard, that is identified on the chart. Depths on older charts were referenced to *mean low water* (MLW), which is the average local height of all low tides as recorded over a 19-year natural cycle. As a mariner, you could be reasonably sure that the depth you would encounter at a given time and location would be as deep or deeper than its charted sounding. Reasonably sure but not absolutely so. Why? Because in most regions low tides occur twice a day, and one tide is often lower than the other. When boating in such a region, the depths you encounter at the lower of the two daily low tides will be shallower than the average of *all* low tides. To minimize this potential hazard, most new charts use the more conservative vertical datum of *mean lower low water* (MLLW), which is the long-term average of the lower of the two daily low tides. With such a chart, you can traverse an area and count on having at least the sounding depth at almost any time except during the lower low tide when half the time the water level can be less than the sounding.

On U.S. charts, depths are generally expressed in feet. In Canada and much of the rest of the world, they are expressed in meters. Occasionally, you will see charts in which depths are expressed in *fathoms* (a fathom equals 6 feet). The units for depth are shown on the chart, usually in the title block.

To make charts easier to read, depth contour lines are drawn through points of selected constant depth. For historical reasons, in the United States these contours are generally plotted at some multiple of a fathom (6 feet), so you often see depth contours at 6, 12, 18, 30, and 60 feet. Elsewhere the contours are generally plotted in multiples of 6 meters, although other increments may be used. You need to look at the printed depths along the contours. You can tell a contour depth from a sounding because it is oriented with the contour, interrupts the contour line, and is printed in the opposite style of the soundings (italic vs. regular type). Cartographers also use color to help identify information. Shallow water is generally shaded blue; deep water is white. (The definition of what is shallow differs from chart to chart, so take a look at the chart's scale before making any assumptions.) Very shallow water that uncovers at low tide is usually shown in green; land is colored in tan. The type of bottom is often expressed by a combination of abbreviations and symbols, a few of which we'll touch on below.

Scales

Charts come in a variety of scales, with the scale indicated as a ratio. For example, on a 1:40,000-scale chart, 1 inch or centimeter on the chart equals 40,000 inches (approximately half a nautical mile) or centimeters (400 meters) in the real world. A 1:20,000 chart is typical for local waters; a 1:10,000 chart may depict a specific harbor; and a 1:80,000 chart depicts a wider boating region. A 1:10,000 chart is considered "large scale"—ideal for navigation in narrow, rock-strewn waters. A 1:120,000 chart is considered "small scale"—excellent for "big picture" cruise planning but insufficiently detailed for picking your way among ledges, buoys, and islands. Large-scale charts show more detail but cover a smaller area. Think of it as "large scale = large detail." The accuracy of charted locations depends on scale. When the scale is larger, charted objects are placed more precisely.

A chart's scale is a ratio of the distance between objects on the chart to the distances in the real world. This small-scale chart shows a large area, stretching from the mouth of Delaware Bay to the Gulf of Maine. This is a 1:1,200,000-scale chart; useful for passage planning.

This coastal chart at 1:80,000 scale is good for coastal passages, but you'll need a larger scale to navigate narrow, complicated inshore waters.

1:40,000-scale chart picks up inshore details you won't find on the 1:80,000-scale chart.

A more detailed harbor chart has a 1:20,000 scale.

Some popular harbors have very detailed charts of 1:10,000 or even 1:5,000 scale. This is an example of a 1:10,000 chart.

Updates

Although the information on charts is updated regularly, the charts themselves are updated only at intervals. Hydrographic organizations worldwide provide regular updates to charts known as *Notices to Mariners* (NTM). And the U.S. Coast Guard provides updated information in its weekly *Local Notices to Mariners* (LNM), a report that you can access on the Internet. To stay current, review these notices, locate a specific chart by its number (which is printed in the margin of a paper chart or the title block of a paper or digital one), and add the corrections to your copy. Today, commercial services can do this work, and you can purchase copies printed on demand that are updated to the date of printing. Revision dates are listed in the title block of the chart.

Chart Grid and Horizontal Datum

To pinpoint our location on the surface of the Earth, we need a system of coordinates. Most nautical charts use *latitude* and *longitude* for this. Latitude and longitude have already been discussed and are explained further below, but it's important to note that there are other grid systems in use throughout the world. It's imperative that your GPS be set to the same grid system that is employed on your chart.

The Earth's shape is not uniform. Although globes depict a smooth, spherical Earth, our planet is oblong and uneven, and we need a mapping grid that takes this variability into account. This framework is called a *horizontal datum*. Today, most nautical charts reference World Geodetic System 1984 (WGS-84) as the horizontal datum. You need to set your GPS to the datum that was used to create your chart. For example, a few old charts in the United States may not have been updated from the older North American Datum 1927 (NAD-27). If you use the wrong datum in your GPS, you could inadvertently create mismatches of hundreds of yards or more, mistakes much like those that bedeviled the old cartographers.

Coordinates

An object on a chart can be located using its nautical position address—its latitude and longitude. The chart provides a latitude scale, usually printed in the left and right margins. The longitude scale is usually printed in the top and bottom margins. Latitude is measured from 0° at the equator to 90° N at the North Pole or 90° S at the South Pole. Lines of equal latitude are called *parallels*. Parallels are horizontal slices through the Earth that are parallel to the equator. The parallel lines form the horizontal grid lines on your chart.

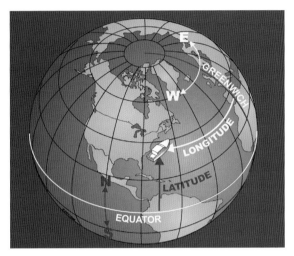

Top: *Latitude* and *longitude* provide a unique address for every location on the Earth. This grid system is based on a mathematical model for the shape of the Earth. Latitude is measured, either north or south, from 0° at the equator to 90° N or 90° S at the respective poles. Longitude is measured, either west or east, from 0° at the meridian (line between the poles) that goes through Greenwich, England, to 180° W or 180° E.
Bottom: Lines of equal latitude are called parallels. The horizontal grid lines around the globe, which indicate equal latitudes, form horizontal circular planes that are parallel to the equator. Lines of equal longitude are vertical planes *(meridians)* that intersect an imaginary line through the Earth between the poles.

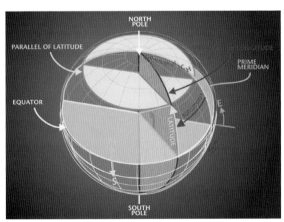

Lines of longitude, or *meridians*, are vertical slices that pass through both poles. Typically, meridian lines are printed at regular intervals on your chart and form the vertical axis of the chart grid. Meridians are numbered from 0° at the prime meridian (which, for historical reasons, passes through Greenwich, England), increasing by degrees both west and east until, on the opposite side of the world, they meet one another again at 180°. All meridians are *great circles*, a great circle being an imaginary line scribed on the Earth's surface by a plane passing through the exact center of the Earth. Except for the equator, however, no line of latitude is a great circle. Any two points on the Earth's surface can be joined by one and only one segment of a great circle, which always defines the shortest distance between those points. Unfortunately, great circles may not make practical courses to follow over great distances because your steering direction will constantly change, and your path will appear curved on a Mercator projection. But no matter. The *rhumb lines*—or courses on a single bearing—we follow in coastal navigation are only slightly longer than their great-circle equivalents. For local navigation, the differences aren't noticeable.

Each spot on the Earth is uniquely identified by its latitude and longitude. Scales on coastal nautical charts are generally divided into *degrees*, *minutes*, and *tenths of minutes* (a minute of angle being 1/60th of a degree). Great Lakes and river nautical charts often have scales divided into degrees, minutes, and *seconds*. (A second of angle is 1/60th of a minute.) One minute of latitude is always exactly equal to 1 nautical mile. This means that you can use the latitude scale for measuring distance on the chart. A minute of longitude, however, is equal to 1 nautical mile only at the equator, diminishing to nothing at the poles. Thus, the longitude scale cannot be used to measure distance.

Chart Symbology

Charts use an array of symbols (see top illustration page 44) to depict rocks and other obstacles, depending on whether the obstacle is always visible, or is covered only at higher tides, or lies below the surface at all tides. If you run aground on soft bottom, often you need only wait for a higher tide to get off. If you encounter rocks or wrecks, however, you risk damaging your boat and possibly sinking—or at least ruining your afternoon! NOAA charts use a symbol that resembles an asterisk (*) to indicate rocks of unknown heights that are *awash* (breaking the surface at low tide). Underwater rocks often are indicated by a plus sign (+). Broader areas of potential danger are often shaded blue and bounded by a dotted line. For example, rocky regions bounded by a dotted line may be labeled with the term "Rk" or "Rks." Other dangerous zones may be labeled simply "Obstn," for obstruction. A sounding inside the blue area usually indicates the shallowest depth. If no sounding is shown, the depth generally is unknown. Regardless, you should avoid the shaded area altogether.

Wrecks, too, are shown by symbols. If any part of the wreck's superstructure is visible at low tide, it's usually indicated by a profile of a half-sunken boat. If only parts of the boat—such as masts or funnels—are visible, the wreck area is circled by a dotted line, the area within is shaded blue, and a solid line with three intersecting hatch marks is inserted into the middle of it all. (This symbol resembles a three-masted boat, with the long line representing the hull.) Usually, the chart also indicates which part of the wreck is visible at low tide—"Masts," for example.

Charts use a symbol language to communicate features.

Restricted areas are generally bounded by a dotted line consisting of T-shaped symbols, often in magenta. Alternatively, dashed lines, either in magenta or black, may surround these and other defined areas. Given the heightened security surrounding bridges, naval ships, and other ships and facilities since 2001, you should consult the *Local Notices to Mariners* for updates and append your charts accordingly.

Charts also use symbols to define specific areas or restrictions.

Navigation Aids

Buoys and beacons help define channels as well as mark a variety of underwater conditions or hazards. Navigation aids are either *lateral* or *informational* in North America. (Elsewhere a *cardinal* system for marking isolated offshore dangers is used in addition to the other systems.) Lateral marks indicate the sides of the channel. The United States and Canada use the "red-right-returning" rule of lateral marking: Keep the red buoys on your right when returning to a harbor, navigating up a river, or traversing the North American coast in a clockwise direction, and keep green buoys to your left. (Elsewhere in the world, the opposite applies.) In serpentine or complex waters, when it isn't absolutely clear which way is toward the nearest harbor or clockwise around the continent, consult your chart. Buoys with red-and-white vertical stripes indicate safe water or a center channel. Informational aids may mark danger or note local rules, such as no-wake zones. Some navigation aids are equipped with lights or audible devices. Charts generally show all significant navigation aids. Though a smaller-scale chart may not show all secondary buoys in inshore waters, it will be apparent from a lack of soundings and other details that larger-scale charts of these waters are needed for safe navigation. However, even a large-scale harbor chart may not show locally maintained, nongovernment navigation aids within a harbor or an approach channel. You'll need local knowledge for these. Government navigation aids are depicted with abbreviations or

The United States uses the "red-right-returning" system. In other words, when you return from the sea, red navigation aids indicate the right-hand side of a navigable waterway; green navigation aids indicate the left side. Navigation aids with vertical red-and-white stripes indicate the center channel and can be passed on either side. Black-and-red aids indicate isolated hazards or danger. If you come to the junction of two channels, the preferred channel is indicated by the top color on a navigation aid. To use the preferred channel, imagine that the junction buoy is the color of the top band. In this figure it is green, indicating that you should keep it to your left. Therefore, the preferred channel is to your right. Buoys are floating navigation aids. Beacons are fixed to the bottom or the shore.

The chart section shown on page 38 is shown here with the symbols for navigation aids added.

The U.S. Coast Guard standard symbols for navigation aids are shown on this and the next three pages. **Above:** The U.S. Aids to Navigation System follows the IALA (International Association of Lighthouse Authorities) -B system, which is also used in Canada, Mexico, South America, Japan, Korea, the Philippines, and the Caribbean. In the IALA-A system used elsewhere in the world, the colors of lateral buoys are reversed—i.e., green buoys mark the right side of the channel, red the left.

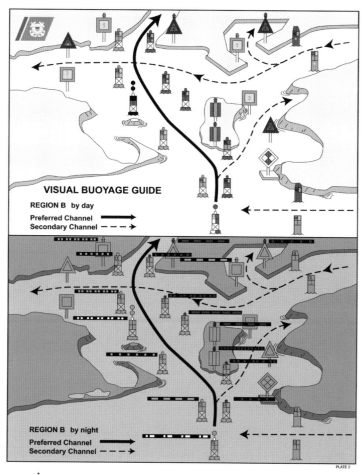

PLATE 2

The lateral-system nav aids from the previous illustration are shown here in idealized fashion as they might appear by day and by night.

symbols that describe their appearance or characteristics. (Please note that charted buoy locations are approximate. Whereas beacons are fixed to the Earth, anchored buoys shift nominally with the tides and can be moved greater distances by powerful storm waves.)

Unlighted fixed nav aids, called *daybeacons*, are usually indicated by a green square or a red triangle. These objects may be on land or in shallow water on poles fixed to the bottom. (Most cartographers further distinguish between fixed and floating nav aids by using italics for the latter.)

Lighted beacons are indicated by symbols that resemble exclamation marks. The solid black dot of the exclamation mark charts the beacon's fixed location; the accompanying magenta teardrop flare helps distinguish the beacon from buoys or other navigation aids. The characteristics of the beacon are printed next to the symbol, indicating the light pattern, color, height, and usually the visible range. The light pattern is often flashing ("Fl"). The repetition interval of the flashes is identified by the number of seconds, such as "4s." If the light has a color, it is indicated by "R" for red, "G" for green, "Y" for yellow, and "W" for white, although most white lights are not labeled. Thus, "Fl R 4s" denotes a red light flashing at 4-second intervals.

Using Nautical Charts

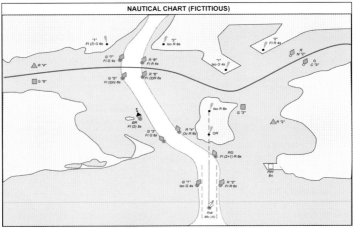

Here we see a visual buoyage guide as on page 47, this time with a corresponding idealized chart segment.

There are prescribed light patterns for certain navigation aids. For example, a lighted center channel (or safe water) buoy will flash a Morse code "A" (short-long) pattern with a white light. A junction buoy will flash a two short plus one short (2 + 1) pattern in the color of the top band (either red or green).

Buoys on NOAA charts are indicated by a small, open, black circle indicating the approximate position and a diamond flare (♦). The color of the diamond corresponds to the color of the buoy. If the buoy is lighted, the circle will be surrounded by a magenta-shaded circle. (Outside the United States, lighted buoys are denoted with a flare just as lighted beacons are, but the approximate buoy location is marked by a small hollow rather than the circle at the base of a diamond.) The color of the buoy is also given in the label, such as "R" for red, "G" for green, or "RW" for vertical red/white. On the water, the buoy's shape and color are significant. Unlighted conical red buoys are called *nuns* (shown as "N" on the chart). Unlighted cylindrical green buoys are called *cans* (shown as "C" on the chart). Lighted buoys are often conical or cylindrical as well, but they may also be a bell buoy, gong, or other *pillar* shape (generally a lattice tower on a flat base), and they have a wider range of colors. In addition to red and green, lighted buoys may be painted red/white, black, or yellow. Their lights are red, green, or white,

U.S. AIDS TO NAVIGATION SYSTEM
on the Western River System

The Western Rivers System of nav aids used on the Mississippi River and its tributaries differs from the U.S. coastal IALA-B system in several respects, among which are that the nav aids are not numbered. The Uniform State Waterway Marking System used on lakes and inland waterways that are not covered by nautical charts, as well as some that are, has been discontinued in favor of the IALA-B system but may still be encountered here or there.

and the light color and pattern are shown on the chart. White lights are used on center channel buoys (red/white) as mentioned above. Buoy sounds are labeled as BELL, HORN, or SIREN if present.

Plotting Tools

Now that you know something about charts, let's look at the tools that are used with them. You will need to get charted information into your GPS, and you should verify electronic positions by nonelectronic means from time to time. For both these reasons, you need the time-honored tools of piloting.

Dividers

Dividers are used to measure distances and latitude and longitude coordinates on a chart. In its basic form, a pair of dividers comprises two arms ending in points, the distance between

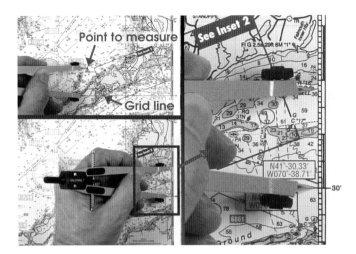

Dividers are used to make measurements on your chart. In this example, the latitude of an object or location is being measured. In the upper-left panel, one point of the dividers is placed on the object and the other point is opened to the closest grid line. Then that second point is traced along the grid line until it reaches the latitude scale on the side of the chart. Now you can read the corresponding value of latitude. In this example, the latitude of our object is 40° 31.84′ N.

which can be adjusted by means of a friction pivot. Friction pivots are quick and easy to adjust but can be inadvertently altered on a moving, bouncing boat. Other pivots use an adjustment screw to fine-tune the position, but setting these can be arduous. The best designs have quick-set capability in addition to an adjustment screw. With these dividers you can quickly open the arms to the approximate setting you want, then turn the screw to fine-tune and lock in the setting.

In addition to a pair of dividers, many mariners like to carry a *drawing compass*, in which a pencil replaces one of the points of a divider. A drawing compass, no doubt familiar to you from school days, is handy for plotting points at specified distances or tracing arcs of specified radii.

Determining Coordinates

To determine the latitude of a spot on the chart, you simply place one point of the dividers on the spot of interest, then adjust the arms to place the other point on the nearest line of latitude. Once this gap is set, move the dividers along the line of latitude to the latitude scale in either margin. Now one point lies on the latitude line and the other marks the latitude measurement for your desired location. In the Northern Hemisphere, the value of latitude increases upward and is read as degrees, minutes, and tenths of minutes north (N).

Longitude is similarly measured by placing one point on the desired location and the other point on the nearest meridian line. You then transfer this setting to the scale in the top or bottom margin of the chart and read the longitude. In North America longitude is read as degrees, minutes, and tenths of minutes west (W), with values increasing to the left.

Measuring Distance

Distance is measured using the two points of the dividers, one point placed on each end of the distance to be measured.

To measure the distance between two locations, place one point of the dividers on the first location and the second point on the other location.

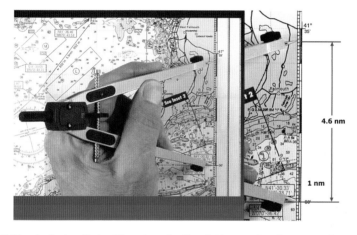

Without altering that setting, transfer the dividers to the distance scale on the chart or to the latitude scale on the side. One minute of latitude (not longitude) is exactly equal to 1 nautical mile, so you can use the latitude scale as a distance scale.

While maintaining that setting, move the dividers to the distance scale on the chart, put one point on zero, and read the distance to the second point. Alternatively, you can use the latitude scale and count the number of minutes (nautical miles) and tenths of minutes between the divider's points. *Note: Most charts have distance scales in nautical miles, statute miles, and kilometers. On the water it makes sense to use nautical miles due to the natural relationship with latitude.*

    If the distance you wish to measure is greater than the dividers can span, you will need to draw a line between the two locations. Now you can use the distance scale or the latitude scale to preset the dividers to a convenient distance—for example, 5 nautical miles. Next, set one point of the dividers on one end of the line and *walk* the dividers along the line by advancing from point to point, counting the number of preset segments as you do so. Let's say that you've set the dividers to 5 miles and are measuring the distance between two buoys that are 12 miles apart. You count off two divider spans for 10 miles, then see that the remaining distance is less than the gap between the divider points. So you close the divider points until they precisely span the remaining distance, then read that distance on the chart scale: 2 miles. Add this distance to the sum of the fixed intervals you just counted, and you get the answer: 12.

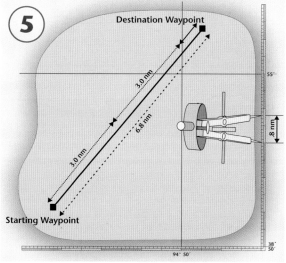

If the distance you want to measure is too large for your dividers to span, draw a line between the locations. Next, set the dividers to a convenient distance, such as 3 nm, using the latitude scale. Walk the dividers from one location toward the other, counting the number of 3 nm increments until the last increment is less than the dividers' preset distance. Now, set the dividers to measure that final increment, and go to the latitude scale to read that final distance. Add all the increments to get the total distance.

Some charts for locations such as the Great Lakes and major rivers use latitude and longitude scales calibrated in degrees, minutes, and seconds, whereas most nautical charts use degrees, minutes, and tenths of minutes. Because minutes and tenths of minutes correspond well with nautical miles and tenths, you may wish to convert any charts that use the more cumbersome seconds. To do so, simply divide the number of seconds by 60 to get tenths of minutes.

Plotting Coordinates on a Chart

Your GPS continually provides the latitude and longitude coordinates for your position, but until you plot this position on a chart, it doesn't mean much. To do this, locate your GPS latitude on the appropriate chart's latitude scale and place one point of the dividers on that spot. Then adjust the dividers so that the second point rests on the nearest latitude line. Now move the dividers along the latitude line to your approximate location (by visually approximating the longitude) and make a small horizontal pencil mark. Then do the same for the longitude. Your current position is at the intersection of the pencil marks.

When you use a GPS, it will provide values for your current latitude and longitude. To determine where you are on the chart, you must plot these values. This process is similar to what was shown on page 50, only this time it's done in reverse. In the last example, we transferred chart information to the scales, but here we'll use the same basic techniques to transfer scale information onto the chart. First, place one of the divider points on the scale mark that corresponds with the GPS-derived latitude value. Then open the dividers so that the second point rests on the nearest grid line. Then drag the open dividers across the chart, stopping when you reach your approximate longitude. ("Eyeball" this location.) Draw a short pencil mark at this point. Then repeat this process to transfer the longitude value. Your location is where the two pencil marks meet.

Parallel Rules

Perhaps the simplest tool for plotting is a set of *parallel rules*. This device comprises a pair of rules that are joined together by two or more swinging hinges. The rules serve as straightedges for plotting courses. The hinges allow you to expand or collapse the distance between the two rules while keeping the rules exactly parallel to each other. This is an easy and accurate way to transfer a plotted bearing line across a chart to the compass rose for measurement, or to transfer a measured bearing (say, the bearing to a nearby lighthouse measured on deck with a hand bearing compass, as described below) from the printed compass rose across the chart for plotting. The mechanics of the process are simple. You merely press down on one rule while swinging the other outward, then press down on the lead rule while you swing the trailing rule after it. Repeat as necessary, thus *walking* the rules across the chart without altering the bearing. This time-honored device is practical for working on charts at home or at sea. With a little experience, the parallel rules can be walked either across the chart or up or down on it to align with the region of interest. And because the compass roses printed on nautical charts allow you to measure directions relative either to true or magnetic north, using parallel rules obviates the necessity for converting from *true* to *magnetic bearings* and back, with its attendant risk of error.

Plotting on a chart often involves transferring a course line to a compass rose, or vice versa. In doing so, it's crucial that the second line is drawn perfectly parallel to the first. Parallel rules are popular for this purpose.

A more modern variation of parallel rules is the *rolling parallel rule*. This device has only one straightedge and moves across the chart on a long roller, which preserves the proper orientation. What the device gains in simplicity, it loses in versatility. It can go only forward and backward, not side to side. A special variation called the *Bi-Rola* has rollers that are perpendicular to each other. By pressing on one or the other, you can move across or up and down to reach any spot on the chart and still maintain an accurate bearing. These devices work well on a chart table but may slip or shift on less uniform surfaces or in rough seas.

The compass rose (which is printed in multiple locations on your chart) provides the chart's fundamental reference for magnetic directions. It is printed in a magenta ink that is distinctive when viewed with red light at night. (Navigators use a red light at night for illuminating charts and instruments, because this color has minimal effect on night vision, which is essential for keeping watch.)

The compass rose has two rings. The outer ring aligns with the chart grid of latitude and longitude lines— that is, with true north; the inner ring aligns with magnetic north. Within the inner ring is a legend that notes the local variation used for the chart. The variation describes both the magnitude of the difference in degrees and minutes between true and magnetic north for the charted location, and the direction of that offset, either east or west. (Magnetic north is moving, albeit slowly, so variation needs to be adjusted for this movement.) In addition, the legend identifies the date used for the variation and the amount by which it will change each year, east or west. You will need to adjust the variation accordingly if your chart is several years old and the annual change is significant.

Many mariners use the compass rose for laying out or measuring a course or bearing. Because the rose is rarely if ever located where you want to plot or measure a course, devices such as parallel rules are used to transfer the direction to or

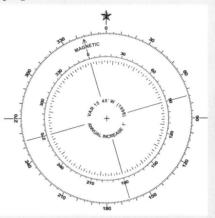

Charts are printed with one or more compass roses. The compass rose has two rings. The outer ring is aligned with the chart grid and true north. The inner ring is aligned with magnetic north. A legend at the center of the rose provides the local variation and its annual change. The compass rose simplifies the labeling of courses and bearings and provides instant reference between true and magnetic north.

If you need to transfer that parallel line to a location beyond the reach of the parallel rules, simply walk them to the location by extending, contracting, and reextending the rules.

from the rose. Make sure you read your direction from the compass rose going the right way—that is, by imagining your boat at the center and reading toward the rose in the direction of the course or bearing.

To obtain the direction of a plotted course using parallel rules, align one rule with the plotted leg, then walk the rules across the chart to the nearest compass rose and read the course in degrees magnetic from the inner ring. The course is now ready to steer provided your steering compass doesn't exhibit significant deviation errors that you can't get rid of. See page 61 for more on deviation.

To plot a compass bearing on a chart, you place the parallel rules over the nearest compass rose. On the inner circle of the rose, find the bearing you measured on deck (either by sighting over your steering compass or using a hand bearing compass) and align one of the rules with this bearing and the center of the rose. Now open the rules and walk them as necessary until the leading rule intersects the charted object on which you took the bearing. This is a line of position, and you are located somewhere along this line.

Protractor Plotting Tool

Alternatively, you can measure courses and bearings in degrees true using a *protractor plotting tool*. These tools are inexpensive

One of the simplest plotting tools has no moving parts. The *rectangular plotting tool* is imprinted with a series of parallel lines. You can move the tool across the chart by drawing intermediate lines, moving the plotter, and realigning one of the printed parallel lines with the plotted line on the chart.

Course and bearing directions can be determined by using the scales on a protractor plotting tool. You need to align the bull's-eye with a grid line while you have the plotter aligned with the course line. You can align the top of the plotter or any of the printed parallel lines with the course line. Finally, you read the course direction from the appropriate protractor scale. Which scale to use? Use common sense. This simplistic compass rose (right) provides you with a sense of direction. Any course or bearing toward the top right of the chart will be between 0° and 90°. By the same token, any course or bearing toward the bottom right will be between 90° and 180°. Toward the lower left will be between 180° and 270°. Finally, toward the upper left will be between 270° and 360° (0°).

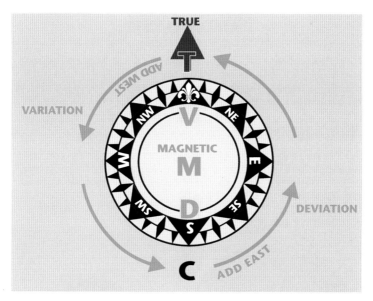

If you plot your bearings and courses in degrees true but steer them in degrees as read on a compass, you'll have to convert from one to the other. This is why so many small-boat navigators prefer to do their plotting in degrees magnetic. When you convert from true to magnetic, you need to add westerly variation—remember, "West is best." By the same token, if your compass has residual deviation (see page 61), to go from magnetic direction to what you would read on the compass, you will add westerly deviation. In other words, going down (T to M to C), you add west. Conversely, going up (C to M to T), you add east. This diagram provides an easy way to remember this—you always add counterclockwise. On the "west" side of the diagram, you add west (either V or D). On the "east" side you add east. If your compass has negligible deviation and you plot courses and bearings in degrees magnetic, no conversions will be necessary.

and reliable. If you're in cramped quarters or on a small charting table, protractors can be less cumbersome than parallel rules. Plus, because a protractor scale is printed directly on the plotting tool, you won't need to access the compass rose for angles. This added flexibility is especially helpful when lack of space forces you to do your plotting on a folded chart. Murphy's Law being what it is, the nearest compass rose is always folded underneath and therefore inaccessible. The simple *rectangular plotting tool* shown opposite was designed by the United States Power Squadrons. Two protractor scales and parallel lines are printed on the template, with one for use with latitude lines and the other (printed in reverse order) for use with longitude lines.

To plot a course, align the course's starting point (whether a navigation buoy or simply a waypoint) on the plotter edge, orient the plotter's bull's-eye on a latitude or longitude line as appropriate, and read a direction in degrees true from one of the protractor's scales. This device takes some practice in order to avoid reading or using the wrong scale, and it requires those pesky conversions between true and magnetic bearings and courses that you can avoid by using parallel rules. Most navigators prefer to use parallel rules.

Compasses

Now that you have the tools to plot your bearings and courses, you'll need tools to measure and steer them. The most fundamental of these is the ship's magnetic steering compass, and no boat should be without one.

Ship's Compass

Even if you use GPS to set and monitor your courses, you will find it easier to steer and hold a course using the steering compass, and it serves as an essential backup when all else fails. It is a wise investment to get the best compass you can afford. Generally, larger is better. The best have a spherical chamber containing a flat or dished card.

The magnetic compass is the most fundamental and important navigation instrument on your boat. Shown here are two powerboat compasses. The compass card is suspended in a liquid-filled bowl of oil and pivots on a fine point. This allows the card to stay level as the boat pitches and rolls. On the left is a front-reading compass. The card is read on its front surface against a lubber line etched in the glass. This style is a little more difficult to use. A top-reading compass card (right) is more intuitive, because its orientation matches directions around you and those of a chart's compass rose. The top-reading card also gains an advantage of some magnification from the fluid-filled bowl. The cards in powerboat compasses are dampened (intentionally slowed) to counteract the dynamic motions of fast boating and thus improve readabilty.

Sailboat compasses are a bit different from powerboat compasses in that they are dampened less and are designed to perform under greater angles of heel. The version on the right is designed for a bulkhead mount and provides a scale of heel as well as compass heading.

All steering compasses are dampened to counteract the quick motions of a boat, but compasses designed for sailboats are dampened differently from those used on powerboats. In addition, many sailboat compasses provide an additional scale indicating the degree of heel for the boat.

To be useful, your compass probably needs to be compensated. Nearby metallic objects on a boat influence the way the Earth's magnetic field affects a compass. These effects are different for each heading, because a change in heading alters the relative alignment of the metallic objects between the compass and the Earth's magnetic field. Most compasses incorporate built-in magnets that can be rotated to compensate for onboard influences. Usually, there is one magnet for north-south compensation and another for east-west. By running known courses, it is possible to adjust these magnets iteratively until the compass readings are quite accurate. Although compensation can counteract most effects, there is always some residual error. Usually, however, you can reduce this error to 2 degrees or less, depending on the heading, at which point you may choose simply to ignore it. If the residual errors are larger, you can construct a deviation table that provides the difference between the compass reading and the actual magnetic course for each direction of the boat. Then you can apply these corrections whenever you steer a compass course by adding or subtracting the deviation as appropriate (see page 59). Compensation to within a degree or two is obviously the more practical solution. Although you can adjust your compass yourself with careful measurements and a lot of patience, this is a challenging task best left to a professional.

Typically, magnetic compass cards are marked in 5-degree increments. This seemingly wide margin between hash marks is okay, because the boat's natural motion makes it difficult to hold a reading to better than a degree or two. The longer hash marks—marking 10-degree increments—are painted to a width of 1 degree, making an "eyeball" estimate of your heading easier. In most marine compasses, the card sits suspended in a thick liquid such as mineral oil, the viscosity of which helps dampen the motion of the boat so that the reading appears relatively steady.

Most compasses present a heading in one of two ways. You can read your heading either against the *lubber line* on the front edge of the compass card (front reading), or across the top of the card against a pointer on the far side (top reading). The latter is preferable because the numbers will increase clockwise, just as the numbers on a compass rose do. The front- or direct-reading card displays numbers in a counterclockwise progression, which can lead to confusion.

Hand Bearing Compass

From time to time you'll want to take visual bearings in order to fix your location, determine your speed, or measure the relative course of a nearby vessel. At such times it pays to have a *hand bearing compass*, which is nothing more than a handheld magnetic compass with a built-in sight. Simply aim the sight at the other boat or charted object and read its bearing off the compass. Hand bearing compasses come in a variety of configurations and cost as little as $25. Some marine binoculars contain an integral compass, which is displayed as you view a distant object; most such units have crosshairs for accurate sighting.

Hand bearing compasses are subject to onboard magnetic disturbances, just as your ship's compass is. These influences

A hand bearing compass is essential equipment on your boat. Taking bearings on landmarks and navigation aids with this device is quick and easy. Shown here is a Ritchie small-boat "hockey puck" hand bearing compass.

may be different at different locations on the boat. Therefore, you should always use the hand bearing compass from a single spot near the helm. (Also, be sure not to brace the compass against any wire shrouds or metal fittings.) To quickly check the deviation of a hand bearing compass, point it at the bow and compare its reading with that of the ship's compass. If they are close, you are in good shape. If they differ (and you know that your steering compass is accurate), apply that difference to any reading you take with the hand bearing compass while on that heading. If the ship's compass reads 5° lower, for example, you need to subtract 5° from each reading of the hand bearing compass. Keep in mind that this deviation will change for every new boat heading. Although the deviation is usually not significant and can probably be ignored, you should check it on all headings to be sure.

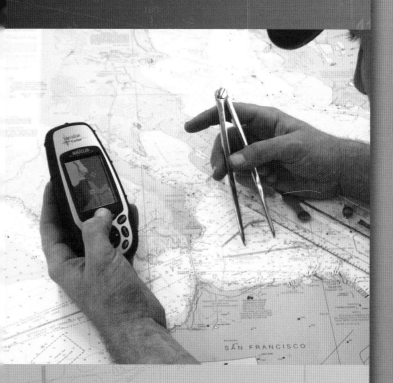

CHAPTER 4

Bob Sweet

Using GPS

Meet Your GPS

All GPS receivers offer similar functions. The generic layout shown here is typical. Use your GPS manual to identify any differences in detail.

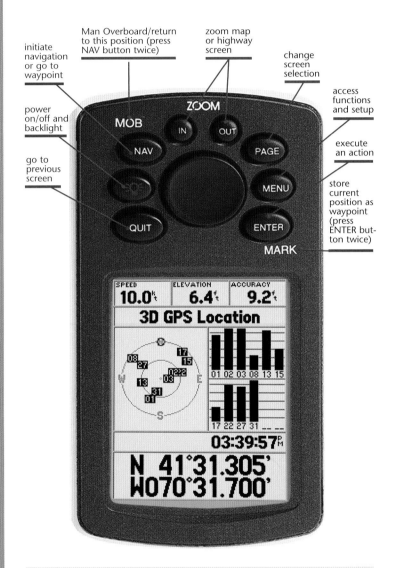

initiate navigation or go to waypoint

Man Overboard/return to this position (press NAV button twice)

zoom map or highway screen

change screen selection

power on/off and backlight

access functions and setup

go to previous screen

execute an action

store current position as waypoint (press ENTER button twice)

Buttons

The many GPS functions are controlled by a set of buttons, restricted in number by the space available. Most of the buttons control how the GPS processes and displays information. The button labeled NAV or GoTo controls navigation functions. Press the ENTER button to execute actions. Press the QUIT or ESC button to revert to a prior screen instead of executing an action. The labels may vary slightly by model, but the general approach is always the same.

Screens

You can select screens as needed. The **Satellite Screen** indicates the quality of the GPS position and tells you if part of the sky is blocked to the GPS antenna. The **Position Screen** indicates the latitude and longitude of your current position and the precise time. (In this example, Satellite and Position appear on one screen; other models present them separately.) The **Map Screen** shows your current position with respect to other objects (waypoints) stored in your GPS, and the active course line. The **Highway Screen** shows a 3-D representation of your active course with your current position in the foreground and your next waypoint in the background. This is likely to be the most valuable screen to keep you on course.

Satellite/Position Screen

estimated accuracy

fix quality

signal strengths

satellite positions

position coordinates

Map Screen

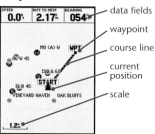

data fields

waypoint

course line

current position

scale

Highway Screen

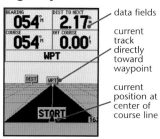

data fields

current track directly toward waypoint

current position at center of course line

Map Screen with Map*

map

track

*some GPS models have the ability to store and display maps

Menus

Use menus to program the GPS, to initiate and control navigation, and to select display format. Most menus are accessed via the **Main Menu** using the MENU (or ENTER) button, or by paging to find the Main Menu screen. In addition, most GPS sets offer screen-dependent menus that control how data are displayed on an individual screen. Access these from the current screen by pressing the MENU (or ENTER) button.

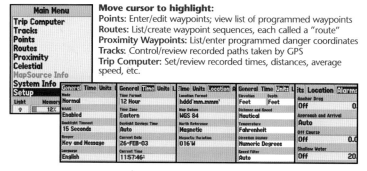

Move cursor to highlight:

Points: Enter/edit waypoints; view list of programmed waypoints
Routes: List/create waypoint sequences, each called a "route"
Proximity Waypoints: List/enter programmed danger coordinates
Tracks: Control/review recorded paths taken by GPS
Trip Computer: Set/review recorded times, distances, average speed, etc.

Using GPS

Where Are You?

your current position
(gull's-eye view)

your current position
coordinates (GPS receiver)

Navigation begins with knowing where you are, particularly as you begin your cruise. The GPS receiver provides that information with great precision in the form of a latitude and a longitude ①, but these coordinates are meaningless until you transcribe them onto a chart. Using dividers, first locate the latitude on the latitude scale with one point of the dividers and then set the second point on the nearest grid line. Transfer this distance across the chart to the region of the GPS longitude ②. Next, mark the longitude similarly and transfer it up along the grid line to refine the position ③. You now know where you are.

Where Are
You Going?

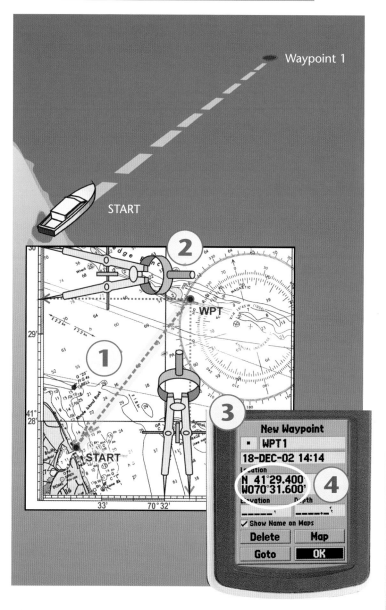

The next step is to determine where it is you plan to go. In this example, you have decided to go to WPT1 (waypoint 1). First, plot this course ① and ensure the path is safe. Second, determine the coordinates of WPT1. Use dividers to pick off its latitude ② and longitude ③. Now, access the New Waypoints Screen ④ and enter the measured latitude and longitude into your GPS (see page 74). Your GPS will now give you the course and distance to WPT1 (see page 68).

Navigating Using GPS

Using the GoTo command (see page 75), enter WPT1. You can select the Highway Screen to display your course ①. It tells you that the bearing to WPT1 is 54° and the distance is 2.17 nm. Steer your boat to 54° and stay in the center of the highway. Alternatively, you can choose to use a different screen, such as the Map Screen, for navigation. Most GPS models alert you with a text message and an audio alarm as you approach WPT1 ②. Your GPS displays the remaining distance as 0.00 nm—you have arrived.

Along the Way

Your GPS continuously updates your position on the Position Screen (latitude and longitude). You can select a number of data fields to present information about your course, speed, estimated time of arrival, and many other choices. It is important for you to prequalify the path from START to WPT1 to ensure that this path is free of charted hazards. As long as you stay on course, you should encounter no charted obstacles.

Marking a Spot

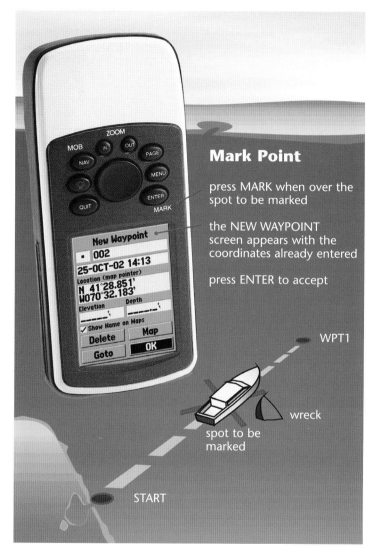

Mark Point

press MARK when over the spot to be marked

the NEW WAYPOINT screen appears with the coordinates already entered

press ENTER to accept

WPT1

wreck

spot to be marked

START

New Waypoint
- 002
25-OCT-02 14:13
Location (map pointer)
N 41°28.851'
W070°32.183'
Elevation   Depth
_____   _____
✓ Show Name on Maps
Delete   Map
Goto   OK

While on the water, you may have occasion to mark specific spots. This is easy using your GPS: just press the MARK key while you are on the spot.

In this example, you have spotted a partially exposed wreck near (not on!) your chosen path. To mark the spot on your course near the wreck for future reference, press the MARK (ENTER) key once. (On many GPS models, MARK is not a key but a second function on one of the buttons—you may need to press the button twice to save the mark.) The New Waypoint Screen comes up with the coordinates already entered and the OK field highlighted. To save this waypoint with the name 002, just press ENTER. Edit the names later, when you're no longer at the helm (see page 74).

Planning an Extended Cruise

Plan a longer cruise using the procedures already described. First draw the course line and determine if the path is safe to travel. Clearly, in this example the direct path will encounter hazards ①, but if you travel first to WPT1 and then on to your destination, you'll have a safe path ②.

destination (DEST)

direct path is dangerous

safe path with two legs

WPT1

START

Measure the coordinates of your destination ③ and ④ and enter them into your GPS as another waypoint (DEST). As long as you stay on the two-legged route from START to WPT1 to DEST you should be safe from underwater hazards.

Alternatively, you can store this sequence as a Route that, once selected, will automate the selection of the DEST waypoint as soon as you reach WPT1.

Repeat this process to plan a cruise of any length and any number of legs within the limits of your GPS model.

Traveling the Second Leg

Now let's look more closely at the second leg. In our example, when you reach WPT1 ①, you need to tell the GPS where you want to go next (unless you're following a programmed route). Use the GoTo command (accessed via the NAV button on the model shown, see page 75) to select DEST as your next waypoint. Now, the Highway Screen displays the new bearing you steer to reach your destination.

Unfortunately, steering this new course doesn't ensure you'll stay on the course line. If there is a cross-wind or current as shown, you may be pushed off your course line ②. Both the Highway and Map Screens show you to be off your prequalified course line.

The GPS continuously updates and shows the Bearing and Distance to the waypoint from your current position. Before taking the direct path to DEST, check it on a chart by plotting your current position and drawing the new course line to ensure there are no new obstacles. In this example, you must return to your original course line for the second leg at ③ before you can proceed safely.

Staying On Course

Let's "rewind" back to WPT1 to find out how to prevent getting off course in the first place. Intuitively, you want to head toward your destination, but clearly that won't work in this example.

Instead, you must turn toward the wind or current if you are to follow the course line—but how much? Your GPS solves the problem. Simply adjust your boat heading until you stay in the center of the highway with the destination straight ahead in the middle of the screen ①.

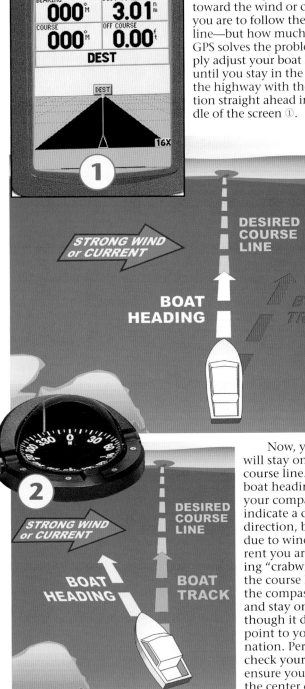

Now, your boat will stay on the course line. Your boat heading and your compass ② indicate a different direction, because due to wind or current you are proceeding "crabwise" along the course line. Note the compass heading and stay on it even though it doesn't point to your destination. Periodically check your GPS to ensure you stay in the center of the highway.

Double-Checking Your Position

Your latitude and longitude as displayed on your GPS look OK, but how do you know for sure? This simple technique will confirm your position rather quickly and without charts.

In advance of your trip, store the coordinates of visible objects into your GPS. Then, on the water, sight on at least one of these objects using a hand-

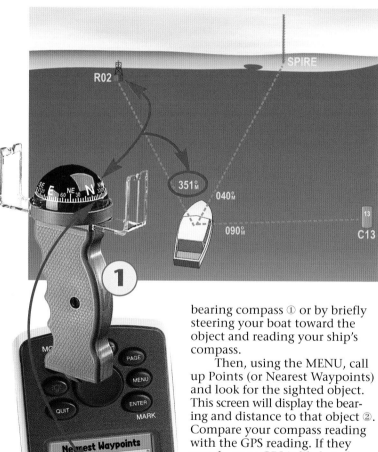

bearing compass ① or by briefly steering your boat toward the object and reading your ship's compass.

Then, using the MENU, call up Points (or Nearest Waypoints) and look for the sighted object. This screen will display the bearing and distance to that object ②. Compare your compass reading with the GPS reading. If they match, your GPS is likely to be accurate. If they don't match, plot your position on charts using the visual bearing(s).

The GPS also displays your elevation; but GPS accuracy in elevation is only 100 feet or so. An elevation error does not mean your horizontal coordinates are wrong.

Using GPS

More on Waypoints

GPS provides your position with high precision, but to use it for navigation you need to enter waypoints. Waypoint navigation involves sailing a sequence of straight-line segments called "legs." The endpoints for each leg are stored in the GPS as waypoints.

Entering Waypoints

Obtain the coordinates of waypoints you plan to use for navigation as shown on page 67. There are four ways to store those waypoints in your GPS. If your model doesn't permit Manual entry use the Scroll method.

Manual: Enter coordinates manually by accessing the New Waypoint Screen. Using the cursor button, scroll down until the coordinates field is highlighted, and press ENTER. You will be presented with a single highlighted character. Use the cursor to scroll up or down to change the character (number) until it corresponds to your desired entry. Then use the cursor to scroll right or left to change the values of other characters. When you're satisfied with the entered values for latitude and longitude, press ENTER to accept. Scroll to "OK" or "Save" and press ENTER to accept. Your GPS will assign a number in the name field. You can change the name (or the symbol displayed with the waypoint) in the same manner as entering values into the coordinates field.

Scroll: An easier way to store coordinates in your GPS is to scroll the cursor on the Map Screen. The cursor's coordinates are shown on the screen. Press MARK to access and edit the New Waypoint Screen, and then Save. For some GPS models, this is the method by which you access the New Waypoints Screen. Usually, it is quicker and easier to scroll to the general area of the desired waypoint, press MARK, edit the details of the coordinates until you're satisfied, and then Save.

scroll cursor to selected coordinate

press MARK
New Waypoint Screen appears
with cursor coordinates shown

edit name or coordinates if desired, then press "Save" to store into GPS

MARK: On the water, mark your current location by simply pressing the MARK key. See page 69.

Computer: Using digital chart software, you can plan routes on a computer and then load the corresponding waypoints and routes via cable into your GPS for navigation. See page 77.

Navigating with Stored Waypoints

GoTo: Use the GoTo button (accessed through the NAV button on some models) to see a list of stored waypoints. Select the desired waypoint and press ENTER. The GPS now computes Bearing and Distance to that waypoint from your current location. However, you must use charts to determine if that path is safe.

press GoTo or NAV ①

brings up Menu Screen; select GoTo Point ②

brings up Nearest Waypoint Screen; select WPT1 ③

select GoTo ④

Scroll: Using the cursor on the Map Screen, scroll to a way-point until it is highlighted and then activate it by selecting GoTo and ENTER. You also can scroll to particular coordinates and use GoTo to create a temporary waypoint. While scrolling, you will be presented with the cursor coordinates and the Distance and Bearing from your current position to the cursor.

use the cursor key

scroll to selected Waypoint; when field is highlighted, press ENTER to activate

current position

Route: The Route function automates the selection of sequential waypoints along your cruise. To create a route, select Route from the Main Menu. Then, in the order you wish to nav-igate them, select waypoints already stored in your GPS. Once this sequence is stored, you can select and activate a Route using the Menu or the NAV button (if your GPS has one). The GPS then will present your entire route on the Map and Highway Screens, and provide Bearing and Distance to each waypoint in the selected sequence. For your return trip, reverse the order of waypoints in a route by selecting Invert Route with the Menu function.

WAAS and GPS Accuracy

GPS fixes are quite accurate. In open water, knowing your position to within 30 to 50 feet ① is extraordinary compared with the accuracy of traditional navigation tools.

However, when you attempt to navigate within a harbor or channel, you may prefer somewhat higher accuracy. You have a choice of two systems to do that—DGPS or WAAS. Differential GPS (DGPS) is a U.S. Coast Guard system designed for mariners. Designed for aircraft by the Federal Aviation Administration, Wide Area Augmentation System (WAAS) also provides excellent service for boaters.

In both systems, fixed receivers at precisely known locations listen to the GPS satellites in view. Atmospheric and other factors cause the signals to produce a fix with some error. By adjusting the signals from each satellite until the right answer is obtained, these stations derive a set of corrections. Each system then transmits these corrections to your GPS.

WAAS transmits corrections at the same frequency as the GPS signals ② via geostationary satellites over each ocean. Once you enable WAAS in your system setup, your GPS receives these corrections and applies them to yield accuracies of 10 feet or better. But beware, your chart is likely to be less accurate than the GPS. Only newer GPS models have the software needed to receive WAAS corrections.

To receive DGPS corrections, you must have a DGPS antenna and receiver on your boat.

GPS accuracy relative to your boat station

GPS advertised (no SA)*

GPS typical

25 ft boat

DGPS

10 ft
WAAS

15 ft

33 ft

50 ft

①

*Selective Availability

WAAS Satellite   WAAS Satellite

②

GPS Satellites

Upload Stations   Upload Station

Users   Monitoring Stations   Master Control Station

Connecting
Your GPS

Your GPS receiver is designed to share its data with other equipment both on and off your boat. Connecting the GPS to a computer is quite easy ①.

The manufacturer of your GPS model can provide you with a cable designed to connect your GPS to the serial port on your computer ②.

The navigation software you select will then tell you how to set up the GPS. Now you can plan and monitor your cruise on a digital chart displayed on your PC.

GPS also can provide data for display on a radar screen or to control the autopilot in an integrated system ③.

connecting cable for a Garmin handheld GPS

GPS communicates with other electronics using a protocol called NMEA 0183. There are only three wires involved: Data In, Data Out, and Ground. The Data Out from the GPS goes to the Data In port on the radar, autopilot, computer, etc. You can supply up to about three devices from a single GPS; however, the Data In port on any device can listen to only one source. You may need to solder wires onto special connectors, available from the GPS manufacturer.

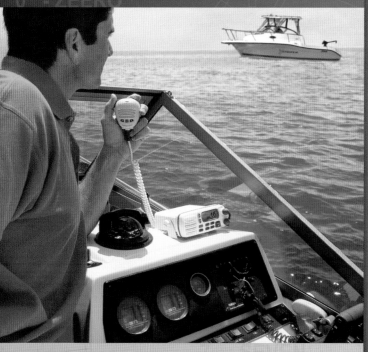

ZULU ALPHA

BRAVO

CHARL

DELTA

ECHO

Y Z A B C

D

FOXT

5

1 - WUN
2 - TOO
3 - THUREE
4 - FOWER
5 - FIYIV
6 - SIX
7 - SEVEN
8 - ATE
9 - NINER
0 - ZEERO

GO

G

H

HOT

RA

OMEO

Bob Sweet

QUEBEC

Using VHF and SSB Radios

Keeping in Touch on the Water

A number of options exist for communicating between boats or with the shore. Here's an overview:

Near Shore

Cellular phones are especially convenient for conversations with those on land. However, the coast guard and other search-and-rescue agencies cannot direction-find an emergency cell phone call, and coverage is limited by the locations of relay towers on land.

VHF (very high frequency) radio (see pages 82–86) is the first choice for emergency calls as well as for routine communications. The VHF emergency channels are constantly monitored by national coast guards. VHF range is slightly greater than line-of-sight, since very high frequency radiowaves bend slightly over the horizon, but boat-to-boat transmissions are generally limited to about 20 nautical miles and may be shorter between powerboats with low antenna heights. Ship-to-shore calls may be possible at up to 30 miles due to the greater height of shore-based antennas.

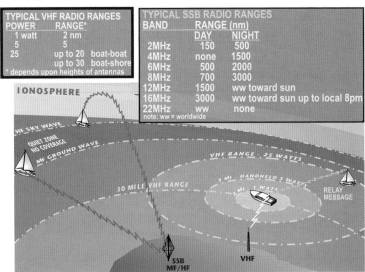

TYPICAL VHF RADIO RANGES

POWER	RANGE*	
1 watt	2 nm	
5	5	
25	up to 20	boat-boat
	up to 30	boat-shore

* depends upon heights of antennas

TYPICAL SSB RADIO RANGES

BAND	RANGE (nm)	
	DAY	NIGHT
2MHz	150	500
4MHz	none	1500
6MHz	500	2000
8MHz	700	3000
12MHz	1500	ww toward sun
16MHz	3000	ww toward sun up to local 8pm
22MHz	ww	none

note: ww = worldwide

Offshore

SSB (single sideband) radio (see pages 88–90) is the popular choice for ship-to-ship and ship-to-shore communications beyond VHF range. Radiowaves at SSB high frequencies (HF) reflect from the ionosphere and thus can reach other transceivers thousands of miles away under the right propagation conditions. You must match your transmission frequency to the distance and atmospheric conditions. At shorter ranges out to 150 to 200 miles during the day (or as much as 500 miles at night), medium-frequency (MF) SSB signals (called groundwaves) wrap around the surface of the Earth. Worldwide weather broadcasts and e-mail services can be received as well.

Satellite phones offer reliable voice, fax, e-mail, and data communications throughout the world but are expensive. One company, Inmarsat, supports regular and emergency distress calls (except in polar regions) using satellites in geostationary orbit. Iridium and Globalstar provide satellite coverage using low orbiting satellite networks.

Ham radio (amateur radio) remains popular among cruisers, since licensed ham operators can speak with other licensed hams on land or sea, often in scheduled group gatherings or "nets," and can ask a shore-based ham to patch them through a telephone line without paying the stiff fees charged by SSB High Seas marine operators.

The General Class License required for voice communications over ham frequencies requires some knowledge of radio theory and ham operating protocol and the ability to receive Morse code at five words per minute. Passing the exam is not difficult, and ham radio equipment is less expensive than SSB while operating at similar frequencies and over similarly impressive distances.

NOTE: Neither ham radio nor a satellite phone is a proper substitute for an SSB marine radio, because the coast guard does not continuously monitor ham frequencies or satellite phone communications. This chapter will therefore concentrate on VHF and SSB radio communications.

EPIRBs (Emergency Position-Indicating Radio Beacons, see page 93) are stand-alone portable units that can be activated in a distressed boat, a lifeboat, or in the water to summon help offshore. EPIRB signals are relayed via overhead satellites to coast guard and other search-and-rescue centers. Modern EPIRBs identify the boat from which they came and even provide GPS coordinates to rescuers, but a beacon does not allow two-way communications.

MARINE RADIO SPECTRUM

GROUND WAVE   REFLECT FROM IONOSPHERE   LINE OF SIGHT

SSB RADIO   VHF RADIO   406 EPIRB

156–163 MHz | 406 MHz |

MF   HF   VHF   UHF

300KHz   3MHz   30MHz   300MHz

1.8   2 3 4 5 6 7 8 9 10   12   14   16   18   20   22   24   26   28   30 MHz

Amateur Radio Bands   Marine Single Sideband

Using VHF and SSB Radios

Meet Your VHF Radio

speaker   distress all-station alert (DSC only)   display   current channel   push-to-talk

change channel   function buttons   received signal squelch

VHF marine radios are available as either fixed or handheld. Virtually all fixed units offer the legal maximum transmitting power of 25 watts, whereas most handheld transceivers (like the one shown in page 84) are limited by battery capacity to no more than 5 or 6 watts. The great advantages of handheld radios are their portability and their self-contained antennas, but their dependable boat-to-boat transmission ranges are limited to 3 to 5 miles or so by power level and antenna height. Fixed radios like the one shown above require a separate antenna, but a good antenna installed high on a sailboat's masthead or a powerboat's flybridge provides much greater communication ranges.

VHF antennas transmit equally in all horizontal directions, but longer antennas provide extra "gain" by focusing the available energy to lower elevations as illustrated below. Gain is described in decibels (dB). Since sailboats heel, a lower-gain antenna avoids missed coverage. Powerboats don't have tall masts that extend range, so they sometimes benefit from a higher gain—say, 6 dB. A 6 dB antenna might be 8 feet long and weigh 5 pounds, whereas a 9 dB antenna might be 24 feet long and weigh as much as 12 pounds.

All VHF radios must have a 1-watt power setting for short-range communications to minimize stepping on other users over a wide area. All radios manufactured since 1987 switch automatically to the 1-watt setting when transmitting on channels 13, 17, 67, and 77 but permit a manual override to maximum power for emergency bridge-to-bridge communications on channel 13.

VHF Radio Controls

A typical VHF radio includes the following features and controls:

Microphone: You must press the transmit button (on side) to talk. Many microphones have remote controls for channel selection, volume, and power level.

Channel Select: Up-down buttons (or rotary dial) to change the active channels for transmission and reception.

Volume: Controls the speaker sound level.

Squelch: Represses all signals below the threshold set by the control, thus eliminating annoying static. Reduce the squelch until static can just be heard, then advance it slightly to eliminate static.

Emergency: This protected switch is found only on radios equipped for digital selective calling (DSC, see page 92). Press only in an emergency. It sends a digital signal on the DSC emergency channel (70) providing your identity and (if interfaced with GPS or loran) your location, and sounds an alarm on all DSC-equipped radios.

HI/LO: Switches a fixed VHF radio between the 1-watt transmit level mandated for short-range communications and the optional high-power level (25 watts for fixed units) required for longer-range communications.

WX: Switches the VHF radio from the communication channels to the NOAA weather receive-only channels. Some models also provide an automated alarm in response to a NOAA weather alert.

DSC: Since 1999, new VHF radio models must be equipped with digital selective calling, or DSC (see page 92). Pressing the DSC button permits you to call another DSC radio whose number is stored in your radio, much as if you were dialing a phone number. The digital signaling alerts the other radio that you have called and automatically switches that unit to the working channel you have selected.

Note: Pre-DSC VHF marine radio models were still recently being manufactured and will remain in use for years to come.

Other VHF Functions

A good VHF marine radio may also offer the following functions:

16/9: Pressing this button immediately sets the channel to 16 (the distress, safety, and calling channel). A second press sets the channel to 9 (the standard alternate calling channel).
Scan: Pressing this button (and on this example, holding the button down for a second) causes the radio to continuously scan through the channels that you have "tagged" until a signal is heard. It will continue scanning after the signal ends until you press the channel select button or the 16/9 button.
Priority Scan: Ensures that channel 16 is scanned between each of the other frequencies on your scan list.
Intercom: Some VHF models can be operated from a remote microphone, which might be placed at the helm while the radio itself is below decks. The intercom function permits direct conversations between someone at the radio and someone at the remote microphone. Such conversations are not transmitted.
Dual/Tri-Mode Watch: Scans the radio between distress/ signaling and intership channels.
Panel Lighting: Illuminates the display and buttons for nighttime use.
Hailer: Interfaces the microphone through external loudspeakers for hailing nearby boats. These hails are not transmitted.
Scrambler: Some VHF radios will accommodate add-on devices to scramble communications on all channels except the emergency channels 16 and 70, so that confidential conversations cannot be overheard.

VHF Use

Recreational boats, in addition to hired vessels with no more than six passengers, are considered "voluntary vessels" and are not required to carry a VHF radio or to maintain a license to operate one domestically (so long as you do not visit or communicate with a foreign port). If you do have a VHF radio, however, you must monitor channel 16, the international distress channel, at all times. Having all radios tuned to 16 increases the probability that a distress call will be heard, and relayed if necessary.

If you carry both a VHF radio and an SSB MF/HF transceiver, you must use the VHF rather than the SSB whenever possible. The reason is simple: VHF communications, unlike SSB, are incapable of hogging a channel over ranges of hundreds or even thousands of miles.

Handheld VHF radios like the one shown at right are not permitted for use on shore. However, you may use yours to communicate with your ship at 1 watt using the ship's name followed by "unit 1." Most handheld radios do not have DSC capability and therefore cannot provide coded distress alerts or position information.

VHF Channels

The marine VHF band falls between 156 and 163 megahertz (MHz). Within this narrow band are many channels, only a few of which con-

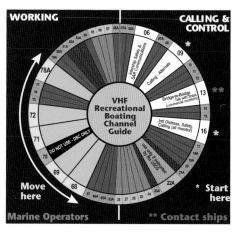

cern the recreational boater. But with these few channels you can contact the coast guard and other rescue services, communicate with other vessels, and call marinas, restaurants, bridge tenders, harbormasters, and other shoreside stations. You can receive marine weather reports and navigational notices, and you can contact shore-based marine operators who, for a fee, will connect you with the land-based telephone grid or with other boats that are beyond your direct VHF range.

VHF CHANNEL USAGE has been established by international treaty and is enforced in the U.S. by the FCC. Recreational boaters should confine their communications to the channels that are drawn wider in the graphic above. You will initiate most calls on channel 16 (or 9 if you are in certain areas, know that it is monitored, or have prearranged this channel). When the other party answers, immediately arrange to switch to a working channel so as to keep CH16 open (see page 86).

CHANNEL 16 is the International Distress frequency and is also used for safety messages and calling (initiating a contact). Anyone hearing a distress call must monitor this channel and await a response from the coast guard. If none is heard, relay the distress call and attempt contact—you may be able to relay communications between rescue personnel and the vessel in distress. When you contact the coast guard on CH16, you will usually be directed to switch to CH22A for further communications.

WORKING CHANNELS are intended for messages about the needs of the ship, including fishing reports, rendezvous, scheduling repairs, and berthing information. General conversation is prohibited, so as to keep the channels as free as possible. Use channel 72 for ship-to-ship messages only.

COMMERCIAL SHIPS are required to monitor channel 13 in addition to channel 16. When crossing paths with commercial ships, you are well advised to contact them via channel 13. Describe your vessel, your location relative to the ship (e.g., "I'm a 30-foot white sloop one-half mile off your port bow"), and what you are planning.

WEATHER CHANNELS are designated for receive-only. Meteorological services (NOAA in the U.S.) broadcast continuous weather reports on these channels. Scan to find the strongest signal for your area. Channels are labeled as WX1, WX2, . . . etc.

MARINE OPERATORS can link you to land lines for a fee. Make advance arrangements or place collect calls.

Using VHF and SSB Radios

VHF Radio Call Procedures

Marine frequencies are crowded. Take the time to pre-plan your call and message and write your station ID information in the blanks below so you have it handy:

Your Boat Name phonetically _____

Your MMSI (if DSC equipped)* _____

Your Call Sign (if you have a license)** _____

*Note: The Maritime Mobile Service Identity, or MMSI, is the nine-digit number that is assigned to a DSC marine radio and identifies its operator just as your telephone number identifies you at home. Only the new, digital radios have MMSIs. If your radio and the one you're calling are both DSC-capable, you can direct your call selectively to the station you want. And in case you're wondering, digital and analog radios can talk to each other just fine.

**Note: If you have an FCC radio license, use the call sign after the name of the boat at the beginning and end of the session.

When You Make a Call

Select: Usually you will initiate a call on CH16 (or CH9 when CH16 is crowded). Set the POWER to LO unless the call is urgent or must reach some distance. If another channel has been prearranged, use it or the listed channel of a shore station.

Listen: You may not interrupt or "step on" other communications. Wait for a brief period of silence. (Set the volume and squelch, then listen.)

Press: After pressing the MIC PTT (push-to-talk) button, wait a second before speaking to ensure that your transmitter is operating and will not cut off the first part of your message.

Speak: Hold the MIC a few inches from your mouth and slightly to the side. Speak normally, but clearly and distinctly. In less than 30 seconds, say " 'Boat A' (up to three times, followed by MMSI or call sign if applicable) calling 'Boat B' (three times), Over."

Listen: Release MIC PTT button. If no answer, repeat in 2 minutes, then again in another 2 minutes. If still no answer, try again after no less than 15 minutes.

Exchange Messages: If you get an answer, listen for " 'Boat B' calling 'Boat A.'" Assuming you and your caller are not using DSC-capable radios, your caller should direct you to a working channel such as "six-ate" (not sixty-eight), then say, "Over." (DSC radios automatically retune from CH70 [the DSC digital call channel] to an analog working channel for the follow-on voice communications.) Tune to the working channel within 1 minute, press MIC, and say, " 'Boat A' calling 'Boat B,' " then provide your message, followed by "Over."

End: After the last message, either party says, " 'Boat Name,' Out."

Radio Speak for VHF and SSB Radios

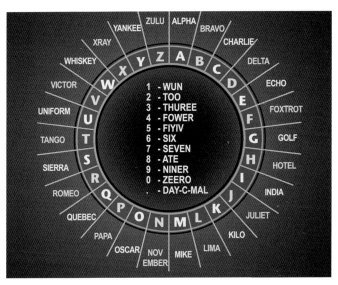

PHONETIC ALPHABET use is recommended when speaking on VHF or SSB radio, because words, letters, and numbers can be distorted over the air, leading to mistakes. The phonetic terms above are internationally recognized. Speak slowly and clearly, emphasizing syllables when spelling out words or numbers.

PROCEDURE WORDS are used as shorthand, as follows:

Over: Signifies that you have ended your transmission but expect a reply.

Out: Indicates that you have completed your communication.

Roger: Acknowledges that a message was received and understood.

Affirmative: Indicates agreement. Alternatively, say "Yes."

Negative: Indicates disagreement. Alternatively, say "No."

Say Again: Requests the sender to repeat the last transmission.

This is "name of boat": Used to identify you.

Wait: Indicates that you must pause, but want the other station to continue to listen, followed by "Wait Out" to resume.

I Spell: Precedes phonetic spelling.

Break: Marks a change in message.

Word after (or before): Points to a specific word.

Silence (see-lonce): spoken by Coast Guard three times to keep routine traffic off an emergency frequency during a Mayday situation, and maintained until lifted with "Silence Fini" (see-lonce fee-nee).

Meet Your SSB Marine Radio

Most SSB marine radios are digitally tuned and provide about 100–150 watts of transmitting power. They can tune in the frequency range from 0.5 to 30 MHz (500 to 30,000 kilohertz), which includes shortwave and ham bands, and they transmit on allocated marine bands.

A typical SSB marine radio is shown below. Models (there are fewer to choose from than is the case for VHF radios) vary by signal quality, power, and the functions offered. SSB radios with DSC capability are available but still very expensive and thus found mainly on commercial ships, where they are required.

microphone   push-to-talk   transmit frequency select   current frequency   enter channel

speaker

power   distress 2182 KHz   speaker volume   received signal squelch   change channel   fine-tune

Microphone: You must select a frequency band and then press the transmit button (on side of microphone) to talk.

Channel Select: Internationally allocated marine frequencies usually are pre-programmed. They can be selected using a digital keypad or (in this model) with two rotary knobs, one to select a frequency band and the other to tune a frequency within the selected band.

Clarity: Fine-tunes the received frequency to compensate for any minor differences between the transmitter and the receiver.

Volume: Controls the speaker sound level.

Squelch: Cuts off reception of all signals below the level set by the control. Adjust to the level at which static can just be heard, then advance slightly to eliminate static. Stronger signals still will be received.

Using SSB Radios

SSB marine radios require a station license to operate. A VHF radio must be installed and used in preference over SSB. Beyond VHF range, SSB provides generally reliable communications, but SSB radios are somewhat more complex to operate. They offer channels in seven frequency bands ranging from 2 MHz (2000 KHz) to 22 MHz (22,000 KHz). The selection of a particular band and channel depends upon the application (voice, digital, or telex), the locations of the two stations, the time of day, the season, and other propagation factors.

The international SSB distress frequency is 2182 KHz, which has a range of up to about 200 miles via groundwave propagation by day, or 500 miles by night. You may need to transmit distress signals on other frequencies in order to reach assistance.

Antenna: The frequencies employed with SSB radios require a much longer antenna than those used with VHF. On a sailboat, the backstay can be converted into an antenna by electrically isolating the top and bottom of the wire. The antenna is connected to an antenna tuner, which matches the characteristics of the antenna to the transceiver for each frequency used. On a powerboat, a whip antenna, typically 23 to 30 feet long, is used. Generally, these antennas must be supported at an intermediate height as well as at the bottom.

Grounding: Effective radiation of MF/HF energy requires a good ground plane (the ocean) and the system must have good coupling between the boat and the sea. This can be accomplished using metallic plates within the hull below the waterline. These plates couple effectively to the ocean at SSB frequencies, even through the hull.

Licenses: To operate an SSB radio, you must have a Station License for your boat and a Restricted Marine Operators Permit (RP) for each user. In the U.S., the Station License is obtained by filing FCC Form 605 and Form 159 (fee processing form). The RP is obtained by filing Forms 753 and 159. These forms can be obtained at www.fcc.gov. These licenses are not required for VHF, radar, or EPIRB used on recreational boats not communicating with or entering foreign ports.

Channels: By international treaties, marine radios are restricted in the frequencies that can be transmitted. The International Telecommunications Union (ITU) has designated frequencies for safety and working channels across the MF and HF bands. Most modern SSB radios come preprogrammed with those frequencies. You can listen to any frequency but must transmit only on allocated frequencies unless you also are licensed as a ham radio operator. The channels are numbered with the first one or two digits reflecting the band; channel 401 is in the 4 MHz band, and channel 2236 is in the 22 MHz band. Separate frequencies are used for receiving and transmitting for each channel. For example, channel 241 transmits on 2.06 MHz but receives on 1.635 MHz; channel 401 transmits on 4.065 MHz and receives on 4.375 MHz; etc.

Calling: You must give your call sign each time you call another vessel or coast station, at the end of each transmission that lasts more than 3 minutes, and every 15 minutes during ship-to-shore calls. In addition, you must maintain a log of all distress, emergency, and safety calls, and a log of all adjustments or maintenance signed by a licensed technician.

SSB Frequencies

The major consideration in using SSB communications is selection of a frequency band. You must transmit on only those frequencies allocated for your purpose within the band you select.

MF/HF radio waves travel beyond line-of-sight, either hugging the Earth (medium frequencies) or reflecting from the ionosphere (high frequencies). The characteristics of the ionosphere change dramatically from day to night, with seasons, and through an 11-year sunspot cycle.

SSB Coverage

```
Range    |---|---|---|---|---|---|----|----|------|------|------|------|-------|
          0  200 400 600 700 800 1000 1500 2000   3000   4000   5000   6000   7000 mi
Night    Range (mi)
2 MHz    |--------500 (groundwave)
4 MHz    |xx200-----------------------2000
6 MHz    |xxxxxx500-------------------2000
8 MHz    |xxxxxx500-------------------------3000
12 MHz   |xxxxxxxxxxxxxxxxxxxxxxxxxxxxxxxxxxxxxxx
Day
2 MHz    |--200 (groundwave)
4 MHz    |xxxxxxxxx
6 MHz    |---------500
8 MHz    |--------------700
12 MHz   |xxxxxx500*-----------------2000
16 MHz   |xxxxxxxxxxxx750*-----------------------4000 .........6000
22 MHz   |xxxxxxxxxxxxxxxxxxx1500*--------------------------------7000
```

xxx Skip zone, no coverage   Min Range-------Max Range
* no coverage until late morning, minimum range for local noon

Nighttime: The ionosphere is lower and less reflective at night, so frequencies above the 8 MHz band may pass right through out to space. Consequently, you will need to use lower frequencies than during the day. Frequencies near 2 MHz can be used out to about 500 miles, propagating as groundwaves, but these medium frequencies may be absorbed and not reflected by the ionosphere to greater distances. Using higher frequencies, you might get reflection and much greater distances via one or more "hops," but these signals may be absorbed and not reflected at shorter ranges, creating a "skip zone." For example, using the 6 MHz band, you may be able to communicate as close as 500 miles or as far as 2,000 miles via multiple reflections, or hops. As soon as these signals reach a time zone experiencing daylight, however, conditions will change, causing the signals to be absorbed and go no farther.

Daytime: The ionosphere is much higher, thicker, and more reflective. Many of the nighttime frequencies will be absorbed. Groundwave propagation still works near 2 MHz and can be used out to about 200 miles during the day, but it is susceptible to interference. Begin with the nominal frequencies shown in the table, and adjust upward or downward to increase or decrease the distance to be reached. Listen to other transmissions at various frequencies and attempt to correlate distance with frequency. Usually, the strongest signal will be received at the highest frequency that just reaches the desired range. PC software is available to help with frequency selection.

Emergency Calls

There are three types of calls (DISTRESS, URGENCY, and SAFETY). These are transmitted on VHF CH16 or SSB 2182 KHz. The procedures are slightly different for each, as follows:

DISTRESS: is reserved for situations involving risk of life and/or grave and immediate danger. It calls for immediate assistance. It has priority over all other forms of traffic. (If you are using a DSC-equipped radio, initiate your Mayday call by pressing the Distress button as outlined on page 92.)

Distress Signal: MAYDAY
Provide the following message:

> MAYDAY, MAYDAY, MAYDAY...
> This is:
> Boat Name _____(repeat three times)
> Call Sign (if you have a license)_____(once)
> MAYDAY, Boat Name_____
> Position is: Lat_____Lon_____, or
> _____nm_____(N,S,E,W) of_____
> Nature of Distress _____
> Assistance Required _____
> Boat description _____
> No. of persons on board _____Other_____
> OVER

URGENCY: is reserved for situations involving the safety of the ship or some person on board that is serious but has not yet reached the level of immediate peril (loss of steering, medical difficulty, etc.). It calls for assistance.

Urgency Signal: PAN-PAN (pronounced PAHN-PAHN)
Provide the following message:

> PAN-PAN, PAN-PAN, PAN-PAN...
> ALL STATIONS (or particular coast guard station) (once)
> This is:
> Boat Name_____(once)
> Call Sign (if you have a license)_____(once)
> Urgency message (assistance required): _____
> Position is: Lat_____Lon_____, or
> _____nm_____(N,S,E,W) of_____
> This is: Boat Name_____(once)
> OVER

SAFETY: is reserved for information regarding navigation safety. The coast guard encourages all mariners to transmit safety messages when they spot a hazard to navigation (buoy off-station, floating log, etc.).

Safety Signal: SECURITE (pronounced SAY-CUR-I-TAY)
Provide the following message:

> SECURITE, SECURITE, SECURITE...
> ALL STATIONS (once)
> This is:
> Boat Name_____(once)
> Channel # for message: _____
> OUT (go to channel, repeat above, and provide message)

Using VHF and SSB Radios

Using DSC-Equipped VHF Radios

DSC (Digital Selective Calling) helps to free up crowded channels and vastly speeds rescue operations. On VHF, channel 70 is dedicated to DSC. (On SSB, the DSC frequency is 2187.5 KHz to call the U.S. Coast Guard.)

DSC transmits a digital signal that includes the MMSI (Maritime Mobile Service Identity) number unique to your boat, as well as your position (if your VHF transceiver is connected to a GPS receiver). It also transmits data about the type of call and the intended recipients. DSC calls can be placed to all users for distress or selectively to a single ship or group for routine message traffic. When not transmitting, your DSC-equipped VHF transceiver monitors channel 70 (SSB monitors 2187.5 KHz), sounds a tone corresponding to the type of incoming call, and automatically tunes to the appropriate frequency for the subsequent incoming message.

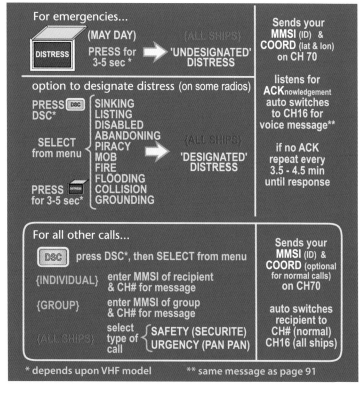

MMSI: You must register your DSC radio. You will provide key information about your identity and boat that will be essential in the event of a distress. To make individual or group calls, you will need the MMSIs of the radios you wish to call. The U.S. Coast Guard group MMSI is 003669999. In addition, local USCG and Canadian Coast Guard stations have individual MMSIs. Contact local authorities for these numbers.

(Note: SSB DSC frequencies include 2187.5, 4207.5, 6312, 8414.5, 12577, and 16804.5 KHz. Ships equipped for GMDSS [Global Maritime Distress and Safety System] will monitor these frequencies in addition to VHF CH70.)

EPIRBs and GMDSS

The Global Maritime Distress and Safety System (GMDSS) provides a worldwide method for monitoring and providing assistance at sea. One of the key components of this system, particularly for offshore operations, is the EPIRB (Emergency Position-Indicating Radio Beacon). Radio reports are preferred, but in some situations the radio may not be available, such as after abandoning ship. For these applications the EPIRB is essential.

An EPIRB is a self-contained radio beacon. Several types and categories are available, but the most current system uses a 406 MHz transmitter to send coded messages to satellites. Two types of satellites receive these messages. Low orbiting satellites receive the message when over the EPIRB and relay it when near a local ground terminal (Local User Terminal). Geostationary satellites are higher and can relay messages immediately.

Each EPIRB is registered, so the ground station knows the identity of the sender and the location, which is ascertained by the satellites. Position location accuracy can be enhanced by EPIRBs that incorporate a GPS unit.

Once an alert is received and verified, the rescue operators attempt land contact at the address and number in the registration. Then a message is sent to the local rescue coordination center that directs the rescue.

The EPIRB is only a signaling device, so the nature of the distress is unknown to rescuers. It is the communication mode of last resort but effective in quick response. The EPIRB can be used only under life-threatening conditions.

Some EPIRBs contain a 121.5 MHz aircraft frequency as well. This frequency originally was intended to be monitored by commercial aircraft, but its use by recreational boaters is prohibited by the U.S. Coast Guard as of 2007.

If choosing an EPIRB, insist on a 406 MHz model. The 406 MHz channel is digital and can pass information quickly. You have a choice of manual or automatic (the latter being activated by immersion), and the option of an internal GPS unit for precise position information that will be transmitted along with the distress signal.

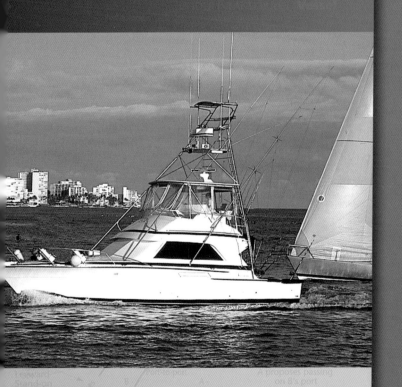

CHAPTER 6

Rules of the Road and Running Light Patterns

Charlie Wing

Why the Rules Matter

We are all familiar with the rules governing vehicular traffic: stay to the right; pass on the left; give way at an intersection to a vehicle on your right; don't exceed the speed limit. These rules are easily remembered because streets and highways are marked with reminders: solid and dashed lines marking traffic lanes, stop signs, traffic lights and speed limit signs.

Piloting a boat is more like driving in an open field—there are no streets, no traffic lights, and no signs. Despite the differences, however, there are remarkable similarities between the rules for vehicular and boating traffic.

The International Regulations for the Prevention of Collision at Sea (COLREGs) are the "Rules of the Road" for the ocean. The United States Inland Rules govern U.S. Great Lakes, bays, inlets, rivers, and waterways that connect to the sea. The boundary between the two jurisdictions is shown as a dashed magenta (red) Demarcation Line on nautical charts. The two sets of Rules are, fortunately, identical in most respects. In this chapter we clearly indicate where they differ.

This chapter does not include the entire text of the 225-page Rules. What it does contain is visual explanations of the rules you are likely to encounter as a recreational boater. In all cases we've provided the corresponding rule number from the official rules.

Purpose of the Rules. The purpose of the Rules is NOT to grant one boat the "right-of-way" over another. Avoiding a collision between two boats requires the participation of both. Rather, the purpose of the Rules is to present, in any situation where two boats encounter one another, guidelines for the action required of each. Under the Rules, one boat is designated the **stand-on vessel**; the other the **give-way vessel**. These designations carry obligations for each vessel to act in a specified way to avoid collision. Note that the Rules do not address situations involving more than two boats. In such instances common sense must be the principal guide.

Application (Rule 1). The Rules apply to ALL VESSELS on the high seas and navigable waters connected with the high seas.

Responsibility (Rule 2). Nothing in the Rules exonerates any vessel or its owner, master, or crew from the consequences of neglect to comply with the Rules or neglect of precaution which may be required by the ordinary practice of seamen or by the special circumstances of the situation.

Key Definitions (Rule 3).

> *Underway:* not anchored, grounded, or otherwise attached to shore. A boat does not have to be moving either through the water or over the ground to be underway.

> *Restricted visibility:* any condition other than night that reduces visibility, including fog and heavy rain.

> *Vessel:* anything that carries people or cargo on or in the water, including kayaks, personal watercraft, seaplanes, and supertankers.

Give-way vessel: the vessel obligated to keep out of the way of the other.

Stand-on vessel: the vessel obligated to maintain its course and speed unless an alteration is necessary to avoid collision.

Power-driven vessel: any vessel underway with an engine that does not fall into any of the other categories defined below.

Sailing vessel: a sailboat underway with sails only, not using an engine.

Vessel engaged in fishing: any boat fishing with equipment that limits its ability to maneuver (nets, trawls, etc.).

Vessel not under command: a vessel unable to maneuver as required by the Rules, due to mechanical breakdown or any other reason.

Vessel restricted in her ability to maneuver: a vessel that, due to the nature of her work, cannot maneuver easily. Examples include buoy tenders, dredges, dive boats, mine sweepers, and tugs with difficult tows.

Vessel constrained by her draft: a vessel that may go aground if it deviates from its course. (The *Inland Rules* do not contain this definition.)

Lookout (Rule 5). Every vessel must at all times maintain a proper lookout by all means available in the prevailing circumstances and conditions (including radar even under conditions of unlimited visibility) so as to make a full appraisal of the situation and of the risk of collision.

Safe Speed (Rule 6). Every vessel must at all times proceed at a *safe speed* so that she can take proper and effective action to avoid collision and be stopped within a distance appropriate to the prevailing circumstances and conditions.

Risk of Collision (Rule 7). Every vessel must use all available means appropriate to the prevailing circumstances and conditions to determine if risk of collision exists. When there is *any doubt,* risk must be assumed to exist. Risk exists if the compass bearing (or relative bearing, if you are on a steady course) to an approaching vessel does not appreciably change as the vessel draws nearer.

Action to Avoid Collision (Rule 8). Action to avoid collision must, if circumstances permit, be positive, made in ample time, and with due regard to good seamanship.

Alteration of course and/or speed to avoid collision must, if circumstances allow, be large enough to be readily apparent to the other vessel; a succession of small alterations of course and/or speed should be avoided.

If necessary to avoid collision or to allow more time to assess the situation, a vessel must reduce speed or take all way off by stopping or reversing engines.

Remaining Rules (Rules 9–37). Rules 9–18 (see *At-a-Glance Guide*) spell out the actions to be taken to avoid collision. Rule 19 (see *What to Do in Fog*) specifies conduct in restricted visibility. Rules 20–31 (see pages 98–103 and 105) describe lights and shapes to display, and Rules 32–37 (see *Sound Signals*) specify sound signals.

Rules of the Road and Running Light Patterns

Power-Driven Vessels Underway *(Rule 23)*

RULE/VESSEL	GROUPS	SHAPES	BOW	STERN
BOTH INTERNATIONAL AND INLAND				
Rule 23(a) Power-driven ≥50 m	2 Mastheads Sidelights Sternlight	None		
INLAND (GREAT LAKES ONLY)				
Rule 23(a) Power-driven ≥50 m	Masthead Sidelights All-around for 2nd masthead + stern	None		
BOTH INTERNATIONAL AND INLAND				
Rule 23(a) Power-driven <50 m	Masthead Sidelights Sternlight	None		
Rule 23(c) Power-driven optional <12 m	Sidelights All-around in lieu of masthead and stern	None		
INTERNATIONAL ONLY				
Rule 23(c)(ii) Power-driven <7 m & <7 kn max.	Sidelights if practical All-around	None		
BOTH INTERNATIONAL AND INLAND				
Rule 23(b) Submarine	2 Mastheads Sidelights Sternlight Flashing Yellow, 1/sec. for 3 sec., followed by 3 sec. off	None		
Rule 23(b) Hovercraft in displacement mode <50 m	Masthead Sidelights Sternlight	None		
Rule 23(b) Hovercraft non-displacement mode <50 m	Masthead Sidelights Sternlight Flashing Yellow	None		
INLAND ONLY				
Rule 23(a) Law Enforcement <50 m	Masthead Sidelights Sternlight Flashing Blue	None		

Rules of the Road and Running Light Patterns

Vessels Towing and Pushing *(Rule 24)*

RULE/VESSEL	GROUPS	SHAPES	BOW	STERN
BOTH INTERNATIONAL AND INLAND				
24(a)/Towing astern (Tow 200 m)	2 vert. Mastheads Sidelights Sternlight Towlight	None		
If vessel 50 m, add	Masthead aft			
24(a)/Towing astern (Tow > 200 m)	3 vert. Mastheads Sidelights Sternlight Towlight	◆		
If vessel 50 m, add	Masthead aft			
24(b)/Composite (treated as single power vessel)	Masthead Sidelights Sternlight	None		
If composite 50 m, add	Masthead aft			
24(c)/Pushing ahead or towing alongside (not composite)	2 vert. Mastheads Sidelights Sternlight	None		
If vessel 50 m, add	Masthead aft			
24(e)/Vessel/object being towed astern (other than 24(g)) (Tow 200 m)	Sidelights fwd Sternlight	None		
24(e)/Vessel/object being towed astern (other than 24(g)) (Tow >200 m)	Sidelights fwd Sternlight	◆		
24(g)/Partly submerged 100 m long (<25 m wide) All-arounds forward & aft		◆		
(25 m wide) Add all-arounds on beams				
Partly submerged >100 m long (<25 m wide) All-arounds forward & aft and every 100 m		◆ ◆ aft fwd		
(25 m wide) All-arounds forward & aft Add beam all-arounds every 100 m		If tow >200 m		
INTERNATIONAL ONLY				
24(f)/Multiple vessels/objects being pushed ahead	Sidelights fwd	None		
24(f)/Multiple vessels/objects being towed alongside	Sidelights Sternlight	None		
INLAND ONLY				
24(f)/Multiple vessels/objects being pushed ahead	Sidelights fwd Special flashing	None		
24(f)/Multiple vessels/objects being towed alongside	Sidelights Sternlight Special flashing	None		
24(f)/Multiple vessels/objects being towed alongside BOTH sides	Sidelights 2 Sternlights Special flashing	None		
INLAND Western Rivers except below Huey Long Bridge				
24(i)/Pushing ahead or towing alongside (not composite)	Sidelights 2 Towing lights NO mastheads NO sternlight	None		

Sailing & Rowing Vessels Underway *(Rule 25)*

RULE/VESSEL	GROUPS	SHAPES	BOW	STERN
BOTH INTERNATIONAL AND INLAND				
Rule 25(a) Sailing only any length	Sidelights Sternlight	None		
Rule 25(b) Sailing only <20 m option	Tri-color	None		
Rule 25(c) Sailing only optional any length	Sidelights Sternlight R/G all-around	None		
Rule 25(d)(i) Sailing or Rowing <7 m	Sidelights Sternlight	None		
Rule 25(d)(ii) Sailing or Rowing <7 m option	All-around or show only to prevent collision	None		
Rule 25(e) Motorsailing ≥50 m	2 Mastheads Sidelights Sternlight	▼		
Rule 25(e) Motorsailing <50 m	Masthead Sidelights Sternlight	▼		
Rule 25(e) Motorsailing <12 m	Masthead Sidelights Sternlight	▼ Optional under Inland Rules		

Rules of the Road and Running Light Patterns

Fishing Vessels
(Rule 26)

RULE/VESSEL	GROUPS	SHAPES	BOW	STERN
BOTH INTERNATIONAL AND INLAND				
Rule 26(b) Trawling, making way ≥50 m	Masthead Sidelights Sternlight G/W all-around			
Rule 26(b) Trawling, making way <50 m	Sidelights Sternlight G/W all-around			
Rule 26(b) Trawling, not making way	G/W all-around			
Rule 26(c) Fishing other than trawling, making way Any length	Sidelights Sternlight R/W all-around			
Rule 26(c) Fishing other than trawling, not making way Any length	R/W all-around			
Rule 26(c) Fishing other than trawling, making way Gear out >150 m	Sidelights Sternlight R/W all-around All-around	gear side		
Rule 26(c) Fishing other than trawling, not making way Gear out >150 m	R/W all-around All-around	gear side		

Rules of the Road and Running Light Patterns

Vessels Not Under Command or Restricted in Ability to Maneuver *(Rule 27)*

RULE/VESSEL	GROUPS	SHAPES	BOW	STERN
BOTH INTERNATIONAL AND INLAND				
Rule 27(a) Not Under Command Making way	Sidelights Sternlight R/R all-around			
Rule 27(a) Not Under Command Not making way	R/R all-around			
Rule 27(b) Restricted in Ability to Maneuver Making way <50 m	Masthead Sidelights Sternlight R/W/R all-around			
Rule 27(b) Restricted in Ability to Maneuver Making way ≥50 m	2 Mastheads Sidelights Sternlight R/W/R all-around			
Rule 27(b) Restricted in Ability to Maneuver Not making way	R/W/R all-around			
Rule 27(b) Restricted in Ability to Maneuver Anchored <50 m	R/W/R all-around W all-around			
Rule 27(b) Restricted in Ability to Maneuver Anchored ≥50 m	R/W/R all-around 2 W all-around			
Rule 27(d) Dredging or Underwater Operations Not making way	R/W/R all-around R/R all-arnd obstr. side G/G all-arnd clear side	obstr. side / clear side		
Rule 27(e) Diving, but unable to display Underwater Operations lights	R/W/R all-around	Int'l Code Flag "A"		
Rule 27(f) Mine-clearing Making way ≥50 m	2 Mastheads Sidelights Sternlight G Δ all-around			
Rule 27(f) Mine-clearing Making way <50 m	Masthead Sidelights Sternlight G Δ all-around			

All Other Vessels
(Rules 28–31)

RULE/VESSEL	GROUPS	SHAPES	BOW	STERN
INTERNATIONAL ONLY **Rule 28** Constrained by Draft Making way If 50 m, add	Masthead Sidelights Sternlight R/R/R all-around 2nd Masthead	cylinder		
BOTH INTERNATIONAL AND INLAND **Rule 29(a)** Pilot Vessel on Duty Underway	Sidelights Sternlight W/R all-around	Int'l Code Flag "H"		
Rule 29(a) Pilot Vessel on Duty Anchored	W/R all-around Anchor Light	Int'l Code Flag "H"		
Rule 29(b) Pilot Vessel off Duty Making way <50 m	Masthead Sidelights Sternlight	None		
Rule 30(a) Anchored 50–100 m	2 W all-around	●		
Rule 30(b) Anchored 7 m and <50 m	W all-around	●		
Rule 30(c) Anchored 100 m	2 W all-around All deck lights	●		
Rule 30(d) Aground 50 m	W all-around forward Lower W all-around aft R/R all-around (if practicable INLAND)	● ● ●		
Rule 30(d) Aground <50 m and 12 m	W all-around R/R all-around (if practicable INLAND)	● ● ●		
Rule 30(f) Aground <12 m	W all-around	●		
Rule 31 Seaplane Underway	Masthead Sidelights Sternlight	None		

Rules of the Road and Running Light Patterns

Sound Signals *(Rules 32–37)*

● = 1-sec. blast; —— = 4- to 6-sec. blast. Repeated every 2 min.

INTERNATIONAL

Meeting or crossing and action required (no answer required):

I am altering my course to starboard	●
I am altering my course to port	● ●
I am operating astern propulsion	● ● ●

Overtaking in narrow channel or fairway and action required (agreement required before action initiated):

I intend to overtake you on your starboard	—— —— ●
I intend to overtake you on your port	—— —— ● ●
I agree to be overtaken	—— ● —— ●
Warning—I dont understand your intentions	● ● ● ● ●
Approaching a bend in a channel	——

INLAND

Meeting or crossing within ½ mile and action is required (agreement by the same signal required):

I propose leaving you to my port	●
I propose leaving you to my starboard	● ●
I am operating astern propulsion	● ● ●

Overtaking in narrow channel or fairway and action required (agreement by same signal required before action):

I propose overtaking you on your starboard	●
I propose overtaking you on your port	● ●
I agree to be overtaken as proposed	● or ● ●
Warning—I don't understand your intentions	● ● ● ● ●
Approaching a bend in a channel or leaving berth	——

IN RESTRICTED VISIBILITY (INTERNATIONAL & INLAND)

Power vessel making way	——
Power vessel underway but stopped	—— ——
Manned tow	—— ● ● ●
Pilot vessel –optional signal	● ● ●

Not under command, restricted in ability to maneuver, constrained by draft, sailing, fishing, towing or pushing, fishing at anchor, or restricted at anchor   —— ● ●

Anchored:
    <100 m—ring bell rapidly for 5 sec. once per min.
    ≥100 m—ring bell 5 sec. forward, then gong 5 sec. aft
Aground: 3 bell claps + rapid 5-sec. bell + 3 claps; repeat all 1/min.
    ≥100 m—add gong 5 sec. aft
    <12 m Inland option—horn, bell, or gong once per 2 min.

What to Do in Fog *(Rule 19)*

Fog Situation	What You Should Do
Regardless of traffic	Maintain safe speed; power-driven vessels sound one 5-sec. blast every 2 minutes. Most other vessels sound one 5-sec. and two 1-sec. blasts every 2 minutes.
Hear sound signal forward	Slow to bare steerageway or stop.
Radar target forward	Slow; do NOT turn to port unless you are overtaking the target vessel.
Radar target aft or abeam	Maintain speed; do NOT turn toward the target vessel.

Light & Shape Definitions
(Rule 21)

Visibility of Lights *(Rule 22)*

Type of Light	Vessel Length, m	Visibility, nm
Masthead	under 12 12 to 20 20 to 50 50 or more	2 3 5 6
Side	under 12 12 to 50 50 or more	1 2 3
Stern, Towing, and All-around	under 50 50 or more	2 3

Rules of the Road and Running Light Patterns

At-a-Glance Guide

Situation: What You Need to Do

ARE YOU IN OR ENTERING A CHARTED
TRAFFIC SEPARATION SCHEME ?

 YES → RULE 10

If using, stay in lane in direction of the arrows on chart

If crossing, do so at 90° and stay clear of vessels in lanes

If sailing, fishing, or <20 m in length, you may use an
inshore zone, but you must not impede a vessel
that is following a lane

Don't anchor in or near the ends of traffic lanes

If risk of collision occurs, use the rules below

NO

ARE YOU IN A NARROW
CHANNEL OR FAIRWAY?

 YES → RULE 9

If crossing, don't impede vessels using the channel

If sailing, fishing, or <20 m in length, don't impede
a vessel using the channel

If overtaking, first obtain agreement by sound signals

Otherwise, keep to the starboard edge of the channel

NO

ARE YOU OVERTAKING OR BEING OVERTAKEN BY ANOTHER VESSEL?

 YES → RULE 13

If overtaking, stay clear; use sound signals if necessary

If you have any doubt, assume you are overtaking

If being overtaken, stand on; answer to sound signals

NO

ARE YOU ONE OF TWO POWER-DRIVEN
VESSELS MEETING HEAD-ON?

 YES → RULE 14

Both vessels alter course to starboard and pass port-to-port.
On the GREAT LAKES and WESTERN RIVERS only, down-
bound vessel should propose method of passage using
INLAND sound signals.

VHF is OK instead of sound signals under Inland Rules.
No answer required under COLREGs.

NO

to Rules 9–18

Illustration of the Rule

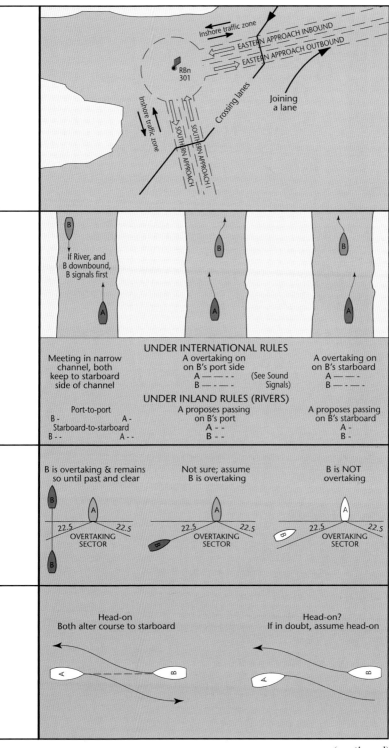

UNDER INTERNATIONAL RULES

Meeting in narrow channel, both keep to starboard side of channel

A overtaking on on B's port side
A — — - -
B — - — - (See Sound Signals)

A overtaking on on B's starboard
A — — - -
B — - — -

UNDER INLAND RULES (RIVERS)

Port-to-port
B -   A -
Starboard-to-starboard
B - -   A - -

A proposes passing on B's port
A - -
B - -

A proposes passing on B's starboard
A -
B -

If River, and B downbound, B signals first

B is overtaking & remains so until past and clear

22.5   22.5
OVERTAKING SECTOR

Not sure; assume B is overtaking

22.5   22.5
OVERTAKING SECTOR

B is NOT overtaking

22.5   22.5
OVERTAKING SECTOR

Head-on
Both alter course to starboard

Head-on?
If in doubt, assume head-on

(continued)

Rules of the Road and Running Light Patterns

At-a-Glance Guide

Situation: What You Need to Do

ARE YOU ONE OF TWO POWER-DRIVEN
VESSELS CROSSING PATHS?

 YES

RULE 15

If other vessel on your starboard, keep clear; pass aft

If other vessel on your port, maintain course and speed

RULE 17

If the give-way vessel is not giving way, the stand-on
vessel MAY slow or turn to starboard to avoid collision

If collision can no longer be avoided by action of the
give-way vessel alone, the stand-on vessel MUST
take whatever action she thinks will best avoid
collision, including a turn to port

NO

ARE YOU ONE OF TWO
SAILBOATS MEETING?

 YES

RULE 12

If on different tacks, the port-tack vessel stays clear

If on same tack, the windward vessel stays clear

If you are on port tack and you are uncertain about the
tack of the vessel to your windward, stay clear

 NO

IS THE OTHER VESSEL
A DIFFERENT TYPE?

 YES

RULE 18

Stay clear of vessels higher than you on the list at right

To claim their special status, vessels must display
shapes during the day and lights sunset to sunrise

See pages 98–103 and 105 for shapes and lights

NO

YOU HAVE MISSED SOMETHING

Slow to bare steerageway or stop and
review the At-a-Glance Guide from the top

Contact the other vessel on VHF Channel 13
or Channel 09 to clarify both vessels' intentions

Illustration of the Rule

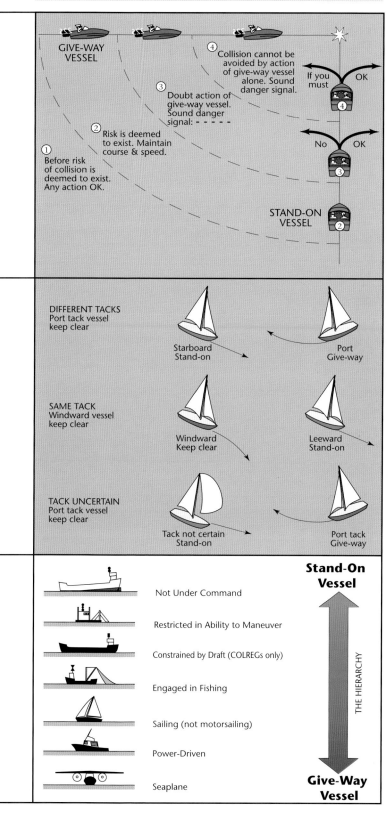

GIVE-WAY VESSEL

④ Collision cannot be avoided by action of give-way vessel alone. Sound danger signal.

If you must   OK

③ Doubt action of give-way vessel. Sound danger signal: - - - - -

No   OK

② Risk is deemed to exist. Maintain course & speed.

① Before risk of collision is deemed to exist. Any action OK.

STAND-ON VESSEL

DIFFERENT TACKS
Port tack vessel keep clear

Starboard Stand-on

Port Give-way

SAME TACK
Windward vessel keep clear

Windward Keep clear

Leeward Stand-on

TACK UNCERTAIN
Port tack vessel keep clear

Tack not certain Stand-on

Port tack Give-way

Not Under Command

Restricted in Ability to Maneuver

Constrained by Draft (COLREGs only)

Engaged in Fishing

Sailing (not motorsailing)

Power-Driven

Seaplane

Stand-On Vessel

THE HIERARCHY

Give-Way Vessel

Rules of the Road and Running Light Patterns

CHAPTER 7

Knots, Splices, and Line Handling

Charlie Wing

Rope Construction

Rope Fiber. Virtually all rope today is manufactured of synthetic materials. Natural fibers have been replaced by chemically engineered fibers with a wide range of desirable characteristics, including high strength-to-weight ratio, high or low elasticity, infinite fiber length, and abrasion, rot, and UV resistance. The table below lists the leading fibers and their characteristics. Nylon and polyester predominate on boats.

CHARACTERISTICS OF FIBERS

Material	Breaking Strength[1]	Stretch %	Abrasion Resistance	Specific Gravity[2]	UV Resistance	Relative Cost
Polypropylene	1530	18–22	Fair	0.91	Fair	Low
Nylon	2600	30–35	Excellent	1.14	Good	Med
Polyester (Dacron®)	3470	15–20	Excellent	1.38	Excellent	Med
Hi-Tenacity Polyethylene (Spectra®)	8160	2.3–3.9	Excellent	0.97	Fair	Hi
Aramid (Kevlar®)	8500	1.5–4.5	Fair	1.44	Fair	Hi
Hi-Tenacity Copolymer (Technora®)	10700	1.5–4.5	Fair	1.44	Fair	Very Hi
Liquid Crystal Polymer (Vectran®)	11600	3.5–4.5	Very Good	1.40	Fair	Very Hi
Hi-Tenacity Polyethylene (Dyneema®)	12000	2.0–4.0	Excellent	0.975	Very Good	Very Hi

Notes: [1]Breaking strength of single-braid 5/16" rope [2]Floats in fresh water if <1.00; salt water if <1.025

Construction. Rope is either cable-laid or braided. Right-handed (the usual) **cable-laid** rope consists of fibers twisted clockwise into yarns, yarns CCW into strands, and 3 strands CW to form the rope. In **braided rope**, fibers are twisted into yarns, 2–4 yarns laid together as strands, and the strands braided into rope. Braided rope may have a uniform cross-section (single-braid), a braided core inside a braided cover (double-braid), a core of straight yarns inside a braided cover (parallel-core), or, in the case of polypropylene, a hollow core inside a braided cover.

	Strength	Flexibility	Stretch	Cost
THREE-STRAND	Medium	Low	High	Low
SINGLE-BRAID	Medium	High	Medium	Low
DOUBLE-BRAID	High	Medium	Low	Medium
PARALLEL-CORE	Highest	High	Very Low	High

APPROXIMATE BREAKING STRENGTHS OF ROPES

| Diameter, inches | 3/16 | 1/4 | 5/16 | 3/8 | 7/16 | 1/2 | 5/8 | 3/4 |
millimeters	5	6	8	9.5	11	12	16	19
Polypropylene Hollow-Braid	550	980	1530	2200	2990	3910	6110	8800
Polypropylene 3-Strand	725	1290	2010	2900	3940	5150	8050	11600
Nylon Single-Braid	940	1670	2600	3750	5100	6660	10400	15000
Nylon Double-Braid	1090	1940	3040	4375	5950	7770	12100	17500
Nylon 3-Strand	940	1670	2600	3750	5100	6660	10400	15000
Polyester Single-Braid	1140	1900	3000	4200	5500	7000	11000	15300
Polyester Double-Braid	1200	2000	3000	4400	6600	8500	14400	20000
with Spectra or Kevlar Core	2300	3800	5700	7600	10200	12800	21800	28800
with Vectran or Technora Core	2720	4500	8000	10000	15000	18000	31000	42300
Polyester Braid with Parallel Core	1600	2700	4400	5500	7400	9600	15000	21600

Knots, Splices, and Line Handling

Selecting Rope for Lines

When selecting a type of rope, keep in mind the desired characteristics for the application. Strength per diameter or weight is rarely the determining factor. For example:

Anchor rodes require high stretch (to reduce shock loading) and high abrasion resistance (chafe is the leading cause of rode failure), but not great flexibility. Choose 3-strand nylon.

Dock lines: require moderately high stretch and strength, flexibility (for cleating), and high abrasion resistance. Choose braided (single or double) nylon, with polyester cover as an option.

Dinghy painters, life-ring lines, and ski-tow ropes must float so they don't get caught in the propeller. Choose polypropylene.

Halyards must not stretch or sail shape will be lost. Choose a polyester braid with a low-stretch core.

Sheets and vangs must be strong and flexible, but also moderately stretchy to absorb shock loads. Choose an all-polyester braid.

DOCK LINES
(Based on 3-strand or braided nylon)

Boat Length	Bow/Stern Lines	Spring Lines	Rope Diameter
to 27'	20'	25'	3/8"
28–36	25	35	1/2
37–45	30	45	5/8
46–54	35	50	3/4
55–72	40	70	1

ANCHOR RODES
(Recommended rode consists of 15 feet of chain plus 200 feet of 3-strand nylon)

Boat Length	Chain Size	Rope Dia.
to 25'	3/16"	1/4"
26–35	1/4	1/2
36–45	5/16	5/8
46–54	3/8	3/4
55–72	1/2	1

LINE GUIDE FOR THE CRUISER AND CASUAL RACER

Application	Polyester Single-Braid (e.g., Regatta)	Polyester Double-Braid (e.g., Sta-Set)	Polyester Braid/ Parallel Core (e.g., Sta-Set X)	Polyester Braid/ Vectran Core (e.g., Sta-Set X+)
Main/Genoa Halyard	Not Rec.	Good	Excellent	Excellent
Main Sheet	Excellent	Excellent	Fair	Good
Genoa/Jib Sheets	Very Good	Excellent	Very Good	Very Good
Reefing Lines	Good	Excellent	Excellent	Good
Spinnaker Halyard	Not Rec.	Very Good	Excellent	Excellent
Spinnaker Sheets	Good	Very Good	Excellent	Good
Spinnaker Guys	Not Rec.	Good	Excellent	Excellent
Foreguy/Topping Lift	Good	Excellent	Very Good	Good
Vang	Good	Excellent	Good	Fair
Control Lines	Very Good	Excellent	Good	Fair
Runner Tails	Not Rec.	Good	Very Good	Very Good
Furling Lines	Excellent	Very Good	Fair	Fair

RUNNING RIGGING SIZE GUIDE (Based on polyester double-braid)

Application	to 20'	20–25'	26–30'	31–35'	36–40'	41–45'	46–50'	51–60'
Main Halyard	1/4"	5/16"	3/8"	7/16"	1/2"	9/16"	5/8"	3/4"
Genoa Halyard	1/4"	5/16"	3/8"	7/16"	1/2"	9/16"	5/8"	3/4"
Main Sheet	5/16"	5/16"	3/8"	7/16"	1/2"	1/2"	9/16"	9/16"
Genoa Sheets	5/16"	5/16"	3/8"	7/16"	v1/2"	9/16"	5/8"	5/8"
Reefing Lines	1/4"	5/16"	3/8"	7/16"	7/16"	1/2"	1/2"	9/16"
Spinnaker Halyard	1/4"	5/16"	3/8"	7/16"	1/2"	9/16"	5/8"	3/4"
Spinnaker Sheets	1/4"	1/4"	5/16"	3/8"	7/16"	1/2"	9/16"	5/8"
Spinnaker Guy	5/16"	5/16"	3/8"	7/16"	1/2"	5/8"	3/4"	3/4"
Foreguy/Topping Lift	1/4"	1/4"	5/16"	3/8"	7/16"	1/2"	9/16"	9/16"
Vang	1/4"	1/4"	5/16"	3/8"	7/16"	1/2"	9/16"	9/16"
Control Lines	3/16"	1/4"	5/16"	3/8"	7/16"	1/2"	9/16"	9/16"

Cleating and Coiling

Cleating. Take a single round turn around the base of the cleat, then engage the horns in a single figure-8. To leave unattended, make the last turn a half hitch for security. A lead-in angle of 10–20° prevents jamming.

The Sea Gasket Coil is ideal for coiling lines not in use, such as dock lines. After coiling the line and wrapping the coil with a couple of turns, reach through the coil and pull a loop from the running end up and over the top of the coil. Pull on the running end to cinch the loop.

The Halyard Coil keeps the long halyard tail off the deck. After cleating, simply coil the halyard, pass a loop from the cleat through the coil, give it a couple of twists and hang the coil from the twisted loop.

Faking Down a long line (such as an anchor rode) is simple to do and prevents tangling as it is paid out.

Flemishing the end of a line makes for a neat appearance and keeps the deck clear.

Short Lines

Long Lines

Dock Lines and Their Uses

DOCK LINE NAMES
1. Bow Line
2. Bow Breast
3. Forward Spring
4. After Bow Spring
5. Forward Quarter Spring
6. After Spring
7. Stern Breast
8. Stern Line or
   After Quarter Spring
9. Outer Stern Line

MOST COMMON
1. Bow Line
3. Forward Spring
6. After Spring
8. Stern Line, or
9. Outer Stern Line

Backing Away From Dock

① Cast off Bow, Stern, and Forward Spring; loop After Spring around cleat and hold.

② Power forward; stern swings out.

③ Back away; retrieve Spring.

Powering Away From Dock Forward

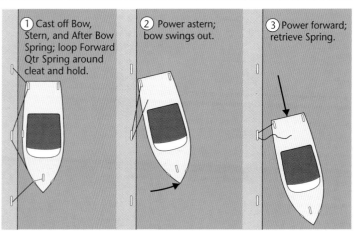

① Cast off Bow, Stern, and After Bow Spring; loop Forward Qtr Spring around cleat and hold.

② Power astern; bow swings out.

③ Power forward; retrieve Spring.

Knots, Splices, and Line Handling

Landing in Tight Quarters

① Approach berth at 45° angle. With bow in, attach After Spring.

② Rudder to starboard; power slowly forward. Stern swings in to dock.

③ Adjust After Spring and secure.

Backing Around Corner of Pier

① Cast off lines; power aft to mid-hull point.

② Place fender and Forward Quarter Spring.

③ Power aft; boat will rotate around corner.

Towing Operations

Towing Alongside

In calm waters and in tight quarters, towing alongside (towing on the hip) gives maximum control to the towing vessel. The bow ① and stern ② lines keep the two vessels pressed together, while the towing strap ③ effects the forward tow, and the backing line ④ allows slowing.

Positioning the tow vessel's rudder and propeller(s) aft of the towed vessel's stern maximizes the maneuverability of the pair.

Towing In Line

In rough waters and for long tows in open waters, towing in line is more satisfactory. A proper tow setup consists of:

① A pair of lines from the strongest points of attachment on the towed vessel, leading forward through the bow chocks. On a sailboat these may be the genoa winches aft or, where keel-stepped, the mast.

② A shackle, connecting lines ① in a bridle.

③ Low-stretch towing line (not 3-strand nylon) adjusted to keep the vessels in step with the waves.

④ A pair of lines attached forward of the towing vessel's rudder and connected in a bridle.

⑤ A bridle from the stern cleats is acceptable, but reduces the maneuverability of the towing vessel.

About Knots

Knotting Terminology

The end of the rope used to tie a knot is its **running end**; the opposite end—usually fixed—is its **bitter end**. The section of rope around which the knot is tied is the **standing part** and a loop in rope is a **bight**.

Knots usually fall into one of three categories:

Bends connect two different ropes, or a rope and an anchor ring.

Hitches fasten the end of a rope to an object such as a piling.

Knots tie ropes to themselves, as in making a loop in one end.

Tying Knots

Square or Reef Knot: good for tying reefing points, but may slip and always jams under high load.

Bowline: single most useful mariner's knot. Never slips, no matter how great the load.

Bowline on a Bight: double the strength of a bowline and can be used as an emergency bosun's chair.

Sheet Bend: for connecting two different size ropes. Simpler, but not as secure as the Carrick Bend, below.

Carrick Bend: best for tying ropes of different sizes and/or types. Used in towing operations. Seizing ends keeps knot open for ease in untying.

Seizing—

Anchor Bend (Fisherman's Bend): except for an eye splice around a thimble, the best way to secure a rode to an anchor. Seizing increases security.

Seizing—

Figure-8: used to keep line ends from escaping blocks. Bulkier and less prone to jam than simple overhand knot.

Knots, Splices, and Line Handling

Round Turn and 2 Half Hitches: allows adjustment of length and tension on a line. A third half hitch increases friction and holding power.

Clove Hitch: for tying docklines to posts or pilings or for hanging fenders from stanchion bases. Easily adjusted and never jams.

Rolling Hitch: grip increases as tension is applied. Used to remove strain from larger line while the line is adjusted.

Becket Hitch or Bend: tied the same way as a Sheet Bend except to a line with an eye. The Double Becket is far more secure than the Single.

Trucker's Hitch: provides mechanical advantage of two when tightening. Best hitch for securing loads.

Whipping

Plain Whipping: simple to produce, but temporary. Start by forming a loop of whipping cord (also called twine or "small stuff") with apex ½" from the end of the rope. Wrap the running end of the cord around the loop 8–10 times, working toward the apex. Pass the cord's running end through the loop, then pull on the bitter end until loop disappears under the turns. Clip the cord ends.

Sailmaker's Whipping: permanent. This version doesn't require use of a sailmaker's needle. Start by unlaying the end of a 3-strand rope about 1 inch and pass a loop of whipping cord around one of the strands, then relay the strands. Whip the rope 8–10 times toward its bitter end with the long end of the cord. Place the original loop back over its strand and pull tight using the cord's short end. Lay the long end back along the strands and tie the cord ends with a reef knot, and clip.

Sewn Whipping: can be used on braided as well as 3-strand rope. Start with two stitches through the rope. Tightly whip the rope 8–10 times toward its bitter end. Keeping the whipping taut, pass the needle through ⅓ (120°) of the rope and pull the cord taut. Now pass the needle through the rope at the other end of the whipping and tighten. Repeat until you have three double stitches spaced at 120° around the whipping. Take one final stitch and clip cord ends.

Splices

3-Strand Splices

Long Splice: doesn't increase rope diameter (for running through blocks) but weaker than the Short Splice.

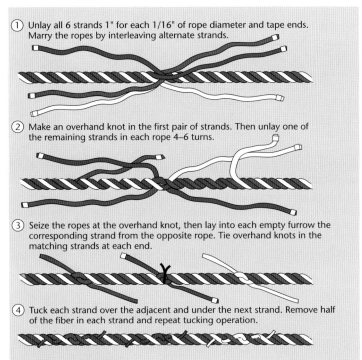

① Unlay all 6 strands 1" for each 1/16" of rope diameter and tape ends. Marry the ropes by interleaving alternate strands.

② Make an overhand knot in the first pair of strands. Then unlay one of the remaining strands in each rope 4–6 turns.

③ Seize the ropes at the overhand knot, then lay into each empty furrow the corresponding strand from the opposite rope. Tie overhand knots in the matching strands at each end.

④ Tuck each strand over the adjacent and under the next strand. Remove half of the fiber in each strand and repeat tucking operation.

Short Splice: retains full strength of the rope, but increases diameter by 40 percent.

① Unlay all 6 strands 1" for each 1/16" of rope diameter and tape ends. Tape ropes to prevent further unlaying, and marry the ropes.

② Remove one of the rope tapes. Cross a strand end over its adjacent and under the next.

③ Continue tucking strand over and under for a total of 4 tucks (6 for nylon).

④ Repeat Steps 2 and 3 for second strand.

⑤ Repeat for third strand against the lay.

⑥ Remove remaining tape and pull on loose strands to snug splice. Repeat Steps 2–5 going in opposite direction.

Eye Splice: most useful splice. Retains 90 percent of rope's strength, compared to 50 percent for most knots.

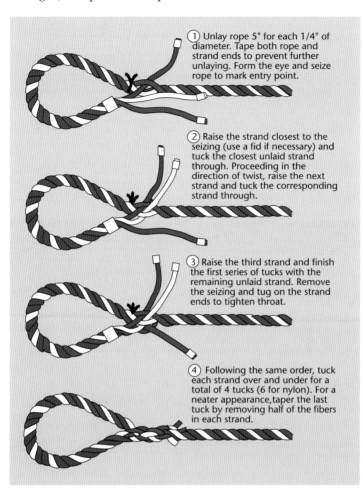

① Unlay rope 5" for each 1/4" of diameter. Tape both rope and strand ends to prevent further unlaying. Form the eye and seize rope to mark entry point.

② Raise the strand closest to the seizing (use a fid if necessary) and tuck the closest unlaid strand through. Proceeding in the direction of twist, raise the next strand and tuck the corresponding strand through.

③ Raise the third strand and finish the first series of tucks with the remaining unlaid strand. Remove the seizing and tug on the strand ends to tighten throat.

④ Following the same order, tuck each strand over and under for a total of 4 tucks (6 for nylon). For a neater appearance, taper the last tuck by removing half of the fibers in each strand.

Back Splice: alternative to whipping rope end; increases rope diameter by 40 percent and provides a handle.

① Unlay rope 5" for each 1/4" diameter. Tape both rope and strand ends to prevent further unlaying. Form a crown knot with the strands as shown.

② Tighten the crown and remove the tape. Moving straight downward, tuck each strand under the 1st strand it encounters.

③ Continue over and under for a total of 4 tucks (6 for nylon). Repeat for the other two strands. Cut ends of strands close to rope.

Knots, Splices, and Line Handling

Double-Braid Eye Splice

An eye splice in double-braid rope is complicated and time-consuming, but the end result is strong, permanent, and attractive. This splice can be made around a thimble for a mooring pendant or anchor rode.

This is a splice which cannot be achieved without a tubular fid—a hollow tube having a pointed end and interior barbs for catching inserted line. The size of the fid must be proportional to the size of the line being spliced:

	Lengths of Tubular Fid Sections		
Rope Diameter in. (mm)	Short Section in. (mm)	Long Section in. (mm)	Full Length in. (mm)
1/4 (6)	2 (51)	3 1/2 (89)	5 1/2 (140)
5/16 (8)	2 1/2 (64)	4 1/4 (108)	6 3/4 (171)
3/8 (9)	3 (76)	4 3/4 (120)	7 3/4 (197)
7/16 (11)	3 1/2 (89)	6 (152)	9 1/2 (241)
1/2 (12)	4 (101)	7 (178)	11 (279)
9/16 (14)	4 1/2 (114)	8 (203)	12 1/4 (311)
5/8 (16)	5 (127)	9 1/2 (241)	14 (356)
3/4 (19)	5 3/4 (146)	11 (279)	16 (406)

STEP 1: Tie a slip knot 8 fid lengths (FL) from end. Mark Point "A" 1 FL from end. Form an eye of the desired size (around a thimble if one is used), and mark Point "B" next to Point "A."

STEP 2: Pry open the cover at "B" and extract a small loop of the core. Mark the core "C." Extract the free end of the core and tape its end. Pinch and tape the end of the cover, as well.

STEP 3: Pull cover back toward slip knot and mark Point "D" 1 short fid length (see table above) from "C." Mark Point "E" 1 short + 1 full fid length beyond "D."

STEP 4: Insert the end of the cover into the fid. Insert the fid at "D" and exit at "E." Continue pulling the cover through until "A" just appears. Remove the fid and the tape.

STEP 5: Now taper the exposed cover. Starting at "A" mark every 7th pic (pair of parallel ribs) running at one angle. Then count off 4 pics from "A," and mark every 7th pic running at the opposing angle. Cut one strand at each mark and remove the cut strand ends. Pull the tapered cover back until the end just disappears.

STEP 6: Insert the free end of the core into the fid. Insert the fid at "A" and exit at "B."

STEP 7: Pull on the core's free end until cover and core eyes match in size.

STEP 8: Insert the core end into the fid again, reinsert the fid at "B," and push it as far as you can into the rope's standing part. Pull the fid and core through the cover and cut off the excess core.

STEP 9: Grip the slip knot and work the cover toward the eye so that "E" and "D" disappear. Continue up to Point "A."

STEP 10: Secure the splice with waxed twine. Take 5 stitches through the throat of the splice, leaving a long tail. Switching the needle to the tail, take another 5 stitches at 90° to the first row of stitches.

STEP 11: Tie the ends of the twine in a reef knot, and trim the ends.

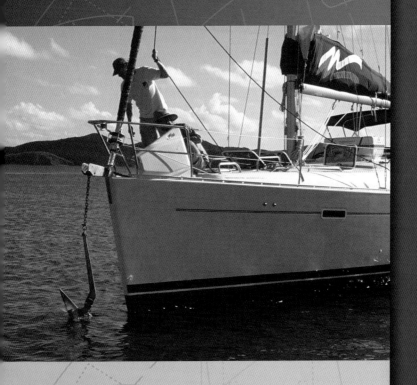

CHAPTER 8

Peter Nielsen

Anchoring

Which Anchor?

Anchors come in great variety. The anchor you might use for a short, sheltered stop is not necessarily the one to use for anchoring overnight. Coastal cruising sailors and powerboaters should carry two anchors of different designs—a primary anchor that you trust to hold your boat in a boisterous anchorage, and a secondary to deploy as a backup when the primary won't do the job alone. Many boats carry a third, lighter anchor to use as a fair-weather "lunch hook" and for other occasional duties. Here's a quick rundown of types:

Plow Anchor and Scoop Anchor

CQR

Holds best in: Firm sand, thick mud, rock, coral, weed
Not so good in: Silt, sloppy mud, gravel
Stowability: Usually stows well on a bow roller; hard to stow belowdecks
Comments: Excellent all-around anchor; the most common primary anchor on sailboats with bow rollers. Designed to bury deeply and provide high holding power in firm substrates. Tends to reset itself quickly when broken out or after a change in the direction of pull. Awkward to stow except on a bow roller, so not often found on small cruising sailboats or powerboats. Most will orient themselves point down when hauled up on a bow roller, making them self-stowing as well as self-launching. Scoop anchors differ from plows in their concave upper blade surface, which enhances their holding power. Popular examples are:

CQR. Hinged-shank plow. One of the oldest anchors still in general use. Immensely popular. Beware poorly made copies. Best if heavier for a given size of boat than most other plows.

Delta. Fixed-shank plow. Valued by sailors and powerboaters for rapid setting, good holding power, and reasonable cost. Awkward to stow and won't fit some bow rollers.

HydroBubble. This plow has a plastic float to ensure that the blade meets the bottom at the desired angle. Sets quickly, holds well, and breaks down for storage, but creates an awkward fit on many bow rollers.

Spade. This scoop anchor has gained wide acceptance among cruising sailors in recent years. Concave blade and weighted tip provide excellent penetrating and holding power in most bottoms. Can be dismantled for storage.

Rocna and **Manson Supreme.** These new scoops have a roll bar rather than a weighted tip to orient the blade's sharp point into the seabed. Set quickly. Expensive and awkward to stow (except in a bow roller).

Claw Anchor

Bruce

Holds best in: Rock, weed, coral, sand
Not so good in: Soft mud, soft sand
Stowability: Awkward to stow except on bow roller
Comments: Like a plow, a good all-around choice as primary or secondary anchor on any boat over 30 to 35 feet. For best substrate penetration, heavier is better. Popular examples are:

Bruce. Rivals the CQR among sailors' longtime favorites. Beware poorly made copies.

Pivoting-Fluke Anchor

Danforth

Holds best in: Sand, soft mud
Not so good in: Rock, grass, clay, weed
Stowability: Light and easy to stow on deck or in a locker
Comments: Features a pair of blades set at right angles to the shank and hinged to penetrate the bottom whichever way the anchor lands. Unexcelled holding-to-weight ratio once dug in, but can be slow to dig in or to reset after tripping. Sometimes prone to trapping lumps of weed or rocks between blade and shank, rendering it useless. Typically the primary anchor on a boat of less than 30 feet without bow-roller stowage. Ideal on larger boats for stern anchor, lunch hook, or kedging when aground. Can also serve as storm anchor, tandem anchor, or in other uses of a secondary anchor. Every boat should carry one. Popular examples include the West Marine Perfomance, plus:

Danforth. Like the CQR and Bruce, has spawned countless imitators. Provides excellent straight-line holding power. Often superior to plows in mud and sand.

Fortress. Lightweight aluminum. Consistently scores very highly for holding power in anchor tests. Breaks down for convenient storage.

Other Designs

fisherman

The **fisherman** anchor is excellent for taking a quick hold in rocks and for penetrating thick weed but needs to be much heavier than an equivalent plow or Danforth. It is awkward to handle, needs to be dismantled for stowage, and can be broken out too easily if a bight of the rode wraps around the fluke or stock. Four-pronged **grapnel** anchors are good in rocky bottoms but are too inherently weak to be used as a main anchor.

If you're going to be anchoring a lot, it's a good idea to carry two anchors of different designs. Shown here (clockwise from top left): Delta, Spade, HydroBubble, Fortress (assembled and disassembled).

Delta

Spade

HydroBubble

Fortress (disassembled)

Fortress

Anchoring

What Size Anchor?

The loads on a boat and its *ground tackle* (the combination of anchor, rope, and chain) are ever-changing and dynamic. Wind and current make a boat sheer about at the end of its anchor rode. Waves make a boat's bow pitch up and down, jerking at the ground tackle. It is the ability of an anchor to withstand such jerking and snatching from varying directions, and to rebury swiftly should it be plucked from the bottom, that is critical.

According to anchor manufacturers' recommendations, the primary or secondary anchor for a 34-foot cruising sailboat could be a 22-pound Delta, a 35-pound CQR, a 33-pound steel Spade, a 15-pound aluminum Spade, a 10-pound Fortress, an 8.5-pound Danforth, or a 16-pound Bruce. Holding power is determined not by weight but by design and the surface area of the blade or flukes. For instance, Spade claims identical holding power for its steel and aluminum anchors, which have identical dimensions apart from weight. Weight, however, is certainly a factor in getting an anchor to dig in and set on a hard bottom, and unless an anchor digs in and sets quickly, its holding power is immaterial.

For decades, the anchoring maxim was "1 pound of anchor for every foot of boat." You could do worse than to follow that maxim today, at least for a plow or claw anchor.

Recommended Minimum Primary and Secondary Anchor Sizes for Sail or Power (pounds)

BOAT LENGTH (FT.)	DELTA	CQR	SPADE (STEEL/ ALUM.)	WEST MARINE PERFORMANCE	FORTRESS (ALUM.)	DANFORTH DEEPSET	BRUCE (CLAW)
20–25	14	25	22/10	6	4	5	11
25–30	22	25	33/15	14	7	8.5	11
30–35	22	35	33/15	14	10	8.5	16
35–40	35	35	44/20	25	15	13	22
40–45	44	45	44/20	40	15	20	33

Stern or **kedge** anchors are the exceptions to the pound-per-foot guidelines for anchor weight. You may have to row these out in a dinghy or carry them out by hand, so you want no more weight than necessary. A pivoting-fluke anchor on an all-nylon rode makes an ideal kedge.

A plow anchor (in this case a Rocna) setting itself in firm sand during beach testing.

Ground Tackle

The other elements of your ground tackle include the rode and connectors. The rode will be rope, chain, or a combination of the two.

Rope. There is only one rope material suitable for an anchor rode—nylon. No other fiber offers such a combination of strength and shock absorption. Traditionally, three-strand nylon has been the rope of choice, but the 8- to 12-strand single-braid nylon (also known as multiplait nylon) now marketed under such brand names as Mega Braid and Brait is an even better alternative, able to absorb more shock energy before failure and less prone to kinking and binding in chain pipes.

BENEFITS OF ROPE

- Elasticity lessens shock loads that can jerk an anchor out of the seabed
- Light and easy to stow
- Inexpensive and easy to replace

DRAWBACKS OF ROPE

- Need to guard against chafe
- Requires greater scope than chain
- Allows boat to sail around its anchor

Chain. For anchor rodes, most boaters use one of four kinds of open-link galvanized chain. *Proof coil* is made from low-grade carbon steel and is the most economical chain for anchor rodes. *BBB* has shorter links and is better than proof coil for windlasses. *High-test* or G40 has a higher strength-to-weight ratio and is made from high-tensile carbon steel. *Alloy chain* is made from steel alloy and is even stronger (and more expensive) than high-test.

BENEFITS OF CHAIN

- Cannot chafe through
- Great strength
- Extra weight on seabed absorbs shock loads and reduces need for long scope
- Boat does not sail around so much on anchor

DRAWBACKS OF CHAIN

- Extra weight can be hard to handle without a windlass and can affect boat trim
- Expensive
- Doesn't absorb shock loads in extreme conditions

By way of example, let's compare nylon and chain rodes for a 32- to 36-foot boat (see the table on page 132):

TYPE AND SIZE OF RODE	AVERAGE BREAKING STRENGTH (lbs.)	HORIZONTAL ENERGY ABSORPTION (ft.-lbs. per 100 ft.)	WEIGHT (lbs. per 100 ft.)
5/16" BBB chain	7,600	0	115
1/2" 3-strand nylon	5,750	67,665	6
1/2" nylon Brait	6,300	114,452	6

Rope or Chain—What's Best for You?

You often see offshore cruising sailboats and trawler yachts anchored on all-chain rodes, but most powerboaters and coastal cruisers use a combination of chain at the anchor end and nylon at the boat end. The chain augments the anchor weight and keeps the pull on the anchor as horizontal as possible. A commonly accepted ratio is 6 inches of chain for each foot of boat length, but a foot of chain for each foot of boat length is better, and a 50- or 60-foot chain allows a much shorter scope to be used than if the boat were anchored with mainly rope rode. Boaters in generally shallow waters (like the U.S. East Coast) can usually get away with using less chain (and even less rope) than those plying deeper waters (e.g., the West Coast or Great Lakes).

Recommended Rode Sizes

BOAT LOA (FT.)	NYLON RODE DIAMETER	CHAIN DIAMETER BY TYPE	WEIGHT (lbs. per 100 ft.) (ALL-NYLON/ALL-CHAIN/ ALL-HT CHAIN)
Up to 25	3/8"/9mm	3/16" Proof Coil	3.5/50
27 to 31	7/16"/11mm	1/4" Proof Coil/BBB	5/76–81
32 to 36	1/2"/12mm	5/16" Proof Coil/BBB, 1/4"/HT	6.5/115–120/70
37 to 44	9/16"/14mm	3/8" Proof Coil/BBB, 5/16"HT	8.2/166–173/106
45 to 50	5/8"/16mm	3/8" Proof Coil/BBB/HT	10.5/166–173/154
51 to 62	3/4"/18mm	3/8" Proof Coil/BBB/HT	14.5/166–173/154

Connectors

Connect your chain to the anchor with a strong shackle (the working load should be stamped on it), preferably galvanized—stainless steel shackles are often weaker than galvanized ones. Making the shackle one size larger than the chain (e.g., 5/16" shackle for 1/4" chain) is a good precaution. Wire the shackle pin so that it can't unscrew itself ①. Do not use a carabiner-type quick link unless you have a small boat that doesn't put much load on its anchor. A stainless steel swivel between chain and anchor is a potential weak link, so if you feel you must use one (in an area of reversing currents, for example), make it top-quality. Always fit a shackle between swivel and anchor to ensure that it articulates properly.

Lengths of chain can be connected with a joining link, but a single length is stronger. There are two equally strong ways to

connect rope to chain: with a rope-to-chain splice ② or with an eye splice (around a thimble) and strong galvanized shackle ③. The former approach is mandatory if you have a windlass.

Anchoring

Choosing
an Anchorage

If you will only be anchored for a couple of hours in settled weather, your biggest worries will be making sure you have enough water underneath you and that the anchor has dug in. But for a longer stay:

- Consult your chart to find out how much depth there is around the anchorage, and the makeup of the bottom. (**S** = sand; **M** = mud; **Cy** or **Cl** = clay; **Si** = silt; **St** = stones; **G** = gravel; **P** = pebbles; **Cb** = cobbles; **Sh** = shell; **Co** = coral; **S/M** = sand over mud; **Wd** = weed.) Avoid unmarked rocks or shoals and obstructions on the bottom that could foul your anchor.
- Check the weather forecast—will the anchorage provide shelter from the forecast wind direction?
- Look at how other boats are oriented. If their bows are not all pointing into the wind there is likely some current running, and this will influence your choice of where to anchor.
- Choose a spot that will have enough depth at low water—at least 6 feet under the keel. The less depth you anchor in, the smaller your swinging circle will be. If you know the local times and heights of low water and high water, you can estimate the height of tide when you anchor using the Rule of Twelfths. The rule assumes, given a 6-hour tidal range, that the tide rises or falls by one-twelfth of its overall range in the first hour, two-twelfths in the second, and so on, in this pattern: 1, 2, 3, 3, 2, 1.
- If possible, anchor on a flat bottom.
- Try to anchor where the effects of swell or wind are minimized.
- Make sure your boat can swing to its anchor without fouling other anchored boats, hitting obstructions, or grounding.
- Take compass bearings of safe routes out of the anchorage in case you have to leave at night.

These boats have taken clearing bearings on dangers at the entrance.

You need to know how much depth you'll have under your keel at low water. The depths marked on your chart and the heights of tide predicted in tide tables both relate to chart datum. If the height of tide at low water is predicted to be +1.0 foot, you can add 1 foot to the charted low-water depth. Allow for the range of tide when determining how much scope you need.

RANGE

MAXIMUM DEPTH H.W.

MAXIMUM DEPTH L.W.

Chart Datum

Anchoring Among Neighbors

Make a circuit of the anchorage to choose a good spot and check out depths and hidden dangers. Now take a close look at your neighbors. Different boats lie differently to their anchors. If possible, anchor next to boats that are similar to yours, and check whether they are anchored with chain or rope.

Observe the unwritten code of conduct. The first boat to arrive gets its choice of prime spots. The last to arrive is the first to move when boats swing too close. Also, don't drop your anchor over someone else's, don't anchor too close abeam of another boat, and respect your neighbors—don't play loud music or make unnecessary noise.

① A long-keeled, heavy-displacement sailboat will tend to lie quietly in most conditions, especially if anchored with all-chain rode.

② A sailboat with fin keel and spade rudder will tend to range from side to side at anchor.

③ A powerboat with little of its hull underwater will typically sail about all over the place when wind and tide are opposing each other, especially if it is on a rope rode.

④ Synchronized swinging circles, when all boats move together to the changing wind or tide, make for a peaceful anchorage.

Unfortunately, while boats will lie predictably when wind and current are in the same direction ⑤, they will be all over the place when the wind and current oppose each other ⑥.

In a river, try to anchor where the prevailing wind blows across the river ⑦. Otherwise you will spend much of your time in an undesirable wind-against-tide situation ⑧.

Anchoring Under Power

The procedure for setting an anchor under power is so simple that it is amazing so many people get it wrong so often. The same rules apply to power- or sailboats.

- Head into the wind or current, whichever is stronger.
- Bring the boat to a dead stop.
- As the boat begins to gather sternway, ease the anchor to the bottom either hand over hand or with the windlass. Do not just let the rode run out uncontrolled ①.
- Apply a touch of throttle in reverse to get the boat moving astern. If it is windy, this won't be necessary.
- Pay out the rode as the boat drifts back, keeping a slight tension on it so it forms a line across the seabed. The boat will probably lie broadside to the wind ②.
- When you have paid out about half your intended scope, snub the rode until you feel resistance from the anchor, then resume easing it out ③.
- Keeping tension on the rode, pay out another quarter of the scope, then snub again momentarily.
- With the boat still moving astern, secure the anchor rode when the desired scope has been paid out. The boat's weight should dig the anchor in solidly; the anchor rode will rise out of the water in a straight line ④.
- To make doubly sure the anchor is well dug in, back down with the engine at half throttle for 30 seconds. The boat should move forward on the rode when you ease the throttle.
- If you don't get your anchor to set the first time, try again. If it still won't set, try another spot.

Common mistakes: letting chain pile up on top of the anchor; letting the anchor go while the boat is still moving forward; going astern so quickly that the anchor does not have a chance to dig in; anchoring too close to other boats.

Most common mistake of all: failing to let out enough scope (see page 136).

Anchoring

Anchoring Under Sail

Upwind: Roll up the headsail as you approach the chosen spot on a close or beam reach. Steer into the wind and let the mainsail luff until the boat stops. Drop the anchor as the boat begins to make sternway, and pay out the desired scope as on page 135. You can lower the mainsail as the boat falls back.

Downwind: Drop the main and play the jibsheet to spill wind and slow the boat as you approach the chosen spot. Roll up the jib completely as the anchor is let go. If you have a rope rode, be careful not to overrun it and get it tangled with your keel or rudder. As you snub the rode, put the helm over so that the boat swings around. The weight of the boat coming onto the rode should dig in the anchor.

Scope

Scope is the ratio of rode length to water depth plus freeboard (i.e., the height of the bow above the water added to the depth of water). If you anchor at low tide, add the expected rise of tide.

4 x water depth all chain

6 x water depth long chain/rope

10 x water depth short chain/long rope

For instance: 5' height of bow + 15' depth + 6' rise of tide = 26'. At the recommended 4:1 scope (all chain) you would let out 104' of rode; at 6:1 (chain/rope), 156'; and at 10:1 (all rope) a whopping 260'.

Adapt these rules of thumb to prevailing circumstances. In a crowded anchorage in settled conditions, you should get by with 3:1 scope on an all-chain rode or 4:1 or 5:1 on a rope/chain combo. Conversely, as the wind and seas increase, let out more rode to increase your scope.

Catenary—the sag in a chain rode caused by the weight of the chain—helps dampen loadings on the anchor and keep a horizontal pull on it.

CATENARY

60 feet

20 feet

Dragging Anchor

Sometimes the anchor won't set even after several attempts. You can either try a different anchor or move to a different spot. Even after you think the hook is set, it may drag when the wind increases or the tide changes and the anchor fails to reset.

How to Tell When You're Dragging

Immediately after anchoring, line up a couple of landmarks or seamarks on either side of the boat. Two objects in line with each other comprise a range; as long as the two objects stay aligned, one behind the other, you can be sure you are not dragging.

The pier and church steeple make a range to starboard. The rock and lighthouse make a range to port.

You are probably dragging if:

- The two objects in a range are no longer aligned
- Anchored boats appear to be overtaking you
- The rode rises up out of the water and then goes slack again
- The boat sheers to one side and does not swing back again
- The boat lies side-to the wind
- You can feel the rode vibrating beneath your hand or bare foot

What to Do When You're Dragging

The first thing to try, if you are dragging into shallow water but are far enough from shore for safety, is to let out more rode (inadequate scope is the #1 reason anchors drag). Often this is all that's required. If you are among other boats, dragging into deep water, or too close to shore, get the anchor up immediately. If your anchor has pivoting flukes, make sure they have not been jammed by a pebble or starfish, and take special care when you try again to make the anchor dig in properly. If you still drag, your anchor may not like the bottom, so it is best to move to another part of the anchorage. On a windy night in an exposed anchorage, the crew may have to take turns keeping "anchor watch." Be careful when you're raising anchor with other boats close abeam. If it's windy the bow of your boat will fall off quickly when the load comes off the anchor, and you will have to use a lot of throttle to keep control.

Anchoring

Anchoring
Tips and Tricks

Weight on rode. An excellent way to reduce your swinging circle in a constricted anchorage is to lower a weight down the rode ①. This can be a dedicated metal weight weighing a minimum of 20 pounds, shackled to the anchor rode, or you can use your kedge anchor. Rode weights also improve holding in strong winds.

Riding sail. A riding sail, attached to the backstay and sheeted in tight, acts as a weather vane to keep the boat facing into the wind ②. It greatly decreases a boat's tendency to sail around its anchor. They are commercially available or you can make your own.

Anchor trip line. When anchoring over rocks or obstructions, you can attach a trip line to the crown of the anchor. If the flukes get stuck, the trip line should release them. The other end of the line goes to a small float ③ that should be clearly marked so that other boats don't mistake it for a mooring buoy. In a crowded anchorage, it makes sense to bring the trip line back on board your boat so that it doesn't foul other boats ④.

Multihull anchoring. Catamarans and trimarans tend to sail around their anchors more than monohulls. This tendency can be minimized by rigging an anchor bridle ⑤.

Anchoring from the stern. In calm, settled conditions, it is possible to anchor from the stern in order to get the breeze flowing through the cockpit and into the cabin. The best way to do this is to lead the main anchor rode back to the stern and cleat it there ⑥. When it is time to leave, or if the wind increases, uncleat the anchor rode so that the boat comes head to wind, then retrieve the anchor ⑦.

Bring anchor cable aft

WIND

Release anchor line so boat comes head to wind

Anchor rollers. On small boats where weight distribution is important, it is often not feasible to keep an anchor on the bow, but if your boat is big enough and coastal cruising figures in your plans, a dedicated bow roller ⑧, ⑨ and anchor locker will be a blessing. Aftermarket anchor rollers are readily available, and fitting them is within the scope of a competent do-it-yourselfer.

Left: Double bow roller.
Below: CQR stowed in bow roller. Danforth stowed in bow-pulpit bracket.

If your boating habits take you into waters where you will often need to set a stern anchor, you will also get good use out of a stern anchor roller ⑩, which can be bolted to the taffrail.

Chafe protection. Nylon rode has many virtues, but resistance to abrasion isn't one of them. A ½"-inch anchor rode can chafe through in a matter of hours when the bow is pitching up and down in a rough anchorage. A length of fire hose (discards from the local fire station or commercial equivalent) is an excellent chafe preventer. Second best is a length of flexible vinyl water hose (used in plumbing). The only practical way to get these onto a nylon anchor rode is to split them lengthwise, and this means they'll work loose more easily. The best solution is to slide the fire hose or water hose over a snubbing line, which is then rolling-hitched to the anchor rode.

Marking your rode. How do you know how much rode you've got out unless you mark it? Commercially made rode markers are available from West Marine, or you can make your own. Plastic cable ties work well on either chain or nylon. They don't interfere with windlass operation and are available in different colors so you can come up with your own code. Leave the tails long; they can cut your fingers if trimmed too short, and they'll be easier to feel in the dark. Webbing markers are another alternative. There's no need to mark the rode more than every 25 or 30 feet.

Anchoring

A spring line on the anchor.
Some anchorages are inherently rolly. Often the boat will ride more comfortably if you fasten a line from the stern quarter to the anchor rode with a shackle or rolling hitch, then ease the rode until the boat presents its bow to the swell rather than the wind ①.

DIRECTION OF SWELL

WIND

SPRING ON ANCHOR

Anchor snubber. If anchoring with all-chain rode, you should rig a nylon snubber line (sized like a nylon rode) from a sturdy deck cleat to the chain ②. Not only will this absorb the shock loads the chain would otherwise transmit to windlass or anchor cleat, it prevents the rumblings of the chain dragging across the bottom as the boat swings from being transmitted to the hull. The snubber should be about 30 feet long so that you can lengthen it as the wind increases. It can be fastened to the chain with a rolling hitch or with a chain claw.

Taking a line ashore. It is often possible to anchor in narrow coves with little swinging room by taking lines ashore ③. The boat should always face open water in case you have to leave in a hurry. Drop the anchor, back into the desired spot, then take lines ashore with a dinghy. This is a good technique to use where the bottom drops away steeply from the shore.

Keeping your rode in order. If you don't have a dedicated chain locker, the best way to keep your anchor rode ready to run is by faking it into a bucket ④. This will ensure that it will pay out without tangling or kinking. Tie the bitter end of the rode to the handle of the bucket, leaving enough free so that it can be cleated off before you drop the anchor.

Setting two anchors. Sometimes it is a good idea to set two anchors. For example, you might want to limit your swinging circle so as to anchor closer to shore; you might be anchoring in a river or narrow cut where the current reverses; or you might want extra security because strong winds are forecast.

The most common way of doing this is to drop your main anchor first ⑤, then fall back until you have paid out

⑤ ⑥

double the desired scope. Release the stern anchor, then pull the boat forward on its bow anchor rode until the scopes are equalized ⑥. Remember that the heavier anchor is always set in the direction of the strongest current, which flows from upchannel if anchoring in a river. When it's time to leave, weigh the downstream anchor first; if the bow is facing downstream, take the stern anchor rode forward outside the lifelines and cleat it off at the bow. Then let the boat swing head to current before dropping back to retrieve the anchor.

The fore-and-aft moor works well most of the time in confined waters. When the wind is blowing from abeam, however, it puts a huge strain on the anchors and may well break out one of them. At such times you can set bow and stern anchors as above, then carry the stern anchor rode forward and secure it at the bow. This configuration is known as a **Bahamian moor**. The stern anchor rode may foul the keel when the boat swings unless you weight it or secure it to the main rode well below keel depth ⑦.

If you are in an exposed anchorage and a change in wind direction is forecast, you can lay out a second anchor from the bow in the direction of the anticipated wind shift ⑧. This is best done with the dinghy. When the wind shift arrives, equalize the two rodes so that they share the strain.

Sometimes you might want to set two anchors from the bow to reduce your swinging circle. An angle of up to 120 degrees between them is fine in

Chain/rope connecting anchors equal to maximum depth

light to moderate winds ⑨, but in strong winds the angle should not exceed 45 degrees, and 30 degrees is better ⑩.

Finally, some long-distance sailors recommend setting **tandem anchors** in strong winds. The technique involves shackling a lighter anchor to the crown of the main anchor. Unless you do this with a length of chain at least equal to the depth at high water, you will find it very awkward to retrieve the second anchor. You need to get the main anchor on deck or in its roller before lifting the second one.

CHAPTER 9

Onboard Weather Forecasting

Bob Sweet

Be Your Own Forecaster

Meteorologists monitor large-scale weather systems and, using computer models, are able to predict with fair regional accuracy what lies ahead for those in a system's path. Before heading out on the water, you should by all means obtain a local forecast, and update it on board if you can. This is your earliest indicator of what may be heading your way. Pages 152 and 153 list some sources of weather forecasts.

But these regional forecasts don't always match the conditions you encounter on the water. For one thing, the precise path of a low-pressure center will significantly impact what happens where you are. For another, a regional forecast cannot account for variations across the region of coverage. On land it rarely matters whether the actual local wind strength is 15 or 25 knots, but on the water it certainly does. Then too, a topographically enhanced sea breeze or a locally generated thunderstorm cannot be covered adequately in a regional forecast. And forecasts prepared for offshore waters—where there are few monitoring stations—may be several hours out of date by the time they reach you.

You'll be better prepared for what's coming if you use your own observations to modify and refine official forecasts. This chapter, which focuses on the temperate regions where most boats operate—between 30 and 60 degrees north and south latitudes—will provide the background you need.

Over the centuries, mariners have developed weather proverbs for interpreting their observations. We'll find out why these four, in particular, have proved reliable:

Red skies at night, sailor's delight; red skies in the morning, sailors take warning . . . (see page 146).

A wind from the west means weather's fair; a wind from the east, foul weather's near . . . (see page 146).

Mackerel sky, 12 hours dry . . . (see page 151).
The higher the clouds, the better the weather . . . (see page 150).

Highs and Lows (Depressions)

Weather maps show the locations of high- and low-pressure centers, around which are lines of equal atmospheric pressure called *isobars*. (The maps also show fronts. See page 146.) Winds blow from high-pressure centers toward lows, but the Earth's rotation deflects the winds so that they tend to follow the isobars at higher altitudes. Due to friction with the Earth's surface, however, ground-level winds over land cross the isobars at about a 30-degree angle toward the low. Over water, where there is less friction, surface winds blow at a lesser angle to the isobars—about 15 degrees toward the low.

In the Northern Hemisphere, winds are deflected to the right by the Earth's rotation and thus spiral outward from highs in a clockwise direction and inward toward lows in a counterclockwise direction. The opposite is true in the Southern Hemisphere, where winds are deflected to the left. Highs can be likened to hills, lows to hollows, and isobars to the contour lines on a topographic map. When the isobars are closer, the slope is steeper and the resultant winds are stronger.

Generally, isobars are more closely spaced around a low than a high, which means the winds will be stronger in a low. Highs are typically broad, ranging up to a thousand miles or more across, while lows tend to be more compact, perhaps 400 or fewer miles across. Within a high, air from the atmosphere is sinking and therefore stable; the air in a low is rising and therefore unstable. Simply stated, bad weather is associated with lows, or depressions, and fair weather with highs.

	HIGH	LOW
Weather	Generally fair	Stormy, precipitation
Temperature	Stable – long periods	Cool to warm changing to colder
Motion (avg) [~West to East]	Winter: 565 nm/day Summer: 390 nm/day	Winter: 600 nm/day Summer: 430 nm/day
Winds	Moderate, rising near edge	Strong and changeable with possible high seas
Pressure [Typical]	Rapid rise on approach, slow decline on retreat	Rapid fall on approach, slow rise on retreat
Clouds	Sparse, mostly near periphery	Wide variety, all altitudes

Passage of a Low

Since bad weather is usually associated with lows, knowing where the center of a low lies relative to your location can tell you a great deal about what to expect. Weather systems move generally west to east, steered along a boundary of major air masses by the planet's high-altitude jet streams—so if a low is to your west, you are likely to experience deteriorating weather as the low approaches. If the low is to your east, the weather is likely to improve as the low moves away. Since clear air refracts sunlight into the red spectrum, this is the reason the red skies proverb proves correct 70% of the time: red skies to the east at sunrise mark retreating clear weather, while red skies to the west at sunset herald its approach. Jet stream locations and the average speed of advance of a low (see page 145 table) vary by season.

To find the direction to a nearby low in the Northern Hemisphere, face the wind and extend your arm to your right. According to Buys Ballot's law, the low pressure will be slightly behind your outstretched arm—15 degrees behind over water, up to 30 degrees over land. In the Southern Hemisphere, use your left arm instead.

Detecting the center of a low in the Northern Hemisphere.

Frontal Weather Systems

The lows that drive our middle-latitude weather form along the boundaries between two adjacent air masses—for example, between the cold, dry air mass that persists over Canada and the warm, moist air mass that recurs over the southern U.S. A low is born when a kink forms along this boundary and begins a counterclockwise rotation (Northern Hemisphere). East of the kink, southerly warm air starts to override colder air to the north and east, while to the west, northerly cold air pushes south and east, displacing the warmer air ahead of it. The resultant frontal boundaries (called *fronts*) separating regions of cool or colder air from warm assume the shape of an inverted V with the low at its apex, as in the page 147 graphic.

The newly formed system migrates eastward, steered by the overhead jet stream that follows and defines the air mass boundary, until the low dissipates several days later. The isobars surrounding the low show distinct bends along fronts, marking abrupt shifts in wind direction there.

A front is named for the relative temperature of the advancing air behind it. A warm front (red line on weather maps) denotes warm air overriding cooler air ahead, while a cold front (blue line) marks cold air overtaking warmer air ahead.

The weather sequence you experience with the passage of a low depends in large measure on whether the low passes to your north or south.

Advancing Weather System

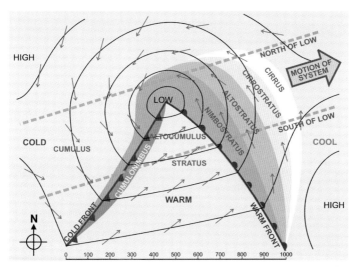

When a low passes poleward of you (i.e., to your north in the Northern Hemisphere), both fronts are likely to pass overhead as shown here by the lower dashed green line. In this illustration the black lines are isobars. The lowest pressure is within the small circle around the low, and each isobar moving outward from the center represents another 4-millibar (mb)[1] increase in pressure. As the system moves overhead, you can visualize the corresponding change in pressure by observing the isobars that pass by. The blue arrows indicate wind direction at each location, with the wind shifts clearly visible. The characteristic progressions of cloud types heralding the approach of each type of front are also labeled. A vertical cross-section along the dashed green line is shown on pages 148 and 149 for the warm front and cold front, respectively.

If the low is moving to your south (as in the upper dashed green line), you may have a period of rain without distinct fronts, as shown at the bottoms of pages 148 and 149.

Because cold fronts move faster than warm fronts, the cold front associated with a mature low (one that is several days old) will overtake the warm front, lifting the warmer air off the ground and forming an *occluded front* (purple line on weather maps) of moderating weather characteristics. The occluded front will usually dissipate within a day or so, and the low itself may dissipate soon thereafter, having traveled several thousand miles since its formation.

The red half circles along a warm front depiction and blue triangles on a cold front point toward the front's direction of advance. Occasionally two fronts meet and oppose each other, forming a *stationary front* that is depicted by alternating segments of cold- and warm-front symbols.

[1]Standard atmospheric pressure at sea level equals 1013 mb, or 29.92 inches of mercury. The actual sea level pressure varies between 925 and 1060 mb (27 to 31 inches).

Advancing Warm Front

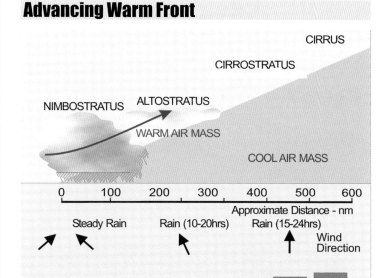

In a warm front, the overtaking warm air rises gradually up and over the cold air, forming a long wedge or incline. When a Northern Hemisphere low is passing north of you, you will see high cirrus clouds (see page 150) up to 24 hours or 600 miles ahead of the warm front, followed by cirrostratus, and the barometer will begin to fall. Up to half a day later, the winds will *back* (change in a counterclockwise direction) from south to southeast, and altostratus clouds will begin to move in under the cirrostratus. As the ground-level warm front continues its approach, the clouds will get steadily lower and thicker while the barometer continues a steady fall. Precipitation will begin up to 200 miles or more ahead of the front. As the front passes, the temperature will rise and the winds will *veer* (clockwise change in direction) from southeast to southwest. Within the warm sector, the wind direction will be fairly steady from the southwest (Northern Hemisphere) while the barometer will be somewhat steady. The skies may clear and the temperature will remain mild. Follow along the lower green line on page 147 to see the progression of isobars and winds.

North of the Low

If you are poleward of an approaching low (upper green line in the page 147 graphic), you will not experience a warm or cold front. Instead, there will be an indistinct transition between the cool air ahead of the low and the colder air behind it, with nimbostratus clouds and steady rain likely. The approaching low will cause changes like those of an approaching warm front, except that the winds will back from east to northeast as the low passes to the south, and there will be no warm sector. Barometric pressures will fall gradually with the approach, then rise as the low moves off, while the winds gradually back into the northwest. The infamous *nor'easters* of the northeast U.S. result when a low stalls near the coast. The northeast winds north of the low dump moisture picked up from the sea.

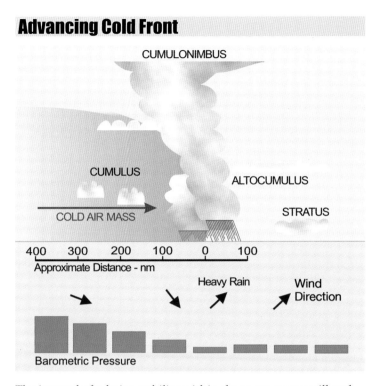

Advancing Cold Front

The interval of relative stability within the warm sector will end with the approach of the cold front. Unlike the slow transition of a warm front, the cold air behind a cold front is shouldering the overtaken warmer air abruptly aloft. This rising warm air cools and can no longer hold all its moisture, becoming highly unstable. Dangerous squall lines can develop 100 miles or more (i.e., several hours) in advance of the front. High storm clouds will pile up, leading to gusty winds, squalls, and possible thunderstorms as the front approaches. The barometer may fall immediately ahead of the cold front, perhaps rapidly—caused by the narrow band of rising air. The period of rain will be brief but could be severe. As the cold front passes, the winds will veer from southwest to northwest with gusts, and the temperature will drop. Cumulonimbus clouds will give way to nimbostratus, followed by clearing. Pressures will rise quickly. Clear, cool, dry weather is the norm, but those gusty northwest winds can continue. An assortment of clear-weather cumulus clouds may be seen.

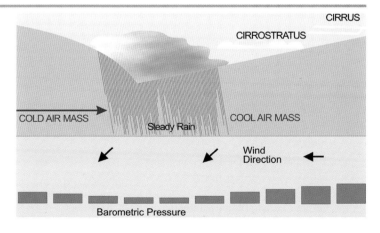

Onboard Weather Forecasting

Cloud Formation

Clouds form when water vapor condenses in cooling air. Since temperatures fall fairly steadily with altitude, rising warm air will cool, and some of its water vapor will condense into water droplets, forming a cloud when it reaches its dew point (see page 157). If the air continues to rise, the clouds will develop vertically (a shape called *cumuloform*). If the air stops rising, the clouds will flatten into a *stratiform* shape. How high and how fast the warm air rises depends upon what is pushing it aloft, and thus cloud shapes are a direct indicator of atmospheric stability. The more vertically developed the clouds, the more unstable the atmosphere.

Cloud Types

Clouds are categorized by altitude: high, middle, or low.

High Clouds (Cirro): Above 20,000 feet consist of ice crystals

Medium Clouds (Alto): 6,500 to 20,000 feet consist of water droplets

Low Clouds: Below 6,500 feet consist of water droplets

Name Clues: Cumulo—bumpy (unstable); Stratus—flat (stable); Nimbo—rain

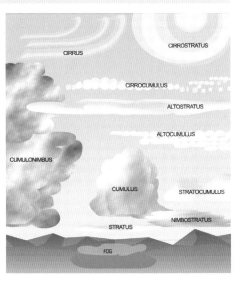

High Clouds

Above 20,000 feet, the water droplets become ice crystals. This makes high clouds wispy and insubstantial. The sun or moon viewed through these clouds will have a halo around it but will not be obscured. High clouds, called *cirro*, come in three varieties, depending on their shapes.

Cirrus clouds, sometimes called "mares' tails," are thin and wispy and often precede a warm front. They usually indicate immediate fair weather, but the approaching front will bring change within 24 hours.

Cirrostratus are flat, like a mild veil across the sky, and suggest that the coming warm front is 12 to 24 hours away.

Cirrocumulus, often called a mackerel sky, are thin and bumpy. These clouds are lower than cirrostratus. They are usually seen in winter and indicate fair but cold weather.

Middle Clouds

Clouds found between 6,500 and 20,000 feet are called *alto*. They are likely to be thicker than the high clouds, are often associated with light rain, and come in two varieties.

Altostratus, at the upper altitudes for middle clouds, are flat and blue-gray in color. When they thicken, long-lasting precipitation often follows.

Altocumulus are fluffy and bumpy. They often appear late in the day and produce brilliant red sunsets. When observed on a warm, humid morning, look for late afternoon thunderstorms.

Vertical Clouds

Some clouds develop vertically to such a degree that they transcend the low, middle, and high categories. Such clouds usually form from convectively rising, extremely warm, moist air or from warm air forced aloft by a cold front.

Cumulonimbus are often associated with thunderstorms and squalls. These clouds can extend from low altitudes to the upper edge of the troposphere at 45,000 feet. This great vertical development is a sure sign of atmospheric instability.

Onboard Weather Forecasting

Cumulus clouds often have significant vertical development (up to 16,000 feet), but are widely spaced and associated with fair weather. They are often left over from cumulonimbus clouds that have dissipated.

Low Clouds

Clouds at altitudes under 6,500 feet are likely to be even denser than alto clouds and are often associated with steady rain. Low clouds are sometimes called, collectively, *strato*.

Stratocumulus are low, lumpy, gray, and quite thick, and often foretell rain preceding a front.

Nimbostratus, thick and dark gray, usually bring sustained precipitation with winds NE to S.

The lowest of these clouds, stratus, are a uniform gray and bring steady but often light rain and drizzle.

Clouds at ground level are fog.

Where Can I Get Weather Forecasts?

Weather forecasts are available from many sources, both government and commercial. The NOAA National Weather Service (NWS) provides forecasts across the U.S. and much of the globe. These predictions are available on the Internet at www.nws.noaa.gov. Regional NWS offices develop local forecasts and operate weather radars to observe storms. These radars and the local forecasts can also be viewed on the Internet. NWS also operates NOAA Weather Radio, which broadcasts local forecasts, including marine forecasts, on VHF radio frequencies. Marine VHF radios enable you to quickly select one of these frequencies, and this is the principal means of obtaining forecast updates on U.S. waters.

Commercial sources include local and national newspapers and media (TV and radio), which develop their own forecasts from NOAA data. Often, local media and services operate their own radars and meteorological equipment to enhance their forecasts. Several services provide round-the-clock forecasts on

NOAA 24-hour forecasts indicate frontal patterns and pressure centers, as in this map of the U.S.

TV, and more recently via satellite. For example, *The Weather Channel* and *XM Weather* broadcast weather information that can be received via a special receiver and displayed on a computer or chartplotter aboard your boat.

Offshore, the principal source of weather information is HF (shortwave) radio via voice or modem (for data or fax). NOAA's Ocean Prediction Center (OPC) is the mariner's weather lifeline. They provide forecasts for the high seas from 65°N to 15° S (except for the Indian Ocean) via radiofacsimile and shortwave radio broadcasts. The U.S. Coast Guard provides radio forecasts in both voice and text (using special printing or display devices) on HF and MF bands, and voice messages on VHF Channel 16 (coastal). USCG also supports NAVTEX, which is part of the GMDSS (Global Maritime Distress and Safety System), providing MF text coastal forecasts to shipboard text receivers out to about 250 miles at sea. Contact www.navcen.uscg.gov for details. A number of global services are available via HF SSB marine radio for offshore mariners—most by subscription.

While NOAA provides broad global coverage, there are many other sources of forecasts and current marine weather data, both government and commercial. For example, around Canadian waters, Environment Canada (weatheroffice.ec.gc. ca/marine) provides marine forecasts. Around the United Kingdom, the Met Office (www.metoffice.com) is the official government source and the BBC is another source (www.bbc.co.uk/ weather). The Bureau of Meteorology provides weather forecasts around Australia (www.bom.gov.au). A number of commercial companies provide excellent resources on the Internet, easily found via a web search.

COLD FRONT—advancing cold air

WARM FRONT—advancing warm air

STATIONARY FRONT—front has stopped advancing

OCCLUDED FRONT—cold front has overtaken warm front—still advancing

TROUGH ("TROF")—isobars make a sharp turn around a low, much like a front, and weather conditions are much like a front

Onboard Weather Forecasting

Making Your Own Forecast

The foregoing elements of onboard forecasting can be combined in various ways to understand what your observations are telling you. Let's look first at the signs of stable or changing weather.

	Continuing Good Weather	Indicators of a Change
Skies	Clear, light to dark blue, bright moon, contrails dissipate	Hazy, halo (sun or moon), thick lingering jet contrails
Clouds	Few, puffy cumulus or high thin clouds, higher the better	Veil of clouds, clouds at multi-layers & directions, cirrus
Winds Seas	Generally steady, little change over day; sea swells same direction	Strong winds in early AM, wind shift to S; seas confused, varying directions
Temperature	Stable; heavy dew or frost at night	Marked changes; increase in humidity
Dew Point	Marked spread between dew point & temperature = no fog	Close spread: probable fog if temperature drops
Barometer	Steady, rising slowly	Falling slowly
Sunrise	Gray sky at dawn or sun rising from clear horizon	Red sky, sun rises above horizon due to cloud cover
Sunset	Red sky, sun ball of fire " or sets on a clear horizon	Sun sets high above horizon, color purplish or pale yellow

Forecasters have great difficulty predicting a low's precise path, but Buys Ballot's Law (see page 146) gives you the local perspective. Here's how to refine a regional forecast with your own observations:

APPROACHING LOW

CLOUDS: high cirrus, gradually lowering and thickening
WIND: backing to SE—possibly increasing
BAROMETER: begins to fall (2 to 10 mb in 3 hours)
SEAS: Offshore swell increases, with decreasing period

What to Expect:
RAIN: within 15–24 hours
If low is W to NW, passing to your north, you will see fronts
If low is W to SW, passing to your south, you will not see distinct fronts

APPROACHING WARM FRONT

CIRRUS OR MACKEREL CLOUDS: front > 24 hr away
LOWERING AND THICKENING CLOUDS (ALTOSTRATUS, NIMBOSTRATUS): front < 24 hr away
RAIN: begins lightly, then becomes steady and persistent
BAROMETER: falls steadily; faster fall = stronger winds
WINDS: increase steadily, stay SE
VISIBILITY: deteriorates, especially in rain

PASSING WARM FRONT

SKY: lightens toward western horizon
RAIN: breaks
WIND: veers from S to SW, may decrease
BAROMETER: stops falling
TEMPERATURE: rises

WITHIN WARM SECTOR

WIND: steady, typically SW, will strengthen ahead of cold front
BAROMETER: steady—may drop shortly ahead of cold front
PRECIPITATION: mist, possible drizzle

APPROACHING COLD FRONT

WIND: SW increases; line squalls possible > 100 mi ahead of front
BAROMETER: begins brief fall, could be rapid
CLOUDS: cumulonimbus build to W
TEMPERATURE: steady
RAIN: begins and intensifies, but duration short (1–2 hr typical)

PASSING COLD FRONT

WIND: veers rapidly to NW, gusty behind front
BAROMETER: begins to rise, often quickly
CLOUDS: cumulonimbus, then nimbostratus, then clearing
TEMPERATURE: drops suddenly, then slow decline
RAIN: ends, gives way to rapidly clearing skies, possibly with leftover altocumulus

Special Weather Topics

Wind Chill

The following wind chill table will give you an idea of the apparent temperature when radiational cooling due to wind is factored in. Wind speed means apparent wind on deck (the vector sum of true wind and your boat's forward motion). Especially in spring and fall, wind chill is directly related to onset of hypothermia.

Wind (mph)	Temperature (°F)																	
	40	35	30	25	20	15	10	5	0	-5	-10	-15	-20	-25	-30	-35	-40	-45
5	36	31	25	19	13	7	1	-5	-11	-16	-22	-28	-34	-40	-46	-52	-57	-63
10	34	27	21	15	9	3	-4	-10	-16	-22	-28	-35	-41	-47	-53	-59	-66	-72
15	32	25	19	13	6	0	-7	-13	-19	-26	-32	-39	-45	-51	-58	-64	-71	-77
20	30	24	17	11	4	-2	-9	-15	-22	-29	-35	-42	-48	-55	-61	-68	-74	-81
25	29	23	16	9	3	-4	-11	-17	-24	-31	-37	-44	-51	-58	-64	-71	-78	-84
30	28	22	15	8	1	-5	-12	-19	-26	-33	-39	-46	-53	-60	-67	-73	-80	-87
35	28	21	14	7	0	-7	-14	-21	-27	-34	-41	-48	-55	-62	-69	-76	-82	-89
40	27	20	13	6	-1	-8	-15	-22	-29	-36	-43	-50	-57	-64	-71	-78	-84	-91
45	26	29	12	5	-2	-9	-16	-23	-30	-37	-44	-51	-58	-65	-72	-79	-86	-93
50	26	19	12	4	-3	-10	-17	-24	-31	-38	-45	-52	-60	-67	-74	-81	-88	-95
55	25	18	11	4	-3	-11	-18	-25	-32	-39	-46	-54	-61	-68	-75	-82	-89	-97
60	25	17	10	3	-4	-11	-19	-26	-33	-40	-48	-55	-62	-69	-76	-84	-91	-98

Frostbite Times: 30 minutes | 10 minutes | 5 minutes

Onboard Weather Forecasting

Thunderstorms and Squalls

Thunderstorms are of two origins: air mass or frontal. The former is created when warm, moist air rises over land, usually during hot, humid summer days. When the resulting cumulonimbus clouds mature, the storm begins, and may bring squalls to coastal waters. It soon dissipates.

Frontal thunderstorms and squalls are associated with the near-vertical wall of cold air in an advancing cold front, which forces warm air aloft at a rapid rate. Especially during spring and early summer, the resulting squalls can be severe, and are dangerous to boaters.

Check forecasts for the possibility of squall-line thunderstorms and be on the lookout. An advancing dark band of vertical clouds, often called a *roll cloud*, will be preceded by strong winds blowing in your direction, followed by heavy squalls from the opposite direction as the storm passes overhead. Severe lightning usually accompanies these squalls.

Severe squalls can precede the arrival of a cold front by up to several hundred miles.

Tropical Storms

The highs, lows, and fronts that sweep west to east in the middle latitudes are absent from the tropics, which are characterized instead by the steady northeast (Northern Hemisphere) and southeast (Southern Hemisphere) trade winds, which converge near the equator in a zone of rising air and light and baffling breezes known as the *doldrums*.

Tropical disturbances take the form of low-pressure troughs or waves that move east to west with the trades, picking up heat energy from warm tropical waters. Some develop into tropical depressions (closed cyclonic circulation with surface winds less than 39 mph) or tropical storms (winds of 39 to 74 mph), and a few become hurricanes (winds higher than 74 mph; known as typhoons in the western North Pacific and cyclones in the Indian Ocean and Australia). The path of a hurricane is hard to predict even with sophisticated computer models, but you will have ample public warning of a hurricane's advance. Use that warning to get ashore and secure your boat. Vessels caught at sea in the Northern Hemisphere should strive to be on the left side of the hurricane's path (facing the direction the storm is heading), where the speed of its advance subtracts somewhat from wind speed rather than adding to it.

What Causes Fog?

The *dew point* is the temperature below which water vapor begins to condense from air of a given humidity. If you know the dew point at ground level, you'll know the temperature at which fog will form. For example, if the current temperature is 65°F and the dew point is 61°F, a mere 4° drop in temperature, such as might occur with the approach of sunset, is likely to produce fog.

The dew point can be measured by comparing the temperatures recorded by the dry- and wet-bulb thermometers in a sling psychrometer. The instrument

A sling psychrometer (with wet- and dry-bulb thermometers) measures the dew point.

is swung until evaporation depresses its wet bulb reading.

The several types of fog that affect boaters are listed below.

Advection	*Conditions:*	light winds (5–10 Kn up to 15 Kn), warm, moist air blown over cold water—air condenses to produce fog
	Clears:	persistent fog that will clear when winds become stronger or change direction
Radiation	*Conditions:*	light winds (5–7 Kn), low lying areas, warm, moist air condensed by nighttime radiational cooling
	Clears:	fog will lift in stronger winds or burn off as soon as the area is heated by the sun
Frontal	*Conditions:*	warm front, warm rain or drizzle falling through cool air can form dense fog
	Clears:	wind shift or passage of warm front

A barometer is a mariner's best forecasting tool. Pages 154 and 155 tell you what the readings mean.

Onboard Weather Forecasting

CHAPTER 10

John Rousmaniere

Heavy Weather Sailing

What Is
Heavy Weather?

Heavy weather is not an absolute wind speed, like (say) 30 knots. Rather, it's when the wind blows so hard and the waves are so big that *your boat* is on the verge of losing control and *you and your crew* begin to feel overwhelmed. This can be 12 knots in a small dinghy, or 40 knots in a big, heavy cruising boat.

Heavy weather can sneak up on you. Because the force of the wind increases with the cube of its speed, a seemingly small increase in wind strength has a big effect on wind force. So be sensitive to your boat's handling characteristics. Always be prepared to change course or **shorten sail**. Your crew should be able to reef in less than 2 minutes. Practice reefing and setting storm sails (see pages 166–69) ahead of time. **Remember this rule: "When you're thinking about shortening sail, it's already too late!"**
Here's a wary guide for shortening sail based on the Beaufort scale of wind forces. For storm tactics, see pages 170–73. NOTE: Every boat has to be handled uniquely. Many boats can usually carry more sail when running or reaching than when sailing close hauled.

BEAUFORT FORCE (wind and waves)	BOAT SIZE AND TYPE		
	SMALL Heavy monohull<30' Light monohull<35' Multihull<40'	MEDIUM	LARGE Heavy monohull>50' Light monohull>55' Multihull>60'
FORCE 5 Fresh breeze, 17–21 knots; 6' seas, some whitecaps	Small jib, 1–2 reefs	Small jib, 1 reef	Medium jib, 0–1 reef
FORCE 6 Strong breeze, 22–27 knots; 10' seas, extensive whitecaps	Small jib, 2 reefs	Small jib, 2 reefs	Small jib, 1–2 reefs
FORCE 7 Near gale, 28–33 knots; 14' seas, some breakers	Storm jib, 3 reefs (or storm trysail)	Small jib, 2–3 reefs	Small jib, 2 reefs
FORCE 8 Gale, 34–40 knots; 18' seas, heavy spray	Storm sails, storm tactics (except heaving-to)	Storm jib, 3 reefs (or storm trysail)	Storm jib, 3 reefs (or storm trysail)
FORCE 9 Strong gale, 41–47 knots; 23' seas, rolling crests, dense foam	Storm sails, storm tactics (except heaving-to)	Storm sails, storm tactics	Storm sails, storm tactics
FORCE 10 Storm, 48–55 knots; 29' seas, all white; survival conditions except for the best-found boats	One storm sail, storm tactics (except heaving-to)	Storm sails, storm tactics (except heaving-to)	Storm sails, storm tactics

Waves are more dangerous than wind. Flying water packs a lot of force. Don't leave loose objects (like sails and fenders) exposed on deck, where a wave can catch and throw them into the cabin or through the lifelines, causing damage to the boat or crew.

The size of a wave depends on several factors: wind strength, wind fetch (the distance over water that the wind blows), the length of time the wind's been blowing, water depth, and current. The biggest seas are caused by winds blowing hard and long over a great fetch; but the worst waves often are the short, steep breakers that appear in the early part of a storm, in shallow water, in rapidly shifting winds, in tidal races, and anywhere the tide runs against the wind. By one estimate, a 1-knot contrary tide doubles the size of a wave, and a stronger current increases it still further. A fast-moving boat may jump off one of these waves and smash down, doing great damage to itself and the crew. Being caught beam-to by such a wave invites being rolled over or stove in by the breaker and filled with water. About one wave out of twenty is a "rogue" that runs at an angle across the others, sometimes stirring up unusually steep, breaking seas.

Therefore, it pays to anticipate areas of rough water and either slow down or steer around them.

Wind against current kicks up a steep chop in a tidal race.

Sailing in a blow is most dangerous when the wind is astern. That's when you're going fastest, when the crew is most exuberant and likely to be careless, when their backs are turned to the waves, and when a small mistake at the helm or the appearance of even a tiny rogue wave can toss the boat over on its side in a wild broach (see page 166).

Author steers downwind in the 1979 Fastnet Race storm. All elements were in the 50s—wind and water temperatures (Fahrenheit), wind speed (knots), and the occasional wave height (feet).

Preparing for Bad Weather

Signs of approaching bad weather include a falling barometer, a swift change in wind speed or direction, ocean waves from a new direction, a mass of dark clouds in the west, fierce lightning, and warnings over the radio or Internet (see *Onboard Weather Forecasting*, Chapter 9). If any of these appears, take the time to carefully gather all the information you can. Sketch a weather chart showing the location of the approaching weather front or center of low pressure, and carefully consider your options. You want to dodge the storm, but may not have time to get to port.

Running off in the Southern Ocean.

Underway Offshore

Plan your strategy. Sail away from the storm, especially the "dangerous quadrant" on its right front (left front in southern hemisphere). To predict the path of a low-pressure storm system, use Buys Ballot's Law: when you face the wind in the northern hemisphere, low pressure is on your right and high pressure on your left. (This is because wind circulates counterclockwise around a northern hemisphere low. The low will be on your left in the southern hemisphere, where wind circulates clockwise around a low.) As a rule, except when the wind is south to southwest, keep the wind in the northern hemisphere on your starboard side in order to sail away from the approaching storm.

Boat A has time to reach harbor. Boat B tacks out to sea and away from the dangerous quadrant (shaded).

Prepare the boat and crew.

1. Check fuel. Now's the time to switch to a full tank.

2. Shorten sail (see page 166).

3. Suit up. With the skipper setting the example, everybody puts on foul-weather gear, life jackets, and (if they have them) safety harnesses, which must always be hooked on when on deck. (See page 172.) Rig grab lines in the cockpit and cabin. Take seasickness medication.

4. Batten down. Shut and dog (bolt down) hatches and ports, install washboards in the companionway. Take loose gear off the deck. If you have protective panels to put over large windows, do it now—especially on the leeward side—to keep windows from breaking should the boat fall on its side. Below, secure personal items, food, dishes, etc. in lockers (which must be shut tight). While the boat's still steady, cook some hot food and heat water to put in thermoses.

Underway, Squalls Near Shore

Follow steps 1–4 above.

When black clouds appear and sweep your way, expect a squall. After plotting your position, decide if you have time to return to harbor. (To estimate the distance to a squall in miles, time the interval between the flash of lightning and the sound of the thunderclap, then divide by 5.) Because squalls are unpredictable, it's often safest to stay in open water, well away from land, shoals, and other boats.

In Harbor

If your boat is in the harbor when a storm approaches, prepare it carefully.

Squall clouds warn of an approaching wind.

1. Reduce windage. Any exposed area makes the boat sail around its anchor or dock lines, snapping them. Strip off *everything:* all sails (including roller-furled sails), the Bimini, ventilators, awnings, the Lifesling, etc. Deflate the dinghy and put it in the cockpit. A hard-bottomed dinghy should be sunk or stored ashore.

2. At the dock. Double or even triple up on dock lines, using plenty of spring lines (they control surges). Tie leather or cloth chafe protection over lines and fittings. Deploy all your fenders, tying plastic milk bottles full of water to their bottoms to keep them from riding up as the boat rocks against the dock.

3. At anchor. Set out all your anchors with plenty of scope.

4. Close all seacocks and other through-hull fittings.

5. Batten down.

6. Get off. The Coast Guard and other authorities are adamant that the dumbest thing anyone can do is stay aboard a boat in a hurricane.

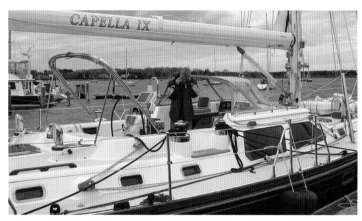

Squall coming: high-windage deck gear cleared away.

Dock lines doubled.

Chafe gear installed.

Boat Care at Sea

Check engine fuel filters often. Rolling and pitching stir up dirt in the bottom of fuel tanks that can stop an engine.

Keep the bilges dry. You don't want water sloshing up into bunks. Pump every hour or half hour, and note in the log how many strokes are needed before the pump sucks dry. To keep water from coming below, tightly shut hatches and ports, close off holes at the partners (where the mast comes through the deck), and aim deck ventilators downwind.

Inspect gear often. In rough weather, chafe (damage from rubbing) occurs remarkably quickly. In addition, halyards and other lines loosen, and tie-downs undo themselves. Take regular inspection tours around the deck and cabin.

Rig preventers. Rolling about in waves causes booms

Multiple chafe points on foredeck.

to fly around, and this has caused serious injuries and deaths. When a sailboat is reaching or running, even in light wind, the boom must be held out by a preventer—a line leading from the boom forward to the deck, through a block, and back to the cockpit. Secure the block to a strong point on deck, and tie the line to a reinforced point on the boom (for instance, a main-sheet block attachment). Most of the time the preventer can be rigged on deck near the leeward shrouds. When running in very large seas, however, lead the preventer forward all the way to the bow so there is little downward pull on it, and if the boom trips in the water, it will lift and not break. Lead the line back to the cockpit so it can be adjusted easily as you ease and trim the mainsheet. In rough conditions, you want to keep people off the deck as much as possible.

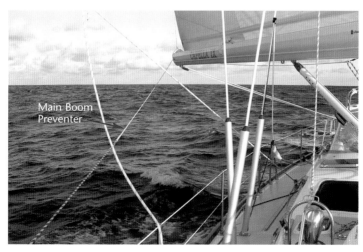
Main Boom Preventer

Heavy Weather Sailing

Strong Wind Tactics

Slow down. When the boat gets uncomfortable, decrease speed. It's amazing how much better a boat rides when you slow down by just a couple of knots. Under power, throttle back on the engine. Under sail, let the traveler down or let the sails luff a little (but not too much or you'll break battens and rip sail cloth). If that doesn't work, shorten sail.

Change your angle to the waves. A comfortable, safe angle often is with the wind about 30 degrees forward or aft of the beam. Big waves directly on the side roll boats violently and may capsize them. Waves on the bow can cause dangerous pounding and wave-jumping. Waves from behind may lift the stern and cause the boat to broach (turn violently to one side) or even pitchpole (somersault over the bow).

Find protection. If the boat is still out of control, get on the tack that has the smoothest water, try stopping altogether, or find some land that provides protection.

Shortening Sail: Reefing

Reducing sail area is often all that's necessary to steady a boat in fresh to strong breezes (17–27 knots) and 6- to 10-foot waves with whitecaps. (This is Force 5–6 on the Beaufort scale of wind forces.)

One way to shorten sail is to douse (lower) or roll up a sail. You can partially or completely roll up or lower the jib, and even sail under one sail alone. **Warning:** Don't sail under jib alone except in smooth water; the mainsail provides considerable fore-and-aft support for the mast in rough seas.

To reef the mainsail:

1. Support the boom, luff the sail. Tighten the topping lift or adjust a rigid, rod-type boom vang so the boom won't drop when the halyard is eased. Then ease the sheet until the sail luffs completely.

2. Reef the sail's luff. Lower the halyard and pull down the luff

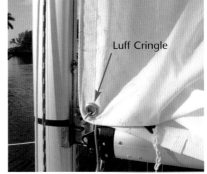

Luff Cringle

until its cringle (the big steel eye) is at or near the boom. (It helps to mark the halyard at this point.) Secure the cringle to the boom with a line or a metal hook. Pull the halyard so tight there are tension wrinkles in the luff.

Leech Cringle

3. Reef the leech. With the sail still luffing, pull on the leech reefing line to haul the leech cringle right down to the boom. This pull will be long and hard.

4. Finally, ease the topping lift, trim the mainsheet, and coil the halyard and reef lines.

5. If the sail's foot is flogging, tie in and tighten reef points—either short lines or a long line led through the grommets (small holes) along the reef.

To shake out (undo) a reef: luff the sail, cast off the reef point, throw off the leech reefing line, throw off the luff, raise the halyard, and retrim.

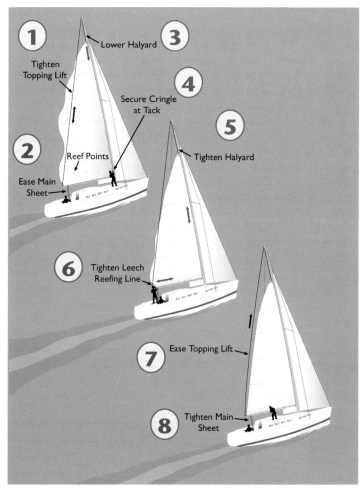

1

Lower Halyard 3

Tighten
Topping Lift

4

Secure Cringle
at Tack

5

2

Reef Points

Tighten Halyard

Ease Main
Sheet

6 Tighten Leech
Reefing Line

7 Ease Topping Lift

8 Tighten Main
Sheet

Heavy Weather Sailing

Common reefing problems:

The reef isn't tied in soon enough. When you first think about reefing, it's probably already too late. Once the boat is heeled over 20 degrees most of the time, think seriously about reefing.

The sail is too full when reefed. The halyard or reefing lines must be tightened all the way. The leech reefing line must be far enough aft on the boom so it pulls *back* as well as down.

The reefing lines stretch. This means they're too small. They should be the same size as the mainsheet.

A fine, rail-down breeze. But when you heel this far, you should think about reefing.

Shortening Sail: Storm Sails

As the wind builds, tie in a second (or third) reef, and then go to the storm sails. The storm trysail and storm jib are set low (to decrease heeling force) in place of the mainsail and regular jib. At first they look ridiculously small, but because the wind's force rises exponentially with velocity, in a strong wind they'll be enough to drive the boat. These sails have no battens, which might break.

The storm jib is best set alone on an inner stay (called the forestay), which keeps the sail area near the mast so the boat balances well and the sail is easy to handle without having to venture out on the bow. If you don't have a forestay, you may be able to improvise one by leading a spinnaker pole topping lift or a spare halyard to the bow cleat and tightening it hard, then hanking the storm jib to it. But the storm jib can be hoisted on the headstay if necessary, even over the roller-furled jib using loops of line that ride over the sail. The storm jib's tack should be on a pendant (short strap) that lets it ride high above any waves that may come on deck.

Storm Trysail

Storm Jib

This storm jib's tack pendant should be longer.

The storm trysail's luff is hoisted like the mainsail's on a mast track or in a groove (true cruising boats have a separate track for the trysail). The tack is secured with a pendant so the sail is above the furled mailsail. The tack is secured with a pendant so the sail is above the furled mailsail. Traditionally a trysail is trimmed through a block on the leeward rail to allow the main boom to be dropped down on deck so it won't swing around. But with the modern rod-type boom vang that holds the boom up, many sailors tie the clew of the trysail to the boom. Some of the load must be carried by the boom's strong points (for instance its end and the eyes for the reefing lines). The trysail can be trimmed in the usual way with the mainsheet and traveler so the boat can sail close-hauled.

Mast Track

Loose Foot

Clew Lashing

Storm trysail set on main boom and dedicated mast track.

Gale and Storm Tactics

There are four tactics for coping with strong winds in conditions when sailing is less important than surviving: heaving-to, lying ahull, running before it, and lying to a sea anchor.

Heaving-To

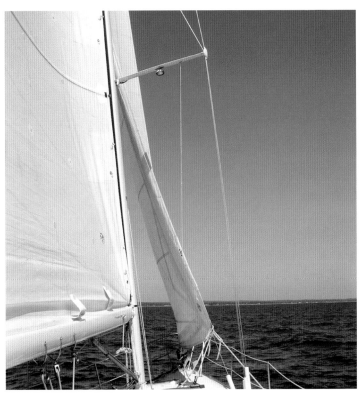

Hove-to with backed jib.

Heaving-to is an excellent tactic for nearly stopping the boat and making it more comfortable in conditions when sail can be carried, which usually means below about 50 knots (Beaufort scale Force 10)—or less in a small boat. Even in lighter wind, it's a fine way to stop while you cook a meal in big seas or wait for dawn to light your way into a strange harbor.

To heave-to. On a close reach at about 60 degrees off the wind, back the jib or storm jib by trimming it flat on the windward (wrong) side. (Alternatively, trim it the usual way, to leeward, and tack without casting off the sheet.) With the jib pushing the bow to leeward and the mainsail and rudder pushing it to windward (the wheel or tiller can be lashed to help achieve this), there is little force left over to push the boat ahead. The boat will jog along comfortably at less than 3 knots. Adjust the mainsheet and traveler so the boat self-steers. Since the boat will make leeway (slide downwind), heaving-to is not a good tactic when you are near a lee shore. Neither is it a safe tactic when the waves are breaking or throwing heavy spray.

Heaving-To
Storm Jib
(Backed)
Storm Trysail
WIND

In a variation of heaving-to called the Rod stop
(named for seaman Rod Stephens), sail on a beam reach at 90
degrees to the wind, roll up the jib (or let it luff), and push the
mainsail or trysail all the way out, securing it there with a line.

Lying Ahull

When the wind pressure on the jib becomes strong enough to
force your bow off the wind despite mainsail and rudder action,
heaving-to becomes unsafe. One possibility then is to lie ahull,
which simply means to douse sails and let the boat drift under
bare poles. This tactic permits the crew to rest, but the risk is
that the boat may lie beam-to breaking seas that could roll it
over. Lying ahull in big breaking seas is not recommended.

Running Before It

Running before the wind is the only *active* storm tactic, mean-
ing that the boat has to be actively steered. Set enough sail to
carry the boat up the faces of big waves, but not so much that
the boat goes too fast when running down the backs of waves
and loses control. With speed up and the waves on your stern,
the force of the waves is less. If you begin to lose control, tow
warps (long lengths of rope with objects—like fenders or sails—
tied on to increase resistance) or a drogue (a parachute or a series
of small parachutes on a line). The loads on warps and drogues
will be powerful. Lead their lines to winches or other through-
bolted fittings, and treat them respectfully. In big breaking seas,
running before the wind often is the best storm tactic for monohull boats, even though they must be steered very carefully and
there is a risk of carrying the boat toward land.

Running before big seas in the Southern Ocean.

Cone configuration and bridle arrangement for a Jordan series drogue. A 30,000 lb. boat needs 300 feet of 3/4" nylon line and 132 cones.

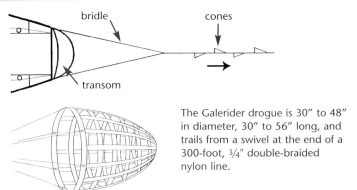

bridle

cones

transom

The Galerider drogue is 30" to 48" in diameter, 30" to 56" long, and trails from a swivel at the end of a 300-foot, 3/4" double-braided nylon line.

Lying To a Sea Anchor

This is the storm tactic often favored by catamarans and tri-marans because their narrow, sharp bows make less resistance to waves than a monohull's wider bow. Under bare poles, the boat lies with the bow into the wind and a parachute-like device called a sea anchor deployed over the bow on the anchor rode or other long line. There is little drift downwind. The crew must be alert to changing wave patterns so the boat is not caught beam-to a big sea. A variation is to heave-to with some sail set and the sea anchor on a bridle. The loading on the lines is very high, so lead them to through-bolted fittings.

A growing body of evidence suggests that monohulls, especially those with fin keels, ride out storms more successfully trailing a drogue from the stern than riding to a sea anchor.

Crew Concerns

Heavy weather is cold, wet, uncomfortable, and discouraging. If it's also demoralizing, the crew may give up just when you need everyone's full attention.

Be optimistic. Under strong, calm, cheerful but realistic, purposeful leadership, many crews have avoided passivity and survived terrible storms on the faith that something better was awaiting them at the other side. Thoughts of family and friends ashore usually provide sufficient motivation to keep sailing, as does loyalty to shipmates and the vessel.

Maintain normal shipboard routines. Serve hot, nutritious food, arrange meals and watches so everyone has time to sleep or at least rest, and keep the cabin neat and dry (with wet clothes and foul-weather gear well away from bunks).

Wear personal safety gear. With the owner and skipper setting the example, everybody should wear PFDs and (if available) safety harnesses, which prevent falls and keep people on board. Put on the harness before you come on deck and hook it in the cockpit before you step out of the companionway. Hook harness tethers into sturdy jacklines on deck or through-bolted fittings. Keep the tether short so any fall won't be long. Clip on all the time, especially when doing a two-handed job—like steering, coming in or out of the companionway, trimming sails, or moving around on deck.

Stay dry. Wear foul-weather gear. A dry body is a warm body, and also an effective body, because symptoms of hypothermia include slow thinking and loss of agility.

Get your rest. Organize the crew in short watches so nobody's exposed on deck for too long. If you can't sleep, at least lie down.

Don't let seasickness catch you by surprise. Take medication early, anticipate drowsiness and other side effects, drink Coke Classic to settle a queasy stomach (some people swear by ginger ale), stay well hydrated, and try to get some food down, even if it's only an unsalted cracker.

Use hand signals. Wind and waves are often so loud that people can't hear each other, so use hand signals. Here are examples:

Trim or ease a line: Point toward or away from the person holding a line.
Lower or hoist a sail: Point down or up.
Stop: Open palm toward the person.
Cleat the line: OK sign (form circle with index finger and thumb).
Change course: Point in the new direction.

A safety harness with two tethers.

Clip your tether before going on deck.

Tether clipped to jackline.

CHAPTER 11

Diesel Engine Care and Repair

Nigel Calder

Meet Your Diesel Engine

Unlike a gas engine, a diesel engine has no ignition system or spark plugs. Instead, diesel fuel ignites "spontaneously" when sprayed into air that has been superheated by compression within a cylinder. This combustion then generates a power stroke. Thus there are three preconditions for a diesel engine to work:

1. An adequate supply of combustion air.

2. Compression of this air until its temperature rises above the ignition point of diesel (this requires a higher degree of compression in colder air than in warmer).

3. Injection of diesel fuel into this cylinder of heated air at a moment that is precisely coordinated with the movement of the pistons up and down the cylinders.

Given air, adequate compression, and proper fuel injection, a diesel engine more or less has to run. Routine maintenance is designed to guarantee these three preconditions; troubleshooting focuses on finding out which of them is missing.

Maintenance requirements and troubleshooting procedures are similar across the variety of diesel engines found in powerboats and sailboats.

Intake silencer · Intake manifold · Oil filler cap · Secondary fuel filter · Fuel injection pump · Dipstick · Oil filler cap · Fuel lift pump · Lubricating oil filter · Marine gear · Fresh water filler cap · Engine name plate (on the rocker arm cover) · Coolant tank / Heat exchanger · Exhaust mixing elbow · Cover · Exhaust manifold · Starter motor · Shift lever · Raw-water pump · V-belt · Alternator

Standard
Operating Practices

Before cranking the engine with the starter motor, check the oil level ① and the freshwater level ②. Also be sure the raw-water seacock is open, the raw-water strainer is unobstructed (see page 184), any "stop" device is not activated (note: many diesels do not have a stop device), and the transmission is in neutral ③.

freshwater expansion bottle

Immediately after the engine fires, be sure the oil pressure gauge is normal or the oil pressure warning light is out. Also be sure that the alternator is charging (i.e., either the ammeter shows charging or the light is out) and that cooling water is coming out of the exhaust ④. (Note: It is important to develop a sense of what constitutes normal flow.)

Troubleshooting

Diesel Engine Care and Repair

Seizure	High exhaust back pressure	Hunting	Rising oil level	Excessive oil consumption	Low oil pressure	Knocks	Misfiring	Loss of power	Poor idle	White smoke	Blue smoke	Black smoke	Overheating	Low compression	Lack of fuel	Cranks, but poor starting	Will not crank	Low cranking speed
																	•	
•								•					•					
								•										•
							•	•		•						•		
							•	•				•				•		
	•						•	•				•				•		
														•		•		
							•	•	•							•		
						•	•	•	•	•						•		
						•	•	•	•	•		•				•		
•													•					
•													•					
•				•									•					
•			•	•									•					•
•		•		•									•					
							•							•	•			
						•	•	•	•			•				•		
								•	•					•		•		
						•		•	•			•	•			•		
													•					
			•			•	•	•	•	•	•			•		•		
							•	•	•	•					•	•		
							•	•	•	•					•	•		
			•								•							
							•	•	•	•				•		•		
				•														
		•							•									
									•									
•			•							•			•	•	•			
•													•					
					•		•							•		•		
•							•						•				•	
•			•														•	

Overview

Bn engine that does not crank almost always has an electrical problem (pages 180 and 181), but occasionally has water in the cylinders (page 182). An engine that cranks slowly and fails to start is probably not compressing the air in the cylinders sufficiently to attain ignition temperatures—the cranking speed will need to be increased. An engine that cranks at normal speeds and does not start (page 183) likely has one of the following: a fuel supply problem; an obstruction of the air inlet or exhaust; or a serious lack of compression. The latter requires a rebuild, and is particularly likely with an engine that has high operating hours, especially if it is harder to start in cold weather.

Possible Causes
Battery low/loose connections
Engine overload/rope in propeller
Auxiliary equipment engaged
Pre-heat device inoperative
Plugged air filter
Plugged exhaust/turbocharger/kink in exhaust hose
Throttle closed/fuel shutoff solenoid faulty/tank empty
Plugged fuel filters
Air in fuel lines
Dirty fuel
Closed seacock/plugged raw-water filter or screen/plugged cooling system
Defective water pump/defective pump valves/air-bound water lines
Oil level low
Wrong viscosity oil
Diesel dilution of oil
Lift pump diaphragm holed
Defective injector/poor-quality fuel
Injection pump leaking
Injection timing advanced or delayed
Too much fuel injected
Piston blowby
Dry cylinder walls
Valve blowby
Worn valve stems
Decompressor levers on/valve clearances wrong/valves sticking
Dirt in oil pressure relief valve/ defective pressure gauge
Governor sticking/loose linkage
Governor idle spring too slack
Blown head gasket/cracked head
Uneven load on cylinders
Worn bearings
Seized piston
Water in the cylinders

Diesel Engine Care and Repair

Engine Cranks
Slowly or Not at All

1. Turn on the ignition, but do not crank. Place the '+' probe of a DC voltmeter on the terminal at which the battery positive cable connects to the starter motor solenoid ① and the '–' probe on the cranking battery negative post (or engine block if the negative post is not accessible):

   • Higher than 12.6 volts: OK

   • 12.4 to 12.6 volts: the battery is somewhat discharged

   • 12.2 to 12.4 volts: the battery needs recharging

   • Below 12.2 volts: the battery is almost completely discharged and needs recharging

   • No volts: a battery isolation switch is probably turned off!

2. Assuming a charged battery, put the meter probes as in (1) and have someone attempt to crank the engine:

   • If the voltage remains the same, either the ignition circuit is defective or the solenoid is out of action. To investigate further, connect a jumper wire or screwdriver blade from the starter motor cable terminal on the solenoid to the ignition switch terminal (the one with a relatively small cable going into the wiring harness ②). If the engine cranks, the switch circuit is defective. If it does not crank, use a screwdriver blade to short the two big terminals on the solenoid ③. **Caution: Sparks may fly—hold the screwdriver**

firmly to the terminals, and MAKE SURE THE SCREWDRIVER DOES NOT TOUCH THE STARTER MOTOR CASE. If the starter motor spins (the engine will probably still not crank), the solenoid needs rebuilding (remove the end cover and check the points). No response means the battery is dead (check it again) or the starter motor is inoperative.

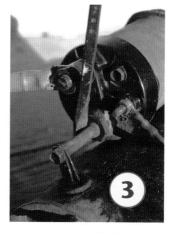

- If the voltage falls a volt or two but then stabilizes, feel all connections and cables in the cranking circuit (positive and negative). If any connections are warm, undo them, clean the terminals, and reconnect. If any cables are warm, they are undersized and need replacing with larger cables.

- If the voltage collapses, the battery is dead or has no remaining capacity, or the starter motor is shorted, or the engine is seized or full of water. Place a socket on the crank-shaft pulley nut (see page 182) and attempt to turn the engine over. If it will not turn, the engine is seized or full of water.

Many cranking circuits on boats suffer from excessive voltage drop as a result of undersized cables. To test this, place the '+' probe of a DC voltmeter on the cranking battery '+' post, and the '−' probe on the terminal at which the starter motor '+' cable or strap attaches to the solenoid ④ and crank. Note the reading. Now place the '+' meter probe on the starter motor case and the '−' probe on the battery negative terminal ⑤ and crank. Note the reading. If either reading is above 0.5 volt, there is excessive voltage drop. Clean all the terminals and try again. If a high reading persists, fit larger cables. (Note: Given a high reading on the positive side of the circuit, before replacing the cables put the meter probes on the two large solenoid terminals and crank again. If that reading is high, the solenoid points need cleaning or replacing.)

Engine Seized Up

When a previously working engine seizes on start-up, suspect water intrusion into the cylinders. In an emergency, to clear the cylinders, CLOSE THE THROTTLE, ACTIVATE ANY "STOP" DEVICE, and flick the starter on momentarily with someone watching the crankshaft pulley:

1. If the pulley turns on the first "flick," do this repeatedly, pausing several seconds between each flick, until the engine turns normally. DO NOT AT ANY TIME HOLD THE STARTER ON UNTIL THE PULLEY TURNS FREELY—YOU WILL BREAK SOMETHING EXPENSIVE!

2. If the pulley does not turn on the first flick, *or if it stops turning at any point when the starter motor is flicked on*, STOP! You can try turning the crankshaft *in tiny increments* by placing an appropriate wrench on the crankshaft pulley nut ①. Better yet, remove the valve cover, identify the exhaust valves (those on the exhaust manifold side of the engine), find all

those that are closed (the valves will not be depressed), and push a coin between the top of the valve and the rocker arm or camshaft to open the valve ②. Flick the starter motor on as above or use the wrench on the pulley nut until the engine turns normally. Remove the coins.

Once the engine is turning over, change the oil and filter. If there is any sign of water in the oil, run the engine for a few minutes and change the oil and filter again. Do this once more after 25 hours of running time.

If seawater has gotten into your engine, quite likely it either siphoned in from the raw-water system or was driven up the exhaust pipe by large seas (sailboats are especially vulnerable when under sail). To prevent these intrusions, any engine installed below the waterline requires a siphon break on the raw-water side (normally between the heat exchanger and the raw-water injection nipple into the exhaust, but sometimes between the raw-water pump and the heat exchanger) and a loop in the exhaust line that remains above the waterline at all heel angles and wave heights. Rectify as necessary.

Engine Cranks Normally But Does Not Fire

Suspect a problem with the fuel supply or insufficient compression of the air in the cylinders. A complete obstruction of the air supply is less likely.

1. Ensure that there is fuel in the tank and any fuel valves are open.

2. Make sure any engine "stop" device is not activated. (Not all engines have such a device.)

3. Be sure the air intake and exhaust are unobstructed (is there a closed exhaust seacock?).

4. If the engine has glow plugs, check to see that they are working (the cylinder head in the immediate vicinity of each plug should be warm).

5. Open the throttle wide, crank 10 to 15 seconds, let the engine rest 2 minutes, and crank again. If the engine now fires, it probably has poor compression and needs an overhaul.

6. If the engine is cranking slowly, check the battery and cranking circuit (see pages 180 and 181). If these are OK, block the air intake while cranking and then remove the blockage while continuing to crank (this will help the engine to crank faster). NEVER BLOCK THE AIR INTAKE ON A RUNNING ENGINE.

7. Still not running? On all but common rail fuel injection systems (some modern engines—check the manual), crack an injector nut ①, open the throttle wide, crank the engine, and check for fuel periodically spurting out of the loosened connection (DO NOT DO THIS WITH A COMMON RAIL FUEL INJECTION SYSTEM):

   • No fuel? Recheck any engine "stop" device. Look for a failed electrically operated shutdown solenoid. Bleed the system (see page 188).

   • Fuel? If the engine has been getting progressively harder to start, it likely has poor compression and needs an overhaul. If the failure to start is a new event, go back to (1) and try again!

injector pipe

injector nut

Engine Overheats

If the raw-water flow in the exhaust is normal, check the freshwater pump belt. If that is OK, check the header tank on the freshwater side of the engine (CAUTION: let the engine cool before removing the pressure cap) ①. If the level is OK, proceed with the next paragraph.

If the raw-water flow in the exhaust is reduced or absent, shut down the engine, then check the raw-water pump belt (note: some pumps are gear driven and have no belt). If that is OK, make sure the raw-water intake seacock is open. (If it is not, the raw-water pump impeller may have been destroyed.) Next inspect the raw-water strainer ②. If it is clean:

1. Close the raw-water seacock, disconnect its hose, and momentarily open the seacock to check for a strong flow. If the flow is reduced or absent, there is an obstruction at the raw-water inlet strainer on the outside of the hull.

2. Remove the raw-water pump cover and check the impeller for cracked or missing vanes ③. If any are missing, track down the pieces (they will likely be in the heat exchanger—see next item).

cracked vanes

3. Check the tube stack in the heat exchanger for scaling (flaking) or obstructions (the tube stacks are often accessed by removing covers at one or both ends of the heat exchanger) ④. If necessary, have a mechanic descale an older engine.

vane pieces

4. Disconnect the raw-water hose from the injection nipple on the exhaust elbow and check for scaling or debris.

If an older engine only overheats when heavily loaded or after a move into warmer waters, suspect a scaled heat exchanger.

Miscellaneous Operating Problems

Exhaust Has Blue Smoke

A little blue smoke is normal on start-up. If it persists after the engine has warmed, the engine is burning oil and needs an overhaul.

Black Smoke

A puff or two of black smoke on sudden acceleration is normal for an older engine. In all other circumstances, black smoke indicates improper fuel combustion:

1. Check the air filter or inlet for obstructions.

2. Break the exhaust hose loose from the water lift muffler and check for carbon fouling in the exhaust ①. (This photo shows a carbon-free exhaust exit.) If more than a thin film of carbon is present, the exhaust needs cleaning (and the cylinder head and valves also probably need servicing).

3. If the black smoke only occurs at high engine speeds, check for overloading (a line around the propeller, a heavily fouled boat bottom, too much auxiliary equipment, etc.). If this is a new boat, the propeller may be oversized.

Misfiring

A rhythmic misfiring means that one or more cylinders are misfiring. A misfiring on start-up that stops once the engine is warm suggests that one or more cylinders are losing compression, and the engine needs an overhaul.

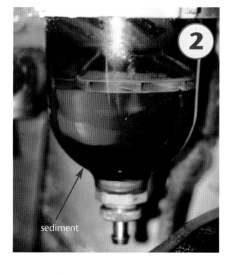

An irregular misfiring suggests dirty fuel (check for sediment in the base of the fuel filter ②), water in the fuel (check for water in the filter), or plugged fuel filters—especially if the misfiring only occurs at higher engine speeds and loads.

sediment

Diesel Engine Care and Repair

Routine Maintenance

The great majority of engine problems are caused by a failure to ensure clean fuel or a failure to change the oil at the prescribed intervals.

Clean Fuel

Dirty fuel is the #1 cause of marine diesel problems. There are four lines of defense to ensure clean fuel:

1. Adequate filtration of everything that goes into the tank. If adding fuel from dubious sources, use a Baja filter or water-separating fuel filter funnel.

2. Take one or more fuel samples from the base of all fuel tanks at least once a year to remove any sediment and water ①, ②, or employ a commercial fuel-polishing service.

diesel
water
sediment

3. Change the primary fuel filter at the specified intervals ③, and clean the tank if the filter is dirty.

4. Change the secondary filter at the specified intervals ④. If the filter is dirty, clean the primary filter and the tank, and check the filter screen in the lift pump. (See page 188 to bleed the fuel system.)

Additional Routine Maintenance

1. Change the air filter at the prescribed intervals (many small diesels do not have an air filter).

2. Periodically tighten the alternator belt. It should depress no more than 1/2 inch at the center of the longest belt run under moderate finger pressure ⑤.

3. Check the heat exchanger for a sacrificial zinc anode (many modern diesels do not have zinc anodes). If present, inspect it monthly until the rate of zinc loss is established. Replace the anode when it is no more than half gone.

4. See also pages 187 and 189.

Diesel Engine Care and Repair

Changing the Oil

Along with ensuring clean fuel, this is essential for long engine life. A marine diesel engine needs an hour meter in the panel so you know when to do oil changes and other maintenance.

1. Run the engine until it is up to normal operating temperature.

2. Pump the oil out of the crankcase with the installed oil-change pump ⑥ or by sucking it out through the dipstick tube ⑦. Marine chandlers sell a variety of manual and electric pumps for this purpose.

12-volt pump

3. Unscrew the oil filter with the appropriate filter wrench. In the absence of a filter wrench, use a spare alternator drive belt. Catch any spills in a disposable diaper or by placing a plastic bag around the filter ⑧.

4. Lubricate the sealing ring on a new filter with clean oil ⑨ and screw it on until hand tight. Tighten a further one-half to three-quarters turn with the filter wrench.

5. Add oil to the appropriate mark on the dipstick ⑩.

Crank the engine and check the oil pressure. (It may take a few seconds to come up to normal.) Inspect the sealing area around the new oil filter for leaks.

Bleeding the Fuel System

Air in the fuel system will stop most diesels. Many modern diesels can be purged of air by opening the throttle wide (on a single-lever engine control, push in the button in the center of the throttle before opening it so that the transmission is not engaged) and cranking 10 to 15 seconds at a time. Allow the starter motor to cool at least 2 minutes between cranks.

With older engines, air must be removed by bleeding the fuel system as follows:

1. Check for a pump and bleed nipple on the primary filter ①. If present, unscrew the bleed nipple two or three turns and operate the pump until fuel free of bubbles spurts out.

pump

bleed nipple

2. If there is no pump on the primary filter, find the engine-mounted fuel lift pump. If electric, turn on the ignition. If manual, find the pump lever ②. The engine may need to be turned over a half revolution to get the manual pump working.

3. Move "upstream" from the lift pump (i.e., toward the point of fuel injection on the engine) to the first bleed nipple in the system, which is normally on the secondary fuel filter, and unscrew the nipple a couple of turns ③.

lever

4. Operate the lift pump until fuel free of air bubbles flows out, catching spilled fuel. Then close the nipple. If the air bubbles don't clear, either the tank is low on fuel or there is an air leak on

the suction side of the pump; check the seal on the primary filter first, especially if it has been changed recently.

5. Move upstream in the fuel system to the next bleed nipple, which is normally on the injection pump, and repeat.

6. Once finished, open the throttle wide and crank 10 to 15 seconds.

7. If the engine does not fire, loosen the injector nuts (see page 183), open the throttle wide, crank until fuel spurts from each loosened connection, and then tighten.

CAUTION: You must never loosen an injector nut on one of the new generation of diesel engines with a common rail fuel injection system.

The engine should fire. Note: You can also bleed a newer engine after a fuel filter change in order to avoid the prolonged cranking that may otherwise be necessary to fill the new filter element with fuel.

Diesel Engine Care and Repair

Winterizing (or Annual Maintenance)

1. In freezing climates all raw-water systems must either be drained or filled with nontoxic (propylene glycol) antifreeze. If draining, remove the raw-water pump cover and pull out the impeller. If adding antifreeze, remove the raw-water hose from its seacock, dip into a bucket of antifreeze solution, and run the engine until the solution comes out the exhaust.

2. Inspect the raw-water pump impeller for signs of wear or cracking. Replace as necessary or at the specified intervals.

3. At least every two years, drain the freshwater side and refill with a fresh ethylene glycol antifreeze solution to restore the corrosion inhibitors.

4. Wash the valves on any vented loops in warm water to clean out salt crystals.

5. Change the engine oil at the end of the season rather than the beginning of the next (this removes corrosive acids from the crankcase).

6. Change the transmission oil.

7. Pump a sample from the base of the fuel tank (as on page 186) and remove any water or sediment. Fill the tank to minimize condensation.

8. Break loose the exhaust hose at the water lift muffler and check for carbon buildup (there should be no more than a light film) (page 185). If present, review the operating practices to prevent long-term damage to the engine.

9. Spray WD-40 or a similar penetrating fluid into the air inlet, then seal the inlet to prevent moisture entry. Place a note in a conspicuous place to remind yourself to unseal this before cranking the engine!

10. Remove the battery from the boat or ensure that it gets charged periodically (once a month for wet-cells; every few months for gels and AGMs).

11. Check the wiring harness and all electrical connections for signs of abrasion or corrosion and rectify as necessary. Spray with a corrosion inhibitor.

12. Check all hoses for signs of softening, bulging, kinking, or abrasion, and all hose clamps for signs of corrosion. Replace as necessary.

13. Every couple of years, or if confronted with unexplained vibration, check the engine alignment.

Recommissioning

1. Unseal the air inlet.

2. Replace the raw-water pump impeller (if removed).

3. Pump a sample from the base of the fuel tank and remove any water or sediment.

4. Replace the battery (if removed).

5. If the engine has a "stop" lever, activate this to prevent the engine from starting, then crank 10 to 15 seconds to initiate oil lubrication. Let the starter motor cool 2 minutes, then crank.

Diesel Engine Care and Repair

CHAPTER 12

Emergencies On Board

John Rousmaniere

Boating is a remarkably safe sport, yet emergencies can and do occur. According to Coast Guard statistics, the most frequent accidents include collisions, falls on deck or in the cabin, groundings, flooding, and fire. We won't talk about collisions here except to say that, like all accidents, they are often caused by alcohol abuse, operator inattention, or ignorance of basic rules. Neither will we address first aid.

Here the subject is onboard emergencies that can damage the boat or cause injury or even death. We'll interject some cautionary words about preventing emergencies.

Crew Overboard (COB) Rescue

If someone (the COB) goes over the side, you have six tasks, none requiring much more than basic boating skills.

1. Organize the remaining crew. Strong, decisive, positive leadership is needed. Note your geographical position. Nobody goes into the water as a rescuer without permission (the only reason to dive in is if the COB is unconscious; the rescuer must wear a PFD and be tethered to the boat).

2. Get buoyancy to the COB. Throw cushions, life rings, or the Lifesling—a retrieval system consisting of a buoyant yoke at the end of a long line tied to the boat. (The boat drags the line and yoke to the swimmer, who gets into the yoke and is hauled to the stopped boat and then out of the water.)

3. Keep the COB in sight. Stay nearby and instruct someone to point continuously at the COB, shouting encouragement.

4. Make a rescue maneuver. You must stay near the COB and get back quickly. There are three simple options:

- **Under power or sail.** *The quick stop:* When the COB goes over, turn the boat into the wind, then circle the COB slowly. Drag the Lifesling or its line into his or her hand, or

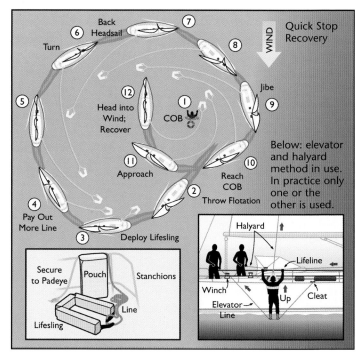

throw a line when the boat stops. If under sail, trim the sails tight and *don't cast off the jibsheet when tacking or jibing.* This keeps the boom from banging around, and the backed jib (headsail) slows the boat and allows quick turns.

- **Under power.** Several yards from the COB, take the engine out of gear and throw a line to the COB or let the Lifesling down to the COB.
  OR (large boat), **the Williamson Turn:** alter course 60 degrees to one side, then turn 240 degrees in the other direction to come back to the COB. Follow the directions above.
- **Under sail.** *The figure eight (reach-and-reach) (useful in strong winds because there is no jibe):* When the COB goes over, get on a beam reach and sail for a few seconds. Tack, reach back below the COB, and head up to the COB, dragging the Lifesling or throwing a line.

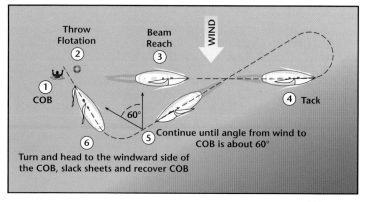

OR heave-to after returning to COB: This leaves the boat jogging along very slowly and, in most cases, self-steering so nobody is needed at the helm. On a close reach, trim the jib flat on the windward side and adjust the mainsheet and traveler so the boat self-steers. In a variation called the Rod stop (named for seaman Rod Stephens), sail on a beam reach, roll up the jib (or let it luff), and push the mainsail all the way out, securing it there with a line.

5. Make physical contact. When the COB has hold of the Lifesling or line, stop the boat by taking the engine out of gear or luffing and lowering sails. Pull the COB to the boat.

6. Retrieve the COB. You usually can pull the COB over either side. But if the boat is rapidly sliding downwind, it may be best to retrieve over the upwind side so as not to drift over the COB. If the COB is in the Lifesling, clip a halyard to it, lead the halyard to a winch, and hoist the victim on deck. (You may need a block and tackle.) Without the Lifesling, the COB can be lifted by strong crewmembers or helped up a swim platform or ladder. Or drape a line over the side, lead the line to a winch, have the COB kneel or stand on it, and use the elevator method to hoist the COB. *Do not try to lift the COB by the boom,* which will likely swing and hit someone, and may be too low.

If You Fall Overboard

Do not try to swim. You won't be able to catch the boat, and you'll wear yourself out. Get rid of objects that weigh you down and assume a fetal-type position—arms folded, knees drawn to chest—to reduce loss of body heat. Blow a whistle, shine a light, or make splashes to attract attention.

Emergencies On Board

Fire

To use a fire extinguisher, aim it at the base of the fire, pull the trigger, and apply with a sweeping motion, side to side.

Three types of fires are typical on boats: combustible materials (Class A), liquids (Class B), and electrical (Class C). The label on the fire extinguisher indicates the type(s) it can handle.

Class A—Combustible material fires (wood, trash, cloth, etc.): Use water or an extinguisher suitable for Class A fires, such as a dry chemical or aqueous foam device. (Halon has been banned.)

Label for a fire extinguisher that can handle three different types of fires.

Class B—Flammable liquid fires (cooking fuel, engine fuel, grease, etc.): Immediately cut off the flow of fuel by turning off the stove or engine *and* the fuel supply at the tank. Do not spray or dump water on the fire (this may spread it). Extinguish a liquid fire with an extinguisher suitable for Class B fires, such as a CO_2, dry chemical, or aqueous foam extinguisher, or cover the fire with a wet towel. Dampen combustible objects to prevent the fire from spreading.

Class C—Live electrical fires: Immediately turn off the power source. Extinguish the fire with an extinguisher suitable for a Class C fire, such as a CO_2, dry chemical, or aqueous foam. Do not use water.

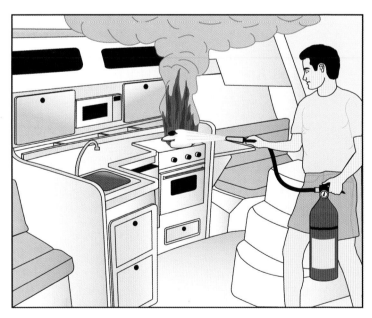

Since a dry chemical or aqueous foam extinguisher will put out all three types of fires, one of these should be your first choice. Smaller bottles are easier to handle than big ones. Dry chemical extinguishers are effective at ranges from 5 to 15 feet.

Taking on Water

If the bilge fills, use all your manual and electric pumps while energetically applying a bucket brigade until you have gotten ahead of the leak. Check the deck, anchor locker, ventilators, hatches, mast, rudder post, propeller shaft, and other gear for major leaks. Water can come from all directions. Also check the bilge, seacocks, and hoses. If a hose is leaking, shut the seacock and replace the hose or tighten or replace the hose clamp. If the seacock or its through-hull fitting is missing or damaged, drive a plug into the hole with a hammer.

If the water is still coming in, there probably is a hole in the bottom. Heel the boat so the hole is as far out of the water as possible and cover it from the outside with a sail or mattress or fill it from the inside with a mattress. Keep pumping and bailing.

An emergency bilge pump may be improvised from the engine's water cooling system. Close the seacock for the water intake and move the hose from the seacock into the bilge.

Running Aground

First, study the situation. Is the boat leaking? What part of the boat is aground? Can you see a safe channel? Check the tide tables. If the tide is flooding, you may float off. If ebbing, move fast!

Back off. Go out the way you came in—carefully, for the rudder may be damaged by a rock. In mud or sand, it may help to rock the boat to break the hold on the boat's keel.

Set out an anchor in a dinghy or by wading. Take a strain on the rode to pull the stern or bow off.

Heel the boat to decrease draft. Put the crew's weight at one side (for example, on the boom) and try to sail or power off.

If the tide is going out, put fenders under the lower side to prevent hull damage and lead a halyard to shore to keep the boat from flopping over in the wrong direction.

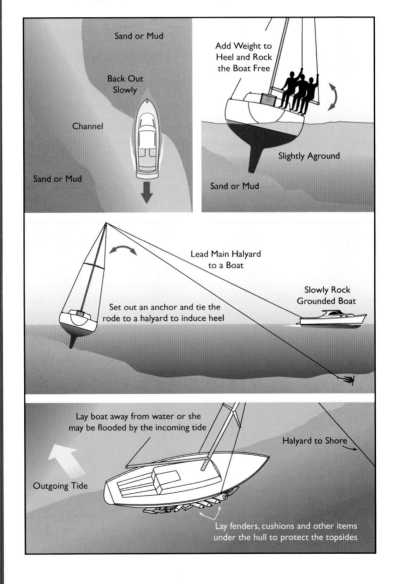

Towing

If offered a tow:

1. Settle terms. Agree on a fee, destination, hand signals, and radio frequency. Avoid a dispute about salvage rights by leaving a crew on your boat and giving the tow boat your line. Be sure to establish a safe towing speed so your boat is not pulled apart or towed under water.

2. Use a nylon line. It stretches and absorbs jerks. Secure it to the largest through-bolted fitting on deck, like a bow cleat, a winch, or the mast. Back up this fitting with another line, pulled taut, or create a bridle as in the illustration. Make sure lines run fair, without rubbing against fittings. A fairlead may have to be improvised on the bow from a sail stop or a short length of line and a block.

3. Start towing slowly. Increase speed and adjust the towline length until your boat is riding in the trough of a wave well behind the tow boat.

4. Shorten the tow line in crowded waters, or tow alongside for maximum control.

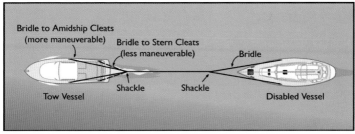

Bridle to Amidship Cleats (more maneuverable)
Bridle to Stern Cleats (less maneuverable)
Bridle
Shackle
Shackle
Tow Vessel
Disabled Vessel

Disabled Vessel
Fenders
Stern Line
Towing Strap
Backing Line
Bow Line
Tow Vessel
Position Tow Vessel Slightly Astern of the Disabled Vessel

Steering Failure

If the steering system breaks, stop the boat and inspect for damage that can be repaired with spare wire, bulldog clamps, shackles, or other fittings. If repair is impossible, call for a tow, attempt to self-steer, or jury-rig a rudder. When the steering cable breaks in a wheel-steered sailboat, you may find a post atop the steering quadrant on which to bolt an emergency tiller.

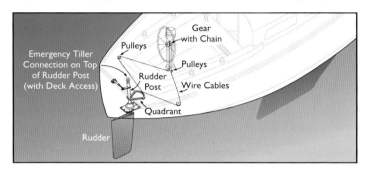

Self-Steering

Powerboats. A twin-prop boat might be steered by balancing the force of the two engines. Single-prop boats usually cannot be steered without a rudder.

Sailboats. Many boats can be self-steered by trimming the sails and finding the right balance between the jib (pulling the bow down) and the mainsail or mizzen (pushing the bow up). A ketch or yawl usually self-steers most effectively because the mizzen balances the jib.

Jury-Rigged Rudders

On powerboats and sailboats, a temporary rudder can be jury-rigged (improvised) by dragging a paddle-like object, some fenders, or another substantial object over the stern and adjusting it with lines to swing the stern. Because the loads are large, the system will break unless it is flexible. In this possible solution, the hinge at the stern must have plenty of give or the jury-rigged rudder will snap; make it from a loose assembly of rope.

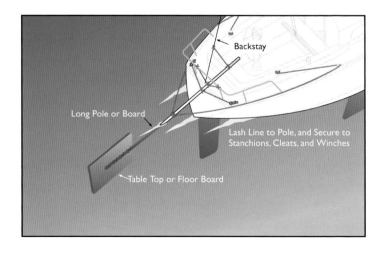

Broken Rigging

If a shroud breaks. Immediately luff the sails and tack the boat to put the load on the other side. If the headstay breaks, immediately bear off downwind. If the backstay breaks, luff up and get the sails down. A stay can be repaired using spare wire and bulldog clamps, or a substitute stay can be rigged using a halyard. Someone may have to go aloft in a bosun's chair.

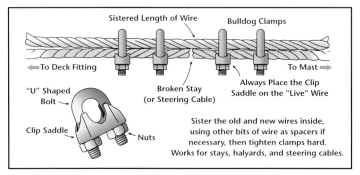

Sistered Length of Wire   Bulldog Clamps

To Deck Fitting   To Mast

"U" Shaped Bolt

Broken Stay (or Steering Cable)

Always Place the Clip Saddle on the "Live" Wire

Clip Saddle   Nuts

Sister the old and new wires inside, using other bits of wire as spacers if necessary, then tighten clamps hard. Works for stays, halyards, and steering cables.

    If the mast breaks. Clear away the mess before it holes the hull by pulling the cotter and clevis pins in the turnbuckles. Wire stays usually cannot be cut. A dismasted boat rolls and pitches violently, so wear and hook on safety harnesses and crawl on deck. A new mast can be jury-rigged by lashing together the remains of sails and spars with line.

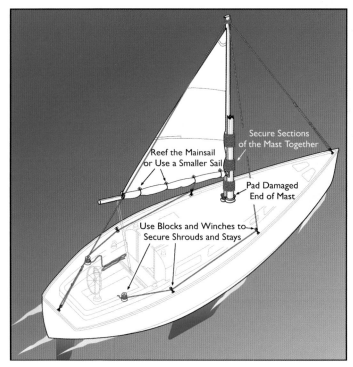

Secure Sections of the Mast Together

Reef the Mainsail or Use a Smaller Sail

Pad Damaged End of Mast

Use Blocks and Winches to Secure Shrouds and Stays

Only a few of the many possible jury-rig possibilities are shown here. Necessity is the mother of invention. Can you use a spinnaker pole as a gin pole to help erect a mast section? Use what you have!

Losing Power
(see also Chapter 11)

Engine shutdowns are often caused by problems with fuel, with the cooling system, or with the electrical system.

Fuel problems cause most engine troubles. If the engine stalls, the fuel may be dirty. Replace the fuel filters. If the engine is still balky, there may be an airlock in the fuel line. Remove it following the instructions in the engine manual.

Cooling problems cause the engine temperature to rise dangerously. Stop the engine and inspect the raw-water intake. The seacock may be closed or the system may be clogged by weed. One sign of a damaged cooling system is that water is not spitting out of the exhaust pipe.

Electrical problems may prevent the engine from starting or running smoothly. No engine will start with a dead battery. Reserve one battery for starting. With a gasoline engine, clean or replace the spark plugs.

Engine Troubleshooting Guide

SYMPTOM	POSSIBLE CAUSE	REMEDY
Engine won't crank.	Starter switches not turned on properly.	Turn on proper switches (consult your owner's manual).
	Battery discharged.	Charge battery or turn battery switches to include house batteries in charging battery. If you get engine started, find out why battery was discharged.
	Starter solenoid or starter defective.	Listen to starter motor when someone else turns ignition switch. If you hear a click and nothing happens, tap side of starter motor once with hammer while trying to start. The starter may start (this is only a temporary fix). Be ready to shut off emergency engine electricity if you hear a loud whirring hum, however. Call a professional.
	Loud, whirring hum.	Severe problem in starter. Turn off power to engine start circuit; use emergency switch if you have one. Don't use starter. Call a professional.
Engine cranks, but won't start.	Out of fuel.	Add fuel and bleed fuel lines if necessary.
	Fuel line valve closed.	Open valve.
	Fuel shutoff cable is shutting off fuel.	Move shutoff cable to ON position.
	Air in fuel line.	Bleed fuel lines.
	Blockage in fuel line.	Clear blockage.
	Very dirty fuel filters.	Change fuel filters.
No water exiting exhaust.	Water intake closed.	Open seawater intake seacock, fast!
	Blockage in seawater intake line.	Clear blockage.
	Defective impeller pump.	Replace impeller.
Engine runs ragged.	Dirty fuel.	Change fuel filters, change to different fuel tank if possible. Have professional clean tanks.
	Dirty fuel filters.	Change fuel filters.
	Blockage in fuel line.	Clear blockage.
	Fuel lift pump defective.	Replace fuel lift pump.
Engine smokes.	Defective injectors.	Replace injectors.
	Serious engine problem.	Call professional.
	Too much oil in engine.	Stop engine; pump excess oil out. Do not run engine in an excess-oil state: Very dangerous!

Additional Possibilities for Gasoline Engines

SYMPTOM	POSSIBLE CAUSE	REMEDY
Engine cranks, but won't start	Defective spark plugs.	Replace spark plugs.
	Carburetor problem.	Call a professional.
	Engine timing problem.	Call a professional.
Engine runs ragged.	Defective spark plugs.	Replace spark plugs.
	Carburetor problem.	Call a professional.
	Engine timing problem.	Call a professional.

(Chart courtesy David Kroenke, *Know Your Boat*)

Emergencies On Board

Preventing Accidents

A few simple routines can keep emergencies from occurring in the first place:

Be careful with alcohol. It spoils good judgment, makes you unsteady on your feet, and causes seasickness.

Know your boat. Have a diagram showing where all important gear is stowed.

Wear a PFD. Almost 75% of all reported recreational boating fatalities are caused by drowning. In almost 90% of these tragedies, the victims were not wearing life jackets or other personal flotation devices (PFDs).

Wear a safety harness. It prevents people from falling overboard in the first place. According to the Coast Guard, 38%

of reported boating deaths are due to falls overboard, and when someone goes over the side the chances of a fatality are one in three. There are some excellent combination PFD-safety harnesses on the market. Put on the harness before you come on deck, and hook it in the cockpit before you step out of the companionway. Hook the safety harness tether into sturdy jacklines or through-bolted fittings. Keep the tether short so any fall won't be long. Clip on whenever you're unsteady, and especially when doing a two-handed job—like steering, coming in or out of the companionway, trimming sails, or hoisting sails.

Prevent falls. One of the main causes of injuries in a boat is a fall on deck or in the cabin. Everybody should wear nonskid shoes. When you feel unsteady on your feet, use grab rails and lifelines or crawl on deck (the best sailors do it).

Tame the boom. A flying boom can cause serious, even fatal, head injuries. Even in light wind, hold it out with a preventer—a line leading from the boom forward to the deck, through a block, and back to the cockpit.

Stay dry and warm. A dry body is a warm body—and

Main Boom Preventer

also an effective body, because symptoms of hypothermia include slow thinking and loss of agility. Wear good foul-weather clothing as soon as the spray begins to fly. Underneath, wear layers of fleece clothing.

Getting Lost

If you don't know where you are, stop the boat (a sailboat can heave-to), take a deep breath, calm down, and think. Using the chart, methodically examine your surroundings as you try to re-create your recent course or courses. Have people with fresh eyes search for landmarks or buoys. Take bearings to any landmarks or buoys you can see or identify. In poor visibility, if you can't fix your position with GPS, either stay where you are or proceed slowly in a direction you know to be safe—toward open water, a bold shore without off-lying hazards, or an aid to navigation that produces a distinctive sound signal and is not close to a reef or other hazard.

Emergency Calls and Signals

Before signaling a Mayday or SOS, ask yourself, "Is this truly a life-threatening emergency? Can I get home on my own?" Every distress call puts at least one other boat at risk.

VHF-FM Radio: Avoiding Collision

Even when you have the right of way under the Navigation Rules, if you feel the slightest concern about a possible collision, talk to the other vessel on VHF Channel 13 (the bridge-to-bridge channel) or Channel 16 (the emergency channel). Even if your message is simply, "I'm the blue sailing vessel on your port bow. Do you see me?," the other captain will appreciate it. When near or crossing shipping lanes in poor visibility, announce your boat's type, position, speed, and heading on Channel 13 or 16. Ask nearby vessels to do the same and say you're standing by on Channel 16. Even if you don't hear a response, you will get the attention of the other vessel's crew.

VHF-FM Radio: Distress Alerts

BY VOICE: Tune the radio to Channel 16, the international distress frequency. (Because VHF has a range of only about 50 miles or less from a typical small or medium-size boat, it may not be helpful at sea unless nearby boats relay your call.) Then *slowly and clearly:*

1. Say, "Mayday, Mayday, Mayday."
2. **Say your boat's name three times, followed by your radio call sign.**
3. **Say "Mayday" and your boat's name again, then your geographical position.** Preferably, give your position in latitude and longitude (read it off the GPS or chart). But it can be a bearing and distance to or from a buoy, a point of land, or other charted object. (For instance, "We're two miles northeast of gong number 1 off Oyster Bay.")
4. **Briefly describe your situation, your distress, and the assistance you require.**
5. **Describe your boat by type, color, and size.**
6. **Say how many people are aboard, and if they need medical attention.**
7. **Sign off (say "over").**

Repeat the above until someone acknowledges.

When USCG or law enforcement officials respond to your call, they will follow a set procedure that you may find frustrating because some questions may not seem relevant to your situation. Try not to be impatient. These professional men and women are doing the job they were trained for. The quicker you provide answers, the quicker the officials will get to the specifics of your problems

BY DIGITAL SELECTIVE CALLING (DSC) VHF-FM RADIO: If your boat's VHF radio is equipped with Digital Selective Calling (DSC), and it is properly installed and registered *(see below)*, distress calls are almost automated.

1-A. Lift the cover and press the DISTRESS button. If the display reads "Undesignated," press the button for three to five seconds. The radio transmits a simple "Mayday" alert in a digital signal containing your identity and location over Channel 70 to the Coast Guard and other ships.

1-B. If the display provides a choice between "Undesignated" and "Designated," selecting "Designated" calls up a menu that allows you to specify the type of trouble you are in. Then press the button for three to five seconds to send the signal.

2. When the call is acknowledged digitally by another DSC-equipped radio, you will hear a tone.

3. If the radio does not switch automatically to Channel 16 for voice transmission, press the CANCEL/CLEAR button.

4. On Channel 16, send a voice message concerning your situation (see above) and talk to rescuers and other vessels.

DSC installation and registration. In order to send complete distress calls, a DSC-equipped VHF radio (1) must be connected to the boat's GPS navigation system receiver; *and* (2) the boat's unique Maritime Mobile Service Identity (MMSI) number must be registered with the Coast Guard; *and* (3) the radio must be formatted with the MMSIs of radios you wish to call. The U.S. Coast Guard's group MMSI is 003669999. Local U.S. and Canadian Guard Guard stations have MMSIs available from local authorities.

Visual Distress Signals

Most boats 16 feet or longer must carry distress signals for use by day. If out at night, they must carry night signals.

Day distress signals. Ignite an orange smoke signal, show an orange flag with a black square or circle, wave hands or honk horns aggressively, or reflect sun with a mirror.

Night distress signal. With a bright flashlight signal SOS (dot-dot-dot, dash-dash-dash, dot-dot-dot).

Day/night distress signal. Fire off a red flare (rocket or hand-held). (White flares are intended to identify a boat when a collision threatens.)

Note: Smoke signals and flares must be replaced by their expiration dates.

Smoke Flare   Flare Gun   Gun shots

Square over ball   Black square and ball on a field of orange   Inverted flag

Morse code SOS   Parachute flare   Waving of hands

Dye in water   Radio MAYDAY   Loud horn

Fire   Smoke canister in water   Red ribbon in water

Evacuating Crew
by Helicopter

1. Wear PFDs and safety harnesses. The boat will roll violently in the helicopter downdraft.

2. The pilot is in charge. He and the rescue crew will communicate by radio, hand signals, or signs.

3. Jog along slowly. Unless otherwise ordered, keep the wind on the port side.

4. Prepare to put the injured crew in a dinghy or a life raft tethered to your boat. Direct evacuation from a low powerboat may be possible, but superstructures and masts will tangle the rescue equipment. (Uninjured evacuees may be instructed to jump into the water.)

5. Don't touch the litter basket or cable before they are grounded in the water or on deck. They carry a violent static electric shock.

6. Leave a written medical report with the person being evacuated.

Rescue Helicopter

Rescue Basket
with Injured
Crew Member

Boat

Life Raft or Dinghy

Abandoning Ship

This is absolutely the last resort. Resist the temptation to get off the boat simply because you are seasick, wet, bruised, and miserable. As the saying goes, "The only time to step into a life raft is when your first step is *up*." No matter how bad the situation may seem, the boat often survives. The crew may be in more danger when abandoning the boat than on board. A life raft is an extremely unseaworthy vessel, a helicopter rescue is hazardous, and it's always risky to bring boats alongside in rough weather. But if the boat is obviously going down, or if there is a serious fire, you have good cause to abandon ship.

1. Bring the life raft on deck and tie its tether to the boat. Or prepare the boat's dinghy.

Ditch Bag

Dye Marker

2. Prepare an abandon ship bag ("ditch bag"). This collection of gear and rations should address the problems of thirst, cold, hunger, wet, and signaling rescuers. Take water (and, ideally, a hand-operated membrane desalinator with which to make more), paddles, food, a knife, a handheld VHF-FM radio, flares, a signal mirror, an EPIRB (satellite radio beacon), a sea anchor, seasickness medication, fleece clothing, foul-weather clothing, blankets, waterproof containers, a small bilge pump, a sponge, etc.

3. Inflate the life raft. Tie tether to boat, throw raft downwind, and pull on tether until raft inflates. It may inflate upside down and have to be righted.

4. Notify others. Using the radio and leaving a note, identify the boat and yourself and say you will return.

5. Abandon ship. Put the gear in the life raft, climb in, turn on the EPIRB, and cut the tether to the boat.

406 MHz
EPIRB

CHAPTER 13

Richard Clinchy

Emergency First Aid On Board

What to Do First

Get the Big Picture

How many people are ill or injured? If more than one, make all as comfortable as possible and treat the most serious first.

Think about causes. Suspect burns after a fire or explosion, wounds after a collision, etc. If victim is diabetic or has history of heart trouble, suspect these causes.

Any risk to others on board? If the boat is taking on water, get life jackets on everyone. If there is a fire on board, maneuver boat to keep smoke and flames downwind.

Know your limits. This chapter focuses solely on the immediate care of emergencies that present an imminent threat to life or risk of serious permanent disability. Do the best you can, and do not be afraid to act, but get professional medical help for the victim as soon as possible.

Injury

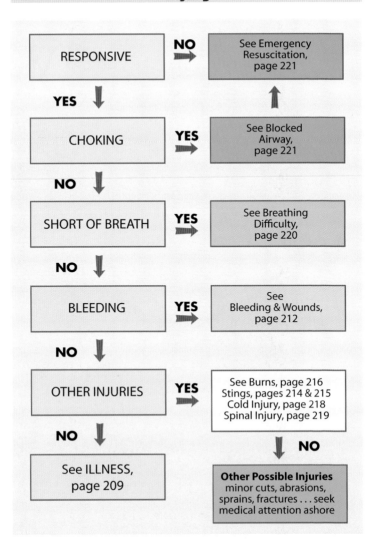

Emergency First Aid On Board

Get Help

Where are you? Write it down. GPS can give you latitude and longitude, or you can note distance and direction from the nearest nav aid or landmark.

If you have a marine radio on board, use it on Channel 16. It is more reliable than a cell phone. For a life-threatening illness or injury or possible loss of the boat, start your transmission stating, "Mayday-Mayday-Mayday." If your radio has digital selective calling (DSC) capability and is linked to GPS, press the distress button. If you call the Coast Guard by radio, describe in as much detail as possible what is occurring on the boat, what emergency action has been taken thus far, and your location.

If you can't get help by radio, use your cell phone and call 911.

When talking to a 911 operator, don't disconnect first. Let the emergency operator control the call.

Illness

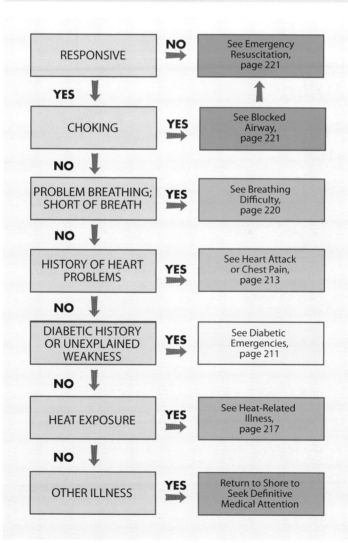

Recommended First-Aid Kit

Your onboard first-aid kit should contain these items at a minimum:

1. Waterproof case (Pelican 1300 recommended)
2. CPR barrier mask—1
3. SAM Splint—1
4. Warming emergency blanket—1
5. Hypoallergenic disposable gloves—3 pairs
6. EMS utility shears—1
7. Triangular bandage—2
8. 1" MAT (Mechanical Advantage Tourniquet)—1
9. Cool Jel treatment for minor burns—small bottle
10. Water-Jel sterile 4" x 4" burn dressing—1
11. Water-Jel sterile 4" x 16" burn dressing—1
12. 3" conforming gauze bandage—3 rolls
13. 1" plastic bandage—25
14. Sterile 4" x 4" dressing—4
15. Germacidal wound wipes—4
16. Aspirin—325 mg buffered tablets
17. Acetaminophen—500 mg tablets
18. Ibuprofen—200 mg capsules
19. Motion sickness medication
20. Diphenhydramine (Benadryl)—25 mg capsules

A kit that precisely matches these specifications can be purchased from the author at Boating Good Samaritan Kit (phone: 850-939-0840; web: www.boating-good-samaritan.com). Equivalent kits are available from West Marine at prices ranging from $80 to $300 (see www.westmarine.com) and from other retailers.

Diabetic Emergencies

1. Most diabetics adequately manage the disease and maintain stable blood sugar levels.

2. The onset of a diabetic coma from insufficient insulin—leaving cells unable to absorb glucose from the blood—is usually gradual and therefore unlikely to reach crisis stage. Blood sugar levels elevate as the condition progresses, leading to severe *hyperglycemia*. Early symptoms include thirst and frequent urination, followed later by nausea, vomiting, shortness of breath, and ultimately coma.

3. *Hypoglycemia*, or low blood sugar—whether from taking too much insulin, skipping food, or excessive stress, exercise, or alcohol consumption—can develop more rapidly and usually without warning (except that the victim is usually aware that he or she is diabetic). Possible symptoms include:

   * Weakness
   * Dizziness
   * Excessive sweating
   * Pale, cold, and moist skin
   * Rapid pulse
   * Headache
   * Poor coordination
   * Shakes or trembling
   * Changes in behavior or mood
   * Seizures
   * Eventual coma

4. The treatment of a victim with low blood sugar is simple and quickly effective if initiated soon enough. Give the victim any food or drink that contains sugar, including soda, fruit juice, ice cream, candy bars, or spoonfuls of table sugar dissolved in water. If the victim loses consciousness, place sugar, cake icing, or similar under his or her tongue.

5. Do not let a recovering victim resume normal activity too quickly. He or she should rest and should be allowed to eat some food that will provide a longer-acting release of sugars into the blood.

DISCLAIMER: This chapter augments but does not replace appropriate training in first aid and CPR. Boaters are encouraged to supplement and confirm information in this chapter with other sources, including recognized training agencies. The author and publisher assume no liability with respect to the accuracy, completeness, or application of information contained in this chapter.

Emergency First Aid On Board

Bleeding and Wounds

1. Don disposable gloves.
2. Press a 4" x 4" sterile dressing on the site of the bleeding.
3. If blood seeps through, add more dressings.
4. Once bleeding is stopped, wrap wound with a conforming dressing.
5. Stop bleeding with pressure and elevation as necessary. If this fails to stop bleeding from an arm or leg, apply a tourniquet and arrange for rapid transport of the patient to a hospital. Any flat, nonstretch bandage, sail tie, belt, or similar can be used as a tourniquet. Wrap tightly, as closely above wound as possible. Damage to the arm or leg is possible after a few hours, but this is preferable to having the patient bleed to death.

Use of the MAT tourniquet. After clipping around limb above wound, cinch strap tight, then tighten further by turning key clockwise. Release by pressing red release button and then lifting the clip.

If professional medical care cannot be reached within 24 hours, it is a good idea to clean the wound daily or whenever a dressing gets wet or dirty in order to minimize infection. Use the following steps:

1. Remove dressings.
2. Wash the wound using soap and clean water. Bleeding may restart. If so, repeat steps 1–5 above.
3. Flush wound with clean or sterile water.
4. Apply fresh, sterile dressings and bandage.

Applying a dressing to a wound.

When an object is impaled in the victim, do not remove it. Instead, stabilize the object using additional dressings or anything else at hand.

If part of the victim's body has been removed as a result of the wound, take the following additional steps:

1. Rinse the removed part in clean water to remove dirt and debris. Do not scrub.
2. Wrap the part in a sterile dressing.
3. Place the wrapped part in a plastic bag or wrap to keep it from getting wet in the following step.
4. Immerse the wrapped part in ice water, but avoid direct contact with ice.
5. Transport the removed part to the hospital with the victim.

Heart Attack/ Chest Pain

1. Common signs and symptoms:
   - Anxiety
   - History of high blood pressure, angina, or heart disease
   - Recent significant exertion before onset of chest pain
   - Chest pain that does not change with the victim's position or breathing
   - Pain that radiates up the sides of the neck or down the victim's arm or arms
   - Complaint of indigestion that is not consistent with recent food consumed
   - Rapid or irregular pulse or complaint of "palpitations"
   - Pale, cool, moist skin
   - Noticeable increase in breathing rate.
2. Place victim in a comfortable position, usually semi-sitting.
3. If the victim has a history of angina and carries nitroglycerin, have the victim self-administer the nitroglycerin. Assist as necessary. Nitroglycerin can be taken at least two more times at 3-minute intervals if pain is not relieved with the first dose.
4. If the pain persists 15 minutes after nitroglycerin, suspect a heart attack. Rapid transport to medical care is vital.
5. If you suspect a heart attack, allow the victim to take one adult aspirin tablet, but give no fluids other than a swallow of water with the aspirin.
6. If there is oxygen on the boat, administer oxygen to the victim at a high flow.
7. Getting a heart attack victim to medical care quickly is critical.

Insect Stings

Insect stings can be painful but are usually not life-threatening unless there is a severe allergic reaction.

1. Insect stings will show redness and swelling at the site of the sting. Pain may be intense initially but then subside to a dull pain.

2. First and foremost, observe for signs of an allergic reaction. What to watch for:

   - Numbness or itching around the mouth and the face
   - Difficulty breathing
   - Tightness in the throat or chest
   - Agitation and anxiety
   - Diminished level of consciousness

3. If an allergic reaction appears to have occurred, determine if the victim carries an anaphylaxis (allergic reaction) kit, typically called an Ana-Kit, which includes epinephrine (Epi-Pen) as well as Benadryl.

4. If so, administer both the oral and self-injected medication as quickly as possible. Time is of the essence.

5. Reassure the victim while preparing to support the victim's breathing and circulation as described on page 221.

6. A large local reaction to a sting does not indicate an allergic reaction but simply that the victim is highly sensitive. Administer a single dose of Benadryl.

7. Absent an allergic reaction, make the victim more comfortable and relieve pain with the following steps.

8. Apply an ice pack to the sting site for up to 20 minutes or until the pain is relieved.

9. If you have acetaminophen or ibuprofen on board, give the victim the normal adult dose.

10. Your onboard first-aid kit should contain some form of sting-relief swabs. Use one directly on the sting site.

11. Continue to watch the victim for at least an hour to be certain that no signs of an allergic reaction (see #2 above) develop.

Note on CPR (see page 221): This chapter provides a quick overview for performing CPR (cardiopulmonary resuscitation) on an adult. Most emergency medical personnel recommend modified chest-compression and rescue-breathing techniques for children and infants. To be fully prepared for medical emergencies, take a nationally recognized course in CPR. Such courses are readily available in all communities and can be completed with an investment of only several hours of time.

Emergency First Aid On Board

Marine Stings

If someone on your boat comes out of the water with welts or severe itching, it's likely that he or she has been stung by some marine organism such as a jellyfish, anemone, or fire coral.

1. Watch carefully for the signs and symptoms of an allergic reaction as explained on page 214.

2. If you see obvious signs of tentacles or debris on the victim, do not touch this material with your hands as you might get stung too.

3. Rinse visible tentacles or debris from the victim's skin surface using salt water. Do not use fresh water, since this will cause additional stinging.

4. If shaving cream and a razor are on board, lather the affected area and shave the skin surface. Discard the removed shaving cream, since it contains stinging cells.

5. Since most marine venoms break down in the presence of heat, put hot packs on the injured area or expose the area to the hottest water that the victim can tolerate for as long as possible.

6. If you have white vinegar or ammonia on board, pour full-strength vinegar or diluted ammonia (1 part household ammonia mixed with 3 parts water) on the injured area to neutralize the toxin. Pour as much as can be tolerated.

7. As with insect stings, acetaminophen or ibuprofen may relieve some of the pain.

8. If the patient can tolerate it, Benadryl (diphenhydramine) may also be useful to relieve the itching that typically follows the initial burning and pain.

Rinsing a jellyfish sting with diluted ammonia.

Emergency First Aid On Board

Burns

1. Most burns on a boat will be contact burns. If burning clothing or other material is involved, make sure it has been removed from the victim.

2. Do not manage burns long-term on a boat.

3. Critical burns that require immediate medical attention and are true emergencies include:

   • Electrical burns

   • Burns around the face

   • Burns covering more than 20% of the body

   • Burns around the genitals

   • Burns involving the fingers and/or toes

   • Significant chemical burns

4. The first step in treatment is to stop the burning. Pour cool, clean water over the burned area to cool the tissues.

5. Remove jewelry, watches, belts, and clothing from the burned area.

6. Cover the burned area with a Water-Jel dressing, or apply Cool Jel to a minor burn before applying a sterile dressing.

7. Protect any blisters that develop in the burned area from bursting.

8. Bandage appropriately and immobilize the burned part.

9. If fingers or toes are involved in the burned area, place small nonstick gauze pads between the involved fingers and toes before bandaging. This will prevent the burned fingers and toes from sticking together.

10. Carefully monitor the victim's breathing and overall condition while waiting for help or returning to the dock.

11. Giving fluids by mouth is a good idea, but do not overdo this to the point that vomiting might take place.

Applying a burn dressing.

Heat-Related Illness

Differentiating between non-life-threatening heat exhaustion and life-threatening heatstroke is difficult even for professionals, so treat any heat illness as an emergency.

1. Anyone who begins to experience even the most minor symptoms of heat illness should drink water and be taken to shore immediately.

2. Early symptoms include:
   - Headache, weakness, nausea, and/or dizziness
   - Elevated body temperature

3. Progressive symptoms include:
   - Skin cool and clammy (still sweating) or hot and dry (no longer sweating)
   - Body temperature above 104°F.
   - Confusion, disorientation, or diminished consciousness

4. Shelter the victim from the heat and initiate emergency cooling.

5. Remove excess clothing from the victim.

6. Immerse the victim in cool water or cover with ice water–soaked towels or cloths.

7. Victim should sip cool water or diluted (50-50) electrolyte drinks if possible.

8. Monitor the victim carefully. If you see any signs of deterioration, apply ice around the neck, scalp, in the armpits, to the flanks, and to the groin area.

9. PREVENTION is the best treatment. Drink plenty of water *before* getting underway. Continue to drink water underway—as much as 2 pints per hour. Intersperse electrolyte drinks such as Gatorade. Avoid beverages containing alcohol or caffeine, both of which increase dehydration.

10. Clear or light-colored urine indicates adequate hydration.

11. Do not overhydrate. Relieve thirst but do not cause bloating.

Cold-Related Injuries

The most serious cold-related injury encountered by boaters is cold-water immersion. Get the victim out of the water quickly. Extended immersion can lead to hypothermia if death does not occur first.

1. Progressive signs and symptoms of hypothermia may include:
   - Shivering or difficulty moving body parts
   - Poor judgment or confusion
   - Apathy
   - Lack of coordination
   - Rapid breathing and/or heartbeat
   - Stupor
   - In extreme cold there will be a loss of the ability to shiver
   - Unconsciousness
   - Slowed breathing and heart rate
2. Handle the victim carefully, since in severe cases the heart may be susceptible to heartbeat abnormalities that can be fatal.
3. Get the victim out of the wind and remove all wet clothing.
4. Dry the victim and do whatever you can to warm the victim without rough handling. Wrap the victim in dry clothing and blankets, use the metallic warming blanket from your first-aid kit, or use another dry person's body warmth.
5. Make sure the victim's body *and head* are covered with dry clothing or wrapped in a heat-conserving blanket.
6. If the victim is capable of swallowing safely, have him or her drink warm, sweet liquids. DO NOT permit alcoholic beverages of any kind.
7. Do not leave the victim alone. It is important to continue to monitor his or her condition.

The HELP (Heat Escape Lessening Position) posture will slow a swimmer's loss of body heat, but the most critical survival factor for a person overboard is wearing a PFD (personal flotation device). The victim's first reaction when falling into cold water is to gasp and then aspirate water. He or she may lose the ability to swim, and only a PFD will keep him afloat.

Spinal Injuries

A serious fall or impact may cause injury to the spinal cord. There is little you can do to treat such an injury, but appropriate management is critical.

1. Suspect injury to the spinal cord and surrounding bony structures if the victim exhibits any of the following:
   - Significant pain or tenderness at any point along the spine, including the bones in the neck
   - Loss of ability to move arms or legs
   - Loss of feeling in arms or legs
   - A complaint of weakness in arms or legs after a fall or being struck by a sailboat boom
   - Loss of feeling or a complaint of pins and needles in any part of the body below the neck following an injury
2. Lay the victim flat on the boat's deck for stability. If he or she must be moved, one rescuer should immobilize the head and neck while others lift the body as a unit.
3. Manually stabilize the victim's head and neck, getting additional help from a cervical collar, life jackets, clothing, towels, etc., as available and necessary.
4. If you need to manually maintain the victim's breathing, use the jaw-thrust maneuver to open the airway. Do not employ the head-tilt, chin-lift procedure.
5. If the spinal cord injury is severe enough, it may be necessary to support the breathing of a fully conscious victim, since the muscles used to breathe may not work properly.
6. Minimize pounding or disturbance of the boat. Focus on a smooth transport rather than speed.
7. Do not allow any handling of the patient that will in any way disturb the immobilization of the victim's body.

Jaw thrust. To open a victim's airway with this technique, put your fingers under each side of the jaw and lift it up *without* tilting the head back. Use this technique when you suspect a neck or spinal injury.

Breathing Difficulty

1. The victim will typically complain that he or she can't catch his breath or is short of breath.

2. First ascertain whether the victim has a chronic disease such as asthma, chronic bronchitis, or emphysema. If not, shortness of breath may be a sign that the victim is suffering from a heart attack (page 213) or sting (pages 214 and 215).

3. Get the victim in a comfortable position—usually a sitting or semi-sitting position.

4. Reassure the victim that help is coming or will be waiting when the boat returns to the shore.

5. Loosen any clothing that might restrict breathing. This includes any tight upper-body undergarment of a woman.

6. If oxygen is on board and someone is trained to use it, administer it to the victim.

7. If the victim's breathing stops, go to page 221 and follow the steps you will find there.

Ventilating with barrier mask. In CPR, give two breaths sufficient to cause the chest to rise, about 1 second each, then do chest compressions. Your first-aid kit should include a barrier mask.

Chest compressions. In CPR, follow ventilations with 30 compressions at a rate of 100 per minute. Then repeat ventilating/chest compression sequence.

tilt chin back

Head-tilt, chin-lift procedure. Use this to open the airway prior to rescue breathing when you are sure there is no neck or spinal injury. If such injury is possible, use jaw-thrust technique (page 219).

Emergency Resuscitation

CPR

1. If a victim has collapsed and is seemingly unresponsive and you have someone else on board, contact the Coast Guard or 911 for emergency help. If you're alone, start from Step 2 before summoning help.

2. Shake the victim and shout, "Are you OK?"

3. If no response, DO NOT DELAY... DO NOT CHECK FOR PULSE. (See page 214 for note on children.)

4. Open the victim's airway using the head-tilt, chin-lift procedure (see page 220). If you suspect a neck or spinal injury, use the jaw-thrust procedure (see page 219). Give two breaths sufficient to cause the chest to rise (see page 220). Breaths are about 1 second each. Have the person who is contacting the Coast Guard or 911 say that CPR is in progress.

5. Begin chest compressions with hands placed in the middle of the chest at the nipple line (see page 220). Compressions should be administered at a rate of 100 compressions per minute. Give 30 compressions and then 2 more ventilations as in Step 4. Watch for the chest to rise. Continue this 30:2 compression-ventilation series for about 2 minutes.

6. If you're alone, call the Coast Guard or 911 after your first 2 minutes of CPR.

7. If the victim has not responded and an automated defibrillator is on board, connect it to the victim and activate it now.

8. Continue compressions and breaths until no one on board is physically capable of continuing or help has arrived.

Choking—Blocked Airway

1. If the victim CAN make noise, don't do anything. Air is moving.

2. If the victim makes no noise or only nods "yes" when asked, "Are you choking?" act immediately.

3. Give abdominal thrusts until the victim breathes or becomes unconscious. If abdominal thrusts don't work, give the victim chest compressions.

Abdominal thrust (Heimlich maneuver) on standing (left) or unconscious (right) victim. For hand position for chest compressions, see page 220.

Nigel Calder, a diesel mechanic, boatbuilder, and marine technical writer, is the internationally acclaimed author of *Boatowner's Mechanical and Electrical Manual*, universally recommended as the first and most essential book to carry aboard for assessing and maintaining your boat's systems. He is also the author of *Marine Diesel Engines*, *Nigel Calder's Cruising Handbook*, and *How to Read a Nautical Chart*, among other nautical books.

Richard Clinchy, PhD, is a paramedic and military and EMS medical equipment consultant with nearly 50 years of prehospital emergency medical care experience and over 35 years as an emergency medical care educator. Formerly chairman of the American College of Prehospital Medicine, he is the author of the Dive/First Responder text and training program and has written or edited seven books on diving and emergency medical care. He is the former Chief, Department of Education, United States Coast Guard Auxiliary.

Bill Gladstone is the Director of Education for North Sails and author of the North U *TRIM*, *Tactics*, and *Cruising* books and CDs. Bill has been teaching sailing for over 30 years. He is the former Commodore of the Yale Corinthian Yacht Club. Graduates of his seminars and clinics are racing and cruising worldwide.

Peter Nielsen is the editor of *SAIL* Magazine and was previously an editor at *Yachting Monthly* in the UK. An experienced mariner who has cruised, raced, and anchored worldwide, he is also the author of *Sailpower*.

CONTRIBUTORS

John Rousmaniere is the author of the best-selling *Annapolis Book of Seamanship*—widely hailed as the best book available on seamanship under sail—as well as *Fastnet, Force 10*; *After the Storm*; and a dozen other nautical books. He lectures widely on seamanship and safety, and won the Captain Fred E. Lawton Boating Safety Award for outstanding contribution to boating safety through the media. He has sailed more than 35,000 bluewater miles.

Bob Sweet is the author of *GPS for Mariners*, *The Weekend Navigator*, and *Powerboat Handling Illustrated*. A former radar and communications system engineer and executive manager of a corporate business unit that helped develop GPS for the U.S. Air Force, he is the Assistant National Education Officer for the United States Power Squadrons. Bob is also a navigation instructor and an avid boater with more than 30 years' experience on the water.

Charlie Wing, author of *One-Minute Guide to the Nautical Rules of the Road*, received his PhD in oceanography from the Massachusetts Institute of Technology. He lived aboard a cruising sailboat for 6 years, during which time he earned a U.S. Coast Guard Captain's license. His frustration with available license study guides led him to create International Marine's bestselling *Get Your Captain's License*, now in its third edition. He is also the author of *Boatowner's Illustrated Electrical Handbook* and *How Boat Things Work: An Illustrated Guide*.

Index